SENTI!

OUTCASTS

WHEN DARKNESS FINDS YOU, BURN IT AWAY
BY ADAM FREESTONE
ALASKA'S MASTER OF IMAGINATION

PO Box 221974 Anchorage, Alaska 99522-1974
books@publicationconsultants.com, www.publicationconsultants.com

ISBN Number: 978-1-63747-048-0
eBook ISBN Number: 978-1-63747-049-7

Library of Congress Number: 2022923073

Copyright © 2022 Adam Freestone
—First Edition—

All rights reserved, including the right of reproduction in any form, or by any mechanical or electronic means including photocopying or recording, or by any information storage or retrieval system, in whole or in part in any form, and in any case not without the written permission of the author and publisher.

Manufactured in the United States of America

Dedication

In loving memory of Justin Freestone, my brother.

1984 – 2022
- You were always there to guide me, to teach me, and to show me the way. Our time together was a true adventure.

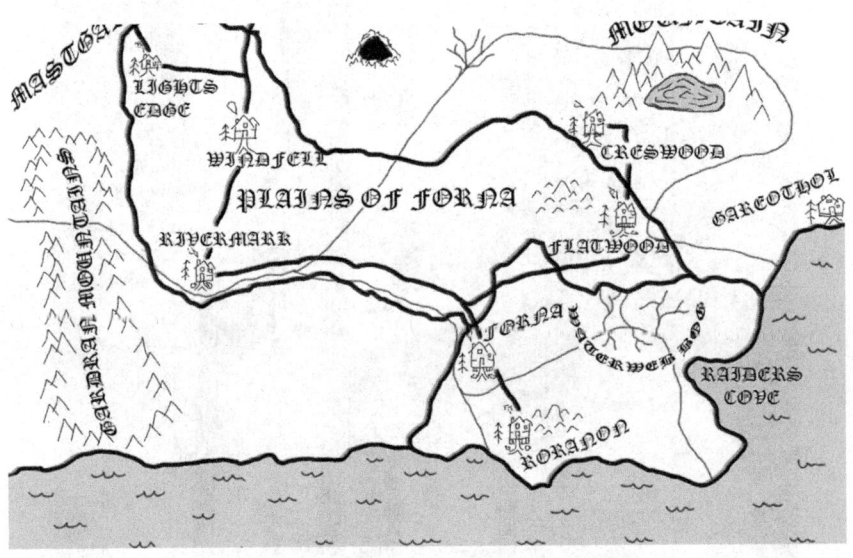

Sentinel Flame
The Story so Far (Recap)

The Sentinel Flame series takes place in a medieval-style fantasy world and is about a boy named Hyroc. Hyroc is different because his face and head resemble that of a wolverine. He has claws, and a covering of black fur, with dark brown stripes running from his sapphire eyes down his back. He knows nothing of his parents or his past, and no one knows what he is. He was adopted by a man named Marcus. Marcus holds a high standing in his town and with a group called The Ministry of the Silver Scythe that he once served. The group's purpose is to seek out any who utilizes dark magic and destroy them and any of their creations. Hyroc falls under their consideration as something to eliminate. Due to Marcus's past work with The Ministry and a favorable reputation with them, Hyroc is protected, though he is still viewed as something evil and often met with disdain from others.

At the age of nine, Hyroc's life takes a bad turn when Marcus falls ill and eventually dies. Marcus' sister June stepped in to care for Hyroc. She has inherited some clout with the Ministry and is able to prevent Hyroc from being killed.

When Hyroc is 15, he accidentally injures another person. The accident removes any protection he had from the Ministry, and he flees for his life. He escapes alone across the Plains of Forna in search of safety. He is ambushed by a group of Witch Hunters. A white bear appears and kills the hunters before mysteriously disappearing.

OUTCASTS

Hyroc arrives at the village of Elswood, which lies at the edge of a vast forested wilderness where The Ministry holds little sway. Hyroc discovers an abandoned cabin outside the village and attempts to make a new life. He is unsure how the villagers will react to seeing him, so he stays hidden until he can determine what they will do. While doing so, two giant spiders attack him. He kills the creatures but sustains a bite in the process and loses consciousness. When he wakes, he again encounters the white bear that killed the hunters. The bear (named Ursa) saved him from the venom of the spiders. Ursa is tasked with protecting him. She then disappears until she is needed again.

Hyroc stumbled upon a girl named Elsa while she was looking for her family's lost goat. Hyroc sees a wolf hunting Elsa and is forced to kill it to keep it from hurting her, revealing his presence to her. Fearing for his life, Hyroc returns to his cabin, ready to run, and watches for signs of pursuers, but no one comes. Thinking he's in the clear, he resumes his normal routine. Days later, he encounters Elsa again. He is surprised to learn that Elsa wants to thank him. Through no fault of Elsa, her oldest brother Donovan and father Svald capture Hyroc. Hyroc is brought to the attention of the village elders so they can decide his fate. Thanks to Hyroc's actions in saving Elsa from the wolf, the elders take no action against him. Though the villagers are perplexed by his appearance and cautious of his intentions, he is allowed to trade with them. Slowly, Hyroc befriends Elsa's family.

Hyroc settles into his new life at Elswood. His sixteenth birthday comes and goes, and winter arrives. While out hunting with Elsa and Donovan, they come across a lone wolf. Before they can slay it, they find a wolf pack surrounding them. The animals behave strangely and have purple eyes. Then they attack. Hyroc is separated from his friends, and he encounters a doglike shadow demon. Hyroc manages to kill the creature. He realizes he has more than just The Ministry hunting him.

Weeks pass, and though Donovan and Elsa are unsettled seeing the shadow demon, they don't tell anyone what happened. But their patients eventually run out, and they come to Hyroc for an explanation. Hyroc answers the best he can but inadvertently raises more questions

Sentinel Flame The Story so Far (Recap)

than answers and only serves to heighten Elsa's and Donovan's growing mistrust. Donovan is suspicious enough to bring his concerns to a man in the village named Harold. Harold, an ex-witch Hunter, ambushes Hyroc and is determined to get the answers he seeks. Ursa shows up and disarms Harold without harming him. She explains the situation to him. At first, Harold is distrustful of her, assuming she is a witch, but she persuades him that neither she nor Hyroc threatens the village. Harold departs peacefully and agrees to only tell Elsa and Donovan enough to exonerate Hyroc.

Hyroc has not seen Ursa since the attack, and he demands answers, the most pressing being who his second enemy is. Ursa is as ignorant about that person as he is, save that they sent the demon from somewhere to the west. He repairs his relationship with Elsa and Donovan, and his life seems to return to normal.

One night, Ursa comes to Hyroc and leads him to a strange stone. When Hyroc touches the stone, his consciousness is taken to an enormous tree inhabited by blue crystalline versions of forest animals. Hyroc is supposed to choose an animal, and he chooses a brown bear. He is brought back from the tree, then to his surprise; he transforms into a bear. Ursa informs him that when he touched the stone, he was choosing what animal he could transform into. His transformation isn't permanent, and he is able to go in and out of his animal form at will. Ursa tells him there are advantages to using his animal form, but there are also dangerous tendencies that it exerts upon its host. Ursa offers to train him to control these tendencies; otherwise, he will succumb to them and become much more animallike. He may even become a danger to his friends. He agrees for Ursa to train him. This means leaving Elswood for a time and coming with her into the untamed wilderness.

When Ursa brings him to a suitable location, she tells him of his origins. He hails from a place called Wulfren. The kingdom was once under threat from invaders, and they had gained favor with a powerful Guardian named Wearla. She bestowed upon the inhabitants of Wulfren the gift of transformation into an animal to fight off the invaders. The invaders were defeated, and there was peace in the land for a time, but the inhabitants of Wulfren used the transformation gift in a way that was expressly forbidden. Because of their misuse of the gift, Wearla curses them. Thus, they became the Wol'dger.

Hyroc is shocked and depressed to learn he is some cursed creature. To him, he is the monster everyone has said he always was. Despite this spirit-crushing information, he moves forward with his training.

When he transforms at the beginning of his training, he is locked into his animal form and cannot transform out of it for the duration of his training. He is also deprived of all human comforts and will have to live like a bear lives. Through a series of tough, grueling, and thoroughly unpleasant tasks that test his resolve to its limits, he learns all the capabilities of a bear and learns how to fight as one and control its dangerous tendencies.

When he returns to Elswood after completing his training, he settles back into his life. He is guilt-ridden keeping his bear form from his friends and desperately wants to find a way to tell them. He doesn't know how to do this without everyone potentially thinking he is a witch and turning on him out of fear.

When he works up enough courage to tell them, disaster strikes. Giant spiders, corrupted by the essence of the demon he had killed, attack and drag his friends away to their nest. With no time to seek assistance, Hyroc rushes off to save them. He tracks the spiders to their lair in an abandoned mine. Hyroc fights his way into the depths of the mine. During one encounter with the spiders, his torch is extinguished, plunging him into complete darkness. When all hope seems lost, a blue flame materializes in his hand. Its illumination saves him and allows him to reignite his torch. Then, the flame mysteriously vanishes. Hyroc reaches the family in their web cocoons. His elation turns to sorrow when he is too late to save the parents of his friends. But Elsa, Donovan, and Curtis are alive. He drags them out of the mine and finds Ursa outside.

When he asks Ursa about the blue flame, he learns that he is a type of Wol'dger known as an Anamagi. He is descended from a group of people that had remained loyal to the instructions of Wearla. Because of their loyalty, she offered to spare them the Wol'dger curse. They refused because they did not wish to be set apart from their brethren. Because of their willing sacrifice, Wearla gave a portion of the power of the Guardians to them and their bloodline.

This dispels any of Hyroc's sadness about being cursed and gives him a feeling of worth. After the parents of his friends are buried, and the remaining family is situated, Ursa offers to teach Hyroc how to use the powers of the blue flame, known as the Flame Claw. Hyroc knows of his origins, but he has learned nothing of his parents. Those questions still linger, and the motives of his unknown adversary remain a mystery.

PROLOGUE

Shrouded by the darkness of night, the carriage moved down the cobblestone street, horse hooves steadily clacking as they pulled it along. Rain rolled off the backs of the animals in the shower of a cold downpour. The streets were empty as anyone with sense had taken shelter from the storm. The carriage came to a stop in front of an imposing circular stone structure that had the shape of a squat domed tower with no windows. The drenched driver dismounted the carriage and opened its door. Out stepped a man attired in fine clothing colored in the orange and black of The Ministry and the symbol of a raven adorned one shoulder. He took a few steps, then turned back to face the carriage. A hooded figure emerged from the carriage, garbed in dark clothing, wearing leather gloves, and a hood partially obscured a plague mask with a beak that pointed downward along its chin. The carriage driver warily watched the figure move away. The two passengers walked into the building.

Once inside, the barefaced man shook the rain from his clothing before removing his cloak and handing it to a guard. He removed a lit torch from the wall and then walked further into the building, with the masked figure following. They descended a stone-stepped spiral staircase. At the bottom, the man pounded his fist on a closed door. A view-slit opened, revealing the face of another guard. The guard opened his mouth to speak, but he recognized the man and nodded in understanding before closing the slit. There was a muffled rattling of keys then the door opened. The man and the figure walked down a long corridor lit by evenly spaced torches. They passed several locked doors, stopping at one where two guards sat with their backs against the wall playing a game of dice on the floor. Upon spotting the new arrivals, the two guards abandoned their game and stood at attention. When they looked at the figure, they stiffened alertly and one grasped the hilt of his swords.

"Do not draw your weapons," the man said sharply. "He will not harm you; I am fully in control of him."

The guards relaxed slightly at the assurance, but the one guard's hand remained in position to draw his weapon. The figure grunted derisively and took a menacing step forward.

"Remain where you are!" the man commanded.

The figure stopped, snapped his masked face toward the man, and growled angrily, startling the guards. "As you command," the figure said in a deep, icy tone laced with hatred.

The man returned his attention to the guards. "Anything to report about the prisoner?" the man said.

"No, sir," one guard answered. "She's not made so much as a peep."

The man nodded. "Open the door," he said.

Cautiously, a guard unlocked the door, opened it, and quickly stepped back.

The door led into a small cell. A woman in tattered clothing with a bruised face sat against the far wall; one arm loosely chained to it. She stood, glaring at the man. "What do you want me to tell you this time, Keller?" she asked acidly. "Or should I address you as Inquisitor?" She pointed at him. "Your apparel seems to belong to one of their rank. I believe congratulations are in order." She spat on the ground.

Keller shook his head in displeasure. "Why must you make things so hard on yourself. I do not relish treating you this way."

"Then release me."

"You of all people know the law. Anyone in contact with a witch or having dealings with the products of dark magic is under suspicion of involvement. Until such time as their name is cleared of any involvement, imprisonment is required."

"Yes, I know the law, but I also thought logic and reason were required in its enforcement. It seems I was mistaken in both cases."

"We are under threat, and we do not have the luxury of using a delicate touch in this matter! Just tell me what I wish to know, and I promise I will end this. The Ministry and I will not bother you any further. You can get back to teaching your students. That is a very important task and you're one of the best. We do not wish to waste your talents. So, why do you continue to resist?"

The woman laughed scornfully. "*Threat?* Keller, it's been three years since he left, and in all that time, there hasn't been so much as a rumor of his whereabouts. If he wanted to harm anyone, wouldn't you have expected him to have done that by now? Why is it so hard for you to understand that he wouldn't do that?"

"Because he's not the only one!" Keller snapped. "We found one in the North Lander Army that invaded two years ago. That creature fought against us; it killed our people. And who knows how many more of those creatures are spread across our lands, killing innocent victims. They are a clear threat to us and must be eliminated no matter the cost. Please, for the sake of our citizens, tell me what I want to know. Don't do it for me, don't do it for yourself, do it for them."

The woman laughed humorlessly. "You haven't changed one bit, Keller. You're still blind to the truth. Yes, there's more of them out there, yes, one attacked us, but they're not Hyroc. He would never commit such a heinous act. We – I taught him the difference between right and wrong. He knows taking from others simply because they are weaker is dishonorable. The pain of that lesson he learned many times over. There is good in his heart, much more than you'll ever have in your blackened soul."

Keller shook his head. "Why do you continue to defend that *creature?* It is an abomination and must be destroyed, along with any other of those foul monsters."

"Monster? The only monster I see is you." she indicated the figure behind him with her chin. "And that *thing* behind you. Yes, I know of its origin. Marcus would be disgusted to see you consorting with such evil. You've betrayed your oath and sold your soul for what, to hunt down an innocent person that hasn't been a threat to anyone? You're the worst kind of hypocrite, Keller. You're no better than those who oppressed and murdered our ancestors."

"I do this because I must. If I have to sacrifice my humanity so others do not have to know what it is to face such horrors, then so be it. I gladly accept the burden."

"Feygrotha probably thought the same thing, that he must also do something terrible in the name of accomplishing what he saw as a worthy goal. You don't know how dangerous your words are or your actions. I truly pity your ignorance and empathize with your coming victims."

"Save your pity and your empathy. It will not dissuade me." His expression softened, and his voice became more polite. "Tell me what I want to know, I beg of you. I do not wish for you to suffer any longer. I wish to see you back at the school, spreading good through your students. Please, just tell me."

"I will not aid you in killing him! You want him; you'll have to find him yourself. I would rather die than help you."

Keller sighed, and his expression became gloomy. "That is unfortunate. But I still have a way to get what you refuse to tell me. I had dearly hoped it wouldn't come to this." He turned toward the figure and waved it in. "Begin your work."

The figure raised its head, revealing two purple flaming eyes behind its mask. "As you wish," the figure hissed as it approached the woman.

"Remember, you did this to yourself," Keller said. "This isn't the fate you had to suffer, June. I hope that *thing* was worth this."

Chapter 1
Widening Divide

The wind rustled the green leaves of the forest trees in the bright summer sunlight. Lively plants filled every space within sight, and a vibrant array of reds, blues, and purples showed as if a painter had laid them down on a verdant canvas. Beyond the whispering of a breeze that kept the air comfortably cool, all was silent and peaceful. Amid such tranquility, someone wouldn't expect deeds of heroism to occur. But as unlikely as that seemed, that is just what happened here.

It was a story of bravery and sorrow, a tale that would be praised by any who heard it and the person responsible for it heralded as a living hero. The first tellers of this story were instead met with disbelief. This was not because they were known for making up stories or exaggerating facts. Their disbelief was directed at the hero of the story. He was an outsider to the villagers, and many distrusted and despised him. In their eyes, he was incapable of such an honorable act. As untrue as this was, he gladly accepted their scorn, for it meant the only people he had left to care about were safe.

But that was not the end of it. As time went on, the ire from the villagers the hero endured slowly drifted onto those he considered to be his family. The villagers wondered if the family was complicit in the deaths of their parents. The help and consideration the family had initially received for their unfortunate circumstance ceased. Soon the family was struggling to provide for itself. The villagers turned their backs on them, giving their plight no heed and viewing them as no better than outsiders. But he would not let the villagers determine their fate.

Hyroc stepped into the river. He wore a brown jerkin and black pants. His snouted face, head, and triangular ears gave him the resemblance of a wolverine. His fur was black with two dark brown stripes that ran from his eyes down the back of his neck. A whitish spot of long-healed frostbite showed on the tip of one ear.

His supple leather boots splashed through the water as he moved into the mottled shade of the trees. An eager look entered his sapphire eyes when he spotted a reddish shape ahead of him. Caught in his snare, he saw a beautiful fox that would fetch a fair price in the village. Drawing his bow, he shot the fox through the eye. The animal fell without issuing any sound of pain. He freed the body and reset the trap. Standing with the fox in hand, he slung the animal over his shoulder and headed back the way he had come.

It had been three years since the spider attack that had claimed the lives of his friend's parents, and Hyroc was now nineteen. He had grown in that time. No longer was he the scrawny schoolboy afraid of bullies. He had strong limbs and a strong chest. His other abilities had also grown in power, due largely in part to the teachings of the white she-bear named Ursa. If the villagers learned of these abilities, they might try to kill him, so he kept them hidden. But those powers were extremely beneficial for him and his friends that had adopted him into their small family.

Hyroc moved through the forest, eventually arriving at his cabin situated in a clearing beneath the towering shape of Wolf paw Mountain. This was his home, but lately, he had spent little time at it. Most of his time was instead devoted to helping his friends at their cabin.

He heard the scraping of claws on bark, and the reddish-brown shape of an adult mountain lion appeared in front of him. Hyroc held his hand out, and the big cat he had named Kit rubbed affectionately

Chapter 1: Widening Divide

against it. Rarely did Hyroc have to feed his companion anymore as the big cat did his own hunting.

After a moment of attention, Kit eagerly examined the dead fox. Hyroc pushed Kit away with his clawed hand as the cougar tried sneaking a bite out of one of the fox's limp legs.

"Hey, stop that," Hyroc said sternly. "You can have it once I've skinned it."

Kit settled into a sitting position with his eyes still fixed on the fox. Hyroc gave an appreciative nod. He moved to a large spruce in front of his cabin. He used a rope to hang the fox from a sturdy branch and got to work carefully skinning it. When he finished, he tossed the bloodied remains of the now fleshless animal to Kit, who promptly tore into it. Hyroc moved to a nearby stream and washed the pelt. Normally, he would spend the next few days stretching and treating the pelt for a higher trading value, but the lower price from selling the raw fox hide was needed without delay.

When the skin was sufficiently cleaned, he rung it out, rolled it up under his arm, and headed back toward the cabin. He moved past the structure and was joined by Kit once he reached the road that led to the village of Elswood. He frowned at the mountain lion, seeing a bloodstain on the big cat's mouth. Using the residual moisture on his hands from washing the fox pelt, he rubbed the red patch away before continuing forward. Having his companion enter the village with clearly visible evidence of a recent kill might be problematic. The villagers already disliked both of them; he didn't want to give them more of a reason by them thinking the big cat had killed someone's livestock.

Upon entering the village, the two of them encountered irritated stairs and muttering from those that dwelt there. Three years ago, this would've been extremely distressing to Hyroc, but now it was merely a nuisance. Simply annoying the villagers with his presence was no longer the only reaction he incurred. Some people were hostile and might even try harming him if so inclined. He had to be careful, for if he got into a fight and hurt someone bad enough, the village as a whole might turn on him. It was a similar situation that had initially started him on this path. But unlike then, the lonely wilderness was not his only choice. He had a home out there, where others of his kind lived. Though an exciting thought, he still had responsibilities to his friends and was honored bound to stay with them. Only once they were safe, and they had their livelihood sufficiently restored would he entertain the notion of leaving. For now, he had to ensure his freedom to enter the village for trade.

In light of his current reality, Hyroc had taken on a new strategy for dealing with the villagers. He always brought his sword and maintained an air of strength. Intimidation was the surest way to avoid a confrontation. If everyone thought serious harm would befall them if they gave him any trouble, it seemed reasonable to think they would avoid bothering him. The technique worked on his bullies at the boarding school in Forna years ago, so, in theory, it should do the same here. He also made sure to bring Kit with him whenever he went to the village. The low guttural growl from the big cat was a frightening deterrent. Still, even as unlikely as a confrontation was, he had to be on his guard. It seemed only a matter of time before some idiot tried something with him. And when that situation arose, he was equipped to fight off an attacker.

He and Kit arrived at the village center and made their way to Anton's furrier shop. The man detested Hyroc, acting as if he were going to kill someone at any moment, but coveted the pelts he delivered. So long as he provided valuable trading goods, their relationship remained functional, if barely.

Anton was out front hunched over a table, working a pelt. He spotted Hyroc's approach and stood straighter with a scowl on his face.

"What do you have for me this time?" Anton said, his tone almost hostile.

That's how most of Hyroc's trades went with the man, no pleasantries, straight to the point, all business. Hyroc unrolled the fox pelt and held it up for inspection.

Anton frowned. "A raw pelt?" he asked unenthusiastically.

"I know; it's a raw pelt," Hyroc said. "But I need the Flecks for it now. How much is it worth?"

Chapter 1: Widening Divide

Anton rubbed his chin thoughtfully. "Well, it seems to be in good condition, no nicks or cuts. I'll give you ten flecks for it."

Hyroc narrowed his eyes. "Ten?" he said in disbelief. "I brought you a finished fox pelt not that long ago, and you gave me thirty for it."

"Yes, but this hide is raw, I have to account for the amount of work I need to put in to finish it, so what I can make off of it is less. Therefore, what I'll pay you for it isn't as much."

Hyroc didn't believe him. A pelt in such nice condition, even raw, was a valuable commodity. Anton was trying to swindle him because he was desperate. That was a new low even for Anton.

"Fifteen," Hyroc said sternly.

Anton rubbed his chin, considering the offer. "Fourteen," he answered. "That's as high as I'll go, and if you don't like that, you can go to someone else."

That was an aggravating dig at Hyroc, considering there were no other furriers in the village, but the price seemed reasonable enough.

"Deal," Hyroc said.

Anton nodded. After accepting the pelt, he laid the coins on the table, unwilling to risk Hyroc touching him and defiling his hands.

Hyroc retrieved his payment, then turned, heading for the bakery.

"Is he always like that?" an unfamiliar voice said.

Hyroc turned to see a tall man adorned in a simple white tunic, pants, and a common pair of boots. He had unkempt blonde hair, a short blonde beard, and wore a copper necklace with a runestone. The man was definitely a stranger, possibly with some North Lander blood in him. Hyroc had heard North Lander raiding parties sometimes sent a scout to check out their target, but the man's clothing and pleasant demeanor made that seem unlikely. There appeared no reason to be rude and Hyroc wasn't about to judge the man solely by his appearance.

"Most of the time," Hyroc said conversationally. "He doesn't like me, but he admires the nice pelts I keep bringing him. That's the only reason he tolerates me." Hyroc paused, giving the man a strange look. "Wait, why are you talking to me? Aren't you a little concerned about—"

Hyroc used his hand to indicate his own face "– this? Me looking the way I do?"

The man waved dismissively. "Trust me, I've seen much stranger things than you," the man said happily. "Have you ever seen an ogre? They're much more frightening." He waved his hand apologetically. "Not that I think you're frightening."

Hyroc nodded. "You also have to take into account their whole eating people thing," he added.

The man laughed. "Yeah, that's probably the scariest part." He held his hand out in greeting but recoiled, startled, when Kit let loose a warning growl.

Hyroc promptly nudged his companion with his boot. "Hey, stop that," he said sternly. Kit stopped growling. "Sorry, he's a little protective. Don't worry; you're safe. He won't do anything now."

The man sighed with relief. "That's impressive that you're able to keep a mountain lion as a pet," he said.

Hyroc stroked the back of Kit's head fondly. "We have a closer bond than most," Hyroc said.

"I believe you. That's a frightening friend you have there." The man cautiously held his hand out again. "My name is Einar."

Hyroc stared at Einar's pro offered hand. It had been a while since anyone wanted to shake his hand. Hyroc stood there a moment before shaking the man's hand. "My name is Hyroc."

Einar's eyes lit slightly. "Hyroc? That's an interesting name. Well, it was nice meeting you, Hyroc. I would like to stay and chat, and please don't take this the wrong way, but I've got to go. I'll be seeing you."

"Yeah, I'll be seeing you." Einar clapped Hyroc on the shoulder as he turned to head toward the village center.

Hyroc cocked an eyebrow as he watched the man leave. *What an odd person,* he thought to himself. Did he just make a new friend? They were both outsiders to the village, so they had that in common. It would be nice for him to have someone new to talk to. Though, he was getting ahead of himself. He knew practically nothing about the man and needed to learn more before he even started entertaining the notion of befriending him.

Continuing toward the bakery, Hyroc stopped again when Kit's ears flicked sideways, and he let out a low growl. Hyroc then became aware of the sound of dog barks getting closer. He tipped his head back with a sigh. That was the last person he wanted to deal with today. Turning, he spotted a brown-haired man of average height in mildly dirty clothing with an ugly beard, and he wore an angry scowl. Running ahead of the man were four rowdy hunting hounds barking at every living thing in sight. They surrounded a barrel where an alley cat hissed angrily. The dogs bayed and jumped at the cat, but the feline was out of their reach.

The owner of the dogs was a man named Jack. Every encounter Hyroc had with the man was unpleasant. He used his hounds for hunting and also kept some livestock on his farm. The man seriously disliked Hyroc and was confrontational whenever the two happened to meet. If one of his animals went missing, he would blame the disappearance on Hyroc, or more specifically, Kit. This was unlikely because Jack's farm was on the other side of the village, and Hyroc had more control over the big cat than anyone beyond his friends knew. It was one of the perks of being an Anamagi. He had the ability to communicate simple ideas and concepts to animals. They couldn't understand the words Hyroc said, but they could understand the intentions they conveyed. If Hyroc showed Kit a certain place and told him not to go there, the big cat would avoid going there while hunting. But Hyroc's communication with his companion was not a guarantee of obedience. Kit, though merely an animal, had a mind of his own, and if he seriously didn't like what Hyroc told him to do, he would not obey.

Hyroc had told Kit to avoid going anywhere near people's livestock and their farms, and he was certain his companion had obeyed. Jack just wanted someone to blame for his loss, and they happened to be his favorite targets.

Jack's hounds abandoned the helpless cat on the barrel and rushed toward Hyroc. They skidded to a halt when Kit roared and swatted his claws at them: this cat could not so easily be bullied. The dogs spread out and cautiously circled the two of them, sniffing rapidly. Kit rumbled out a low growl to warn the dogs into maintaining their distance. Jack pointed an accusing finger at Hyroc as he moved in to speak. Hyroc folded his arms in anticipation.

"That filthy cougar of yours killed another one of my pigs last night!" Jack said pointedly. "That beast is nothing but trouble and needs to be –"

"Needs to be what?" Hyroc interrupted. "Killed because you don't know how to keep your animals in their pens?"

Jack glowered. "Getting rid of that cat wouldn't be such a bad thing; most everyone in the village wants something done about it. Beasts like that don't belong around people, and neither do you."

Hyroc used his hand to indicate the direction of Jack's farm. "Your farm is on the other side of the village, nowhere near my cabin. There are farms much closer to me that would be much easier targets for him, and they haven't had their animals disappear."

"That's because they're probably afraid of you, wouldn't tell anyone even if that cat got one of theirs, but I'm not afraid of you. Your murdering the Shackleton's parents don't frighten me."

Hyroc narrowed his eyes, his face warming. He jabbed his finger angrily at Jack. "Don't go there!" Hyroc said fiercely. "That's a lie. A rotten lie. They were good to me, better than a lot of people I've met, and I would *never* have hurt them."

Kit's growling intensified. Glancing over, the four dogs had started moving too close to the big cat. They were now entering the danger threshold on Kit's personal space. Hyroc had instructed Kit on being nonaggressive unless either of them were attacked while they were in town, but there was only so much his companion would tolerate. Kit would attack in moments if they didn't move back.

"I've heard the story about you trying to save them from monsters and whatnot," Jack continued. "Don't believe them. I think it's a bunch of –"

Hyroc indicated the dogs. "Your dogs, they're too close!" he interrupted. Kits growling continued to grow more agitated.

"What, my hounds making your beast uncomfortable?" Jack scoffed.

"Yes, and they seriously need to back off."

"They'll back off when the two of us are done with our conversation."

"No, you don't understand. He's about to –"

Kit roared and tackled one of the dogs. The two animals writhed violently on the ground. The dog yelped frantically and desperately squirmed to escape as the big cat tore into it. Kit found the dog's neck and sank his teeth into it. The dog cried out in pain, then stopped moving.

Jack's eyes erupted with rage. "YOU KILLED MY DAMN DOG!" he bellowed. He reached for a knife, but Hyroc drew his Falchion sword first. Hyroc took a few steps back, his sword held at his side. Kit backpedaled to join him.

"Don't take this any further," Hyroc said. "I tried to warn you that would happen."

Jack pointed an accusing finger at Hyroc. "I'll get you; I'll get you for this."

"I'm sorry," Hyroc said, backing away. He watched Jack pick up the dead dog and walk away. Hyroc breathed a sigh of relief, sheathing his sword. That wasn't good. The thing he was trying to avoid pretty much just happened. And to make things worse, he almost instinctually used his Flame Claw to form a shield with his empty hand. His time in Elswood nearly came to an abrupt end.

Kit looked up at him with a guilty look in his eyes. Hyroc stroked the cat's head. "No, it's all right. You didn't do anything wrong," Hyroc said comfortingly. "Those dogs shouldn't have gotten that close. Jack was so bent on blaming me for everything he didn't even notice."

"Well, that could've gone better," a familiar voice said.

Hyroc looked up to see Harold leaning against the nearby Black Spruce Tavern, smoking a pipe. Hyroc sighed. "I guess it was bound to happen sometime. The man definitely has it out for me."

"Well, ol Jack there has never been known for his brains," Harold said.

"Or bathing," Hyroc noted.

Harold cracked a smile and nodded. "It's tough dealing with those types. I have had more than my share of them. But it's a lot worse when they're drunk." Harold indicated the door to the tavern. "Come on inside, let's talk a minute. I think you could use that."

Hyroc nodded his agreement and headed inside. The tavern was sparsely occupied, with it still being relatively early in the day, and they easily found a place to sit near the fireplace.

"It's been a while since I checked in on the four of you. Is everyone getting by all right?" Harold asked.

Hyroc sighed. "We're getting by, even if just barely. We're running low on food, and I came into town to buy some."

"I can come by today or tomorrow; I've got some extra deer meat I don't need."

"Yeah, that would be a big help."

"It's a damn shame. You should be treated as a hero after what you did to save the Shackletons. Most of the Light Walker I've fought with wouldn't have even thought about doing that. If you going into that spider-infested mine all by yourself isn't bravery, then I don't know what is."

Hyroc sighed. "It's just the way things ended up."

"You deserve better. Everyone here treats you like dirt and despises you. You don't belong here with these people. You belong with your own kind, where people can appreciate what you do. How's that trip of yours coming?"

Hyroc was quite a long moment. "I know where to go, but I'm still working on my course. Once I've figured that out, it's just a matter of supplies." Harold nodded. "But I can't leave until the Shackletons are back on their feet. I'm responsible for them."

Harold laughed mockingly. "It still amazes me how anyone can think anything bad about you. You're making sure your friends that are in a bad spot are taken care of, you coldhearted bastard."

Hyroc couldn't help smiling. He clapped a friendly goodbye on Harold's shoulder and left the tavern. From there, he finally made it to the bakery.

Chapter 2
An Unpleasant Request

Hyroc moved down the trail that led to his friend's cabin holding two cloth-wrapped loaves of bread. Even after two years, he sometimes caught himself hoping to hear the sound of an excited dog rushing to greet him. There were a lot of things he missed about this place, and it stung whatever he remembered the Shackleton's parents. He still looked forward to coming here, but its appeal had been significantly diminished. The nightmarish events of the past tainted everything here.

He found Elsa out in front of the cabin placing fish fillets on a smoking rack, and Donovan and Curtis were working a hide in the back. Curtis was now twelve and had grown significantly. He was fully capable of hunting and put as much effort as he could into any work that needed doing. Unfortunately, Hyroc's relationship with the boy had taken a turn for the worse. In some way, Curtis blamed Hyroc for the death of his parents. This saddened Hyroc, but he empathized with the behavior and felt no ill will toward the boy. Curtis' world had been shattered with the death of his parents, a feeling Hyroc was more than familiar with, and grief had a way of changing a person.

While moving toward Elsa, Hyroc spotted the raven Shimmer perched on the cabin's roof. He stood on one foot and, in the other, held a small twig of a branch covered in crowberries that he was eating. The bird had become friendlier to Hyroc, but they still didn't have a warm relationship. When Hyroc's mentor, Ursa, had completed training him in the use of the Flame Claw, it was time for her to leave. She didn't want to depart and leave him and his friends to fend for themselves at such a strenuous time, with so few resources, but her Guardian oath would not allow her. She made mention of sensing some sort of disturbance that had her concerned. He didn't want her to go, but it had to be done. It just saddened him whenever he wondered if he was ever going to see her again.

Shimmer had instead decided to stay. He served Ursa, but he had sworn no binding oath and was free to make his own choices. Ursa said he was impressed by Hyroc's braving the dangers of the spider nest to save his friends and wished to be of further assistance. Shimmer then seemed to have taken a liking to Elsa. He followed her and often found a perch on her shoulder.

"Elsa," Hyroc said. When she turned to look at him, he indicated the loaves of bread. Her expression turned relieved.

"Looks like we might be having a proper meal tonight," she said happily. She used her hand to indicate the cabin. "Go ahead and set that inside, then I need to talk to you about something."

Hyroc nodded and stepped inside the cabin. "Harold's also going to stop by later today or tomorrow with some meat," he said as he came back out.

"Good, that'll be a huge help," Elsa said.

"What'd you want to talk to me about?"

Her expression became more serious. "I've been giving this a lot of thought, and I hate asking it of you, but we need a bear."

Hyroc shot her an indignant look. He hated hunting bears. Ever since he had gained his ability to transform into a bear, the thought of killing one or even seeing one dead greatly disturbed him. Ursa had explained this was due to his animal form. His repugnance came from him essentially seeing himself in the animal's position and imagining what fear and pain the animal had felt when it died. It was as if he was

Chapter 2: An Unpleasant Request

killing some part of himself when he brought down one of the animals. She said it was normal, but that didn't make it feel any better.

"Elsa, please don't make me do this," Hyroc pleaded.

"I'm sorry, I know you don't like doing that," Elsa said unhappily. "But we're struggling just to get by. We desperately need the meat, and the hide from a big bear will go for enough Flecks to keep us going for a while, maybe long enough for us to get back on our feet."

"Why does it have to be a bear? We can accomplish the same thing by going after deer. We just need a few more to make up the size difference. I can step up my hunting. It's a lot easier for me to find game than you and your brothers. I can track by even the faintest scent in my bear form, I'll bring Donovan along with me, and we can get this done in a couple days."

Elsa shook her head and used her hand to indicate the smoking rack. "Between those two loaves of bread you brought and these fish, there's nothing else. All it would take is one bad day where we don't get anything, and we're starving. And we don't have enough money to buy any food right now. We don't have the time to do it your way, and it's dangerous for you to spend much time around us as a bear. I don't think I could forgive myself if something bad happened to you because you were helping us. But if you know of a better way, please tell me. I won't make you get a bear if you give me a better option."

Hyroc pondered their predicament a moment but shook his head. There didn't seem to be a better option. "No," he said. "I can't figure out anything else to do without us risking starvation." He sighed in resignation. "We have to get a bear."

Elsa nodded. "You also know where one is. I feel terrible asking this. Our best bet is to go after your sparring partner."

Hyroc stared at the ground blankly, feeling a tremendous amount of guilt. Several months after Ursa had departed, while out hunting in bear form, he encountered a fairly large male brown bear. It was bigger than him, but it seemed more docile than the bears he had normally dealt with. Instead of showing aggression or charging him, the bear simply showed a body posture that told Hyroc not to get too close. Then after a few moments, the beast returned to its business. Then some days later, when Hyroc checked the area again, the bear was still there. As the two continued encountering each other, the bear steadily became more and more relaxed. Hyroc then got the idea to try play-sparring with his lumbering neighbor. Without Ursa, he had no one to practice his bear fighting with. Cautiously he tried it, and to his surprise, the bear joined him. Though the match was rough, his sparring partner refrained from inflicting any serious harm on him. After that, every month or so, Hyroc would return for another bout to keep himself from getting rusty at it.

Hyroc had a fondness for the bear, but now, he had to kill it. It didn't feel right at all. But when it all came down to it, this was just another wild animal. The well-being of the Shackletons, Kit, and himself was of far more importance. Killing the bear would keep them all alive.

"I agree," he said. "I know where he usually sleeps, and even if he's not there, I can still find him while I'm in my bear form."

Elsa cocked an eyebrow. "You'll be in bear form?" she questioned. "Isn't that a little risky?"

"He's a pretty big bear. You'll definitely need me in bear form to fight him. I can take him in a short fight, so I'll need the three of you to help me bring him down. Besides, I go through there all the time in my bear form and I've never seen anyone there. I'm confident I'll be okay."

Elsa nodded. "Alright, as long as you're sure about it, that's how we'll do it."

"Just promise me one thing, Elsa. Don't ask me to do this again."

She studied him thoughtfully. "We shouldn't be desperate enough to need one again, but I promise I won't ask for your help hunting a bear again."

"And the three of you are cleaning the carcass on your own. I'll carry some of the meat if I need to, but that's as much as I'll do."

Elsa nodded. "I already wasn't going to ask that of you. You'll have done more than enough."

Hyroc nodded. "Thank you."

Chapter 2: An Unpleasant Request

Elsa lightly clapped her hands together. "Alright, now I just need to get my brothers over here for dinner, and we can plan this out." She glanced anxiously at the fish. "Or at least as much of a dinner as we can make."

Chapter 3
The Last Time

Hyroc sat on a tree stump, gazing up at a clear starry night sky. A torch held by Donovan flickered mildly, casting strange shadows onto the grassy ground. He scratched his chin absentmindedly, where a faint covering of hair had begun to grow. Donovan was proud of its appearance; it seemingly made him feel more manly, but Hyroc couldn't understand why. The beard was just more hair. Maybe it was because people possessed so little hair on their bodies that they got excited over any increase, no matter how small. Hyroc shook his head. Maybe someday, he'd understand.

Curtis sat on the ground, sharpening arrowheads. The boy was a proficient hunter for someone his age and a pretty good shot with a bow. He lacked the strength for the heavier draw of their larger hunting bows and was confined to one that was much lighter. The bow lacked the power to take down big game, but Curtis often came home with fowl or rabbits. He did his fair share of work.

The three of them looked up when they heard the clack of hooves. Elsa came into view clad in her hunting gear and leading a donkey. They were going after a good-sized bear and would need the help of a pack animal to carry home all the spoils from the kill.

"Everyone ready to go?" Elsa asked. The three of them nodded, and Curtis hurriedly stuffed the sharpened arrows into his

Chapter 3: The Last Time

quiver. She focused her gaze on Hyroc. "So, what's the plan for this part again?"

Hyroc stood before speaking. "So, I have to be in bear form for us to have any chance of taking him down without any of us getting hurt or worse," he said.

"So, we shouldn't shoot you?" Donovan said sarcastically.

Hyroc and Elsa shook their heads.

"No, I'd rather you didn't," Hyroc said, mildly annoyed.

"Just checking. You don't want me to get confused and –"

"Donovan, stop talking," Elsa interrupted. Donovan gave a small defeated wave and took a step back. "This is serious! We're hunting a bear *at night*. Our prey can see much better than we can, and obstacles we can see by day are nearly invisible, making it much easier for one of us to hurt ourselves. I only chose to do it this way to make sure no one sees us hunting with Hyroc while he's in his bear form. So, we all really need to focus on what we're doing. Got it?" Donovan nodded. Elsa gestured for Hyroc to continue.

"I'll be in bear form," Hyroc continued. "I need the three of you to focus on the other bear's shoulder." Hyroc slapped his shoulder. "Right here. That's mostly your job with the spear Donovan." Donovan held up the spear, its steel head showing bronze in the torchlight. "You disable that shoulder, and he won't be able to defend himself properly. His neck will be exposed, and I can go in for the kill."

"What do you want Curtis and I doing?" Elsa said.

"Honestly, you two pretty much just need to shoot him without hitting me. Try to aim at the shoulder if you have a clear shot, but the important thing is for you to keep shooting him. Get enough arrows in him, and he's going down."

"Sounds simple enough," Donovan said.

Hyroc laughed humorlessly. "Simple for you, maybe, but you're not the one who will be distracting him. Trust me. This will probably go straight to the Sunless Plain as soon as we find him." Donovan gestured his agreement.

Hyroc took a breath, then removed his gear and jerkin. He indicated the donkey. "Make sure you've got a firm grip on those reigns. He's probably going to bolt. I've never transformed in front of him." Hyroc dropped down onto his hands and feet. He looked up at Elsa. "Ready?" She nodded, tightening her grip.

Hyroc closed his eyes and concentrated on seeing a full moon. It took him a moment to quiet his anxieties about the coming fight before the image appeared. He felt his body growing heavier and strength seeping into his muscles. The process concluded, and he was a bear.

The donkey brayed out in alarm and yanked on its reigns as it turned to run. Elsa maintained her grip and lurched toward the donkey to throw her hand on it. Donovan ran over and wrapped his arms around the struggling animal. The donkey continued to cry out in alarm, but slowly it calmed. After a few minutes, it had settled down enough for it to be led by the reigns once again. It continued to watch Hyroc nervously, but they were able to get it moving.

Hyroc waved a paw unenthusiastically toward the forest. "Let's get going," Hyroc said. He took a deep breath through his nose, smelling for a scent. "Follow me." They moved forward, their minds attuned to hunting.

Hyroc tested the air with his nose. Their quarry was close. The bear wasn't far from where he usually sparred with the animal. He hoped it was bedded down for the night and allow them some element of surprise.

Hyroc turned toward his friends and waved his paw in the direction of the bear. "He's over there," he whispered. "Everyone ready?" His companions nodded. He ignited the blue flame of his Flame Claw in one paw and visualized it forming into a ball. The flame molded into an orb of blue light. Then he made it rise into the air above their heads. He kept it relatively dim so it would add to the light of Donovan's torch instead of overpowering it. They were far enough from the village that no one would see him using his Flame Claw.

Chapter 3: The Last Time

They heard a twig snap as something moved through some bushes. Donovan tightened his grip on his spear, and Elsa held her bow at the ready. Hyroc took a breath to calm himself for what he was about to face. This was what Ursa had to trained him for. Hyroc growled out a deep, challenging call. The sounds of movement ceased and were followed by a deeper return call. Hyroc swatted the trunk of a birch tree with his paw, causing a strong thump, and drug his claws down it for good measure.

The lumbering shape of a brown bear stepped through the foliage in front of them. It lifted its head in surprise, noticing the four of them, seemingly confused by the presence of the three hunters behind Hyroc. Time seemed to freeze as each studied the other. With a twang from their bows, Elsa and Curtis shot an arrow. Curtis' arrow missed its mark, hitting the bear's chest while Elsa's struck true in its shoulder. It was a good hit but nowhere near disabling for the beast. Hyroc charged forward, attacking before their quarry had a chance to escape. He tackled the bear and nailed it in the head with a swift paw strike. The bear shook him off and hit him with several violent strikes. Each hurt but did nothing to hamper Hyroc. The bear grabbed him by the shoulders and moved to sink its teeth into one. Donovan arrived and rammed his spear into the bear's shoulder. It grunted in pain, loosening its grip. Hyroc shoved the bear backward, hoping to unbalance his opponent. It took him an incredible amount of effort to move the beast. He lurched back, allowing an opening for Elsa and Curtis to take a shot. An arrow hit the bear in the side, and another hit it in the neck.

The bear stumbled sideways, showing its wounds were starting to take an immense toll. Hyroc struck the bear's head to further disorient it and used the opening this created to bite the animal's injured shoulder. His opponent roared out in pain, shoved hard against Hyroc's chest, and raked its claws across him, trying to shake his grip loose. Hyroc let go and lurched backward when the bear turned its head to bite him in the neck. It slashed its claws toward him, but he dodged out of the way. The bear tried again, but Hyroc noticed it had caught sight of something else, and this strike wasn't aimed at him. He heard Donovan yell out in pain but didn't dare turn his head to see how bad his friend had been hit. The strike left the bear vulnerable, and Hyroc threw himself into his opponent to knock it off its feet. As soon as the bear hit the ground, Hyroc buried his teeth into its neck. He violently shook his head until the bear stopped fighting him.

When it seemed safe, Hyroc rose to his feet and turned to see the extent of Donovan's injury. Donovan limped toward him, holding his hand over a bloody spot on his leg. Despite the blood, it didn't seem to be anything fatal.

Donovan swore. "I'm okay," he said angrily. "The stupid bear saw me coming and nicked me with its claws when I came in to help your big butt!"

"I'm sorry," Hyroc said apologetically. "I thought he was going to be too preoccupied with me to pay any attention to you." A weak-sounding groan drew Hyroc's attention back to the bear. It was breathing shallowly and continued to moan in pain. Hyroc waved his paw at Elsa and indicated the bear. "Elsa, he's in pain." Elsa nodded and shot the bear in the heart. It breathed out one final quiet moan before dying. Hyroc studied the lifeless animal, feeling a stab of guilt. Though they desperately needed this kill, it didn't make him feel any better.

"I'm sorry your sacrifice was required, brother," Hyroc said in a quiet, respectful tone. "You were a big help to me. Be on your way in peace."

Hyroc turned his attention to Donovan. "Let me see that," Hyroc said.

"It's really not that big of a deal. It's just a little blood," Donovan said dismissively.

"Yes, but you're not going to want to walk all the way back to your cabin in that condition."

"I know that, but after what you just went through, I don't want to –"

"I'm perfectly fine, even after that," Hyroc interrupted. "I appreciate the concern. Let me fix it."

Chapter 3: The Last Time

Donovan nodded. Hyroc lifted his paw over the injury, and a blue glow emanated from it. He slowly moved his paw up and down. The wound knit together, followed by the rip in Donovan's pants. Hyroc felt a slight drain on his Quintessence and extinguished the glow.

His Flame Claw allowed him to heal wounds, but his abilities were fairly limited in this regard. He could only heal minor injuries, such as scrapes, cuts, and burns, but anything more serious was beyond him. It was also a drain on his strength, so he rarely utilized the ability. He usually reserved its use for hindering wounds that impaired movement. They couldn't afford to have any injuries that prevented anyone from providing.

Donovan breathed a sigh of relief. "That feels better," Donovan said thankfully. "That's very nice."

"It's better just not to get hurt in the first place," Elsa said.

"Those are mighty words from someone who stood back and let me and Hyroc do all the work."

Elsa smiled. "That's one of the perks of being the oldest." Donovan shook his head humorously. "Alright, Hyroc, you did your part. We'll take care of the carcass. We just might need you to help us carry some of it back."

Hyroc nodded and moved away. He sat down after a couple of steps and watched the starry night sky. A strange sense of unease settled over him as if he were being watched. He looked around but couldn't see anything other than the torchlight his friends worked under. Hyroc smelled the air, and nothing stood out. The heat of the fight with the bear was only making him feel strange for the moment. In a little while, he should start to feel normal again, or, at least, what was normal for him.

Chapter 4
A Curious Find

The leaves quietly rustled as Hyroc pushed a flimsy branch aside with his hand. In front of him, he saw a grouse pecking the ground. It was a warm sunny day, with some small fluffy clouds spread across the sky, and a breeze kept the air at a comfortable temperature. He pushed his shoulder against the branch to hold it in place while he readied an arrow. A reddish-brown shape burst through the foliage, landing on the bird. Hyroc yelled out in alarm and jerked his bow up an instant before he let his arrow fly. The arrow struck the trunk of a tree just above Kit's head. The mountain lion let loose a surprised yowl and threw Hyroc an alarmed glare.

"Sorry!" Hyroc yelled, gritting his teeth. "I didn't know you were there. You should know better than to pounce on something I'm aiming at. I almost shot you."

Kit relaxed noticeably, but he continued to flick his tail around angrily. He picked up the lifeless bird in his jaws and walked over to Hyroc. Hyroc grabbed the carcass and secured it to his belt.

Donovan came into sight with a startled expression on his face. "What happened?" he asked. "What was all that yelling about?"

Hyroc used his hand to indicate Kit. "Oh, nothing," he answered. "Kit just tried getting shot."

Chapter 4: A Curious Find

"He wanted to see how it felt on the receiving end of a hunt, eh?" Donovan said. Hyroc gave him a flat look. "Well, I'm really glad that didn't happen." He forced out a cough before changing the subject. "I assume you got something." He indicated the dead grouse.

"Yeah, a little grouse."

Donovan nodded. "Which way do you want to go now?"

Hyroc gave their surroundings a quick glance and pointed forward. "I guess we should keep going this way. I've seen deer tracks sometimes in a spot a little further ahead." Donovan nodded.

Close to the area Hyroc was leading them, they came across dear-sign. It seemed relatively fresh, and they followed the trail. After an hour or so of tracking, they spotted something, but it wasn't what they were expecting. They found the deer or what was left of it.

In front of them lay a mutilated deer. The ground was covered in dried blood. The animal's chest was ripped open at the sternum, and its innards were hanging out. Its head and legs were missing, and its spine was broken in several places. Flies swarmed over the body, and though the air held the smell of rot, the stench wasn't overpowering, suggesting the deer had been killed within a day or two. They had come across animal kills before, but none had been anywhere near as grisly as this.

Donovan and Hyroc exchanged a surprised glance before moving closer.

"What in the *shadow* could've done this?" Donovan asked, disturbed. Hyroc shook his head. Donovan crouched down beside the carcass to have a closer look. He drew his hunting knife and probed into the animal's chest cavity with the blade.

"You didn't do this, did you?" Donovan asked.

Hyroc shook his head. "Definitely not," he answered. "It's been quite a while since I solo hunted as a bear. But I wouldn't have wasted all the good meat on the body."

"Didn't think so." Donovan pulled his knife back, wiped it off on the ground, and wiggled it while looking thoughtful.

"What are you thinking?" Hyroc asked. "Did you find something?"

"Well, if I'm looking at this correctly, beyond some nibble marks, hardly anything on this deer has been eaten."

Hyroc focused more closely on the carcass, realizing Donovan was right. There were no major bite marks or the usual chunks of missing flesh from a predator feeding on the carcass. This was more unclear for the animal's chest, but when he examined the innards, though a substantial amount of damage had been done to them, he saw no evidence of anything being eaten. Whatever had killed this deer definitely had no interest in eating it. An animal didn't do this. Hyroc felt the cold tingle of apprehension running up his neck.

"Did something kill this deer for the fun of it?" Donovan said. "Or, do you think this is *him* again?"

Was this the doing of Hyroc's unknown adversary? This person had sent a Shade Hunter after him. That person was responsible for sending him and his friends down such a painful and sorrowful course. Had *they* found him and returned to finish their task? Hyroc felt the power of his Flame Claw tingling in his arm. He was now a lot stronger than he was back then. He was not such an easy target anymore. If they came for him, they would have a fight on their hands.

"I don't know," Hyroc said. "It might be *him*."

"We need to let Elsa and Harold know," Donovan said. He sighed. "And it might be time for you to move along."

Hyroc shot Donovan a shocked look. Leave Elswood? Leave his friends, the only kind of family he had. He had been planning to do so eventually to find others of his kind, but that time had seemed far off, nothing to rush into. But now, that was forced upon him. In mere days he could be leaving everything behind.

Hyroc covered his face with his hand. He didn't know if he could do it. He would be leaving the only family he knew. Lonely isolation would fill their place. He had been there once before and didn't know if he could do it again. How was it possible for his life to change so suddenly? Mere minutes ago, his life had seemed relatively bright and full of potential. Now, it was clouded with darkness.

Chapter 4: A Curious Find

Donovan gave him a comforting pat on the shoulder. Hyroc lowered his hand and stared blankly off into space.

"We should get going," Donovan said. "It's not safe here."

Hyroc sighed in resignation. This wasn't what he wanted. He glanced toward the deer carcass as he stood, and the deer's missing head caught his notice, triggering a thought. He moved to the deer's gaping chest wound and reached inside.

"Hyroc, what are you doing?" Donovan asked, sounding perplexed. "I don't think you want to get any of that on you. Elsa would have a fit if you came inside the cabin like that."

Hyroc ignored Donovan and kept feeling inside the deer. Eventually, he removed his gore-covered hand, feeling the rush of apprehension. "It's not there," he said, shaking the remnants of the deer's insides from his hand. "I don't know if this was *him*."

"What do you mean? What's not there?"

Hyroc indicated the carcass. "The heart, it's missing."

Donovan cocked an eyebrow. "Okay, so the heart is missing. H*e* probably removed it so he could summon another one of those nasty Hunter demon things you killed a couple years back."

Hyroc shook his head. "No, this isn't for another demon. It doesn't quite work that way. Basically, to summon a shadow demon, the summoner has to sacrifice a body part, like a finger, in order to control the demon. So, whoever removed this deer's heart and head isn't going to summon a shadow demon, which means we're dealing with a witch. They can use a deer head, its antlers, and a deer heart for some of their rituals. So, we're dealing with a witch." He narrowed his eyes, the full weight of what he said donning on him. They were dealing with a *witch*! This was a person who could kill him in any number of nightmarish ways and harm who knows how many villagers. This wasn't his unknown adversary. This was something worse.

Hyroc swore. "It's a witch," he said darkly.

"So, we should *really* tell Harold!" Donovan said eagerly. Hyroc nodded.

Kit began to growl quietly, and a feeling of unease suddenly settled on them. Donovan leaned in toward Hyroc. "We're being watched!" Donovan softly hissed out of the side of his mouth.

Hyroc readied himself to use his Flame Claw to form a shield. He and Donovan scanned their surroundings cautiously. They couldn't see anyone, but the feeling of being watched remained.

"Turn slowly back the way we came," Hyroc whispered. Wordlessly they turned and headed away from the carcass. When they were a few yards out, they quickened their pace. They now had another dangerous opponent to deal with.

Chapter 5
Something Amiss

Hyroc found Harold sitting at a table inside the Black Spruce Tavern eating lunch. He and Donovan had decided to split up after their discovery. Hyroc was taking care of informing Harold while Donovan alerted Elsa and Curtis. Harold spotted him and gave an inviting wave.

"Good afternoon," Harold happily said as Hyroc settled into a seat across from him. Harold indicated a piece of meat on his plate. "You should really try this pork. The cook is trying this special herb rub, and it's –"

"We've got a problem," Hyroc interrupted.

Harold gave him a confused look. "Problem?" Harold questioned. "Already? Elsa told me the four of you could relax a little because that bear you killed set all of you up for a while. Did I misunderstand something? What's this problem you're talking about?" Harold took a bite of pork.

Hyroc leaned in. "I think we've got a witch," he said quietly.

Harold choked on his bite of food. "You what now!"

"I think we came across evidence of a witch." Hyroc quickly recounted his and Donovan's discovery of the deer and included all the details he noticed.

Harold rubbed his chin, looking thoughtful before speaking. "Yes, that seems a reasonable assumption," he answered. "I'm guessing only you and the Shackletons know about this?"

Hyroc nodded. "So, what are we going to do? Are you going to tell the village elders so they can get the villagers organized to go after the witch?"

Harold shook his head. "That would be a bad idea."

Hyroc shot him a stunned look. "What do you mean 'that would be a bad idea?'" he hissed in a whisper. "It's a *witch,* and they usually *kill* people. That absolutely seems like a pretty good reason to tell someone!"

"No, it's a bad idea because the elders are likely to send those villagers after *you.*"

"What? Why would they come after me? I had nothing to do with this. And I'm the one telling them. Why would I tell them if I was the one responsible? That doesn't make any sense. I would have to be the dumbest witch there's ever been."

Harold laughed humorlessly. "You think they're going to rationally contemplate the situation? The Shackleton's parents were killed not long after you arrived. That didn't improve the villager's trust in you because a lot of people think you had something to do with their deaths. Then suddenly, you tell them of a witch in the area. Do you think it would be a big stretch for them to think this is all of your doing? And even if they don't reach that false conclusion, they'll likely run you out of the village anyway simply because you seem to be some kind of portent of doom, and it's simply too dangerous to have you around."

Hyroc stared at him, nearly dumbfounded. "That's preposterous. They could not possibly think something so ridiculous."

"This isn't about their thoughts being unreasonable, Hyroc. If people fear something enough, logic doesn't exist. The only thing people will listen to is that fear. It won't matter if you're guilty or innocent. They will kill you simply to alleviate their fear. It's a powerful feeling, and when it's taken root, people stop listening to the voice of reason."

Chapter 5: Something Amiss

Hyroc ran his hand through his head fur. This situation was so frustrating! He was trying to do the right thing. But if he did *that*, it would only cause him more problems despite what should be seen as clearly honorable intentions, intentions meant to keep people from harm.

"Then what are we supposed to do?" Hyroc snapped.

"I think you know the answer to that," Harold said.

Hyroc blew out a breath. "We have to do it ourselves."

Harold nodded. "It was once my job to hunt down witches such as this. Even without the help of the other villagers, our adversary is at a great disadvantage. There's five of us and only one of them." Harold indicated Hyroc's hand and gave a dangerous grin. "And I know you've got a few tricks of your own. We can handle this without more help."

Hyroc felt a surge of confidence. Harold was right. They could do this. Hyroc was Anamagi, the Guardians had bestowed their power upon him, and like them, he hunted the darkness. This witch was just another opponent to be defeated.

"Alright," Hyroc said. "If that's what needs to be done, let's get to it." Harold nodded his understanding. "What do we do?"

Harold glanced around to make sure no one was watching them. "Nothing for now," Harold said. "We know there's a witch about, but we don't know where they are or what they're doing. We're going to watch and listen, alright. But as soon as we know where they're at —" Harold used a finger to make a slicing motion across his throat.

Hyroc nodded. "Do you have any ideas about what I should keep an eye out for?"

"Look for any more indicators of the witch's activity, and keep an ear out for any strange rumors. It's probably safe to assume that witch isn't one of the villagers. Try to keep track of any newcomers. A stranger was responsible for that necromancer crisis."

A thought came to Hyroc. "Stranger?" he said. "Before the bear hunt, I did come across a new face. His name is Einar. Do you think he's the witch?"

—43—

OUTCASTS

Harold scratched his chin thoughtfully. "Maybe, it is odd this all started up shortly after his arrival." He focused on Hyroc. "But, then again, the same things were thought about you when you first arrived here. It could merely be coincidental. We need to be absolutely certain about this before we act. If we're wrong, we may very well end up killing an innocent person. And if we tip off the witch before we're ready, we may very well end up as their next victim."

Hyroc nodded, suddenly feeling the weight of his actions bearing down on him. He held someone's life in his hands. Whether they lived or died was now up to him. There was no margin for error. He needed to make sure before he acted on his thought.

"There is an easy enough way to find out," Hyroc said. "Don't you still have a Perception Orb?"

Harold nodded. "I do," he said. "You want me to use it on him."

"Yep."

"Alright, let's get started." Hyroc and Harold stood.

Harold grabbed Hyroc by the shoulder as he turned to leave. "I'm going to follow you from a way's back, just in case he's in the village."

Hyroc nodded and left the tavern. He scanned the village center but didn't see Einar. From his first meeting with the stranger, he wasn't sure what the man did in the village. The man's simpler clothing suggested he was in need of work, but acquiring food and supplies to continue a journey somewhere was another strong possibility. Hyroc glanced through the various village shops trying to decide which seemed the most likely. His concentration was broken by the sound of barking dogs.

Hyroc rolled his eyes. This was an even worst day for this to happen. He had more important things to worry about than Jack and his dysfunctional mutts right now. He turned toward the sound to see only two dogs rushing toward him. They stopped before Kit even had a chance to growl.

"Aye, I see you there, you filthy devil!" Jack snarled, pointing an accusatory finger at Hyroc.

"Do we really have to do this right now?" Hyroc said, annoyed.

—44—

Chapter 5: Something Amiss

"Yeah, we're doing this *right now*. I said I'd get you for this, and now you're getting it."

Hyroc sighed his resignation. Jack closed the distance and threw a haymaker at him. Hyroc sidestepped the strike and slapped the man's fist down. The man turned and took another swing. This strike was harder but wild, and Hyroc dodged it by taking a few steps back.

"Fight me, coward!" Jack growled.

Jack's dogs edged closer, yipping and barking excitedly. He moved in toward Hyroc to swing. Hyroc used his forearm to block the man's strike and rammed his fist into his opponent's abdomen. Jack gasped in a mixture of surprise and pain. Hyroc pushed the man back as he struck twice more. Jack fell to his knees, holding his stomach and breathing heavily. When the man spit out a mouthful of blood, Hyroc turned away and returned his attention back to his original task.

"I'm not done yet," Jack yelled.

Hyroc heard the sound of a blade slipping out of a scabbard. Kit roared as Hyroc turned his attention back on the man and was surprised to see Jack charging toward him with a knife. Hyroc reached down to grab his sword. He was thunderstruck to see someone slam into Jack. The figure knocked Jack off his feet, dropped to the ground on top of him, and wrestled the knife from his grip. The man tossed the knife aside, pulled Jack's upper body up by his tunic, and nailed him in the face with his fist, sending the man back down a final time. Jack made no attempt to stand.

The unknown man stood and dusted himself off before facing Hyroc. Hyroc was baffled to see that the person was Einar.

"That was a sneak move there!" Einar said, shaking his head in disapproval. "Coming after you with a knife when you're back was turned. Definitely a coward's move. What did you do to piss him off like that?" Einar briefly examined his scraped-up knuckles.

"I'm really not sure," Hyroc said. "He's just always seemed like he hates me."

"Some people are just like that, I guess."

"Thanks for the help there."

Einar gave him a dismissive wave. "No need to thank me, I didn't want to see anyone get stabbed. I see you're no stranger to a fight. Those hits you got in looked painful. I don't think I would've gotten up after that."

Hyroc shrugged. "Some people are too dimwitted to know when to quit."

"Ain't that the truth. I hear you and your friends took down a brown bear." Hyroc nodded. "Congratulations on that! I've never gone after a bear before; that sounds pretty dangerous. How'd you four manage it?"

Hyroc studied Einar carefully, trying to think of the best way to explain the bear hunt without mentioning any of his abilities.

"It was really pretty simple," Hyroc lied. "We piled some stinky fish carcasses in a pit we dug on an animal trail where we found some fresh bear-sign. We made a tree blind and waited for the bear. The smell finally drew it in, and we took it down with a few arrows aimed at its vital areas."

Einar nodded, looking impressed. "That's smart being in the trees like that," he agreed. "I definitely wouldn't want to be on the ground with an angry beast that could easily rip a person to pieces." Einar looked oddly disturbed by his words. "What I overheard from one of the shopkeepers made it sound as if you wrestled it to the ground and killed it with your bare hands."

Hyroc let out a forced laugh. "That's unbelievable!" he said, faking humor. "That sounds like someone who let their imagination run wild."

"I think everyone's got at least one of those for a neighbor."

Hyroc nodded. "So, what brings you to Elswood, if you don't mind my asking?"

"Work mostly. I'm one of the farmhands at the Devery farm just outside of the village. I got tired of all the hustle and bustle in the towns and cities, I wanted something quieter, and this place has plenty of quiet."

"Yeah, it's pretty nice."

Chapter 5: Something Amiss

This was the man they thought was a witch? He was mild-mannered and had even saved Hyroc from a potential stabbing. The only thing the man might be guilty of was being too polite and agreeable. That didn't exactly fit the picture of a heartless sorcerer that mutilated animals to perform bizarre rituals. He seemed like the last person they should suspect as being a witch.

"Well, I should probably get going," Einar said. "I was sent to buy some tools for the farm."

"Alright, have a good day," Hyroc said.

"It was nice seeing you again." Einar pointed a thumb over his shoulder toward Jack. "And hopefully, *he* learned his lesson." Einar turned and headed to a shop.

Hyroc looked toward the Black Spruce Tavern to Harold leaning against the wall. Harold gave him a strange look, and Hyroc shrugged in response before walking over to him.

"Hmm, I've got the feeling he's not a witch," Harold said. "My Perception Orb didn't indicate anything."

Hyroc nodded. "The only stranger we know about is not a witch. What should we look for next?"

"We need more information, so, for now, our only choice is to watch and listen."

"And hope we don't fall into a trap in the meantime," Hyroc said gloomily.

Chapter 6
Elusive Prey

Hyroc tossed a rock into the lake beside the Shackleton's cabin. The stone skipped once across the water's placid surface before plunging out of sight. Kit was crouched at his feet, lazily watching. Behind them, Elsa, Donovan, Curtis, and Harold sat around a small map of the surrounding area. For the last week now, they had diligently searched for the witch, but they weren't any closer to figuring out where the witch was.

"We know they aren't anywhere on the mountain," Elsa said. "The four of us have been all over it, and there's no sign of anyone living there, and we couldn't find any evidence of rituals or anything that might resemble an altar."

"Even the mountain lion cave or anywhere else where someone could take shelter?" Harold asked.

"We checked all those. They were empty," Donovan said. "Nothing bigger than a shrew seems to live in them."

"I even checked while in bear form for a scent," Hyroc said, reaching down for another rock. "And found nothing."

Harold nodded. "I've run down every strange rumor I've heard," he said. He thumbed toward Hyroc. "And beyond some entertaining speculation about you, I didn't find anything," Hyroc smirked, then tossed another stone. It hit the water and plunged straight down. "I

Chapter 6: Elusive Prey

also talked to a bunch of people, and none of them were good candidates as a witch, nor did they tell me about anything useful."

"With a Perception Orb?" Hyroc said.

"Yes, I made sure to bring it with me; no color changes." Hyroc nodded and tossed another rock. It skipped twice before sinking. Harold paused, looking thoughtful a moment. "Though I did hear mention of two farms having one of their livestock animals get mutilated. I checked into them, and each animal was missing its head. When I looked for a trail, I couldn't find anything. And it's obviously too dangerous to have Hyroc take a closer look."

"I probably still wouldn't find anything even if I did," Hyroc noted. "As careful as this witch has been not leaving a trace, they're probably using some form of magic to remove anything that might lead us back to them."

"That seems a reasonable assumption," Harold agreed.

Hyroc threw another stone; it skipped only once.

Donovan energetically indicated Hyroc. "Wait, Hyroc, what about that little tree trick Ursa taught you," he asked. "Where you talk to the trees. Could that help?"

"I don't think so," Hyroc said.

"Tree trick?" Harold said questioningly. "You can talk to trees now?"

Hyroc sighed. "It's a little hard to explain," he said. "I'm not really talking to them. It's more like I'm reading their feelings."

"Trees have feelings?" Harold said skeptically.

"Sort of. They're not feeling in the way any of us understand them. Trees and other forest plants are almost not even aware of their surroundings. They have feelings, in a way, but trees are incredibly slow and resistant to expressing them. It's more like they're reacting to a change in the forest. Think about the way plants droop when they don't get enough water and then perk up when it rains."

"Or when a tree gets a deep scrape in its trunk," Elsa interjected. "And it oozes sap."

Hyroc pointed at her eagerly. "Yes," he agreed. "Something damaged the tree, and the tree reacted. But the sap doesn't come

—49—

immediately. It takes a while before it starts flowing. Basically, that's what we're dealing with. I don't ask the trees questions, and they don't answer. The trees react, and I read the impressions they give me. All the trees are connected, and from the impressions I get, I can tell if there's been a change elsewhere in the forest. But what I can tell from this is fairly limited. I can't figure out the exact location of a particular animal, but I might be able to tell the general area of where it resides depending on how much of an impact it has on the forest. So, if I was, let's say, looking for a specific squirrel, I probably couldn't find one because they're small and do practically nothing to a tree. But, if a herd of deer came through and all of them were rubbing their horns on trees, then the trees would notice. It has to be something significant for them to notice."

"So, if a bunch of people started cutting down trees," Harold said. "You could figure out if that was happening?"

Hyroc nodded. "Yes, I could tell if large numbers of trees were getting cut down, and similarly, I could tell if magic was used, witchcraft in particular, or if there was a shadow demon. The trees have a very strong reaction to both. But I can only use this ability where there is a forest. It's so difficult to tell what the trees are feeling that if there isn't a large enough number of them, there just isn't a big enough concentration of reactions for me to tell anything. So, this ability would be useless somewhere like the planes of Forna because there are too few trees."

"That makes sense, I think," Harold said. "I say you should at least give it a try. We don't have any more leads. What could it hurt?"

Hyroc nodded. "Alright," he said.

The five of them moved toward the edge of the clearing. Hyroc found a birch tree and placed his hand on its cool white bark. Concentrating hard, he began to feel something. Slowly a wave of impressions gently washed over him. They felt faint and distant, as if he were trying to listen to whispering barely within earshot. He could tell there had been a mild forest fire somewhere to the north. Then he found what seemed to be the forest reacting to a recent surge of power.

Chapter 6: Elusive Prey

The power felt dark and foreboding, seeming to indicate the use of witchcraft. It seemed half the forest had felt the ripples of that power, which made finding even a general area for its origin almost impossible. The only thing he could confirm was the power had occurred somewhere to the west of Wolf Paw Mountain, which the Shackleton's cabin sat near. A strange, disturbing sensation caught his attention. It didn't feel like it came from the presence of a shadow demon or someone using magic. It felt as if a crazed animal had torn through part of the forest. The trees here had sustained a high number of broken branches, and deep marks had been cut into their trunks. When he focused on the feelings, he narrowed it down to a familiar part of the forest to the east. He withdrew from the trees. Their impressions faded until Hyroc felt them no more.

"Well, there definitely seems to be a witch," Hyroc said. "The only thing I can figure is the witch might be somewhere west of the mountain."

"Anything more specific?" Harold asked.

Hyroc shook his head. "Sorry, that's all I've got."

"That's not very helpful. West of the mountain is an enormous swath of forest."

Hyroc shrugged. "But there was something else. Something had done a lot of damage to some trees."

Harold looked intrigued. "Doesn't sound like much, but you never know; we should look into it. But do you know where?"

"I think it's to the East. I'll show you. But no guarantees that I'm right. Trees aren't exactly specific, and Ursa only showed me how to do this a couple of times."

It was nearing dusk by the time the five of them arrived at the area of damaged trees. The impressions Hyroc had gotten from the trees were a lot vaguer than he was expecting, and it had taken them a few hours of searching to stumble upon what they were looking for. The whitish tips of broken branches adorned almost every tree they could see, and numerous branches and limbs lay strewn across the ground. Deep claw marks covered the largest trees, and they were missing a significant amount of bark. But most disturbing of all, some of the claw marks were high above the ground, suggesting something big had done this.

"Did a bear do all this," Donovan asked, awestruck.

"Unless it's bigger than any I've ever seen," Harold said. "A bear didn't do this." Harold used his hand to indicate some claw marks above him. "I don't see any marks higher than that, so I'm assuming that's as far as he could reach." He steadily moved his finger down, counting to a certain distance, then stopped. "That's probably about the height where the witch's head or shoulders should be." Harold studied the marks thoughtfully, then jabbed a finger forward in surprise. "Shadow, he's at least eight feet tall!"

Donovan, Curtis, Elsa, and Hyroc exchanged shocked looks. Their adversary was huge!

"That's, that's taller than me on my hind legs in bear form," Hyroc said, shocked. "He's got a whole foot on me."

"And that's if we're right," Donovan noted. "This witch could be even bigger than that. What'd this guy do to himself?"

"I don't know if I can fight something that size, even if I am a bear."

"I don't know if we've got a choice," Elsa said gloomily. "You see what this person did to these trees? What would've happened if they stumbled across someone?"

"I think we would have a horrible, disgusting mess made out of people," Donovan said unenthusiastically.

"If this guy goes to one of the farms or, Hallowed forbid, gets into the village, a lot of people are going to die."

"So, is the witch mutilating animals and using their heads in some kind of dark ritual to do this?" Donovan said.

"I don't know," Harold said. "In all my time with The Ministry, I've never seen anything like this. But why? As careful as this witch has been hiding their presence –" Harold used his hand to indicate the whole area "– why do this? Why leave it here? Why do something that so obviously makes his presence known?"

Chapter 6: Elusive Prey

Hyroc pondered the conundrum. This did indeed seem out of character for their witch. Their target had been incredibly careful to avoid notice or any evidence that could lead them to him. But then he decides to destroy a bunch of trees and doesn't even try to conceal what he did. Anyone who found this spot would know none of this was natural, think a witch was involved, and alert the village. That would be an extremely dangerous situation for a witch. Though witches are powerful, they're not powerful enough to fight an entire village. They might kill a few people, but the weight of numbers would easily overwhelm them.

So, why be so careless? This area wasn't often visited by the villagers, making it a not terrible spot to do whatever he was doing here. But why risk it? All it would take is a hunting group passing by for him to be discovered. And this evidence would remain visible for months or even years. He had the power to get rid of it? This didn't seem to follow any kind of logic. It was almost as if he was begging them to find this. Hyroc paused. What if they were meant to find this? Why would he want them to find this? Why would he care? The five of them should be no one to him unless Hyroc's other adversary was responsible and had sent this witch after him. The Shade Hunter had failed to kill him, so it seemed reasonable to think his adversary would send something more dangerous.

Were these trees meant to taunt him and make him afraid? The situation was admittedly unsettling, but he had faced nightmares before and emerged victoriously. It would take more than this demonstration to frighten him. But if these trees were meant to send him a message, then the witch was definitely coming after him. He had learned from his bullies; attacks of words always came before things escalated into a fight.

"I think he wanted us to find this," Hyroc said. Everyone looked at him skeptically. "He wanted me to find this to tell me he's coming for me."

"You mean the *other guy*," Elsa said. "The one who sent the shadow demon. You think he sent this witch after you."

-53-

"He wants to finish what he started. That's the only thing that makes sense." Hyroc used his hand to indicate the trees. "As careful as this guy has been this whole time, that's the only thing that explains all this here."

"Or he could just be an unstable psychopath," Donovan added. "And he suddenly snapped and took his madness out on these trees."

Hyroc shook his head. "No, this seems too deliberate and focused. I don't think a random crazy person could do everything this witch has done." He indicated a branch. "Besides, none of these breaks are recent. If it was a recent break, the inner bark should be moist and sticky, but it's not. It's dry and crumbling, suggesting it has been broken for a while, a couple of weeks at least."

Elsa grabbed a branch to feel the broken end. "He's right," she agreed. "The texture on this is wrong for it to be a recent break. That's a good catch."

"So, what, the witch snaps, does all this damage, then goes back to being careful, and doesn't come back to try and hide anything. That doesn't seem likely."

Donovan sighed.

Hyroc blew out a breath and turned toward Harold. "So, what's the plan?" he asked. "Are you going to inform the town elders?"

"I might have to," Harold said unhappily. "Whatever the witch turned themselves into is clearly dangerous, and whatever they're planning threatens the whole village. I'm sorry, many more lives than just yours are at stake here."

Hyroc stared at the ground. Telling the village elders about all this would end his life in Elswood. They would think he was involved or chase him out simply because he seemed to attract trouble to the village. Even if he helped them kill the witch, it probably wouldn't matter to them. He would have to leave his cabin either way.

"But I'll hold off on that as long as I can," Harold said. "I'll only do that as a last resort when we have no other option. I just wanted you to be prepared for that if things go that way." He focused on Elsa and Donovan. "But, Elsa, and Donovan, if something happens to me before we get this guy, it's up to you to tell them what's going on." They nodded their understanding. "But, first things first. Hyroc, I need you to see if you can pick up a scent."

Hyroc nodded, removed his shirt and hunting gear, and settled on to all fours. Then he transformed into a bear. He took a deep whiff through his nose. A musty scent belonging to an animal permeated the area, but it was unlike any animal he had ever smelled. It had an incredibly wild and vicious tone to it. Just from the smell, it seemed this thing could easily kill all five of them. When he walked past the farthest damaged tree, the scent vanished. It didn't fade away as it should have. It was simply gone. The witch had used magic to remove any lingering scent beyond the trees. He followed the edge of the area with the smell. It led him in a full circle around the trees, but he found no trail leading away.

Hyroc shook his head. "Nothing. He removed any scent trail that led away from these trees," he said angrily. "There's nothing here we could use. I don't know what else to do."

Harold sighed. "We keep looking," he said. "There's not much else we can do. We keep our eyes open, keep listening, and we keep looking until we find him."

Hyroc glanced toward the enormous claw marks on the trees. It seemed more likely the witch would find them first.

Chapter 7
Frustration

"You need to come up with a plan, Hyroc," Elsa said sternly.

"I know, I know," Hyroc said irritably.

Hyroc and Elsa stood in the village center. The sky was overcast, and they felt the occasional wet line of a raindrop land on their heads. With Hyroc likely having to leave Elswood at a moment's notice, Elsa was helping him prepare for the journey. Hyroc knew this was the prudent thing to do, but he was having a hard time focusing. Thoughts about the witch that hunted him clouded his mind. What was his enemy doing? They had no idea. Even Harold, the ex-witch Hunter, the man who should have all the answers, was stumped. For all they knew, a building would shatter into splinters from something smashing through it, or one might spontaneously erupt into flames and announce the arrival of their adversary. None of them could even be alone for fear of an ambush. Not that it would probably make a difference, considering the enormous size and killing power the witch had bestowed upon themself.

"You're going to need food," Elsa insisted. "Do you have any dried meat saved up that you could use?"

"I don't know," Hyroc said. "Maybe. I haven't been up at my cabin for days."

"Hyroc, you need to figure out if you need to buy any more food."

Chapter 7: Frustration

"I know that, Elsa!" Hyroc snapped. *"You don't think I know that."*

"I'm only trying to –"

"Stop it, Elsa!" Hyroc interrupted. He spoke more softly. "Just, stop." He threw his arms down to his sides in frustration and moved away from her in the direction of a shop. He needed to be alone. Elsa sighed but didn't pursue him.

He arrived at a shop's window and stared absentmindedly through the glass at the wares inside. He knew he needed to prepare for his inevitable departure, but he couldn't concentrate. His mind was consumed with thoughts about the witch. That seemed the only thing he was capable of thinking about.

"You don't look like you're having a very good day," a familiar voice said.

Hyroc turned his head to see Einar coming out of the shop's door. "You could say that," he said in a subdued tone.

"Want to talk about what's bothering you?"

Hyroc absolutely wanted to vent everything to Einar, but telling the man about anything involving the witch was a horrendous idea. "I don't know."

"If you don't know, then you probably should talk about it." Einar waived his arm invitingly toward the Black Spruce Tavern. "Come share a meal with me. We can talk about what's going on. I know you'll feel a whole lot better."

That was an enticing idea for Hyroc. He couldn't talk about the witch directly, but he still might be able to talk about his problems if he was careful. He needed this.

Hyroc nodded, and the two of them headed into the tavern. Einar ordered them a plate of cheese and bread.

"So, what's going on?" Einar said.

Hyroc swallowed a bite of cheese before speaking. "I don't think I can stay here much longer," he said, waving his hand in frustration.

Einar cocked an eyebrow. "Is what's his name, Jack, hassling you again? He must be the dumbest person in the world to bother you after what I did to his face."

Hyroc shook his head. "No, no, it's not that idiot. It seems this whole village wants me gone. I'm tired of people that want to hurt me coming after me when I'm not doing anything wrong," Hyroc said, actually meaning the witch instead of the villagers.

Einar finished a bite of bread. "I understand why you feel that way," he said. "But I don't think you can ever escape people like that, no matter where you go. There are those kinds everywhere. You can never escape them, no matter how hard you try. Their ch –" Einar began coughing as he choked a little on a piece of food. He pounded on his chest, which seemed to alleviate his discomfort. "Sorry, food down the wrong pipe." He cleared his throat before continuing.

"Leaving might be more comfortable, but everything else tells you staying is probably a better option. Sure, there's people that don't like you, people that despise you, people that want to control your every action, but that's their problem. They're the ones suffering."

Hyroc studied Einar thoughtfully. He'd never thought about people's behavior toward him that way. The villager's animosity was disconcerting, but they physically didn't do anything to him. Their bad thoughts didn't control him, it controlled them. They were the ones he should feel sorry for.

"That's a nice way of looking at things," Hyroc agreed.

"Not too bad for a forest wondering foreigner, eh," he said happily. For an instant, Hyroc thought he saw sadness in Einar's eyes. It felt strange the man could exhibit two opposing emotions at the same time. Maybe the man's being here had resulted from something painful. He knew practically nothing about Einar, and the possibility of learning something piqued his interest.

"Where are you from?" Hyroc asked. "If you don't mind my asking."

"Not at all. I'm from the North."

Hyroc cocked an eyebrow. "So, you are a North Lander?"

"Through and through, but don't you worry, I never raided anyone's land. I was a simple farmer, no different than anyone here. I had land for grain and milk from a wooly cow."

Hyroc laughed. "A woolly cow? That's a thing?"

Einar nodded, not showing any signs of humor. "Sure is. How do you think they survive the winters? But I'll tell you. It's no fun milking one when winter closes in." He stood and indicated a height up to his waist. "Snow up to here, I had to trudge through sometimes." Einar sat back down and tore off a bite of bread.

"I'm glad I don't have to deal with that," Hyroc said. He looked thoughtful. "How did you end up here?"

Einar sighed, staring off a long moment before answering. "Well, the land my farm sat on was owned by a Jarl. He was fairly generous compared to some of the others I heard about. He didn't demand much of our crops, only enough to feed those within his counsel and some to store. During hard years, he was forgiving of late or diminished quotas, rarely disciplining anyone for small contributions. Then one year, we had a long, cold winter, colder than any in living memory. The snow remained late, shortening our already short growing season. By fall, we knew we didn't have enough food to make it through the coming winter. Shortly after the cold months arrived, everyone was on the verge of starvation. We were forced to eat anything we could find. We quickly emptied our hunting grounds of game and were forced to travel farther and farther away from our homes.

When I went out on one hunting trip, I downed a large buck. It was big enough to feed my family for weeks."

Einar looked distant. "But my jubilation turned to ash. As I began the tough journey back to my home, dragging my prize through the snow, I was surrounded by a group of men. They informed me I was trespassing on another Jarl's land, and only the deer was for him to hunt. As punishment, I was forced to become their slave. They made me work on one of his farms. The farm owner I was given to was a harsh taskmaster. He worked me hard, often until my fingers bled. After some months, I was able to escape. But when I reached my farm, everything had been abandoned, and no one remained alive. I didn't find the bodies of my wife and daughter, but even to this day, I don't know if they live.

I was captured by slavers shortly thereafter. Before they could reach the nearest market, I escaped their grasp. I wandered through the forest for days, weeks maybe, until I came across this blessed village. You pretty much know the rest from there."

Hyroc stared at Einar in shocked empathy. That was an awful story! Einar's journey to Elswood made even his look like nothing. This man had been through incredible hardships. Slavery? He shuddered to imagine what it would be to be made a serf in some unknown place, have no freedom, treated as a thing to be owned. And even through all that, the man had come through it and retained his ability to feel happiness.

Einar laughed half humoredly. "Not the happiest story *I know*," he said. "But that's all behind me. And I'm ecstatic to be here where I don't have to worry about anyone with darkness in their heart controlling me." With a visible effort, he stopped himself from laughing.

Einar's behavior seemed strange to Hyroc, but after being an abused serf for who knows how long, he assumed he would probably pick up a few unusual habits as well.

"And I'm happy for you," Hyroc said, unsure how to respond.

"So, who was that young woman with you?"

"Oh, that's Elsa. And before you go making this weird, she's like a sister to me."

Einar nodded. "I see. So, you're not related?"

"No, not by blood, but she's still family to me."

"Is she with anyone?"

Hyroc shot him a strange look. "You mean like courting?" Einar nodded. Hyroc's expression became more serious. "Did I mention she's like a sister to me?"

Einar looked suddenly confused. The two of them studied each other for a long awkward moment. A smile burst across Einar's face, and he laughed. He slapped Hyroc on the shoulder.

"You thought I was serious?" Einar said happily.

Hyroc felt his face warm with embarrassment. He had just been duped. He shook his head and smiled in mild humor.

Chapter 7: Frustration

"I really had you going for a second, didn't I?"

Hyroc sighed in amusement. "I can't believe you got me with *that*."

"Happens to the best of us. Besides, I think you needed that. Feel better?"

Hyroc nodded. "Yeah, I feel pretty good. Thanks."

"You're welcome. Besides, I don't think I'm in any condition to please a pretty lady like her. She deserves better."

"Don't sell yourself too short. I'm sure you can find someone." Hyroc suddenly felt a stab of loneliness. He quickly pushed it away.

"Maybe." Einar paused. "But I think I've talked enough about me. What do you do around here?"

Hyroc thumbed in the direction of Wolf Paw Mountain. "There's not much to tell. I live in a cabin up near the mountain. I trap and hunt up there."

"And that's where you and Elsa live?"

Hyroc shook his head. "No, she lives with her two brothers a little way to the east, out near the lake. I spend a lot of time with them hunting and preparing animal pelts."

"I assume you like it there."

Hyroc sighed. "It's pretty much the only place here where I feel welcome. No one else here has shown me the kindness that they have." Hyroc saw a flash of excitement in Einar's eyes when he said that. Einar was an outcast like he, and Hyroc empathized with the man wanting to find a place where he too could feel welcome.

Einar nodded. "You live so far from the village; do you have problems out there with wolves or bears?"

Hyroc kept himself from smiling. It was actually a bear that kept everything away. "No, we have our own special ways of dealing with the animals."

Einar nodded, seeming a little impressed. "What do the four of you use to hunt with?"

Hyroc raised an eyebrow. "With a bow. Why are you so interested in how they hunt?"

Einar shrugged. "I don't know, you needed to talk, and I wanted to keep this conversation going. We started talking about hunting, so I was just trying to keep going along with that subject, and hunting implements seemed a good place to go. But now I don't know what to discuss because I think we've reached a dead end with this conversation."

"Sorry, I didn't mean to keep going on and on like that."

Einar waved dismissively. "It's okay. I could tell you really needed to talk to someone. Did you get everything off your chest?"

Hyroc pondered the question. His mind seemed clearer, and thoughts of the witch weren't crowding his mind. He seemed able to think about other things.

Hyroc nodded. "I think so," he said happily.

Einar smiled and clapped him on the shoulder. "Glad I could be of a slave." He shook his head. "Excuse me, I meant, glad I could be of service. Thinking about my past seems to have twisted up my tongue."

"I know what you meant," Hyroc said. "Thanks."

"You're welcome. I look forward to doing this again sometime." Einar suddenly looked distant.

"As do I." Einar still looked distant. Hyroc frowned. "umm, Einar, are you alright?"

Einar shook his head as if waking from a dream. He smiled. "Sorry, I just remembered something and got distracted. Anyway, I need to get going."

"Thanks for listening."

Einar nodded and headed out the door.

Hyroc studied the empty plate on the table. Eventually, he stood and left the tavern. Elsa met him outside.

"Feel better?" she asked.

Hyroc nodded. "Yeah, let's get back at it."

"Okay, what are you running low on?"

"Some more food might be nice."

Elsa made a beckoning gesture toward the bakery.

Chapter 8
Foreboding

Hyroc lifted a finished deer hide toward the sun for inspection. It looked good, and he could sell it. He was saddened, knowing this might have been the last deer he would ever hunt in Elswood. Trips with his friends in search of game might be a thing of the past. He pushed the thoughts aside; he needed to focus. There would be time to think about such things later.

"Are you almost done?" Donovan said insistently. Hyroc and he stood outside of his cabin at the foot of Wolf Paw Mountain. Donovan maintained watch on their surroundings, searching for any signs of the approach of their adversary. "We're exposed up here, and I don't want to spend another moment here longer than we need to."

Hyroc continued to examine the deer hide as he spoke. "I know, Donovan. But I've got us covered." He pointed at a large spruce beside the cabin. "Kit's up there, and if anyone heads our way, he'll notice them long before they get here."

Donovan gazed up at the tree, spotting the mountain lion balanced on a branch with his head resting on his paws, fast asleep. "You sure about that?" Donovan said skeptically. "Because it looks to me he's dead asleep up there."

"Trust me, he'll notice. Cats don't go all the way to sleep; not the same as you or I. He can go from resting to running in an instant."

Hyroc pointed skyward to the black feathery shape of Shimmer circling overhead. "We've also got an eye in the sky."

"I'm a little uncomfortable with the idea of putting our lives in the hands of your napping kitty up there or that little birdie."

Hyroc glanced toward him. "You understand Shimmer's not a regular bird, right?"

"Just because he's got some weird silvery markings on his neck doesn't mean we should rely on him."

"Well, he seems to understand everything we tell him to do, and he was one of Ursa's servants. I'm pretty sure he can do a lot more than any bird you've ever seen."

"I've seen someone train a magpie so it almost sounds as if it's speaking, but we both know it's not," Donovan scoffed. "It could be something similar with him for all you know. How are you still not done over there?"

Hyroc slung the deer hide over his shoulder. "Yes, I'm done," he said as he stood. Donovan nodded. Hyroc made a clicking noise when the two of them turned to leave. Kit scrambled down the tree to join them without showing the slightest sign that he had been asleep a second before. The three of them moved down the trail that led away from the cabin.

They moved past the Shackleton cabin to the road. Hyroc froze when he stepped onto the road. Numerous rows of heavy boot prints lined the dirt. He'd never seen this amount of disturbance on the road. He even managed to discern hoof marks from a horse or two. The prints were uniform and neat, suggesting they were made by marching soldiers. That meant only one thing. The Ministry was here! Had they finally found him? Had the thing he feared for nearly four years finally happened? Maybe not. The soldiers had passed by the trail that led to his cabin, indicating they may not even be aware of him. There could be another reason why they were here, something unrelated to him. He needed to find them to make sure.

"I wonder what happened to get these people's attention," Donovan said, studying the tracks.

Chapter 8: Foreboding

"I think these people are from The Ministry," Hyroc said. Kit stepped forward to curiously sniff the prints.

Donovan shot Hyroc a stunned look. "The Ministry?" he exclaimed. "I thought you were done with those people, and they didn't know where you went."

"I still think they don't. They moved past the trail that leads to my cabin. If they were after me, you would think they would've gone straight to my cabin?"

"That's a good point, but why would they come here if they didn't? Maybe they're after the same witch we are?"

"That's possible, but as far as I can tell, beyond the five of us, no one even knows about that witch, and he's been very careful to keep his presence concealed. But we can only be sure if we follow those soldiers."

Donovan looked at him, baffled. "Are you crazy?" he said. "You said these people want to *kill you*, and you're going to follow them? That seems like a moronic idea. Did you get knocked in the head by something we don't know about?" He reached over to feel Hyroc's head.

Hyroc jerked his head away in irritation. "My head's fine," Hyroc said. "I know following them is not the safest thing to do, but we need to figure out why they're here. Besides, I'm going to stay out of sight. If you don't want to come with me, I understand."

Donovan sighed. "I would never leave you to deal with something like this alone. I'm with you."

"Good."

The three of them cautiously moved down the road toward Elswood. They didn't spot any soldiers until the village came into view. The soldiers wore orange and black clothes, and each had a badge on their chest with the mark of The Ministry, a raven, and a scythe. They stood in the village center, talking to villagers.

"Stay here," Hyroc quietly said to Kit when they arrived at the edge of the trees outside of the village. Kit grumbled quietly in annoyance and crouched amongst the foliage. "Good boy. We'll be right back."

Silently, Hyroc and Donovan navigated their way around the village outskirts, searching for a way to get closer unseen. They found a toolshed outside of a shop, and it was close enough for them to safely listen.

Nearby, a soldier had dismounted from his horse and held the animal's reigns while he spoke to a villager. The man's clothing was nicer than that of his companions, and he seemed to be of the Light Walker rank. Light Walkers were relatively low on The Ministry ladder. They were charged with taking care of mundane matters and assignments. They also possessed a limited amount of authority and control over small groups of soldiers.

"...Have you seen anything suspicious lately," the Light Walker said calmly.

The villager, a brown-haired man with a short brown beard, shook his head. "No, sir," he said. "I've never seen any trouble here."

The Light Walker nodded and dismissed the man. He moved over to a woman who held a basket and wore a light blue dress and a scarf on her head. "You there," the Light Walker said. He made a beckoning motion. "Come, I wish to speak with you." The woman stopped, looking confused as she walked toward him. "I am a Light Walker of The Ministry of the Silver Scythe in search of those who would wield the powers of darkness. Have you seen or heard about anything strange in this village?

The woman shook her head. "No, sir," she said. "Everything's been quiet around here."

The Light Walker looked skeptical. "Are you sure? There's been nothing?"

"Nothing, sir."

The Light Walker let her be on her way. He stood against his horse with his hand on his chin, deep in thought. He knew something was off about everyone's story.

Hyroc breathed a sigh of relief. Despite how much the villagers wanted him gone, they were unwilling to reveal anything to The Ministry. At least for the time being, his secret was safe.

Chapter 8: Foreboding

Whenever a witch was revealed to The Ministry, they were quickly dealt with, but things didn't normally end there. He remembered reading at the boarding school about many accounts of what happened after a witch had been killed. The Ministry didn't simply pack up and leave. Often, Inquisitors were dispatched to interrogate every citizen who had any involvement with the witch or was suspected of having any. Their intentions were to root out any traces of witchcraft. The Inquisitors always seemed to find supposed witches or accomplices of witches. Many times, these people would be executed or imprisoned.

Hyroc often wondered how many of those unfortunate souls were innocent. How many were simply using their Quintessence in constructive ways, and their power was mistaken for witchcraft. Fear of witches had warped The Ministry's understanding of magic, and all magic was grouped into the category of witchcraft. They saw all magic as evil. The only way magic could be considered as good or evil depended on how the person wielding it decided to use it. And magic was a part of every living thing. Everything contained some amount of Quintessence, but the quantity within living things was usually too small to be of use in casting a spell. Only a relative few possessing a large reservoir of Quintessence could use magic. If a normal person even tried to use their Quintessence, they would be knocked unconscious because their Quintessence reserve was insufficient to complete a spell. Quintessence was vital for life and similarly as important as breathing. If a spell drained more Quintessence than the body contained, the person was knocked unconscious. That was the body's way of severing its connection to the spell and preventing the person from dying. Depletion of Quintessence was just as deadly as someone bleeding out.

Hyroc's thoughts were interrupted when he saw the Light Walker making a beckoning motion towards someone out of sight.

"What do you think they're looking for?" Donovan said.

"I don't know. They don't seem to have anything specific in mind. They're checking for anything unusual."

Donovan sighed. "Damn, I was hoping we got lucky, and they were hunting our witch," he said, disappointed. "But no, that would've made things easy."

"Where's the fun in doing it the easy way?" Hyroc joked.

"I don't want fun. I want to stay alive and be done with this whole witch situation."

Hyroc returned his attention to the Light Walker. A hooded figure came into view wearing leather gloves and dressed in a ratty-looking dark blue robe. A couple of the soldiers glanced nervously toward the figure, and some stepped back to get out of the way. The person's face was concealed behind what seemed to be a gray plague mask with a beak that pointed downward along the chin instead of outward. From the reactions of the soldiers, Hyroc wondered if the hooded figure was a leper. He had never seen one before, but they were often depicted as wearing similar attire to hide the deformities and sores caused by their condition. Those persons were sometimes known to work with The Ministry as Light Bringers, researchers that studied witchcraft as his foster father Marcus had done. From his childhood, Hyroc remembered Marcus telling him about such occurrences. Beyond hiding their diseased skin, they usually seemed like a regular person. He had sort of looked up to them because they were different as he was, and no one wanted them around. However, he didn't understand this mask. He'd seen some drawings of lepers with face coverings or masks of silver, but nothing near this daunting.

"What do you have to report, Light Walker?" the figure said. The person spoke in an icy tone that made the hairs on the back of Hyroc's neck stand. If this person was a leper, they had some serious throat issues that affected their ability to speak or were just plain unpleasant. Hyroc knew he probably wouldn't be in a good mood dealing with leprosy.

"No one seems to know anything," the Light Walker said.

"Are you sure they're not hiding anything?"

Chapter 8: Foreboding

"I believe they are, but these villagers on the fringes are often suspicious of strangers and are reluctant to reveal anything to outsiders. It's probably nothing. They're likely —"

"Nothing!" the figure snapped. He moved uncomfortably close to the Light Walker. This gave the Light Walker a start, and the man's horse nervously brayed as it pulled against its reigns. "They're hiding something, and you think it's *nothing*. Secrets are only hidden when others can use them against those who experienced them."

"But if we press them too hard, we could turn them against us in the process and only make things more difficult for us."

"Are you challenging my judgment?"

The figure held its gloved hand in front of the man's face. The man tensed but began to relax a moment later. The Light Walker leaned forward defiantly. "You know the limits of this arrangement." The figure made an angry hissing noise and drew their hand back to their side.

"Yes, I remember, Light Walker." The person's voice was even colder and angrier sounding. "I am forced to recognize your authority. But if it were up to me, I would remove your head with my bare hands."

"But it's not. Remember your place, and do what we brought you here to do."

"Yes, Light Walker, I am subservient."

Though that's what the person said, Hyroc knew they didn't mean a single word of it. This person appeared very interested in killing this Light Walker, but some arrangement with The Ministry prevented them from doing so. What could they have over someone like this that gave them control? Holding their family hostage seemed a reasonable conclusion, but Hyroc had a hard time believing that as sour as this person was.

And what was the figure brought here to do? They could be good at finding things, though Hyroc had never heard about a leper-tracker. Or they were good at getting information out of people. The thought of some form of torture being used on the villagers of Elswood disturbed him. He didn't hold them in high regard, but he wouldn't wish torture upon them. So far, the villagers were reluctant to divulge anything to the new arrivals, but his presence wasn't a secret important enough to keep under pain of torture. The Ministry would surely learn of him if things went that far.

"Alright, let's get out of here," Hyroc said. "I've heard enough."

"About time," Donovan said, relieved.

"We need to get back to your cabin to let Harold know about this."

Chapter 9
Shroud of Knives

"Do you see anyone following us?" Hyroc said before climbing over a chest height wooden fence. Kit effortlessly bounded over the fence.

From the other side of the fence, Donovan put a hand above his eyes to block out the sun as he looked behind them. "No, I think we're good," he said.

They rushed across the field in front of them, garnering strange looks from the farmhands working there. On the other end of the field, they encountered another fence and moved into the forest beyond it. From here, they watchfully wound their way toward the road. When the road came into view, to avoid being seen by any Ministry soldiers that might be on it, they remained in the forest as they moved along it.

"You do know what this means, right?" Donovan said as they pushed their way through the trees. "If anyone tells them about you, it won't be safe for you to live here anymore."

Hyroc grit his teeth in displeasure, he had been trying to avoid thinking about that. The arrival of those soldiers probably meant the end of his life at his cabin and Elswood. But worst of all, it would mark the end of his time with the Shackletons. They were family to him. He had no one besides them. It hurt for him to even think about leaving them. But he would be putting more than just his own life at risk. If The Ministry found him with them, they would be counted as accomplices and likely executed along with him. He had to put their needs above his, no matter how much it hurt.

"I know," Hyroc said unhappily. "And if the soldiers stay, it'll also be too dangerous for me."

"We're going to hate saying goodbye to you, but it's what's got to be done."

Hyroc sighed. His predicament was aggravatingly familiar. Not long ago, he had to say goodbye to someone he cared deeply about. "Never turn back," was the last thing he ever heard from her. Words he hated, words he would hear again.

"But first things first," Hyroc said. "We've got a witch to take care of. Only once we've dealt with him will I leave."

"This feels awful," Donovan said. "That no one in the village will ever know that you helped keep them safe."

Hyroc clapped him on the shoulder. "I know, but I'm fine with it. That's just where I ended up. The only thing that matters is that I was here."

"Good way of looking at it, I suppose."

Soon the clearing around the Shackleton cabin came into view.

"I wonder if Harold will have –" Donovan said before cutting himself off. Kit started growling. Donovan quickly fit an arrow to his bow, and Hyroc drew his sword. They saw Harold lying on the ground, his head bloodied. "CURTIS!" Donovan yelled when he saw his little brother lying on the ground toward the back of the cabin where they chopped wood. He broke into a run.

"Go check on him," Hyroc said. "I'll take care of Harold." He was relieved when he saw Harold still breathing. The man was unconscious and bleeding from a gash on his head. Kit rapidly sniffed him, seeming apprehensive. Hyroc used his Flame Claw to perform a healing spell on the wound. Steadily the skin knit back together, and the bleeding stopped. Hyroc gave Harold a gentle shake to try and wake him. Harold suddenly jerked into activity and tackled Hyroc. His eyes were wild, and he reached for a knife. Kit roared, breaking Harold out of

Chapter 9: Shroud of Knives

his frenzy. He turned his head to see Kit standing beside him with his teeth bared. Harold slowly lifted his hand in an attempt to calm the big cat.

Hyroc thrust his hand out as he spoke. "Kit, no! We're fine. We're all fine."

Kit closed his mouth, but remained where he stood, giving Harold a dangerous glare.

Harold tentatively held his hand out, keeping it between him and the mountain lion as he got off Hyroc. He settled into a sitting position. With a grimace, he lifted his hand to his head.

"Harold, what happened?" Hyroc insisted.

"That sneaky bastard got me from behind!" Harold said, banging the side of his fist onto his leg.

Hyroc glanced up to see Donovan carrying Curtis over to him. His little brother was also unconscious, and his head had blood on it. When Donovan set Curtis down, Kit turned his attention from Harold to the boy. The big cat sniffed him intently. Hyroc pushed his four-legged companion's head away so he could heal Curtis' injurie. Curtis moaned, but his eyes remained closed.

"He's not waking up," Donovan said, concerned. "Is he okay?"

Hyroc leaned back, trying to catch his breath. Healing Harold and Curtis had taken more out of him than he expected. He felt noticeably fatigued from the amount of Quintessence he had expended. Kit studied him, looking alarmed.

"He's alright," Harold assured. "Just give him a moment. He'll come to."

"Hyroc, you, okay?" Donovan asked.

Hyroc waved dismissively. "I'm fine. That just took a lot out of me," he said. "I just need a minute." He pushed Kit away when the large feline came in for a closer inspection. Kit pulled back with an irritated glower.

"Harold, where's Elsa?" Donovan said.

"I don't know," Harold said. "I heard Curtis yelling right before I got knocked on the head."

—73—

"Elsa!" Donovan yelled as he stood. They heard no response. Donovan continued calling out, his voice becoming steadily more frantic. "She's not here." He turned toward Harold. "What happened? Where's my sister?"

"He must've taken her," Harold answered. He pulled a handkerchief out of his pocket and began wiping the blood from his head.

Donovan shook his head. "He? You mean the witch?"

"Afraid so."

"How? How did you let this happen? You were supposed to protect us."

"He got me from behind. I didn't see it coming."

"You didn't see it coming? You used to be a Witch Hunter: you know how to deal with these people! How could you let him sneak up on you?"

"I wish the situation had gone differently, but he got the drop on me; boy, that's what happened. My experience doesn't mean a damn thing if I don't see my enemy coming."

"He was probably using a dampening spell of some kind to cover the sound of his approach," Hyroc interjected. "That's what I would do if I didn't want anyone to hear me coming." Donovan threw his arms out in frustration.

"It wouldn't surprise me," Harold agreed. "I was keeping a very close eye on everything, along with Elsa and Curtis. There's no way we would miss someone coming unless they had an advantage. We still haven't figured out what kind of witch he is or what dark art he prefers. He could know how to do any number of things."

"The only thing we do know," Hyroc said. "Is this guy has done some kind of alteration to his body. Remember what we saw with those trees? He's got some pretty nasty claws. And he's smart. He'd have to be to remain hidden from us."

"Don't forget, patient," Harold added. "He waited until you two had left, attacking us when we were vulnerable. He must've been watching the cabin, waiting for an opening."

"I don't care how smart he is!" Donovan said. "My sister has been kidnapped by a psychopath that butchers animals and, Hallowed

Chapter 9: Shroud of Knives

knows, even reads entrails for predictions of the future. We need to go after him and kill him before he sacrifices her to whatever thing he worships."

"That's what he wants us to do," Harold said. "He wants us to recklessly rush after him so he can kill us. This is a trap. We need to think carefully about our next move."

"He's got my sister! Whether this is a trap or not, it doesn't matter. We have to go after him."

"I know he's got your sister: you don't need to remind me. But where do you suggest we start?" Harold waved his arm to indicate the whole clearing. "Because I don't see a trail anywhere that we can follow. This guy doesn't leave traces behind."

"Then what, we do nothing?"

"No, that's not what I'm saying...."

Hyroc narrowed his eyes as the dark shape of a bird descended toward them. Shimmer landed on the ground in front of him. The raven fluttered his wings and cawed anxiously.

"I think I know how we can find him," Hyroc said. Donovan and Harold looked at him with intrigue. Hyroc lowered himself onto one knee. "Do you know where he took Elsa?" Shimmer jumped around excitedly while cawing. "Can you lead us to him?" Shimmer bobbed his head in what appeared to be a yes and took flight.

"Never thought that bird would be this useful," Harold admitted.

"We know where he is now," Donovan said eagerly. "I think we need to pay him a visit."

"Do you feel up to this, Harold?" Hyroc asked.

Harold slowly rose to his feet. A second later, he stumbled. Hyroc caught the man to keep him from falling.

"I would only slow you down," Harold said. "You'll have to go on without me."

"Hyroc, can't you help him with that?" Donovan said.

Hyroc shook his hand. "No, fixing that is beyond me," he said. "I can fix the wound on his skin, but I can't do anything deeper than that."

"It's okay. I know the two of you can do this. I'll catch up when I can."

Donovan and Hyroc nodded.

"Well, I'll need more than just this to go after him," Donovan said, raising his bow. He unstrung it, slipped it over his shoulder, and strung it again, so the wood of his bow rested diagonal across his chest and abdomen. Then, he grabbed his spear that was propped against the cabin. "Alright, I'm ready. Let's hunt this coward."

Chapter 10
Darkness Comes

Hyroc, Donovan, and Kit swiftly moved through the forest. They had just crossed the lower flanks of Wolf Paw Mountain, moving west. Shimmer circled overhead, but whenever he needed them to adjust their course, he would start cawing and fly off in the direction he wanted them to go. It would have been faster for Hyroc to turn into a bear to track the witch by scent, but it was difficult for him to use his Flame Claw in that Form. His hands were natural focusing points for directing his Quintessence into a spell. Hands were more dexterous than heavy bear paws, and he would lose a lot of his agility for directing a spell while he was a bear. The loss of agility could cause him to miss an opportunity to attack with a spell or create an opening the witch could exploit. His natural form seemed the safest option. It would be an even fight, and though it would be tough, he figured he could beat his opponent.

Except, that only holds true if the witch was completely human. From the claw marks on those trees, they were likely dealing with someone who had altered themselves and now possessed huge claws. The depths of those marks suggested the witch was incredibly strong. Then to further compound the issue, this person was capable of using magic. Hyroc and Donovan could be heading into a fight with a super-strong beast-man that wielded powerful magic. Hyroc could turn into a bear to counter the man's strength and similarly, his Flame Claw for the man's magic. But the witch could easily outmatch him in either case, and with only Donovan as backup, their chances of victory seemed grim. If they waited and tried to bring others to tip the scales in their favor, Elsa would probably be dead. Neither of them could allow this, no matter their odds.

It was a situation all too familiar to Hyroc. He remembered how it had felt two years ago, seeing the giant spiders at the Shackleton cabin, seeing the whole family missing, fearing the worst. He had acted on a tiny glimmer of hope back then. His courage had driven him into the foul heart of the spider's nest to save his friends. But he was only able to rescue three. He helped bury the Shackleton's parents. Would there be a funeral today? Would he help lay Elsa to rest when this was all over? Hyroc pushed the thought aside. It was too painful for him to even consider. He had to focus. Their enemy would only use these feelings against them. For all he knew, this was part of the witch's plan; unsettle them with fears of what might be, so they were easier to kill. No. He wouldn't allow it. Only the witch would perish today!

They had spent hours heading west, and it was nearing dusk when they stopped to catch their breath.

"Hallowed," Donovan cursed. "How far did he take her? We've been at this for hours?"

"I've started wondering that too," Hyroc agreed.

"Are you sure we're going in the right direction? That bird could be leading us nowhere."

Hyroc made a waving motion at Shimmer, signaling for him to land. The raven spiraled down onto the branch of a tree beside them. "You're sure that witch went this way?" Shimmer bobbed his head and cawed eagerly. "He seems confident."

"Does he know how much farther?" Donovan said.

Shimmer extended one wing. He jabbed it several times in the direction they were going and cawed excitedly.

Chapter 10: Darkness Comes

"I think we're close." Hyroc turned to Kit. "Okay, buddy, I need you to stay here." Kit let out an unhappy yowl. "I know you want to help us deal with *him*, but it's too dangerous. He's unlike anything you're used to. He can do things to hurt you without even touching you. Believe me; it's too dangerous. You need to stay here." Kit rumbled his frustration and settled down on his belly. "Good boy. And if you see anything coming back this way, and it's not us, get out of here."

"Anything I should know before going into this?" Donovan asked anxiously.

Hyroc shrugged. "Don't touch any runes or symbols you see because they might explode. Don't step into any white circles because something bad might happen, and if you see the witch making any hand motions toward you, move because he is probably going to send something at you."

"So, don't touch anything weird, watch my feet, don't get hit, and kill the witch, simple enough."

Hyroc smirked. "I think you're the only person that would say anything about this is going to be simple."

"Probably because you know more about this stuff than I do, and I don't know how dangerous this actually is."

"Probably," Hyroc agreed. "They say ignorance is bliss."

"Well, whoever *they* are, I don't think they've come against a witch. Let's get to it before our nerves stop us."

Hyroc nodded, and they moved forward.

Hanging in the trees, Hyroc and Donovan started seeing charms made from a mixture of animal bones, sticks, teeth, and feathers. Next, they came across fox skulls stuck on top of wooden poles and strange rust-colored symbols adorned them. Past these, they entered a small clearing. Lit torches ringed the area, and a tight cluster sat in the middle. Flies buzzed around the decaying heads of two rams staked near the cluster. White circles of differing sizes had been drawn on the ground at the center, and a large animal heart sat in one. Beside the heart, in one of the largest circles, knelt the shape of a man. His clothing was made from a combination of cloth and animal hides, and a headdress of deer antlers adorned his head. Smoke rose from a stone bowl in front of him, and the air smelled of burning sage. He held a dagger in one hand and wafted the smoke over his head with the other.

Hyroc and Donovan scanned the clearing, surprised the man's form appeared unaltered. The types of changes to his body they expected would be noticeable even from a distance. The only explanation Hyroc could think of was that the man had used magic to damage those trees only to make it appear as if a beast with large claws had done it. The witch undoubtedly intended for everyone's imaginations to conjure a nightmarish creature to haunt and unnerve them. That had worked on them to some degree, but there was no monster here – just a man.

"So, you have finally found me." the man said in a calm, emotionless tone. He rose to his feet.

"You had to know this would happen eventually," Hyroc said.

The witch turned to face him. The man had a thin face devoid of any hair, and it had scars that possessed a strange kind of symmetry. He had dark brown eyes, and his visage gave him the skeletal resemblance of a featherless bird. A line of reddish-brown rune tattoos stretched across his right temple.

"I did," the witch answered, seeming to pay no attention to Donovan as he moved closer. "But not so soon." The witch waggled his dagger skyward, revealing tiny golden loops set into the ends of his fingers on that hand. "I was not expecting that bird of *hers* to bring you to me."

"Where is she!" Donovan demanded, jabbing his bow menacingly at the man. "What have you done with her?"

The witch continued talking without paying any attention to Donovan's words. "I wanted you to suffer a bit more first, to see those you love dead, and for you to feel the full depth of despair. But no matter, this minor inconvenience doesn't change things. Your life will be extinguished regardless. It just won't be as clean for either of you."

Chapter 10: Darkness Comes

Donovan sent an arrow flying. The witch made a flicking motion with his empty hand. The arrow burst into flame and turned to ash. Hyroc broke into a run with his sword drawn. The witch flung one arm out, made a fist with the other, and punched toward Hyroc. Several torches lifted out of the ground and shot toward Hyroc. He dove out of the way, rose to his feet, hooked his arm in front of him to form a barrier with his Flame Claw and deflected a better-aimed torch. Flames flared behind him as the projectiles smashed into the ground. Hyroc formed a blue fireball in his hand and flung it toward the witch. With a look of surprise, the witch feverishly rotated one arm. Dry leaves flew to the witch, exposing an invisible cone of swirling air in front of him. The fireball crashed into the swirl, dissipating in a short-lived tornado of blue fire before it could do any harm.

The witch flicked his hand again to immolate another arrow from Donovan. Donovan fired two more arrows in rapid succession. The witch made a half-circle motion with his hand, and the arrows turned and flew back at Donovan. Donovan flung himself to the ground an instant before the arrows thunked into the dirt. He jumped to his feet, abandoning his bow, and retrieved his spear he had staked into the ground a few steps away. He charged toward the witch but lagged behind Hyroc, who had used the distraction to try and close the distance on their adversary.

The witch formed an orange fireball in one hand and used the one with the dagger to make a punching motion toward Hyroc as he threw the fireball. Hyroc formed another barrier, but the ball hit with far more force than he expected. He staggered sideways from the force of the blow and felt a noticeable drain on his Quintessence. The witch snapped his attention to Donovan, who was almost within striking distance. He made a pulling motion toward himself with his dagger hand and squeezed the other into a fist. Donovan yelled out as roots burst from the ground and wrapped themselves around his arms and legs, immobilizing him.

The witch threw another fireball at Hyroc. Hyroc dodged sideways, narrowly avoiding getting hit, and dashed behind a pine tree.

Roots popped out of the ground at his feet and started snaking their way up his legs. With a straining motion, Hyroc shoved his hands downward. A swarm of small blue flames shot out of his hands and consumed the grasping roots. He hacked off the bristling branches from the tree he sheltered behind when they started moving toward him. An instant later, the tree started falling his way. With most of the tree's roots turned to ash, there wasn't enough remaining to keep it upright. Hyroc darted out of the way of the falling trunk as it crashed to the forest floor.

He jolted to a stop to keep Donovan's spear from impaling him as it sailed through the air no more than a step away. When he stole a glance at the witch, he saw numerous shards of wood rising toward the palm of the man's hand. The witch gave Hyroc a malevolent smile before sending the shards hurtling toward him. Hyroc formed a barrier to protect himself as he ran for cover amid the storm of projectiles. Each individual strike drained a feeble amount of his Quintessence, but when combined with hundreds of strikes, it was overwhelming. A flurry of wooden spikes shattered on his barrier while others zipped past his head. He could feel himself hemorrhaging energy. He couldn't maintain his barrier under the barrage for long. The cover offered by a tree was right in front of him, but it felt as if it was miles away. He jumped behind the nearest trunk, and the cool night air resonated with thumping impacts as the shards embedded themselves in the trees.

Hyroc breathed heavily, and he could feel the fatigue from the use of his Flame Claw slowing him down. He looked down and was dismayed to find a small piece of wood protruding from his arm. The pain didn't seem to start until he removed it and flicked the blood-covered shard away.

The witch appeared stronger than him with magic and more experienced in its uses. He wasn't going to win this through the brute use of his Flame Claw. Hyroc stole a glance around the tree. His opponent was only a couple of strides away, but he couldn't cover the distance before the witch hit him with a fireball. He could block it with a

Chapter 10: Darkness Comes

barrier, but after the assault of wood shards, he doubted he would have enough remaining strength to attack.

"Wol'dger, your friend need not die," the witch said. "Give yourself up, and I will let him live. Your life for his."

Hyroc knew the witch was lying. Even if he gave himself up, there was nothing keeping him from killing Donovan afterward. But, he still might be able to play this to his advantage. The witch didn't seem to know a whole lot about him, so the man could think he was naïve and trusting. He could use that arrogant assumption to get close enough to strike. Or the witch could fry him as soon as he came out from behind the tree.

"You won't hurt him?" Hyroc said.

"I will not if you trade your life for his," the witch said.

"Give me your word that you'll leave him alone."

"You have it."

"Don't trust him!" Donovan yelled.

The witch made a fist, and a root covered Donovan's mouth.

"Alright, I'm coming out."

Donovan yelled into the root.

Hyroc emerged from the tree with his sword sheathed and one hand behind his back. The witch beckoned him forward before putting his free hand behind his back. Donovan desperately yelled an incoherent warning. When the witch moved his hand back into sight, it glowed with fire.

The witch gazed at him gleefully. "Fool, I lied," he said coldly.

Before the witch could attack, Hyroc quickly moved his hand out from behind his back and threw his hunting knife. The blade spun through the air and stabbed into the witch's casting hand. The flame vanished as the witch yelled out in pain from the knife sticking through his blood-drenched hand. Hyroc rushed forward as he drew his sword. The man thrust his dagger at Hyroc. Hyroc blocked the blow, deflected two defenses strikes, slashed across the man's abdomen, and rammed his blade into his adversary. The witch gasped while staring at him unblinkingly.

—83—

"I lied too," Hyroc said. He placed his foot on the man's chest and wrenched his sword free. The man fell to the ground unmoving. Hyroc looked at Donovan to see the roots retreating from him.

Donovan shook his head. "*Shadow*, I thought you were really giving yourself up there," he said with relief. "Glad you had a plan."

"Well, I knew his word meant nothing, so I used that against him," Hyroc admitted. "Didn't think it was going to work."

Donovan pointed at the witch. "Did you really get him?"

Hyroc glanced over at the growing pool of blood beneath the man. "Yes."

Donovan turned his attention to their surroundings. "Elsa!" he called out.

Hyroc's concern for Elsa suddenly rushed back into his mind. In the exhilaration of the fight, he had almost forgotten about her.

Hyroc joined in, calling her name. They heard no answer, nor did they see any sign of her. She had to be here; this was where the witch was.

A cold choking laugh emanated from the witch. Hyroc turned toward the man clinging to his last moments of life. "You are both fools." He laughed again. "You have eyes, but you do not see."

"What don't we see?" Hyroc prodded.

"The great circle, it rises to fruition even now. Soon blood will cover the ground, and laminations will fill the air."

Hyroc felt a prickle of fear at the man's words. They were missing something. There was more to this! They weren't out of danger yet.

"Enough speaking in riddles," Donovan demanded. "Where's my sister?"

The man laughed. "Hidden until the time is right."

Donovan drew his hunting knife and held it to the man's throat. "What have you done with her?"

"I left her for the wolf. He will finish my work for The Eagle, who sees all."

Donovan grabbed the man by the shirt. "I've heard enough of your meaningless dribble," he yelled. "Tell me the truth! Where is my sister?" The life left the man's eyes as he died. Donovan shoved the body back down and faced Hyroc. "Were you able to make anything out of what he said?"

Hyroc shook his head. "No. Sounded like nonsense from a dying man," he said.

"Where could he have taken Elsa? I assumed she would be right here."

"This is his ritual ground. Maybe he's got some sort of shelter nearby. From what I've read, witches don't normally perform their rituals at the same place they live because if something goes wrong, they could destroy their house. So, maybe we just need to go a little further forward, and we'll find her."

Donovan nodded. "I'll go check around." He moved off to retrieve his spear before checking the edges of the clearing.

Hyroc gazed thoughtfully at the white circles. They reminded him of something, but he couldn't think of what. He looked toward the heart and up at the ram heads. Symbols were carved into each animal's forehead, and they had a subtle glow to them. Ursa had taught him that symbols, runes, and even words could be infused with magic to perform complicated spells. If it was glowing that meant it was active and doing something.

Hyroc scrutinized the heads, heart, and white circles. He noticed the ram heads and the deer heart were arranged in a triangle. Those three things were doing something, but what? He could destroy them, but without knowing what their purpose was, he didn't know if that would accomplish anything. Hyroc racked his brain, trying to remember anything about this arrangement. The rams symbolized strength, so they might be adding strength to something. That meant they were maintaining or feeding into an active spell. The heart was supposed to imbue the power of that animal on someone. So, the witch may have been siphoning power from the heart in order to cast some sort of spell that required more Quintessence than they had. He needed the strength of the rams to maintain the spell and energy from the heart to empower himself. Was it some sort of control spell? But to control

OUTCASTS

what, a shadow demon? The ram heads would serve no purpose in a summoning ritual. When someone summoned a shadow demon, in order to control it, that person had to sacrifice a part of their body. Once completed, as long as the summoner held the sacrifice, the demon was under their control, and nothing more was required to maintain the charm. A demon seemed unlikely.

Then the mutilated trees popped into his head. They were marked up as if some beast had decided to rip into them. He had assumed the witch had altered themselves to have claws, but that clearly wasn't the case. The witch did all that with magic, but doing so would cost a significant amount of Quintessence. And to expend that on something so pointless seemed a situation a witch would want to avoid. If they had nothing in reserve and ran into armed villagers, they would certainly die.

Hyroc glanced toward the dead witch. He felt a growing sense of alarm. He moved over to the body and began examining it. He made sure the man had no claws on his hands and feet. Even if a shadow demon was not involved in this ritual, a shadow demon could still be responsible for the damage to the trees. Hyroc searched the man's body, but he found no amulet or other container that stored the sacrificed body part required to control a demon. The words, "Hidden until the time is right," rang through his mind. He felt a swell of anger rush through him. This was a trap, and they had fallen right into it! The witch wasn't what they should have been hunting. There was something else out there that had Elsa. How could he have missed it; the evidence was right in front of him! He pushed the thoughts aside. He could be angry later. Right now, he needed to focus, focus on Elsa.

He took a deep breath. He needed to figure out what Donovan and he were facing. The witch had said something about a circle rising, a lot of blood, and a wolf. Hyroc paused. Rising circle that actually sounded familiar. He glanced toward the darkened sky. Through the trees, he saw the silvery shape of the moon rising. The witch meant the moon. But what about the wolf? What did that mean? Dread engulfed Hyroc. The witch was talking about a werewolf! He had thought those

Chapter 10: Darkness Comes

were a myth. From the stories about them, a werewolf was a person that transformed into a fierce beast during a full moon. They possessed massive slashing claws and a tremendous amount of strength. The person lost control of themselves and would tear apart anything that moved.

But that was also confusing. Unlike shadow demons, werewolves were immune to being bound and controlled. Yet, the witch had created a ritual to control something that couldn't be controlled. Hyroc forced the question to the back of his mind. Figuring it out wouldn't eliminate the danger to Elsa. They would have to deal with the werewolf regardless of the answer.

He needed to figure out where to go and do it fast. Once the full moon arrived, Elsa was good as dead if they didn't find her. He thought back to what the witch had said about blood covering the ground. He had clearly meant the werewolf and seemed to mean a lot of dead people. A chill ran through Hyroc. The only place with a lot of people was the village. The witch had sent the werewolf to transform there! It would kill everyone in sight. There would be a tremendous death toll if anyone in the village proper survived at all. Could he fight a werewolf? He had no idea. He was liable to die horribly if he even tried. But Elsa would die along with countless others if he didn't try. No matter his feelings toward his treatment from the villagers, they didn't deserve to be torn to shreds.

"Donovan," Hyroc started yelling.

Donovan came into sight running. "What, what, did you find something?" he said eagerly.

"Yeah. Did you find anything?" Hyroc said, hoping his conclusion was wrong.

Donovan shook his head. "There's no sign of her."

Hyroc sighed. "I know where she is."

"Alright, where?"

"In the village."

Donovan looked skeptical. "The village? Umm, why would the witch take her there? There are Ministry soldiers all over the place. Wouldn't they, well, kill him?"

"It's not the witch. There's something we missed."

"I don't think I'm following you."

"We don't have time for me to explain everything. Whoever took Elsa is a werewolf. The witch sent the werewolf there with Elsa, and that's where we need to go."

"Why there?"

"Because the witch wanted me to suffer the guilt from the death of so many people or something. We surprised him by finding him before he was ready, but his plan was already in motion."

Donovan pointed with his spear toward the dead witch. "But we killed the witch, should that get rid of his control over the werewolf."

"I have no idea. That's how it works with controlling a shadow demon, but people aren't supposed to be able to control a werewolf."

Donovan indicated the ram heads. "And what's all that about?"

Hyroc shrugged while shaking his head. "I don't know. He did it for a reason. But we don't have time to figure it out."

"Great, we're heading into another situation blind."

"And the only chance we have of saving Elsa is to get to her before the moon fully rises."

"That's not a lot of time. We need to move!"

Shimmer alighted onto the ground in front of them. He looked around, seemingly confused. Hyroc knelt down in front of him. "I need you to go find Harold and get him to go to the village and be ready for a fight. Can you do that?" The bird hopped angrily and took to the air.

Hyroc and Donovan exchanged a look before quickly heading off.

Chapter 11
Unfortunate Soul

Elsa drifted back into consciousness, but a fog hung over her mind. She opened her eyes to see trees. A torch burned in front of her, and a bronze setting sun dimly illuminated the forest as the sky slipped into night. A deep throbbing pain permeated the back of her head, and her hair felt cold there. When she tried to move her hands, they were restrained by a rope. Pushing her mind a little further, the last thing she remembered was helping Curtis work a hide at the cabin. Something behind her startled Curtis, and he yelled her name in warning. Before she could turn, something heavy hit her in the back of the head, and everything went black.

Movement caught her attention. When she looked at it, she saw the shape of a man sitting beside her. She lethargically recognized him. She had seen Hyroc talking to him. Einar was his name.

"Einar?" Elsa said.

Einar stood and turned to look at her. "You're awake," he said despairingly. "I had hoped you wouldn't before it was time."

"Where am I? Why am I tied up?"

"Because he made me, I didn't want to."

"He? Do you mean the witch?"

He nodded.

"Why are you helping him?"

"I wish I was gifted with the option of choice. I want more than anything to say no."

"I don't understand."

Einar held his hand up to her. She saw a glowing orange rune on his palm. "I am bound to *him*, and I have to do as he commands."

"Bound to him? The witch?"

Einar nodded. "Yes, him."

"How? I thought only shadow demons could be bound."

Einar looked surprised. "You know more about this than I expected."

"My friend Hyroc explained some of that to me."

"It seems I have underestimated him. Or rather, *he* has."

"Most people do. They usually can't see past his appearance."

"That is very unfortunate."

"Is he why you're being forced to do this? Are you going after Hyroc?"

Einar nodded. "He seems to be a decent person."

"He is. But if you're here to kill him, why bother getting to know him?"

"My master wanted to know as much about your friend as possible. He wanted to find the best way of attacking him." Einar sighed unhappily. "And that was his heart." He gave her a look of resignation. "It was you and your brothers. The three of you are the only family Hyroc has. My master wanted to tear you away from Hyroc. He wanted to destroy everything your friend holds dear in order to erode his resolve. The pain this caused him was intended to make him easier to kill."

"That's disgusting," Elsa said venomously.

"Unforgivable," Einar agreed. "An act deserving of the worst kind of death." He looked at Elsa sympathetically. "You all seem like good people."

"Why didn't you try to warn us?"

"*He* wouldn't let me! I was screaming in my head to tell you what was happening. No matter how hard I pushed, I could say nothing."

"How is he able to control you?"

Chapter 11: Unfortunate Soul

Einar sighed in frustration. "Despite my ordinary appearance, I am not like everyone else. This is the one thing your friend Hyroc, and I have most in common. Did he tell you how I came to your village? What I went through to get here?"

"Yes. I'm assuming that was a lie?"

Einar nodded. "It was a lie, but all lies are based on the truth. Indeed, I was a farmer in my village. And we were in the midst of a winter famine. Instead of being taken prisoner by another Jarl, that was when the witch captured me. He forced the tainted blood upon me. Ever since then, I have been his puppet."

"Tainted blood? What is that?"

Einar squeezed his eyes shut. "The beginning of my nightmare that there is no waking from. It is the blood of a moon wolf."

A surge of fear shot through Elsa. "Moon wolf! You don't mean – "

Einar opened his eyes to look at her. He nodded somberly. "Yes, a werewolf."

"You're a werewolf."

"Not just a werewolf, I am a blood werewolf. I am cursed with the transformation, but the beast does not overwhelm me. I am able to control the beast's power. And save for a full moon, I can transform when I wish. But it comes at a terrible price. That control leaves me vulnerable to being bound to the will of another." He stared off, seemingly lost in thought.

"What happened to your family?"

A tear ran down Einar's cheek. "*He* forced me to do it! I remember every one of their faces, their screams of terror. I found all of them. The men, the women, and the children; it didn't matter. They all met their fate at my claws. Not even my wife was spared. I'm not gifted with the loss of memory that a werewolf experiences after transforming. I remember everything I did to them. Her face, along with all the others, is seared into my eyelids. I see them whenever I close my eyes!"

Elsa felt a stab of revulsion at the story. She couldn't comprehend how horrible it would be to kill everyone she cared about and be powerless to stop it. This man wasn't her enemy. He was a victim.

"That's terrible," she said. "Is that what your master wants you to do here?"

Einar gave her a sorrowful look. "It is. We are just outside of your village." He grimaced angrily. "When the moon rises, I will transform into the beast. You –" he stuttered as if the words caused him pain. "You will be the first I kill. Then, I will move on to your village." Streams of tears flowed down his face. "I am so sorry."

"Einar, listen to me. It doesn't have to be this way. You can let me go. I can warn everyone."

Einar shook his head. "I want to. *Shadow*! I want to set you free more than anything in the world. But I cannot break free of *him*. My course is set. I can't change it. I'm sorry." He shot her a compassionate look. "With any luck, the lives I take tonight will be the last. My master is dead, and with his death, I can feel his dominion over me weakening. After this night, I will finally be free."

"There's nothing you can do? How do you know there's not something you haven't tried yet?"

"I've tried everything! I must fulfill my master's –" he grunted in pain and doubled over, holding his stomach. His eyes suddenly gained a glow, his hair thickened, and some of his teeth were more triangular. "It's nearly time," he said with labored breathing. "There's nothing I can do. Please forgive me. I will spend the rest of my life trying to make up for what I've done and what I'm about to do."

He raised his head, looking at something that had caught his attention. Elsa became aware of the sound of voices and the jingling of metal. She immediately started yelling for help.

"No, no, not more lives!" Einar yelled despairingly. "Not more faces to haunt me."

The voices became more excited and rapidly moved toward her. A small group of Ministry soldiers came into view dressed in black and orange. "What's going on here?" a soldier holding a lantern demanded as he stepped forward.

"This man kidnapped me and tied me up here. He was about to perform some kind of terrible ritual." The last part was a lie, but she didn't have time for the truth and needed to say something that would drive them to action. The soldiers drew their weapons and moved toward Einar. One split off to walk over to Elsa.

"No, don't come any closer." Einar pleaded. "Run away! You must flee." His voice was deeper and had gained a growling tone. "My master's wrath is not meant for you."

"Miss, I'll have you out of there in no time," the soldier said as he stepped up to Elsa. He sliced through the ropes. "There you go."

"Thank y —"

A terrible roar ripped through the air. Else and the soldier turned to look at Einar. Crouching where there had once been a man was a huge hairy shape covered in blonde fur. It rose to its full height, towering over the soldiers. It had thick arms and legs, and powerful muscles covered its body. Enormous black claws protruded from its fingers. The face had a long snout, and large deadly teeth protruded from its mouth. The creature's eyes glowed brightly, burning with primal rage.

The werewolf rushed forward and tore through the soldiers. Screams and yells of terror filled the night air. Elsa stood transfixed by the violence, unable to move. She mastered herself and forced her eyes away from the carnage. She grabbed the soldier by his shoulder. "Run!" she commanded. The soldier's face was white, and he gave her a wide-eyed fearful look. The two of them turned and ran as fast as they could.

The screams rapidly diminished until no one was left to make a sound. Another roar erupted. The sounds of something big tore through the trees and underbrush. It sounded as if the whole forest was being uprooted behind Elsa. The sounds were quickly gaining. Out of the corner of her eyes, she saw a hairy mass flying toward the soldier. The man yelled as he was knocked face-first to the ground. Elsa glanced over to see the werewolf sink its teeth into the soldier. The soldiers screamed as the creature violently shook him like a ragdoll.

Elsa dashed off to the side and hid behind a tree. Her heart hammered away in her chest harder than she had ever felt, and her breath came in gasps. She cautiously glanced around the tree. The werewolf crouched with one arm braced against the ground. It waived its head from side to side, and she could hear it sniffing. It snapped its head toward her. She lurched back behind the tree. Heavy footfall moved toward her. She frantically looked through her surroundings, searching for anything useful. There was plenty of cover, but she couldn't reach any without being seen by the creature. The footfall grew louder. She turned her attention to the tree she hid behind. It was a cottonwood, and the branches were low enough for her to reach. She jumped up to grab a branch and hauled herself up. When she turned to grab another branch, she saw glowing eyes staring at her. The creature's head was nearly level with her. "Einar, you've got to fight it. You're stronger than this," she said.

The werewolf regarded her with a predatory glare. "Can't fight," the creature said in a deep snarling tone. "Must kill for dead master."

The werewolf slashed its claws at Elsa. She back stepped the swipe, feeling a rush of wind. The creature tried again. She dodged the strike, but it connected with the branch. With a loud snap, the branch fell away from the tree along with her. Elsa landed hard on her rear, but she was low enough that the impacts didn't harm her. She scrambled to her feet and ran. The werewolf easily caught up to her. She tripped over a tangle of roots and barely managed to stay standing, but she lost all her momentum. Knowing it was now pointless to even try escaping, she turned to look her enemy in the eye.

"Einar fight it," she pleaded

The werewolf came to a stop in front of her. "Can't. I sorry, Elsa. Must kill," he growled.

Elsa took a deep breath, preparing for the end. Killed by a werewolf definitely wasn't how she had imagined going out. She hoped it wouldn't hurt, much.

The creature paused, sniffing. Elsa opened her eyes a crack. A large dark shape exploded through the foliage. A blue glow radiated from the shape as it surged forward. The werewolf growled fiercely, its body going rigid. The shape rose up on two legs and struck the werewolf in

Chapter 11: Unfortunate Soul

the head with a glowing paw. The werewolf flew backward, smashing into a tree. The shape looked at Elsa with blue eyes. She felt a flood of relief. It was Hyroc! Donovan arrived at her side.

"Are you hurt?" Donovan asked breathlessly.

"No, I'm fine."

Donovan nodded. He handed her a bow and quiver. She realized the bow was Hyroc's.

"I promise, I'll explain later. Right now, we've got a monster to kill!"

The thought sickened Elsa. Einar was doing this against his will, and none of it was his fault. He was a tormented victim. He was forced to do terrible things he had no ability to stop. But no matter how unfortunate the situation was, Einar was going to kill everyone he came across. He had to be stopped, or many others would die. It was one man or the entire village. She knew they had to do this. She nocked an arrow and took aim.

Chapter 12
The Face of Death

Hyroc locked eyes with the werewolf. He saw in them an untamable firestorm of feral rage. This creature's only purpose was to end lives. It did not kill for food or feel sympathy or remorse. It was unbelievable this thing had been a man. Hyroc knew the man had no control over their actions, but it didn't matter. Unwilling or not, this soul would kill the three of them without hesitation before moving on to the villagers. No matter how awful it felt to stop him, it was their only choice. Hyroc wondered if he might be able to injure the werewolf enough to disable him until the moon disappeared and the threat vanished. But, holding back could have deadly consequences. He didn't know how strong or how resilient this creature was. Restraining his strikes and prolonging the fight was dangerous against an opponent with unknown capabilities. Attacking full force was the surest strategy. He had to attack with the intention of killing. If the opportunity to disable the werewolf presented itself, he would take it. Unless that happened, he had to be prepared to take this man's life. He wasn't facing someone; he was facing a monster.

Hyroc charged forward. The werewolf had recovered from his initial strike and was beginning to stand straight. Hyroc struck his opponent with his thick bear claws in a flurry, opening up several bleeding gashes. He then sank his teeth into the creature's shoulder. It growled

Chapter 12: The Face of Death

ferociously in pain. The werewolf grabbed the back of Hyroc's neck and wrenched his head back. It used its other hand to immobilize his right paw. Hyroc attempted to heave himself out of the creature's grip, but he barely moved. He knew his adversary was strong, but this was beyond anything he anticipated. The werewolf looked him in the eye and roared. The sound ripped through the night air. Hyroc felt his feet leave the ground as his adversary picked him up. He was by no means a small bear, and it alarmed him to see how little effort the creature seemed to be putting into this. The werewolf threw Hyroc. Pain shot through the side of Hyroc's body as he landed on his side, and the air was knocked out of him.

The werewolf stomped toward him, then jolted backward. It growled angrily as two arrows struck it in the chest. Elsa and Donovan had finally gotten a clear shot. The beast snapped its gaze toward them and moved in their direction. Two more arrows hit the creature, but that didn't slow its pace. Hyroc regained his breath, summoned a fireball into his paw, and flung it at his opponent. A cloud of blue flame exploded around the werewolf, filling the air with the smell of singed hair, and it stumbled from the impact. Hyroc roared to pull the creature's attention toward him. The werewolf turned to give him a deadly glare and answered his challenge with one of its own. Two more arrows struck it in the back, but his adversary barely seemed to notice.

Hyroc felt a thrill of fear when the werewolf dropped down onto all fours and tore toward him. He backpedaled, so he wasn't a stationary target. The werewolf slowed slightly to stand on two legs when it was upon him. It slashed its claws toward him, but he summoned a barrier to block the strike. Its claws skirted the barrier, consuming hardly any Quintessence. Hyroc had directed the barrier forward, which left his sides vulnerable. The werewolf swung with its other hand from the side and nailed Hyroc in the head. The impact knocked his head sideways, causing him to lose focus on the barrier, and he saw black spots pop in front of his eyes. He saw the creature lung forward to grab him and twisted his body out of the way. As his opponent flew past him, he smashed it in the back with a powerful paw strike. This drove the creature onto the ground. Hyroc threw himself onto his opponent, hoping his weight would keep it pinned down, and savaged the back of its neck with his teeth. The werewolf threw him off. It spun around and struck sideways at him with its claws. Hyroc ducked the strike, but it decapitated a sapling behind him. Hyroc lurched forward, throwing all his weight into the beast in an attempt to unbalance it. The creature seized his front legs to stop him and shoved him away. Hyroc slid backward. His adversary rushed forward and grabbed him by the neck and shoulder. Hyroc had just enough movement in his neck to ram his head into the creature's jaw. Its teeth clacked together as its head was jerked back. The creature's grip loosened enough for Hyroc to break free. It seemed he had at least one advantage in this fight; his head was harder than his enemy's.

The werewolf gave Hyroc a vengeful look and growled loudly, with its teeth showing in an angry snarl. Hyroc stepped sideways to give Elsa and Donovan a clear shot. An instant later, another arrow struck his opponent. When a second arrow hit, the creature staggered and roared in pain. Hyroc assumed that had been a shadow killer arrow. Those had heads of silver and werewolves were supposed to be vulnerable to such weapons.

His enemy turned and stalked away from him. Hyroc felt a wave of dread wash over him when he realized the creature was heading toward the village. It would mercilessly kill anyone that crossed its path! Hyroc sprinted after it. He was gaining on the werewolf until it dropped down to all fours; then, it pulled away. Light from the houses was visible. People would die if he lost sight of his adversary. He lifted a paw and made a sharp, sweeping motion. A wall of blue fire blazed into existence in front of the creature. It stopped abruptly and threw up an enormous clawed hand to shield itself against the heat. It howled in frustration as it turned back toward Hyroc and moved away from the flames. When the beast's attention was again fixed on him, he dismissed the flames. He was starting to feel the strain from using his Flame Claw.

Chapter 12: The Face of Death

The werewolf reached over and yanked the shadow killer arrow from its body. Hyroc grimaced, realizing it would take a minute or two for Elsa and Donovan to catch back up and that he was alone for the moment. He moved in a circle around the werewolf, trying to buy time. The creature studied him predatorily, figuring out the best way to kill him. It came toward him at a cautious pace, and Hyroc mirrored this. Without notice, it broke into a run. Hyroc entered a defensive stance. Suddenly, the werewolf jinked to the side. It moved so swiftly that Hyroc hardly had any time to reposition himself. He swatted at his enemy, but the creature dodged his attack. It slashed its claws across his hip and sank its teeth into his shoulder. Hyroc yelled out in pain and answered with several hits directed at the creature's head. This drove his adversary back, and his opponent came away bloodied.

Hyroc was hurting, but beyond the pain, his injuries had little impact on his ability to fight. But he couldn't withstand many more wounds of that magnitude. He hoped Elsa and Donovan would soon rejoin the fight. He had a slim chance of victory without them.

He caught a glimpse of a small light out of the corner of his eye. When he turned his head, he saw the figure of a man moving toward them with a lantern. It was a villager! All the commotion had attracted someone's attention. "Who's there?" the man called out in a cool tone. The werewolf looked at the man hungrily and darted toward him. "Run," Hyroc yelled. The man dropped his lantern as he turned to flee.

Hyroc pursued, but the injury to his leg hindered his ability to run at full speed. Dread engulfed him; he wasn't going to get there in time! He watched helplessly as the werewolf overtook the man and brutally attacked him. The man let out a short scream. Hyroc felt sick seeing the savagery with which the creature dispatched the man. Not even animals killed with such violence. His enemy was so focused on brutalizing the man's lifeless body that it didn't even see Hyroc's next attack. He struck with both paws, digging his claws into his opponent. The creature arched its back in surprise and backhanded Hyroc.

Hyroc stumbled back, amazed by the amount of force even that hit had delivered.

The werewolf turned its head as a figure appeared in a nearby doorway with a lantern. They were now in an alleyway close to the village center. This was the one place Hyroc wanted to avoid taking their fight. The noise of their conflict would wake the entire village, and with that, people would come out to investigate. That would put even more lives in danger.

"Get back inside!" Hyroc yelled. The man swore before disappearing back inside and slamming the door behind him.

Hyroc tackled his adversary. The creature braced itself by grasping his shoulders to maintain its balance. He used his paw to sweep the werewolf's legs out from under it. When it fell, Hyroc struck with a powerful downward blow, but his enemy managed to roll out of the way. It rose faster than Hyroc could react and slashed him in the side. Luckily, it was a glancing blow that merely caused him to hurt and bleed instead of inflicting something grievous. Hyroc managed a few quick hits and shoved the creature away as hard as he could. The werewolf quickly regained its footing and slashed at Hyroc with both hands. Hyroc formed a barrier to block the attack. The impact drained a substantial amount of his Quintessence, far more than he had expected. He wouldn't last much longer without help.

A ripple of pain flowed through the creature's body when a throwing ax and an arrow hit it in the side. Hyroc glanced over to see Harold and Curtis. Curtis used a less powerful bow that was incapable of doing any real harm to his target, but each hit was still enough to annoy and distract the creature. The werewolf wrenched the ax free of its body, releasing a stream of blood, and tossed it to the ground. Hyroc threw himself onto his opponent's back and gave it a strong bear hug, trying to hold it in place long enough for Curtis and Harold to get another hit in. Curtis let two arrows fly. Harold drew a second throwing ax and hurled it into the werewolf.

The creature vigorously tried to break free of Hyroc's hold. It couldn't get a good grip on him when it reached back. The creature

Chapter 12: The Face of Death

snapped its head back and nailed Hyroc in the nose. He lost his grip, and the werewolf shoved him off. It wheeled around and savagely hit him in the head multiple times. The strikes disoriented him, causing him to lose his footing. The world spun dizzily, and fuzzy colored spots erupted in front of his eyes. Hyroc saw the creature readying another attack, but his ability to react had been temporarily knocked from his head.

Harold rushed toward the creature yelling and swinging his sword menacingly. The creature lurched backward to avoid the blade, its attention now firmly fixed on the Witch Hunter. The werewolf swiped at Harold. He ducked the blow, brought his sword up, and stabbed the creature in the abdomen before breaking off to put space between them.

The creature savagely growled as it turned toward Harold, blood streaming down its leg. Harold moved in a circle, ready for its next strike. It stalked forward and swung at him with its uninjured arm. Harold backpedaled out of the way, tapping the tip of his blade into the back of its hand. His adversary pulled its hand back, looking at him wrathfully. It dropped onto all fours and lunged at him. He flashed his sword in front of him menacingly to deter the attack, but his opponent paid no heed to him. It purposely caught the blade on the back of its uninjured forearm arm. Harold attempted to reset his position after striking, but the werewolf backhanded him. Harold flew back, rolling when he hit the ground. He lay in a heap, unmoving. His enemy took a step toward him but turned when an arrow stuck in the back of its neck. It fixed a murderous gaze on Curtis and rushed at him.

Hyroc's disorientation faded, allowing him to focus again. He darted toward the werewolf and intercepted it as it neared Curtis. The creature lost its balance when Hyroc tackled it from the side. He came down on top of his opponent, biting and clawing at whatever he could reach. The werewolf howled in anger as it grabbed him by the shoulders. It kicked him in the abdomen while using its hand in a throwing motion to shove him away. When Hyroc landed, he attempted to stand, but a hard punch to his head from the werewolf laid him out on his stomach. His enemy rose into a crouch and fell upon him to maul the back of his neck. Dizzily Hyroc swept his paw to encircle the werewolf's jaw with a thin barrier before it could fully open its mouth. Only a minimal amount of Quintessence was required for this. The front of his opponent's face slammed harmlessly into the back of his neck. The werewolf shook its head and then started pulling on the barrier around its snout. Each tug drained a more noticeable amount of Quintessence. Hyroc dismissed the barrier when he regained his footing.

The werewolf suddenly arched its back and howled in pain as three arrows struck it in the back. Hyroc stood on his hind legs and used his paws to deliver a series of punishing blows to his adversary's head and chest. His opponent kicked him in the stomach, causing him to stumble backward, and struck him in the head. Hyroc fell down to all fours. The werewolf took the opportunity to put some space between them. It ducked an incoming arrow, but another nailed it in the side. Focusing its gaze on what Hyroc assumed was Elsa and Donovan, it reached back and removed three of the arrows in its back. When Hyroc rejoined the fight, Elsa and Donovan took the opportunity to rush over to Harold. They hoisted him up onto their shoulders and moved him to safety.

As Hyroc drew closer, his opponent snapped its head to look off to the side. Following its gaze, he was dismayed to see a line of lanterns approaching them from the other side of the village. The sounds of battle had drawn a group of villagers! The lanterns resolved into a group of men and women armed with pitchforks and scythes. The werewolf turned and moved toward them. Two more arrows struck it, but the creature seemed oblivious. Hyroc silently cursed the witch for the spell that forced the werewolf to focus on the innocent citizens of Elswood.

Hyroc summoned a fireball. His opponent wouldn't ignore this. Just for good measure, he infused the flaming blue orb with extra impact force and threw it at the creature. The werewolf stumbled as the ball struck it in the back, and patches of fire appeared across its

Chapter 12: The Face of Death

fur. The group of villagers gasped in shock as the blast of fire illuminated their enemy for an instant. They rapidly retreated as they yelled in alarm. Soon everyone in the village would be aware of the conflict. They needed to end this! The werewolf turned toward Hyroc and roared savagely. Hyroc took a few heavy breaths when the fatigue of his waning Quintessence sapped his strength. He had almost nothing left to use his ability, and he couldn't handle this for much longer.

His opponent dropped to all fours and tore toward him, leaving behind a trail of blood. Arrows whizzed past Hyroc as he prepared to defend himself. The werewolf rose back onto its legs when it was upon him. It came at him with an arm stretched out for a slashing attack. Hyroc darted forward, getting inside his enemy's reach. He grabbed the werewolf and jerked its upper body sideways. The werewolf staggered and grabbed Hyroc's shoulder to maintain its balance. Hyroc shoved the creature away and remorselessly slashed into it with his claws. He felt hot sticky blood cover his paws and run down his front legs. The werewolf seized both his paws with one arm in an impossibly strong grip. It slashed the side of his face and burrowed its teeth into his shoulder just next to his neck. Hyroc screamed in pain as his adversary made jerking motions with its head. He desperately struggled to free himself from his adversary's grip, but he remained immobilized.

He saw the glint of a spearhead as it stabbed the werewolf in the side. The creature howled angrily. Hyroc felt its grip loosen. He fought through what remained of its hold and freed himself. Hyroc fell to the ground breathing in heaving gasps from a mixture of pain and fatigue. He looked up to see Donovan pull his spear free of the werewolf's flesh and dodge a wild backhand. When the creature turned to make another strike, Donovan shoved his spear into its abdomen. His adversary shuddered with pain and made no move to retaliate. Donovan used the opening to slash across the middle of the creature and follow through with another stab. With almost no warning, the werewolf swiped Donovan with its hand. The spear remained embedded in the creature as Donovan went flying. He landed hard on his back and was unconscious. The werewolf removed the spear and cast it aside.

A four-legged shape appeared on a roof behind the werewolf. It jumped, pouncing on the creature's back. The shape resolved into the familiar form of Kit. Hyroc looked at his companion anxiously. He had told Kit to stay out of the fight! The mountain lion anchored his claws into the werewolf's shoulder and viciously bit the side of its neck. His adversary sharply shook its upper body, trying to dislodge the big cat, but his claws kept him in place. The werewolf reached back and slapped the feline away as if he were no more than an irritation. Kit landed with a thump. He weakly yowled in pain as he lay on the ground.

Dread engulfed Hyroc at the realization that they weren't going to win this. Only Curtis and Elsa remained in the fight. Elsa put two arrows in the left side of the creature's chest, aiming for its heart. Her kill shots seemed to have no effect on the werewolf. She sent her next and last arrow flying at her enemy's head. The beast jerked its head sideways out of the way.

Hyroc gazed at their adversary in amazement, seeing its body bristling with arrow shafts and how it still seemed capable of fighting at full strength. Just a fraction of those would have easily brought down a fully grown moose buck and then some. This thing had withstood everything the six of them had thrown at it as if their efforts were little more than a nuisance. Its body was riddled with wounds, and it didn't care. Even with the aid of his Flame Claw, they were outmatched. They had merely caused their enemy pain, nothing more. None of them had any more fight in them. He, and his friends, along with everyone in the village, would be killed by this monster. He had failed. His best wasn't enough, and there was nothing he could do.

He watched Curtis rush to the side of his fallen brother. The boy shook Donovan, desperately trying to wake him. Curtis raised his head to look at the creature, tears streaming down his face. Hyroc felt a stab of guilt seeing the despair on his young friend's face and knowing the boy's life would soon come to a violent end. Hyroc felt a tear run down his face. "I'm sorry, Curtis, Donovan, Elsa, and Harold," he whispered. He looked up toward the sky. "I gave it my best, but it wasn't good

Chapter 12: The Face of Death

enough." He grit his teeth angrily. It hurt knowing he couldn't keep the promise he had made to Svald and Helen that he would protect their children. How could he face them when his time came? They would be disappointed.

The air suddenly crackled with energy. It was so heavily laden it almost made it hard to breathe. A bright white glow filled the village center. Hyroc, Elsa, and the werewolf gazed in wonder at the source of the light. Curtis stood at its center with his hands stretched forward, one behind the other. Crackling tendrils of lightning crept erratically over his body, and a streamer of lightning formed in Curtis' hands. It began to grow in size. Hyroc felt hairs all over his body stand on end as the energy intensified. Curtis snapped a determined, wrathful glare at the werewolf. The creature howled in rage as it ran toward Curtis. The boy flung his hands forward, and a blast of lightning slammed into the creature. The impact knocked it off its feet and sent it hurtling through the air as fire blossomed across its body. When the werewolf landed, it struggled to its feet. The left side of its chest and its arm was black with burned flesh. Its arm dangled uselessly at its side, and it seemed to be having trouble standing in place. The light faded from Curtis, but he nearly toppled over from exhaustion. Hyroc knew his friend had just used Quintessence!

Hyroc pushed a flurry of thoughts away and returned his attention to the werewolf. He felt a thrill seeing the weakened state of his adversary. The creature was vulnerable; they could defeat it! Summoning the last of his strength, Hyroc charged at the creature. It took a swing at him with its working arm, but he effortlessly dodged it as he came at his enemy from its exposed side. He rammed into the werewolf, sending it to the ground. Hyroc bit into his adversary's uninjured arm just below the shoulder. He bit down as hard as he could. He tasted blood. Then, something crunched between his teeth. The werewolf let loose an almost deafening howl. Hyroc pinned the creature beneath his paws and bit into its neck. He viciously shook his head from side to side to maximize the damage. Elsa joined him with Donovan's spear in hand. She shoved the steel spearhead into the right side of the creature's chest, aiming for its heart. She repeatedly stabbed it, huffing from a combination of exertion and anger. It was the kind of sound that only someone who had lost all hope and regained a glimmer could make. The creature struggled wildly, but Hyroc held it firmly in place. Elsa yelled, throwing all of her strength into her next strike. The creature gasped and went still. Hyroc was so focused on attacking his enemy that he didn't even notice.

Elsa nudged him with the shaft of the spear. "Hyroc," she said. "Hyroc! That's enough. It's over."

Hyroc pulled his head back, breathing heavily. He sat and used the back of his paw to wipe the blood from his mouth. The werewolf began to change. Its hair and claws receded, and its body slowly started shrinking. Hyroc looked into its eyes, and they had lost the fire of wild fury. They now looked human. Hyroc was thunderstruck to realize he recognized the face of Einar. He was the werewolf! Hyroc had a polite conversation with the man mere days ago. Einar had seemed to be such a kind and gentle person. Hyroc thought he could be friends with him. It seemed impossible that he was hiding this terrible secret.

A tear ran down Einar's reverting face. He gazed at Hyroc with a look of relief, relief knowing he would never be used to hurt anyone ever again. He mouthed the words, "I'm free. Thank you." A moment later, life left him. Hyroc and Elsa breathed a sigh of relief, but Hyroc couldn't help feeling mournful about what he had done. He had no choice in his actions. He had to take a life to save many more. It was necessary, but the witch had taken his innocence from him. There was no going back. He couldn't help hating that witch.

"Are you alright?" Elsa asked.

Hyroc nodded. "I'm fine. It's just blood," he answered. "And you?"

"I'm good. We need to check on the others."

Hyroc stood and followed her over to Curtis. The boy sat on the ground uninjured with his eyes open, but he was dazed. His eyes sluggishly flicked over to look at them. The magic he used seemed to have taken quite a toll on him. They left Curtis where he was and moved on to Donovan. Donovan lay on his back unconscious and had a bleeding

Chapter 12: The Face of Death

gash across his forehead. Elsa sat him up before shaking him. It had no effect. Hyroc stepped over to him impatiently and roared in his face. Donovan's eyes flew open with a start.

"Shadow!" Donovan yelled wildly. "Where's that beast?"

"Relax, we got it," Elsa said.

"You did?" Donovan breathed a sigh of relief. He grimaced and moved his hand up to his head to feel the gash. "Oh. My head. *Ouch.*"

Elsa removed a handkerchief from one of Donovan's pockets and pressed it over the wound. "Hold this there. You've got a pretty nasty cut," she insisted.

He did as instructed. "What happened? All I remember is something heavy hit me."

Elsa and Hyroc exchanged a look. "Well, we're not entirely sure what happened," Hyroc said uncertainly. "I think Curtis used magic, and that saved us."

Donovan looked confused. "Magic? Maybe that thing hit me a lot harder than I thought because it sounded as if you said magic."

"That's the only thing that makes sense from what we saw."

"Okay then, my brother can use magic." Donovan suddenly looked alarmed. He rapidly glanced around until he found Curtis. "Is he alright?"

"He's fine," Hyroc assured. "He's just in a bit of a stupor. I think the magic took a lot out of him."

Donovan nodded. "What about Harold?"

They looked at the spot where they had left Harold. He slowly got to his feet when they saw him. He brushed some dirt from his pants, retrieved his sword, and moved toward them. Other than some scrapes and bruises, he seemed fine, but when he walked, he held his arm at his side as if injured. A quiet yowl drew his attention to Kit. He was relieved to see his companion coming to him. The big cat walked with a minor limp, and when he came to a stop, he put his paw down tenderly. Hyroc lifted his paw for their established greeting when he was in bear form, but Kit remained where he was. He yowled again, seeming irritated.

-107-

"I'm sorry you got hit," Hyroc said. "But it's over now. That thing's gone." Kit looked over at Einar's body. "Thank you for trying to protect me." The mountain lion studied him before rubbing against his outstretched paw, seemingly pleased by his compliment.

Hyroc lowered his paw, noticing lanterns and torches popping up in the darkness all around them. Everyone was coming out to see what had caused such a disturbance. As soon as anyone saw him, they would assume he was a witch. They would see Einar's mangled body and conclude he had brutally murdered the man. That was the farthest thing from the truth, but, in his bear form, there was no way to persuade them otherwise. But worst of all, they would view his friends as accomplices. The four of them had fought to save the lives of the villagers, and no one would know. They would become enemies for their selfless efforts. They would be viewed as being just as dangerous as he was. Elswood, the only place they knew, was no longer their home.

"Elsa, we need to move," Hyroc urged.

She nodded. "I'll get Curtis," Elsa said.

She helped her younger brother to his feet and led him away. Donovan retrieved his spear before joining them. Hyroc used his paw to indicate to Harold what direction they were heading and, with Kit following, limped after his friends. They moved toward the outside of the village, passing darkened figures beginning to appear in doorways. Behind them, they saw a line of lanterns stretching across the village center. If they got caught in a fight here, the sheer number of the villagers would easily overwhelm them. Soon the figures were calling questions out to them. They were almost to the edge. Even more points of light had appeared behind them, and they seemed to be gaining. The last building was within sight – just a little further.

Hyroc suddenly detected a strong smell of metal and wood. Kit growled as the four of them came to a stop when a group of soldiers approached from the outside of the village, cutting off their escape route. When they turned to go back the way they had come, they saw another group emerge from an alley. They were trapped!

Chapter 12: The Face of Death

The group behind entered a defensive poster, and the one in front formed a fighting line. "What goes on here?" said a Light Walker on a horse behind the line of soldiers. His eyes narrowed when he focused on Hyroc. "A witch," he spat. "You're not getting away to terrorize anymore." He thrust his sword toward them. "Soldiers, advance. Kill them all!" The fighting line steadily moved toward them.

Hyroc stared with dismay at the wall of shields and swords coming toward them. It seemed an unbreakable line of metal. In his weakened and injured state, he didn't have any Quintessence to spare for a spell. If he fully depleted his internal reservoir of Quintessence, he would be rendered unconscious from his body, preventing him from killing himself by him losing all of it. He was still in somewhat of a fighting condition, but attacking the soldiers in front was suicide. Their only chance was to break through the group behind them. They only had mere moments before they were smashed between both. It was their only chance.

"Attack the back!" Hyroc yelled. He charged toward the group, and Donovan followed suit. The soldiers tensed in preparation to defend themselves. One of the soldiers stiffened and fell face-first with an ax buried in his back. Another cried out in pain with his back arched. The man collapsed to reveal Harold standing behind him with a bloodied sword. The nearest soldier turned toward Harold and slashed at him with a sword. Harold dodged the first, then blocked a second strike. He kicked the soldier in the side of the leg to unbalance his opponent, then punched the man in the face. The soldier fell to the ground, disoriented. His remaining companions converged on Harold.

Harold looked toward the four of them. "GO NOW!" he commanded as he fended off strikes. "Get out of here. I'll hold them off."

The four of them darted past the soldiers distracted by Harold and moved into a side alley. When they emerged from the other side, it was clear. They saw a clump of lanterns from soldiers moving around the buildings to intercept them. They ran into the trees and moved at an angle away from the village to try and lose any pursuers. Soon, there were no lanterns in sight.

"Hyroc, you smell anything?" Elsa said.

Hyroc shook his head. "I think we lost them." Elsa nodded. "We should split up. I'll head to my cabin to grab some things, and the three of you need to head to yours and do the same."

"Sounds good. You'll meet us at the hideaway?"

Hyroc nodded.

"Wait!" Donovan interjected. "What about Harold. We have to go back and get him." Hyroc and Elsa exchanged a look. "We can't just leave him."

Elsa put her hand on his shoulder, looking sad. "Donovan, we can't. Soldiers will be all over the village by now."

"We have to. After everything he's done for us, we can't abandon him."

"Donovan, he sacrificed himself so we could escape. He didn't want us to come back for him. He's gone." Donovan opened his mouth to argue but closed it. He hung his head shamefully. "I know, I know. We need to get moving." Donovan nodded as he wiped his eye. "We'll meet you there, Hyroc." Hyroc nodded, and the four of them split off into the night.

Chapter 13
Outcasts

Hyroc rushed through the darkened forest. Leaves and spiny pine needle covered branches brushed across his face as he hurried on his way. He barely noticed through a cloud of pain. The exhilaration from his battle with the werewolf had faded, and he felt the full intensity of every wound he sustained during the fight. He was exhausted, his strength was spent, and sheer force of will was the only thing keeping him going. With every passing second, The Ministry soldiers drew closer to not only locating his home but the home of his friends.

This wasn't supposed to happen. Hyroc had accepted that his days in Elswood were coming to an end and that he would have to leave. But with Curtis unexpectedly using magic to light up the entire village with a brilliant lightning bolt, his plan was a bit more complicated. He doubted anyone had witnessed Curtis' new ability, but plenty of people had seen the five of them in the village center. And with the ruckus they had caused fighting the werewolf, it was no stretch of the imagination that The Ministry would link all of them to some kind of witchcraft.

Curtis, Donovan and Elsa were witches, witches that associate with an aberration such as he. Despite their actions preventing the slaughter of the villagers, no one was aware of the reason for their involvement, nor was that how things appeared. Because Einar had reverted back into a human when he died, it looked as if they had murdered an innocent man with the aid of witchcraft. It was a terrible combination that practically guaranteed a death sentence for all of them.

Elswood was the home of his friends, it was the only thing they knew, and they had to abandon it. Hyroc couldn't help thinking of the boarding school and the boy whose leg he broke. It was an accident, he merely wanted to help another student that was being bullied, but it didn't matter. All they saw was a monster that was too dangerous to have in their midst. Just as that had ended his time in Forna, the fight with the werewolf had ended their time in Elswood. There was no place for any of them here anymore.

Hyroc stumbled, nearly losing his footing. He came to a stop beside a tree to rest a moment, leaning against its rough trunk for support. His body urged him to sleep, but he fought it off. He glanced behind him, spotting a patch of his blood smeared across a leaf. His bleeding would make an easy trail for his pursuers to follow. In his present weakened condition, escape seemed impossible, but he had a trick to turn his predicament into an advantage. Ursa had taught him a magic technique that allowed him to erase all traces of his trail within a small area. If he wanted to, he could eliminate his blood trail, but he had an idea about how to use that. He was on his way to his cabin, and he would use his own trial to lead his pursuers there. Once he collected his things from his cabin, the structure was no longer of use to him. After he departed, he would remove any traces of him moving off to rendezvous with the Shackletons at their secret spot. He hoped the Ministry soldiers that tailed him would waste time at his dead-end and give his friends and him fewer of them to deal with while they escaped.

With every step, the mixture of pain and fatigue yelled for him to stop moving and lay down. Hyroc knew if he did, he would fall asleep. After taking a deep breath, he laboriously continued limping on his way. His progress felt agonizingly slow, but he couldn't force his body to move any faster. At any moment, he expected to hear

Chapter 13: Outcasts

the baying of bloodhounds or the sound of twigs snapping as many men approached.

He breathed a sigh of relief when his cabin finally came into view. He pushed the cabin door open with his paw and entered. This was the first time he had attempted this while in bear form, and it was a much tighter squeeze than he expected. His wounds stung as they came into contact with the edges of the doorframe, but he was able to enter. As he turned toward his bed, he bumped into the stool and small table near the fireplace. He used his snout to flip open the lid of a chest at the foot of the bed. It contained various supplies and keepsakes. He grabbed a small wooden box with his teeth and set it on the bed. It required far too fine motions for him to open in his current form, so he magicked it open with his Flame Claw. The box contained a necklace with a small dark red ruby.

Ursa had given him the necklace as a parting gift. Beyond its beauty and the sentimental value it possessed, it acted as a container for Quintessence. Energy could be funneled into it and stored for later use. Hyroc was supposed to fill it with small amounts of his own Quintessence whenever convenient, but he had neglected that task somewhat because he disliked the feeling of fatigue that accompanied doing so. It was still partially full, but he chided himself for his reluctance. A full energy store would have absolutely come in handy at this moment. He could be in real trouble because it wasn't.

He held his paw over the necklace and siphoned the energy from the gem. The harshness of his fatigue melted away, and he felt strength returning to him. His recuperation ceased unsatisfactorily, far short of fully restoring him, leaving his body demanding more. Still, he now had enough strength to comfortably expend Quintessence on needed spells without feeling weak. He moved his paw toward his body and began healing his injuries.

A frantic surge overcame him when he didn't feel his necklace with a silver disc that had his name etched into it. He quickly felt across his body but didn't find it. The necklace was his only link to his past and was very precious to him. He normally took it off while he was in bear form because he risked being identified by the villagers if he didn't. He had been focused on saving Elsa that he had forgotten to take it off and give it to Donovan for safekeeping before they found the werewolf. He glanced behind him to see if it had fallen off when he came through the cabin door. No necklace. He squeezed back out of the cabin to search.

Minutes passed. It was still missing. He lifted his head and groaned unhappily, holding back tears. His only link to his real mother was lost! The werewolf had got him with its claws multiple times and had likely severed the chain with one of those strikes. It was back in the village! But there was another problem created by its loss.

There was a chance that The Ministry would assume an unidentified witch had converted Elsa, Curtis, Donovan, and Harold to the dark arts. That assumption would still lead to Ministry hunting parties coming after them, but potentially at a lower intensity. But with his necklace in the village, which would easily identify his presence there, that wasn't the case. They had been hunting him for years and were specifically driven to eradicate him because, to them, he represented something especially evil and dangerous. They viewed him as the creation of a witch that no good could ever come from. He was tainted by darkness and needed to be killed for the safety of everyone in Arnaira. Now that they knew he was here, they would pursue him with more fervor, and that would make it much harder for him and his friends to evade The Ministry. He took a deep breath and moved back into the cabin. There wasn't anything to be done about it.

He resumed healing his wounds. What he could reach in his bear form was limited, and he was only able to mend a few of his wounds. The worst ones were beyond his reach, and he would have to endure them until he could transform back into his normal self in a few hours.

Hyroc magicked the necklace into the air and put his head through it. Next, he moved to the wall where he usually hung his clothing. A large knapsack with a leather strap for a handle hung there, and Hyroc wiggled his head through it. Once in position, the knapsack

Chapter 13: Outcasts

drooped loosely under his neck. Using his teeth and paws, he began piling his belongings, food, and whatever supplies he could find into it. Kit entered the cabin as Hyroc worked. The mountain lion studied him before sauntering over to a smaller sack that hung on the wall and pushed his head through it. Hyroc gave him an appreciative nod and put some extra things into the smaller bag.

When the sacks held as much as they could carry, Hyroc exited his cabin, carefully contorting his body to avoid spilling the contents of his knapsack. He waited for Kit to join him before he started closing the door behind him with magic. He cocked his head, mildly confused. Why was he closing the door? He wasn't coming back. He gazed into the cabin as a wave of sadness enveloped him. For the last four years, this had been his home. He remembered how excited he had been to find this place abandoned. Rain would no longer affect his sleep; he would have a fire to keep himself warm and have the comfort of a bed. Now, all he felt was dismay. He studied what remained; the things he had no room to carry. There was so much he had worked hard to create that would be left behind. What he left would either gather dust and cobwebs where it lay, or someone would claim it as their own.

There was some irony there. He had claimed the cabin and its contents left from the previous owner, and someone would probably do the same to him. For an instant, he felt as if he was eight years old again, turning from the headmaster's office, Marcus's office. It seemed the only thing he ever did was walk away from the things he cared about.

Hyroc closed the cabin door. He might as well try to be as polite as he could to the next owner if there was another owner. There was a good chance after The Ministry finished ransacking his former home trying to learn something useful about him, they would brand the structure as an evil place. Then, no one would come near it, and not necessarily because the villagers were scared of something associated with something that once touched something that may have come into contact with witchcraft. But because anyone discovered having come

–115–

to it would face the very real wrath of The Ministry and all the bad things that accompanied dealings with them.

He scanned their surroundings, taking everything in and giving himself one last memory of this place. Taking a deep breath, he and Kit moved off into the trees, saying goodbye to their home.

Hyroc headed northeast toward the river. Every mile or so, he cast his trail-removing spell. He continued along the river before turning south when he came upon a tree marked with the shape of a bear paw carved into it. He arrived at the meeting spot, where Elsa, Donovan, Curtis, and a donkey laden with saddlebags waited for him.

"There you are," Elsa said, relieved. "We were concerned about leaving you alone with those injuries, and we were starting to wonder if we should go looking for you."

Hyroc used his paw to slip the knapsack off his head and set it on the ground before speaking. "I know those must've looked bad, but beyond the blood, they weren't serious," he said, thankful for their concern.

Elsa nodded. "Anyone follow you?"

He shook his head. "I made a false trail and used my trick to erase any trail I made, so we're good. Did the three of you get away clean?"

"Yes."

"There's something we need to discuss before we talk about anything else," Donovan said, looking serious as he finished strapping supplies to the donkey.

Hyroc cocked an eyebrow. "What?"

"That werewolf bit you, and from the stories I've heard, that now means you're going to turn into a werewolf next time the moon rises. How are you going to deal with that?"

Hyroc nodded his acknowledgment. "Oh, that. You don't need to worry. I'm not going to turn into a werewolf. Wol'dgers are immune to that. Ursa said it's due to our curse. It cancels out that issue or something along those lines. I didn't quite understand all of her explanation. But the important thing is nothing is going to happen."

Donovan nodded, relaxing. "Oh. Well, good to know."

Chapter 13: Outcasts

"Is Curtis alright?"

Donovan looked thoughtful, glancing at his younger brother. "He seems alright. He came out of that stupor he was in after doing that *thing*. When we tell him to do something, he listens, but he's not talking."

Hyroc nodded. "The first part of that is good. Pretty sure he'll come out of his silence when he's ready. The whole thing was probably just a lot for him to take in."

"So," Elsa said. "What's your plan from here?"

Hyroc blew out a breath. "Well, our first priority is to get away from The Ministry. We evaded them for now, but they'll be out looking for us. Once we're –"

"Us?" Elsa said, giving him a confused look. "What do you mean by us?"

Hyroc returned an equally confused look. "Yes, *us*. We were all –" he trailed off as a realization occurred to him. They didn't know. They thought they were merely helping him escape and that their lives would go back to normal when he was gone. They didn't know they could never return to their home. If The Ministry caught them, they would all be hung. They didn't know they were outcasts just as much as he was. He would have to break their new reality to them.

"Elsa, you and your brothers, have to come with me," Hyroc said sternly. "They're hunting you as well. None of you are safe here anymore."

Elsa and Donovan looked perplexed. "They're hunting us?" Elsa questioned with obvious disbelief. "That can't be right. Why would they be coming after us? We helped kill that *thing*."

Hyroc shook his head. "That doesn't matter."

Elsa shook her head. "That doesn't make any sense. I understand they would come after you for –" she indicated Hyroc's body with her hand "– looking like that, using magic, and speaking like a person when you're a bear. Normal animals don't do any of those things, and they would think you're a witch. They would come after *you*. They have no reason to come after *us*."

–117–

"No, Elsa, they have a lot of reasons to do that. The three of you fought alongside me to kill that werewolf. That makes the three of you my accomplices. To them, you participated in whatever unnatural or dark ritual I was supposedly performing. That makes you just as guilty as me and another enemy to be brought to justice for witchcraft. Then you remember how Einar's body reverted back to human form after we killed him. Well, unless someone saw that change, it would essentially look as if the four of us suddenly decided to murder an innocent man. They could hang the three of you for that alone. And you helped me, a witch, commit what they see as a random act of brutality. Also, you have to think of what Curtis did. There is no way that blinding light went unnoticed. Also, people there had to have recognized you three, and it seems reasonable to assume The Ministry will tie all of you to some type of witchcraft. You're now witches. The three of you, for certain, face a death sentence after all that. If you stay, you'll die."

Elsa shook her head in disbelief. "What about the other villagers. They've known us since we were children. They know we would never be a part of something wretched. They will vouch for us. They wouldn't simply throw us to the wolves."

"Would they?" Hyroc questioned. "What happened after word about the spiders that killed your parents and grandfather spread through the village? How many people came to help your family after that?" Elsa drew her lips into a line, her expression turning impassive. "Harold, out of everyone in the village, was the only one who helped us. One person! No one else. Do you remember the rumors? Everyone scorned you because I was involved. They thought the four of us had murdered your parents. Those are the people you expect to protect you? The three of you would be strung up for a short drop by morning."

"Rumors are just talk," Elsa noted. "How could everyone –"

"Elsa!" Hyroc snapped, cutting her off. "You don't know these people as I do. They will kill you, Donovan, and Curtis without a second thought. I've lived under their threat for my entire life. I know what they're capable of. No amount of reasoning or logic will get through to them. Your only option – our only option, is to leave."

Chapter 13: Outcasts

Elsa bowed her head and held one hand against the side of her head in frustration. Donovan reached out to put a reassuring hand on her shoulder, but she pushed it away. She raised her head and stepped over to the donkey. She rummaged through a side saddlebag, removing a needle and thread.

"Alright, we don't have a choice," Elsa said as she moved back over to Hyroc. "We have to figure out where we're going and what we're doing. But while we do that, you need to get that hip stitched up."

Hyroc grimaced in dismay. "It's fine. I can heal it when I transform back and am able to reach it."

Elsa put a hand on her hip, looking displeased. "And when will that be?" she said skeptically.

"In a couple hours. Morning at the latest."

Elsa shook her head. "So, you'll be bleeding all over the place until morning, leaving a nice clear trail for The Ministry to follow."

He waved his paw dismissively. "No, I can cover that with my trail-removing trick. It's not going to be a problem."

"Yes, but you told me that the more things you have to remove with that trick, the more it saps your strength and weakens you. If I stop the bleeding, that's one last thing to put a strain on your magic, or whatever it's called, and you can stretch it out farther. And that also goes for healing that wound. Didn't Ursa tell you something about, "if you can do something without magic, it's much less draining than doing something with magic, and the lower effort option should always be your first choice."

Hyroc sighed, remembering Ursa had said that. "Are you sure we've got time for this?"

"The sooner I start, the sooner we can leave," Elsa said obstinately. "Now, lay your *fat butt* down so I can get to work."

He grumbled angrily and lay down on his side in front of her.

Elsa settled down on her knees. "What do we need first?" she asked as she threaded the needle.

"We need a –" Hyroc grunted in pain when he felt the stab of the needle.

"It couldn't have hurt *that bad*. I barely did anything."

He took a deep breath to retrieve his line of thought. "We need a map," he continued. Donovan reached into Hyroc's knapsack, retrieving his map. He unrolled the map on the ground in front of Hyroc's face, placing four stones at the corners to keep it flat. Hyroc tensed from another needle stab as he spoke. "Put a finger on Elswood. It's toward the top right." After a moment of studying the map, Donovan put his finger on Elswood. "We're here at Elswood. To the south of us is the main road. It would be suicide for us to go anywhere near it because that's where The Ministry trackers will be coming from, so no –" another stab "– roads."

"That only leaves us with the forest," Donovan interjected.

"We can use that to our advantage," Elsa said, peering over at the map. "The four of us know every tree and rock in the woods around here. The same can't be said for those newcomers. We know all the trails and can move a lot faster than any of them."

"They'll also be slowed down by the rougher terrain amongst the trees because of their armor," Hyroc said. "And they won't be able to use men on horses." He sucked air through his teeth when the next needle stab stung a lot.

Donovan glanced over at Hyroc. "Okay, so, which direction do we go? You're the most experienced with things outside of Elswood, Hyroc. What do you think?"

"We're in your hands for this," Elsa added.

Hyroc raised his head to get a better angle on the map. He carefully scanned it with his eyes. They couldn't go south, and the edge of the map cut off anything to the north and east. So, unless they wished to go get lost in the uncharted wilds, the west was their only course. A vast woodland wilderness lay in their path, but past it was an area of open ground, and he saw the names of towns there. If they went straight through the forest, they would emerge onto the open terrain. And if they covered their trail as they traveled through the trees, it seemed impossible that The Ministry hunters could follow them. The only problem was navigating that labyrinth. Even if he climbed a tree

Chapter 13: Outcasts

to look at their surroundings, the map would be practically useless. But he had an idea how to get around that.

"Shimmer," Hyroc called out. "Are you here?" He heard an excited squawk in response, and the raven glided down in front of them. "We need to travel through the forest to the west. Do you think you can guide us to the other side like how you led us to that witch?" Shimmer looked thoughtful and nodded. "Good. Can you also guide us through the easiest terrain, so we can stay ahead of The Ministry?" He appeared to be deep in thought for a long moment before nodding. "Yeah, he seems confident he can guide us."

"Guide us where?" Elsa prodded.

"To the west. Shimmer is going to guide us through the forest to that open area on the map."

She glanced at the map and then at Shimmer.

"That bird led us to that witch when you were in trouble, Elsa," Donovan said. "It may not have been where you really were, but I think that was just because you were moved while he came to get us. I trust him."

Elsa nodded. "So, your plan is to go to the west. Then where to?"

"Beyond Arnaira." Elsa and Donovan shot him a surprised look.

"We're leaving Arnaira?" Elsa questioned.

"Do you even know what's out there?" Donovan said skeptically. "This is a lot farther than your trip from Forna."

Hyroc breathed out a sigh. "To be honest, I really don't know what's out there. But I have heard about a kingdom to the west. Mastgar, I think is its name. It's supposed to be inhabited by witches, sorcerers, and savage unconsecrated people."

They stared at him, stunned. "THAT'S WHERE YOU WANT TO GO!" they both exclaimed simultaneously.

"You want to go to where you know there's evil people that would probably cut our hearts out if they got the chance?" Donovan said in disbelief. "I think that monster hit you in the head a lot harder than you let on."

"You've heard all the horrible things that people in the village said about me and the things they said that I did. But you know I'm nowhere

—121—

close to what those rumors suggested. You heard Harold's story about that little girl. She helped others and was labeled a witch. Who's to say what The Ministry says about Mastgar is even true. Those witches and sorcerers they talk about could just be people using magic. People like me." He indicated Curtis with his chin. "People like Curtis. The Ministry paints anyone who uses magic as dangerous and evil, regardless of how it's used. You both know that's not true. You're friends with me. Magic can be used for good or bad just as it's everyone's choice if they decide to be good or evil."

They both studied him intently, considering his words.

"I understand what you're saying," Donovan said. "But I'm not thrilled by the idea of us heading to a place we hardly know anything about. What if you're wrong? What if Mastgar is as bad as The Ministry says?"

"I agree with Donovan," Elsa said. "Going in their blind isn't the best idea. We should try to come up with something else."

"What else is there?" Hyroc said. "The Ministry is hunting us!" He indicated Curtis by raising a paw. "Your little brother's been labeled a witch. They won't stop coming after him as long as he draws breath. He's not safe anywhere in Arnaira. Your only choice is to leave and go to the west. It's risky, I know, but we have no other choice. This isn't our home anymore."

Donovan and Elsa looked at each other before answering.

"If you think it's what we should do," Elsa said. "Then I trust you."

"I trust you," Donovan said.

Hyroc nodded.

"Supplies are going to be a problem, though," Elsa said. She thumbed toward the donkey. "Counting what you brought, if we're careful, we've got maybe two weeks stowed away on the donkey. But if my figuring is correct, it'll take us three weeks or more to get through the forest. And it's still a long way to the western border."

"We're all expert hunters," Donovan said. "So I think we can make up what we're lacking by hunting and gathering as we go."

"Maybe," Elsa said uncertainly. "But it's going to be rough."

"There's a couple other tricks I think I can use to help us out," Hyroc said.

"Okay, what about after we get to our first destination? I'm not confident we're going to find enough food to get us to the border. The number of things we can hunt will go down drastically once we reach that flat area. It'll be near impossible to sneak up on game out in the open."

Hyroc looked at the map with an unpleasant expression. "Which means we'll have to stop somewhere for provisions." He bowed his head and sighed.

"I don't think that will be a problem," Donovan said. He studied the map before continuing. "Yeah, on the map, there's a town not far from the edge of the forest. We can get our supplies there."

Hyroc gave him a questioning look. "Don't you think I'll look a little out of place there?"

Donovan waved his hand dismissively. "No, not you. I understand it would be a terrible idea for you to go there." He used his hand to indicate Elsa and him. "But I bet the two of us could without anyone thinking twice."

"We probably could," Elsa said. "Hyroc, you know more about these things than us. Do you think word of us would reach that village before we got there?"

Hyroc glanced between Elswood and the indicated town. "It's pretty far away from here," he said. "We might have enough time to get there before anyone knows about us. But I can't be certain."

"Even if it does, I doubt any of those soldiers got a good enough look at the three of us for anyone to draw an accurate bounty poster. And unless The Ministry really puts the screws on everyone in the village, I wouldn't expect anyone to give a good description either. No one there trusts The Ministry all that much and won't lightly give them information for fear of it being turned back on them, even if it's about us."

"But if your thinking doesn't hold, we'll have to steal the supplies, or we'll starve," Hyroc said grimly.

Their expressions turned more serious.

"Let's just hope it doesn't come to that," Elsa said with forced expectation. "Okay, we figured out everything we're going to do, but those things are a long way off. We need to focus on what's going on right now. We still need to get away from Elswood without The Ministry finding us." She paused to let their situation sink in. "Ministry soldiers are probably all along the road to the south." She used a finger to trace their course across the map. "So, I think we should go north across the river, then west past the mountain. After that, we'll head in a northwest direction to keep away from any Ministry search parties."

"I'll be removing any traces of our passing," Hyroc added. "So, there shouldn't be anything for them to follow."

Elsa nodded. "That will make it much easier," she said. "And when we're far enough away, we'll head straight west until we hit the end of the forest." She turned her attention to Shimmer. "Alright, pretty bird, it's all up to you to keep us on the right track and keep us ahead of The Ministry. You ready for this?" The raven bobbed his head and cawed excitedly. "Good boy," she said as she stroked his head. Shimmer eagerly pushed his head up into her hand.

An orange light formed at the base of Wolf Paw Mountain. Hyroc rose to his feet to get a better look. A stab of sorrow struck when he realized the light was in the same place as his cabin. It was a fire! They were burning down his cabin, his home. Another light appeared closer, at the edge of the lake. Elsa, Donovan, and Curtis exchanged a look, then turned their attention on Hyroc. They knew the second light was their cabin burning down. They were all outcasts without a home.

"We only have one option," Hyroc said sympathetically.

Chapter 14
Worthy Cause

Keller crouched beside the body of a man lying on the ground. Blood covered the corpse, and it had numerous lacerations spread across its flesh. The most noticeable was a deep stab wound to the right side of the man's chest, where his blackened skin indicated that he had been severely burned before he was stabbed in the heart. Lastly, he had a grievous opening in his neck. Beyond his mangled tissues, an absurd number of arrows protruded from his abdomen, back, and chest. Keller could only wonder what this man had done to attract the attention of such deranged savagery. Were they stalking him, or was he merely a target of opportunity in the wrong place at the wrong time? What were they hoping to achieve by killing him in such a sadistic manner? Was it a part of some dark ritual, or were his attackers enacting some larger scheme? A second villager had been killed near the edge of the village, several soldiers had been slain farther out, and there was hardly anything left of them. What did causing the gruesome deaths of all these people accomplish? It was baffling. Killing them seemed completely senseless. Maybe there was no pattern. Maybe it was as simple as the witches wanted to kill people, came out, did just that, and there was no other reason.

He rose to his feet when he saw a Light Walker on horseback trotting over to him. Ministry soldiers filled the space all around him, and simple wooden buildings radiated outward. The village of Elswood was quite unremarkable, nothing more than a backwater settlement with little to offer. It seemed the perfect place for his target to hide. Though it was surprising the villagers hadn't disposed of such an aberration on sight, and even more so that they had allowed it into their midsts. He shook his head. These villagers were ignorant fools! They should have known better. They allowed the creature to live among them and, by so doing, allowed its darkness to spread. The burn marks on the body before him were clear evidence of witchcraft. Their tolerance allowed the evil of witches to fester, and some of the villagers were seduced by the dark arts.

"Anything to report?" Keller said.

The Light Walker dismounted and gave him a quick salute. "According to some of the villagers, they saw a great and terrible beast. They fled at the sight of this creature, and many returned to their homes to hide. But some of the citizens report seeing several blue lights, followed by a brilliant flash that turned the night to day for an instant."

Keller nodded. "Those are clear indications of witchcraft." He glanced over to a disturbed patch of ground, noticing a bear's paw prints with other tracks he didn't recognize. "It seems our prey has grown in its power." He shook his head dismissively. If only the Council of Seven had listened to him sooner. He could have avoided all this death. "It can turn into a beast, a bear from the looks of the tracks, or some hideous altered version of one."

"We also found this," the Light Walker said. He handed Keller a broken bronze necklace chain with a disc of silver attached to it. The disc was covered in specs of blood and had animal symbols etched into the front and back and the name Hyroc.

Keller sneered at it, showing teeth on one side of his mouth. Hyroc was the name that fool Marcus and his idiot sister had used when referring to the creature he now hunted. It sickened him just imagining anyone humanizing that abomination through the use of a name. He glanced over at a hooded figure wearing a plague mask with a beak that pointed straight down.

Chapter 14: Worthy Cause

Keller examined the chain, noting a clean break that indicated something sharp had cut through it. He looked around thoughtfully. If anyone had been brave enough to attack the Hyroc creature, why had no one come forward? He shook his head. He was putting too much thought into it. One of the dead soldiers had probably gotten a lucky stab in on the creature with their blade before it killed them, and that was *what had severed it*. He put the necklace in his pocket.

"It's familiar with using witchcraft," Keller said. "And even managed to convert others to its evil." He indicated with his chin a clump of bootprints. "It appears even I underestimated the danger it posed. I have not, however, underestimated its affinity for evasion. Neither it nor its followers are getting away."

"You don't know what you're hunting," a voice said with a laugh.

Keller turned. Harold stood with his arms and legs bound. Flaky red blood covered his head, and a wound on his side steadily issued blood into a growing red stain on his clothes. Untreated, the injury would eventually end Harold's life, but Keller was unconcerned with the man's health; that wouldn't matter soon.

Two soldiers forced Harold to stand on a tall stool meant to help a rider step into the stirrups of a horse. A third soldier approached while they held him in place. The soldier used a length of rope to measure Harold's neck in preparation for hanging him.

"You deceive yourself."

"Deceive?" Keller scoffed. "I was not the one seduced by evil, Witch Hunter."

"What you call evil is nothing of the sort."

"I'm sure that's how all traitors justify their actions. They talk about how they were doing the right thing as they turned on their countrymen."

"I am not the traitor here, Keller. You are. You've betrayed everything you ever stood for. All for a crusade to take innocent lives."

"Some think my methods are callous and brutish, but we are facing dangers that threaten us all. We cannot afford the niceties of polite culture in the fight against such darkness."

"The ends justify the means?" Harold prodded. "Every monster has echoed that sentiment to justify their actions. How far will this go?"

"It ends when these creatures are cleansed from our lands."

"Creatures?" Harold questioned. "So, there are others."

Keller nodded. "We killed one that dared join our enemy."

Harold laughed scornfully. "You're never going to get this one. He's more clever than you."

Keller pointed angrily at the corpse. "Clever? Its cleverness is carved into that man's body! You doubtlessly stood by as it and its accomplices hewn his body to satisfy whatever morbid ritual they performed."

"That's what you think happened?" Harold spat.

Keller held his hand up to stop the work of the soldiers. "If you know better, then enlighten me."

Harold indicated the corpse with his chin. "That man turned into a monster! He was the deadliest thing I've ever seen. We threw everything we had at him. If not for Hyroc, who you so callously condemn, and his accomplices, everyone here *would be dead*."

Keller shook his head. "You expect me to believe such a ridiculous story." He waved his hand in a circular motion to signal for the soldiers to resume working.

"No," Harold said venomously. "I don't expect anything to penetrate that black hole in your chest that you call a heart."

"You're trying to tell me *that thing* saved this village? Next, you'll tell me it wouldn't hurt a fly. Or, better yet, that it's a kindhearted soul. I know how dangerous that creature is, and I will not be dissuaded from hunting it by your lies."

Harold sighed. "The truth is right in front of you, and you can't see it. Your target, Hyroc, has more honor than your despicable heart will ever know. He has power, but he's only ever used it for good. Actual good, not the kind of good you keep lying to yourself about doing. You're not going to find him. He'll slip through your fingers again."

Keller smirked. "That's where you are mistaken. I've learned from my past failures. I know how to find him. He will not escape this time."

Chapter 14: Worthy Cause

Harold studied him pensively. "This misguided cause of yours will consume you, Keller. And I pity you and your coming victims."

Keller signaled to the guards. One slipped a hood over Harold's face, and another kicked the stool out from under him. Harold's body dropped, supported only by the rope strangling him. His legs kicked for several long moments before going still. Keller turned away from the man's lifeless body to the Light Walker beside the horse.

"Let the hunters know it's time to start their pursuit if they haven't already," Keller commanded. "And send word for an inquisition in this village. I fear evil runs deep here."

"Yes, sir," the man said. He saluted before mounting his horse and trotting off.

"You would be wise to heed that man's words," the hooded figure with the plague mask said, watching Harold's swaying body. "This path could very well be the end of you. An outcome —"

Keller fixed an irritated glare on the figure. "I don't recall asking your opinion," he interrupted. "Nor would I listen, especially to you. I brought you here for one reason and one reason only. Now, get to it."

Chapter 15
Wanderers

Hyroc pushed through a patch of leafy underbrush. The orange glow of sunrise radiated from the horizon, illuminating steely gray clouds that covered the sky. He limped forward through the shadowed forest. Ahead of him, Donovan held the reigns of their supply laden donkey, carefully guiding it across the uneven terrain. Elsa and Curtis walked side-by-side, forming the front of the group. No one talked, as everyone was focused on moving silently and avoiding giving away their location. Shimmer circled overhead, guiding them on their course. Putting their fate in the care of a bird was not a choice they were all completely comfortable with, but he had been helpful in guiding them before, so it seemed a relatively good idea for now.

Hyroc was grudgingly still in bear form. Enough time had passed for him to transform back to his natural state without hurting himself, but remaining in it had been necessary. His heightened sense of smell, granted by his bear form, allowed him to smell the Ministry hunting parties. He and his friends had hoped to depart Elswood before their adversaries got moving, but they seemed to have gotten organized much faster than they had anticipated. He was able to tell what direction their pursuers were coming from and help to adjust their course to avoid them.

Chapter 15: Wanderers

Only one group had come close enough to be a threat. These pursuers had avoided detection by Hyroc due to the wind direction. When he was finally able to scent them, the hunters were nearly on top of them. The group came from the north, and the river was to the south. Hyroc discerned two hunting parties, one near the river's far shore and another farther away to the east. If they tried to escape across the river, they would be seen. They were trapped! Thinking quickly, Hyroc enveloped them in a bubble that contained their scent. He wasn't skilled enough to maintain the spell while they moved and was forced to make it stationary. He had smelled dogs in the group from the north, so he transferred the scent of him and his friends to a river crossing in front of them in order to create a false trail. Many tense, frightening minutes passed, but that group took the bait. The four of them then slipped behind the hunters and continued on their way.

He and his friends came upon a low spot. Donovan deftly guided the donkey down an incline. As Hyroc navigated behind him, he stepped wrong and stumbled. He careened down the slope in an uncontrolled run, unable to stop. Hyroc managed to direct himself away from running into Donovan and the donkey below him. His bulk hitting them at that speed would certainly hurt them. He flew past in a flurry of feet as he descended. He came to rest when he slammed into the trunk of a cottonwood at the bottom. Pain flared through his side, and he felt something pop. Blood oozed out of the wound on his side he sustained from his fight with the werewolf. He had broken one of his stitches. He growled in frustration and pain.

"You okay?" Elsa and Donovan called as they moved to him.

"I'm fine," he answered. Other than gaining a bruise from his impact with the tree, he didn't seem to have any new injuries. He limped away from the tree to lay down in a patch of moss. If he let himself, he would quickly fall asleep. He was so tired. Using his Quintessence to create a false trail earlier had taken a lot out of his already depleted strength, and his wounds were only adding to the problem. He took a deep breath and raised his paw. It glowed blue;

then, the light vanished when he cast the spell to remove any traces of their passing. He only made the spell remove traces for about half a mile, reducing the amount of strain placed on him. He felt the spell siphon off his waning Quintessence. It was a minor drain, but with so little remaining, it felt as if he were on the verge of collapsing from exhaustion. They hadn't stopped moving since last night. He felt his eyes growing heavy.

"You can't sleep yet," Elsa said, insistently nudging him in the jaw with her knuckles. She crouched down beside Hyroc to have a look at his stitches. "I think some of your stitches came out. I'll have to fix that." She retrieved the needle and thread from one of the saddlebags on the donkey. She poured water from a waterskin on the needle and wiped it off on an unsullied handkerchief from her pocket before getting started.

"How are we doing with The Ministry?" Donovan said, patting the donkey on the head.

Hyroc sniffed. He picked up the scent of a hunting party, but it was faint. They were far away. "No one's close," he said. "I think we're in the clear."

Donovan nodded gladly.

"Don't go getting overconfident with that," Elsa advised. "We might've gotten away from them, but we're still being hunted. Remember how many times you thought we lost a deer's trail only for us to find it again. We're the deer this time. All it would take is a single mistake, and they're right behind us again. Keep your guard up, and focus on what you're doing." She paused to stand up and start cleaning the needle. "Hyroc, has enough time passed so you can transform back?"

Hyroc nodded. "Yeah," he said.

"Then you should probably go ahead." She replaced the needle and thread in the saddlebag.

"You sure? There's still that group out there. I won't know if they start closing the distance."

"I know, and I'm sure."

"Besides," Donovan added. "And no offense. But if you're several hundred pounds lighter, we can carry you if need be. If you fall asleep now, there's no way we can move your big butt."

"I also wouldn't mind ridding myself of my cumbersome and pain-racked posterior for a while," Hyroc noted. He rose up on all fours and closed his eyes. His pain and fatigue hampered his concentration, and it took him several minutes to initiate the transformation process. When he was back to normal, he opened his eyes and was mildly surprised to see enormous ragged tears in his jerkin. He slipped off what remained of it, along with his cloak that had also sustained damage, before standing and placing them in one of the saddlebags. When he had regained his strength and had Quintessence to spare, he would mend both with his Flame Claw. He belted on his sword and knife. Then he retrieved an empty knapsack, though he was unsure what he was going to be putting in it.

"You good?" Donovan asked.

Hyroc nodded. "Lead the way."

Shimmer alighted onto the ground in front of them. The bird studied them before turning, cawing, and fluttering his wings in the direction they needed to go.

They moved steadily in a northwesterly direction away from the triangular shape of Wolf Paw Mountain. The morning came and went as they pushed their way through the trees. Near noon, they took a short rest and ate some smoked jerky strips. The food was a welcome relief since none of them had eaten anything in almost a day.

Though it did little for his fatigue, Hyroc was gladdened to know the food would help restore some of his Quintessence. Quintessence naturally regenerated on its own over time, but the process was extremely slow. Unassisted, it could take days before it was fully restored. But if a person rested or ate food after using their Quintessence, their recovery was much quicker.

When they moved out of the low spot again, the terrain roughened. Ruts and shallow ravines appeared in their path, along with steadily thickening clumps of spiny devil's club. Thankfully, when they

OUTCASTS

reached a very daunting swath of the plant, Shimmer guided them along the outer edge of it instead of through it. They wound their way through the forest and eventually returned to their original bearing to the northwest. Near dusk, they made camp under the growing shadows of the trees.

"No fire tonight, Donovan," Elsa said when she noticed her brother gathering firewood. "They might see it. We're still not very far out from Elswood."

"I was going to make a pit fire," Donovan said in answer.

Elsa shook her head. "It's too risky, even for a pit fire."

Donovan sighed, dropping his bundle.

"Donovan, we need to leave as little evidence of our passing as possible," Hyroc said, indicating the discarded wood. "I can use my spell to get rid of everything, but the more I have to alter, the more it takes out of me. Every bit of Quintessence I use for that, the less I have left to protect us with if we're discovered."

Donovan threw his arms up in irritation. "Okay, what am I supposed to do with it then?" he said.

"Just take them away from camp and dump them somewhere, somewhere that won't indicate the direction we're going if they happen to be discovered. That way, when I cast the spell, I can omit any alterations regarding the wood you collected. You didn't chop any of that, did you?"

"No, I didn't chop anything! Do you think I'm stupid?"

Hyroc shot him a perplexed look. "I wasn't trying to say you're stupid. I just needed –"

"To tell me what to do," Donovan interrupted.

Hyroc felt his face warm. "What's that supposed to mean?" He attempted to stand, but he moved wrong, and pain flared through his side. He let out a weak groan and went back down, holding his side.

"You're always –" Donovan continued.

"Stop it, both of you," Elsa interrupted when she came between them. "It's been a long day for all of us! I know we're all tired, but we can't waste our time fighting with each other." She focused on

Chapter 15: Wanderers

Donovan. "Donovan, please take care of that firewood. It needs to be done." With a sigh, Donovan nodded and began disposing of the wood. Elsa then turned to face Hyroc. "And you need to be careful not to pop another stitch. You bleeding all over the place won't help matters either." Her expression turned more compassionate. "You need to rest. You could barely walk by the time we got here. You're exhausted and can't afford to push yourself any further. Sleep."

Hyroc blew out a breath and nodded. He indicated the saddlebags on the donkey. "Just toss me my cloak and torn-up jerkin, so I have something to cover myself with." She shot him a mildly annoyed and expectant look. He felt confused when she didn't move then he realized what she was waiting for. "Please."

Elsa nodded her satisfaction and began looking through the saddlebags.

"Wait," Hyroc said, an important thought coming to him. "Who's taking –"

"First watch?" Elsa interrupted. "You don't need to worry about that, I know." She tossed his things to him. "Stop worrying and sleep."

He settled down into a crook between two tree roots. Kit appeared from the bushes and sauntered over to him. The big cat lay down beside him with his head in Hyroc's lap. Hyroc obligingly scratched under his chin before laying back with his head against the tree's trunk and closing his eyes. He instantly fell asleep.

Chapter 16
Trust

A hand gently shook Hyroc from his sleep. He opened his eyes to see Elsa standing over him with Shimmer perched on her shoulder. The raven loudly squawked as if adding emphasis.

"You need to get up. We're about to move out," she said.

Hyroc saw Donovan and Curtis working to untie their donkey from the trunk of a tree. They seemed almost done. Why did no one wake him earlier when he could have helped?

He rubbed the sleep from his eyes. "Why didn't you wake me when you got started?" he asked.

"You needed the sleep more than we did."

"You shouldn't have done that," Hyroc said, mildly annoyed. "Slowing us down with The Ministry following us isn't a good idea. I don't need special treatment."

Elsa laid a comforting hand on his shoulder. "Hyroc, there really wasn't much you could have done to help us. It's okay. That didn't slow us down."

Hyroc blew out a breath. "Just don't do it again."

Elsa drew her mouth into a line, shaking her head. "Alright. Make sure you eat something before we go." She stood and walked over to help her brothers.

Chapter 16: Trust

Hyroc stretched his arms but abandoned the movement when a surge of pain shot through his side. He grimaced as he held his side. The pain from all his wounds steadily burned back into existence and was joined by intense itching. Fending off the urge to scratch, he used the trunk of a tree to help him stand. He limped over to the donkey and tore a small chunk of bread from a loaf in one of the saddlebags. He stuffed it in his face before turning his attention to his jerkin and cloak. His fatigue had mostly vanished, and a significant amount of his Quintessence and strength had returned. He held his ripped jerkin with one hand and used his Flame Claw in the other to mend it. The spell required little Quintessence to cast, but his inability to use it yesterday was a stark reminder of the danger they were in. In likewise manner, he repaired his cloak before dressing himself.

"Good to go?" Donovan said, taking the reins of the donkey.

"Almost. One last thing." He lifted his hand, and a blue glow emanated from it as he cast his trail removal spell. He made sure to avoid any intention of altering the firewood Donovan had collected. The behavior of spells was largely dependent on the intentions of the caster. This allowed Hyroc to interact with objects or materials he was unable to see. It was impossible for him to think of every single thing he and his group may have disturbed, but where his thoughts failed him, his intentions made up for it. His desire to remove any traces guided the spell to do what he wanted. The only restraint was the amount of Quintessence required to cast the spell. The more things the spell had to deal with, the more it drained the strength of the caster. If the drain was more than the caster could handle, they would be rendered unconscious. The spell would, however, perform the caster's intention for as long as their Quintessence lasted before failing and resulting in an incomplete casting.

Hyroc nodded to Donovan, and they continued on their way. They had barely taken a full stride before Kit padded up beside Hyroc. Shimmer spread his wings and took to the air from Elsa's shoulder.

"I was thinking we should continue to the northwest until about noon," Elsa said. "Then, if everything looks good, we should be clear to head straight to the west."

Hyroc nodded. "What about The Ministry?" he asked. "Any sign of them this morning?"

Elsa shook her head. "I checked for smoke trails at first light, and I couldn't see any through the trees."

"Did you ask Shimmer?"

"I did. He flew up to see, and when he came back, he seemed to indicate some raising smoke." She indicated the direction behind her. "But from how calmly he acted about it, they're probably pretty far away."

"Let's hope so. I know he's proved himself in the past, but I don't know how comfortable I am with trusting him to relay that kind of information accurately."

"He's all we've got without you going *bear*." Hyroc opened his mouth to encourage the idea, but Elsa cut him off. "No, we're not going there, Hyroc. There's not much we can do for you if something happens while you're transformed. It's not up for discussion." Deflated, Hyroc sighed. "Besides, as soon as we come across a rise, we can check."

The morning passed without any significant obstacles blocking their path. As planned, they altered their bearing at noon and moved west as straight as possible. The ground steadily rose into a mild ridge soon after. The trees thinned along the top, giving them a relatively clear view of their surroundings. They saw no trails of smoke rising above the trees, but all that meant was their pursuers hadn't lit any fires for a while because they were busy chasing them. They would have to wait for the fading light of dusk or the first light of morning to see any smoke columns from cooking fires.

The five of them moved on after a short rest. Past the ridge, the terrain remained mostly flat for the rest of the day before beginning a downward slope near dusk. There was enough light for more travel, but the slope would act as a cold-sink that funneled cooler night air to the bottom, so they made camp at the top. They opted for another

Chapter 16: Trust

night without fire which would have only added to the unpleasant chill of the cold-sink.

Hyroc jolted awake in a startled fit. He breathed heavily, and his heart hammered away in his chest. It was the dead of night. He focused and forced himself to slow his breathing. It was just a nightmare.

"You alright?" a voice called out.

Hyroc looked over to see Elsa sitting against a tree with her bow laid across her lap in a ready position. He took a deep breath before speaking. "I'm – I'm fine," he said.

"Trouble sleeping?"

Hyroc nodded. "You could say that." He stared at the ground despondently.

"Nightmare?"

Hyroc didn't answer as he continued to gaze at the ground. It seemed so silly to think about something as childish as a nightmare. But this one had been different. He had never experienced a nightmare the likes of this. It had seemed as real as Elsa or her brothers.

"Want to talk about it?" Elsa said gently.

Hyroc shook his head. "No, I'm fine."

"You sure? It seems to have really gotten you worked up."

Hyroc studied her darkened face thoughtfully. He felt as if he were being immature to even think of talking about something as trivial as a nightmare, but he had a strong inclination to discuss this one.

Hyroc sighed, sitting straighter. "It's about – it's about Einar," he said. He threw a hand up in exasperation. "I'm looking at his face, his human face. He's lying down, and I'm standing over him. There's fear in Einar's eyes. He looks scared to death. He's pleading with me, begging me not to hurt him. Then –" Hyroc paused, reluctant to say what happened next.

"Then?" Elsa pressed.

Hyroc took a breath. "Then, I come down on top of him and bury my teeth in his neck. Only, I'm in my bear form. I mercilessly savage him with my jaws. What I do is so violent! He's yelling in terror, cold heart-stopping terror, the whole time, but I can't make myself stop. It goes on and on. Then, I wake up."

Elsa studied him thoughtfully. "That's awful."

"I tore that man to pieces! I talked with him. I even shared a meal with him. And then I killed him. After all that, I killed him."

"Hyroc, he was going to kill you, me, my brothers, Harold, and everyone in the village. You made the right choice."

"I know that. I know there was no other choice for us to make. But why does it feel so wrong? Why does the right choice feel so terrible?"

"Because you took a life," Elsa said, her voice comforting. "My father once told me if I have to take a life, it's supposed to feel bad. You're not supposed to like it. That guilt you feel lets you know you still have a heart. The guilt warns you not to needlessly take life and only kill when it's necessary when there are no good choices."

"But I killed him so brutally, as if – as if I was some kind of monster."

"Hyroc, you're no more a monster than I am. I helped end his life as well, remember?" Hyroc looked at her, taken aback. He had almost forgotten she had been a part of the fight. She hadn't taken a life until then, either. She, too, was coping with what she had done. He felt somewhat better knowing he wasn't alone in this.

"And if I'm a monster, so is Donovan, Harold, and Curtis," she continued. "If it wasn't for that lightning bolt my youngest brother threw, we wouldn't be alive to talk about this. He saved our lives. Do you think he's a monster?" Hyroc shook his head. "We did what we had to. It was a terrible, awful thing to do, but it was the right thing. My village would have been wiped out if we hadn't. Would that have been better? Of course not. You didn't have a choice in the way you killed him. We would have died if you tried any other way. It's not a good feeling, I know, but we did the right thing. No matter how horrible any of us feels, it was the right thing to do. We both saw the look on Einar's face before he died. His eyes weren't full of hate; they weren't full of anger; they were filled with relief. He was happy, knowing he would never be used to harm anyone ever again. You weren't the one that set

Chapter 16: Trust

him on that path. That witch did this, not you. If anyone is to blame, it was that *evil man*. Would you say ending him was a bad thing?"

Hyroc shook his head. "He would have just continued on with his plan if I hadn't stopped him."

Elsa nodded with a proud look on her face. "Exactly. It shouldn't feel good to take a life, but it was the right thing to do. We need to take comfort in that."

Hyroc took a breath. "Thank you, Elsa."

"You don't need to thank me. We're family." Hyroc couldn't help smiling, but his joyous expression vanished an instant later.

"What did you just think about?" Elsa questioned.

"I just thought about what Harold did. He was a friend, and we didn't even try to go back for him. With us talking about doing the right thing, I can't help but wonder if that was the right choice."

"I've been doing a lot of thinking about him too."

"With everything that's happened since that night, and us trying to stay ahead of The Ministry, this is the first time I've been able to think about him again. I doubt he's even alive anymore."

"Part of me hopes he is, but I know not to fool myself into thinking that. All I can say is he knew the cost of what he did."

Hyroc nodded. "Why do you think he did it? Why he sacrificed himself?"

Elsa leaned forward with a somewhat perplexed look on her face. "It was you. You gave him something he was willing to die for."

"Me? Really?"

She nodded. "People treated you as if you were a bad omen, and yet you did something completely selfless when you saved my brothers and me from the spiders. He was haunted by The Ministry needlessly killing a young girl who had used magic to help her neighbors. I think he was trying to redeem himself from his involvement in that, and he found it with you."

"I was a worthy cause?"

"Yes. He was not going to stand by and let what happened to that girl happen for a second time. And he would not have wanted you to feel guilty for his sacrifice. He sent us away because he would have rather died ensuring our escape than live knowing any of us had gotten hurt trying to save him. We would not have gotten away if we had gone back for him. He knew this and did it willingly."

Hyroc wiped away a tear.

"Honor his memory." Elsa picked up a waterskin beside her and held it toward the night sky. "To Harold." She took a drink, then tossed it to Hyroc.

"To Harold." He drank. "Be at peace, friend. You deserve it." He tossed the waterskin back to Elsa.

"Go back to sleep with your mind at ease," Elsa said.

Hyroc settled back into a comfortable position and quickly went back to sleep. He had no nightmares the rest of the night.

Hyroc chewed a bite of bread as he watched the sunrise. Its light illuminated thin strands of cloud that ran across the sky. To the east, he could see a growing patch of dark clouds where a storm was forming. It was moving toward them, and if it continued on its course, they would have rain by the end of the day. A downpour wouldn't make sleeping at night or travel comfortable, but it might bog down their pursuers and erase any signs of their trail Hyroc may have missed. The Ministry would lose them. It seemed their plan had worked. Hyroc couldn't help smiling at the thought. He hadn't actually expected it to work. He and his friends had escaped and outsmarted The Ministry. That was quite a feat for anyone to accomplish, let alone anyone as young and as seemingly inexperienced as the four of them were.

Hyroc took his last bite of bread before brushing the crumbs from his hands and donning his bow and quiver. He walked toward Donovan, who was getting the donkey ready for travel. The animal tensed when it saw him approaching and brayed with displeasure. Hyroc made a calming shushing noise and gently stroked the donkey's head.

"You're okay, you're okay," he whispered. "No one's going to hurt you." The donkey relaxed. The animal had been around him a lot and was familiar with him, but sometimes he would catch the animal wrong, and it would randomly become nervous. Kit had acted in a similar manner when Hyroc first gained his transformation ability, but that had not lasted for long. The big cat's behavior eventually returned to normal, and he acted the same whether Hyroc was in or out of bear form. Hyroc suspected the donkey's reaction was from it being descended from a herd animal. Those kinds of animals were especially keen on watching for predators. His appearance could be triggering that instinct and making the animal fear him as it would a wolf or bear.

"Looks like we might have some rain later on today," Hyroc said to Donovan, then indicated the dark mass of precipitation to the east.

Donovan looked and shook his head. "I'm sure that'll be pleasant," he said sarcastically. "We won't be able to light a fire if all the wood is soaking wet."

"Not necessarily," Hyroc said. He held his hand out, and a small blue flame appeared. He lazily rolled it around his fingers as he spoke. "I'm not exhausted anymore, so I don't see any problem with me using my Flame Claw to get a fire going. It won't matter how wet the wood is; it'll still burn."

Donovan studied, Hyroc's hand a moment. "But won't the rain keep putting the fire out? And if I understand how this whole *magic* thing works, you'd have to keep casting your spell to keep it going, which would only tire you out and not really accomplish anything."

Hyroc frowned, dismissing the flame. "Yeah, I think you're right."

"I mean, don't get me wrong, I'll definitely enjoy being nice and toasty, but I don't want to have to carry you the next day because you wore yourself out."

Hyroc gave him a flat, slightly annoyed, humored look. "Donovan," Hyroc said sarcastically. "You're such a fantastic person. I wouldn't want to inconvenience you that way."

Donovan patted him on the shoulder. "I know you wouldn't."

Hyroc pushed his hand away. "Well, at least the rain will keep The Ministry off our trail."

Donovan's demeanor turned uncertain. "True. I just hope they haven't figured out where we're going."

"We have a lot of forest to cover. I'm pretty sure they have no idea."

"It's the 'pretty sure' I'm worried about."

Hyroc waved his hand dismissively. Elsa and Curtis joined them, and they moved off. Donovan stopped at the top of the sloping ground they had decided to wait on descending the night before. Hyroc, Elsa, and Curtis exchanged a confused look.

"Everything all right, Donovan?" Elsa asked.

A long moment passed before he answered. "I just realized this is the farthest from home I've ever been," Donovan said. "Me, you, and Curtis have never been more than two days' walk from home. One more step and we've been further than we've ever been."

Elsa laid a reassuring hand on his shoulder. "And we'll do it together, as a family." Elsa signaled for Hyroc and Curtis to stand beside her. "On three, everyone take a step forward. One, two, three." The four of them simultaneously stepped forward. Now the real journey had begun.

Chapter 17
Guidance

A mild sprinkling of rain pattered the leaves as Hyroc picked his way through the trees. Kit slinked beside him, barely making a sound. They emerged from the branches into an area of open grassy ground, and a shallow, gravelly river flowed to their right. On the far shore, the river cut into the base of a hill. Fireweed dominated the hill and much of the surrounding terrain, with patches of sweet clover, monkshood, and reeds.

Their camp sat at the foot of a solitary cottonwood tree. It was just after sunrise, and Donovan worked to ready the donkey for travel. Curtis stomped the remains of a smoldering fire to extinguish it. Hyroc moved toward the hill where they had planned to cross the river. It had been three days since they had started down the incline that signified they were farther from home than ever before. They hadn't seen any signs of The Ministry, and by everyone's reckoning, they had evaded their pursuers. Hyroc walked unhindered because the day before, he had been able to remove the stitches on his side. The assistance of some healing from his Flame Claw had accelerated the process, allowing him to avoid several days of discomfort.

Elsa was at the river gathering up a dropline she had placed across it the previous night in the hopes of snagging fish.

"Did you get anything?" Hyroc hollered.

She reached down and held up a trout of moderate size. In answer, Hyroc held up two grouse with one hand. She smiled and nodded appreciatively. Shimmer descended from the sky with his black feathers silhouetted against a gray sky. Elsa obligingly held an arm out for him to land on. He gently touched down on the pro-offered perch holding a twig with berries. He held it out to her, and she let him drop it into her hand. She affectionately stroked the top of his head with one finger in thanks. The raven straightened his back seemingly pleased by the praise.

They were now in the riskiest part of their plan. They only had enough food for two weeks of travel, and it would take them an estimated three weeks to get through the forest. Rationing their food to make it last for an extra week wouldn't be pleasant, and traveling while doing so would sap their strength. If they ran into The Ministry or anyone hostile in that weakened condition, their chances of survival were nonexistent. And the three weeks were just to get through the forest; they still had to get to the nearest town. There might be a garrison of Ministry soldiers in that town, or wanted posters plastered across every building, and Witch Hunters hungry to collect a bounty. They had to keep their strength up to deal with any obstacles in the way of their escape. None of them were certain they could find enough food for that. Their gambit could end in disaster.

Elsa stuffed the fishing line into a small satchel and got to work gutting the fish. Hyroc joined her to take care of his two grouse. They wouldn't eat the meat from these until dinner when they could cook them. Donovan and Curtis led the donkey across the river just as Elsa and Hyroc finished. They disposed of the innards in the river and joined Donovan and Curtis.

An hour before midday, they reached the edge of the open area and reentered the cool mottled shade of the forest. The white trunks of birch trees populated the terrain, and the leafy canopy offered some cover from the rain. Startled squirrels darted out of sight among the branches as the group passed, followed by an angry chitter from unseen places. Hyroc readied his bow after the first few sightings, hoping for a lucky shot on the move. He caught glimpses of movement but never got a clear shot. Deer tracks came into view beside a patch of red-topped mushrooms. Despite the marks leading in the opposite direction they were traveling, Hyroc had to resist the urge to pursue the animal that would provide them with an abundance of meat. Their course meandered a little to the southwest when Shimmer led them around a patch of rougher ground.

Hyroc stopped when he saw a dark brown four-legged shape off in the trees. At first, he thought it was a deer or moose. When he focused on it, it had a body similarly shaped to that of a moose, but he noticed its back appeared covered in bluish-green moss, and the same material was hanging off of horizontal paddle-shaped horns in long strands. He strung his bow and started to aim an arrow at it, but Elsa pushed his arms down.

"No, don't," she said. "Leave this one alone. That's called a Boenake. They're very rare. This is only the second time I've ever seen one. It's supposed to be good luck to see one."

"What is it?" Hyroc asked curiously. "Some kind of deer?"

"Nobody knows. But I know you don't want to kill one."

The Boenake looked toward them. There was intelligence in its eyes which gave the impression that it was trying to figure them out as well.

"Safe journey, Anamagi," Hyroc thought, a voice whispered quietly in the back of his mind. The Boenake turned its head and walked out of view behind a stand of cottonwood trees. Elsa smiled at Hyroc and continued moving forward.

The birch trees merged with leafless pines and fir until the white trunks vanished. As the sun sunk toward the horizon, they encountered the edge of a marsh. They made camp for the night on the last portion of solid ground.

The group was spared rain for most of the night, but shortly before first light, the clouds broke into a downpour. Sleeping in the rain wasn't an appealing idea for any of them, especially Kit, so they got an early start on the day. They continued west along the marsh edge until the ground opened up into an area of shallow water. The shore curved to the south, but Shimmer made no indication they should go around it. Assuming that meant something worse awaited them to the south, they started slogging through. The water was relatively clear, allowing them to easily see the bottom and anything that might trip them. Fortunately, it was shallow enough that their provisions remained dry on the back of their donkey. Small white flowered lily pads proliferated the area, as did green water grasses and thin stalked plants with yellow flowers. Blue dragonflies zipped around infrequent tiny islands of reeds and clumps of mossy ground, and the calls of cranes rippled through the treeless space.

Not long after starting their push through the marsh, many buzzing things found them. Most were flies and gnats that were no more than nuisances that floated in front of their faces, but a significant amount was mosquitoes. The downpour should have helped ward them off, but they seemed determined to receive a toll of blood from the group. After several long minutes of aggravated swatting and winged things trying to fly into everyone's ears, Hyroc had enough. Using his Flame Claw, he summoned a dome that prevented their tiny adversaries from entering. It was a welcome relief, but it proved a big enough drain on Hyroc's Quintessence that he wasn't comfortable with maintaining the spell for long. They were in no danger from The Ministry, so there was no pressing need for him to preserve his Quintessence, but he was hesitant about using it too much simply for convenience. There were other dangers to consider. If they startled a large animal, or Hallowed forbid, encountered something worse, he would need the energy.

After an hour, to everyone's dismay, Hyroc dismissed the dome. The annoying insects quickly returned. Donovan grumbled quietly about the decision, which made Hyroc feel guilty, but he remained stoic. They unhappily continued through the marsh for most of the day; then, they again arrived at solid ground covered in trees. After everyone emptied the water from their sodden boots, they moved on. It stopped raining shortly after, and with most of their gear waterlogged, they made camp early to give their things plenty of time to dry.

Chapter 17: Guidance

When night arrived, Donovan took the first watch, followed by Hyroc. They had arranged for him to do so when it was darkest because his Wol'dger eyes gave him better vision at night. He sat with his back to the fire in order to preserve his night sight and laid some arrows out in front of him to sharpen. As he worked the heads with a whetstone, a strange sound caught his attention. When he listened more closely, it sounded as if someone was crying. He looked over his shoulder to where everyone was sleeping. He saw the shapes of Elsa and Donovan around the fire, but Curtis's spot was empty. Was Curtis crying? Hyroc gathered up his arrows and walked toward the sound. He found Curtis on the ground, bent over a protruding tree root crying into the crook of his arm.

"Curtis, are you alright?" Hyroc asked tentatively.

Curtis looked at him with reddened eyes. "It's all my fault!" he yelled.

Hyroc stared at him, perplexed. "What's all your fault?"

Curtis angrily through both arms out. "Everything! Why we're out here, why we have no home." He struggled to continue speaking as he held back tears. "If I – if I – if I hadn't done what I did." He broke back into sobbing. "If I wasn't a witch, none of this would be happening. The Ministry is after us because I used witchcraft."

"It's not your fault," Hyroc said comfortingly. He set his bow against the trunk of the tree and crouched beside Curtis.

"Yes, it is! I used witchcraft. Only evil people use that. That man who took my sister used it."

"No, you're not evil. What you did is not the same as what *he* did. I know because me and you're brother fought him. He tried to make a tree strangle me. Do you want to make a tree do that?"

Curtis shook his head. "No."

"I know you wouldn't."

"You do?" He sat straighter and wiped his eyes on the back of his sleeve.

"Of course. I've known you for four years; I would've noticed by now if you were a bad person."

"Then why is The Ministry after us? I thought they only went after someone if they were a bad person."

Hyroc scratched the back of his head. "That's complicated," he said. "The reason for what they do is sort of a misunderstanding."

"Misunderstanding?"

Hyroc nodded. "Yeah. You've heard about Feygrotha and what he did to Arnaira?"

"Yes, my mother told me –" he trailed off, his eyes looking distant.

Hyroc knew Curtis was thinking about the death of his parents. It had been two years since they were killed by enormous spiders, and the sting of their loss had not diminished. It was still just as painful for his younger friend as it had been the day it happened.

"Well, because of what Feygrotha did," Hyroc continued, trying to keep Curtis' thoughts away from that terrible memory. "Everyone was so afraid of it happening again that they forbid every kind of magic and labeled everything as witchcraft."

"So, what I did wasn't witchcraft?"

"Nope."

"But why is everyone afraid of it if good people also use it?"

"I don't quite understand that part myself, and it's difficult to explain what I do know. But I think the best way to look at this whole thing is magic is neither good nor bad. It depends on how it's used." Curtis' expression turned confused. He didn't understand his explanation. Hyroc glanced around for inspiration, focusing on the tree as an idea came to him. "Okay, okay." He raised his hand and summoned a blue flame. "We have this flame here I created using magic." He used his other hand to snap a twig off the tree and dip it in the flame. The twig burned with blue fire, but the flame turned orange when he pulled it away. "This twig is burning, and uncontrolled fire destroys things." He dismissed the flame, licked his thumb, and extinguished the twig between it and his forefinger.

Hyroc looked at Curtis thoughtfully for a moment, figuring out the next example. "Now, hold out your hand." Curtis did as instructed. Hyroc reached over and scratched it with his claws,

Chapter 17: Guidance

drawing blood. Curtis yanked his hand back, shooting Hyroc a betrayed glower.

"Ow, that hurt!" he snapped.

"I know. I'm sorry. That was part of my explanation. Now, give it back." Curtis gave him a defiant glare. "I'm not going to do anything to it, I promise. Please give it back." Curtis cautiously gave him his hand. Hyroc held it and used magic to heal his cut. When he released Curtis' hand, the boy marveled at it. "I used magic there to heal that scratch. "See, I decided to make the fire burn something, which is bad. Then, I decided to make it heal you, which is good. My magic didn't decide to do that. I made it do what I wanted. So, magic is only good or bad depending on how you use it."

"So, if I want to hurt or help someone, that's all up to me?" Curtis asked. Hyroc nodded. "But I used magic to hurt that man who was a monster."

"You did, but you did it to help me, your brother, and your sister. If you hadn't done that, we would have all died, including everyone in Elswood. You saved the whole village with your lightning bolt. Do you think that was a bad thing?"

He eagerly shook his head. "No."

Hyroc gazed at him fondly. "I never thanked you for that," he admitted. "Thank you, Curtis."

"You're welcome," Curtis spoke again after a long pause. "But if people have to choose to do good or bad things with magic, why do they call it witchcraft?"

"Because everyone's forgotten that. All they see when someone uses it, even if it's used to heal someone, is the bad. To them, it's dangerous and unnatural, and only evil things can come from it."

"That's why they're after us. They think I'll hurt someone." Hyroc nodded. "And they're after Elsa and Donovan because they think they'll hurt someone too."

"It doesn't matter that neither of them used magic. The Ministry would've come after them simply because you were their brother. Your brother and sister wouldn't give you up, so none of this is your fault."

Curtis nodded absentmindedly. "What if we tried talking to –"

Hyroc interrupted him with a dismissive wave. "It wouldn't matter. They wouldn't believe you regardless of how much sense you made. When people are scared enough about something, they stop listening. It's a harsh lesson I've had to learn." He sighed. "It's why we have to leave Arnaira. We won't be safe as long as we stay."

An awkward silence settled between them and was eventually broken by Curtis. "I wish I wasn't so helpless," he said with a sigh. "I wish I could use magic to help protect us. Maybe then things would be easier."

"You can't expect to learn how to use magic in just a couple of days. I didn't even know how to start a campfire, let alone throw fireballs, until about two years ago. It just takes time and practice."

"But you can turn into a bear. I know I could do more if I could at least turn into an animal."

Hyroc shook his hand dismissively. "That's different. I don't even understand how it works, but trust me, it takes a lot of effort just to master how to walk as a bear. You remember Ursa, that white bear that trained me?" Curtis nodded. "A big part of learning how to use that form involved me eating meat and fish raw." Curtis gave him a disgusted look. Hyroc pointed at him with a smile. "That's exactly what I thought about it. I don't quite know how I made it through that or what that taught me about moving around as a bear. But the point is, you'll be ready when you're ready. I know it's frustrating, but you shouldn't feel bad for not knowing how to use magic to help us. Besides, you saved our lives. That's more than enough."

"Alright," Curtis said with a sigh.

Hyroc paused as a thought occurred to him. "Well, actually, there is something I know that might help you learn how to use magic." He held one hand out flat, and a small blue flame appeared. Then, he made a grabbing motion at it with his other hand. The flame swirled into a ball. Hyroc made several pulling motions around the ball. Slowly the ball spread out and formed into a four-legged shape. The shape gained definition, becoming a stag made out of flame that walked in place in Hyroc's hand.

Chapter 17: Guidance

Curtis stared at it in awe. Hyroc lowered his hand so Curtis could see the animal better. "Ursa showed me this while she taught me how to use magic. The trick is not to lose your concentration on what you're making. But concentration is not the only thing it requires. Your mind and your intentions form the magic into what you want." Hyroc raised his other hand and flexed it in front of Curtis for emphasis. "But you need your hands to shape it. That's why you saw me moving my hand the way I did while I made that stag." Hyroc flicked his finger at the shape, causing the stag to distort before returning to its original shape. "Those movements give it the shape of an animal. Otherwise, it would have remained a flame."

"How do you know the way you need to move your hand?" Curtis asked.

"There's not really a set way you need to move your hand, I sort of just feel what needs to happen to what I'm making and move my hand in the way that seems right. It's similar to making something out of clay. You don't know how you'll need to move your hands at the beginning; you just know what needs to happen with the shape of the clay for it to become a pot. You shape the clay with your hand and make adjustments to its shape until it's a pot. Get it?"

"I think so," Curtis said.

The stag vanished, and Hyroc put his hands down. "Now you try. Start by raising your hand flat with the palm up." Curtis did as instructed. "Now picture a bolt of lightning forming in your hand and for it to stay in place." Curtis concentrated on his hand then a near blinding white light blazed in his palm. Hyroc put his hand up to shield his eyes. "Good. Now focus on dimming the light so we can see it without us losing our eyesight." Slowly he reduced the light, revealing a bright line that stretched across his hand. Good. Now try to turn it into a ball." The line shuddered but remained a line. "Use your hand. Keep your focus on that bolt and use your hand to help turn it into a ball. Remember, go with the movement that feels right." Curtis lifted his other hand and made a squeezing motion at the bolt. The line of light began bending erratically in all directions, but it slowly curved into a frayed ring of lightning. "That's really good. Now picture what animal you want that ring to turn into and hold it in your mind." Curtis made several slow, deliberate hand movements. The ring collapsed inward before flattening out. The light shuddered violently and, with a loud snap, disappeared in a shower of sparks.

Curtis frowned and sighed angrily.

"Hey, you shouldn't be so hard on yourself," Hyroc said. "You got farther than I did on my first try. It took me almost a month just to learn how to turn mine into a ball of fire." Curtis nodded. "Just keep practicing until you turn it into an animal. Now, let's get you back to the fire before your sister notices you're gone and starts worrying."

When Hyroc put his hand on the trunk of the tree to help himself stand, he felt a sense of unease radiating from the tree. He leaned forward to see around the tree and scanned his surroundings, but he saw nothing suspicious.

"Did you see something?" Curtis asked curiously.

Hyroc held his hand up to signal for Curtis to be quiet. He closed his eyes and concentrated on the tree. He didn't feel anything of interest from the tree in the area around him, but far away, there seemed to be a dark void. It seemed odd there would be a shadow demon in the middle of nowhere, and if it had been anywhere near him, he would have sensed it. The void could simply be an area without enough trees for him to be able to discern anything there. It seemed to be emanating from the direction of the marsh, so that seemed the most reasonable explanation. The unease was likely due to his watchfulness for signs of pursuit from The Ministry. They weren't absolutely sure they had escaped. That was probably just making him paranoid. Several days had passed with no indication of the hunting parties closing in on them. As diligent as he had been in removing their trail, things wouldn't take a turn for the worse overnight. It was all in his head. He returned to himself and stepped away from the tree.

"No, it was nothing," Hyroc said. "Let's go."

Chapter 18
Memories

The sounds of breaking camp drew Hyroc from his sleep. When he opened his eyes, the sun was peeking over the horizon. Clouds from a dispersing storm covered the sky in ragged cauliflower-shaped patches. He ate a small piece of bread before donning his gear and moving off to check for food in the short time he had while his companions finished working. He wound his way through the trees to an animal trail where he had placed a simple spring snare. The sapling he had attached the trap to stood upright with something dangling from it. He found a young deer rabbit with knobs of horn that had just begun to bud from its head hanging by its back legs. The animal started struggling when it saw him approaching. He deftly stabbed it through the heart with his knife, set the carcass on the ground, undid the trap, and gathered up its materials before butchering the rabbit. As usual, he pressed his boot firmly down on the animal's head and yanked on its back legs. The animal's spine came loose from its body and drug all the innards out with it. He tossed the undesirable bits into the forest and carried what remained of the animal in one hand as he retraced his steps to camp.

"You got something?" Donovan said when Hyroc returned.

Hyroc happily held his prize up as he moved toward the donkey. "Just a little deer-rabbit," Hyroc said, stowing away the meat in a saddlebag.

Donovan reached into his pocket and retrieved what looked to be a squirrel's tail. "Well, I think I got the world's dumbest squirrel," he said with mild amusement. "Right after I took over watch for you, I was sitting with my back against the tree, and I felt something touch my shoulder. I glanced over to see a squirrel crawling down my body, completely oblivious to me. So, I grabbed it and broke its neck before it even knew what had happened. Then I had it with my breakfast."

"That's pretty lucky," Hyroc said, congratulatory.

"And you didn't share?" Elsa interjected as she finished checking the straps that held everything on the donkey.

"There was hardly any meat to share," Donovan said. "It was only about two bites."

"I know. I'm just messing around," she said. "We ready?"

Everyone nodded, and they headed off.

Away from their camping spot, the ground steadily descended. The shade grew darker, and the air cooler. When they reached the bottom, the terrain turned muddy at a spring with a tiny trail of water flowing down toward another depression. Thick foliage and devil's club crowded the stream, preventing them from seeing how far it ran. The spring sat within a rocky outcropping on a raised parcel of land. Clearwater gathered in a bowl-shaped indent, which formed the beginning of the stream. They stopped here to refill their waterskins and to wash the dirt from their faces and hands. When finished, they continued.

The muddy ground didn't go on for long, quickly returning to dry, root-riddled forest. At this lower elevation, little sunlight filtered through the trees, giving the air an unexpected chill. They came across a towering slab of vertical gray rock protruding from the ground, and they followed Shimmer along the base of the cliff. Around midday, the ground slowly started to rise. Loose rocks littered the area, forcing the

Chapter 18: Memories

four of them to crowd around the donkey to help support it in case it slipped. They moved up the incline carefully. Any mistake here could lead to a serious problem for everyone.

The donkey froze when they tried to lead it over a patch of bare rock. There was no dirt to add traction to their steps, and slipping was of greater concern. They were nearing the top of the slope, but they were up against the rock face on one side, and the ground dropped off on the other. Backtracking to find an easier way was far more dangerous than proceeding, so they were forced to continue. Donovan and Hyroc grabbed the back of the animal, with Elsa tugging on the reins, and pushed the reluctant animal forward. Despite it braying in protest, it began moving. The animal lost its footing with one of its back legs. The shift of the donkey's weight was more than Hyroc and Donovan could handle. It slid toward the drop-off, threatening to drag them over the edge with it. Almost completely by instinct, Hyroc flung one arm toward the back legs of the animal to form a barrier beneath it. The donkey instantly came to a stop as it regained its footing. Hyroc heavily breathed as he looked at the floating blue shimmer that signified the presence of the barrier. If not for his action, the animal would have plummeted to its death, probably along with one of them as well. They rapidly guided the animal back onto solid ground before breathing a collective sigh of relief.

"You two alright?" Elsa said, concerned. Hyroc and Donovan nodded before saying they were fine. "That scared the life out of me. I for sure thought someone was going over the edge."

"If not for Hyroc's trick there, one of us would have," Donovan admitted, indicating the blue shimmer Hyroc had created. "Thank you for that."

"You don't have to thank me," he said, then dismissed the barrier.

"You kept me from going off the cliff! I think I really do." He affectionately clapped Hyroc on the shoulder.

They more carefully led the donkey across the rock slab. The slippery surface continued for a few more steps; then, dirt returned to the ground. Their path widened and slowly merged with the top of the

–157–

incline. For the first time since morning, they entered warm sunlight. They moved north to put some distance between them and the cliff so they didn't risk re-encountering it. When they were satisfied with the distance, they regained their westerly course. The tree covered terrain remained relatively flat until they made camp at dusk.

The next morning, while Hyroc searched for extra food in the time it took his friends to ready the donkey for travel, he came across fresh deer sign and tracks. Hunting the animal down would delay their departure, but at the rate they were going through their provisions, the meat from it would be a big help. Besides, they hadn't so much as seen a hint of The Ministry following them. They had lost their pursuers, and there wasn't much reason for them to move as fast as they possibly could. A day spent hunting wouldn't harm them.

Hyroc headed back to inform the Shackletons of his discovery. When he explained his reasoning for going after the animal, it took hardly any effort to convince Elsa and Donovan to do so. They were well aware of the food situation, and without The Ministry threatening their lives, they thought it a prudent idea. It was Donovan's turn to lead the donkey, so he and Curtis followed Hyroc and Elsa from a distance as they tracked their quarry.

"Can I ask you something?" Elsa said quietly.

"What?" Hyroc said without looking at her as he examined the leafy stem of a plant for deer sign.

"Do you miss it? Your life in Forna?"

Hyroc turned to give her a surprised look. Why did she want to talk about that? He thought they had more important things to worry about right now.

"Why do you ask?"

Elsa shrugged. "You don't talk about Marcus and June much, but when you do, you speak fondly of them. Do you miss them?"

His mind turned to the few happy memories from his childhood about his adopted father. The man had protected him from The Ministry during his early years and had done more for him than any

Chapter 18: Memories

other person. The man's unexpected passing from fever had thrown his life into chaos. A myriad of unpleasant memories and feelings of loneliness filled his mind. June was the only one who had imparted any sort of happiness into his life during that time. He didn't know if he could have gotten through it without her.

Hyroc pushed the memories aside and forcefully returned his attention to tracking their deer. Now was not the time to consider such things. He moved forward toward fresh deer tracks, hoping Elsa would drop the subject.

She walked up beside him. "It seems they were good to you?" she continued without seeming to notice his reluctance .

Hyroc sighed. She wasn't going to let it go without an answer. "Yes," he reluctantly said. Maybe she would stop now.

She nodded. "Do you miss them?"

Nope, not good enough. She wanted a lot more than that. Hyroc continued to move forward as he talked. "Yes, I miss them," he admitted.

"Tell me about them."

Her words unexpectedly stirred up some unpleasant memories. Hyroc turned to face her. "Why are we talking about this," he said, a little sharper than he had meant.

She looked taken aback by his words. He felt guilty about his reaction and opened his mouth to apologize. "I didn't –"

"Because we're leaving our parents behind," Elsa said, cutting him off.

Hyroc felt his guilt turn into a knot in his stomach. He had almost forgotten about Helen, Svald, and Walter. His friend's parents and grandfather had died two years ago when spiders had killed them. The images of their dead faces filled his mind's eye. He remembered every detail as if it were in front of him. He even remembered the wretched smell of death that permeated that spider colony. It was a miracle he was able to save anyone that day. If he had taken any longer, he would have mourned the loss of everyone that day instead of just three. This was a difficult time for them, and he needed to listen.

"I want to know how it is for you. You're like a brother to me. I want to know about them."

Hyroc nodded shamefully. He took a deep breath. He described how he remembered Marcus and June looked. "When I was younger, I did almost everything with Marcus, but sometimes his duty to the boarding school got in the way."

"He taught at a school?" Elsa said.

"No, he never taught for as long as I went there. He was the headmaster."

"You went to school?" she said, awestruck. "You mean you know how to read, write, and all that stuff." Hyroc nodded. "No wonder you're so smart."

Hyroc smirked appreciatively. He would have smiled, but he was cautious about exposing all of his sharp teeth. It was a habit he was trying to break himself of around his friends. He had implemented the technique during his childhood in the hopes of alleviating the fear strangers showed toward him. Around his friends, there was no need for it.

"And your adopted father was the headmaster," she continued.

"Yeah," he said happily. "There were certain *perks* that came with our relationship. I was never punished as much as some of the other kids, but that's not to say I wasn't ever punished. Marcus still kept me in line. He was also the one who taught me how to duck hunt. Some of my best memories of him occurred during those hunts. It was just the two of us out there, and I didn't need to worry about the way I looked."

Elsa nodded. "Duck hunting on the lake was the first place my father took me to hunt," she said.

"They're not easy to hit, are they?" Hyroc noted.

"Only when they're not standing still." Hyroc couldn't help quietly laughing.

The happiness faded from him, and his eyes looked distant. "He died not long afterward."

"I'm sorry to hear that."

Chapter 18: Memories

Hyroc took a breath. He examined the broken branch of an alder before continuing to talk.

"After he passed, my care fell to June. She didn't do as well as Marcus, but she cared about me and tried as hard as she could to protect me."

Elsa nodded. "Since he was gone, what happened with the school? Did June take over?"

Hyroc shook his head, knowing things would have gone much differently for him if she had been able. "No, she wasn't knowledgeable enough for it or some other nonsense. I really can't remember. A new headmaster arrived, and, well, he was less understanding than Marcus, to say the least. He was appointed by The Ministry, and though he wasn't overly out to get me, he did not miss an opportunity with me. Also, his choice of decor in the headmaster's office was quite disturbing. I had nightmares about some of the things I saw there."

"Don't worry. I won't ask you about that."

Hyroc nodded his appreciation. "Granted, the things I've seen since then would probably put those to shame."

"What happened after that?"

Hyroc took a breath. "Everything sort of went straight to the Sunless Plain. My life was completely turned upside down at that point, and I was introduced to the joys of bullying."

Elsa shot him a compassionate look. "June didn't protect you?"

"No, she did, or as much as she was able to. Marcus had a lot of influence with the town and The Ministry from past service and was able to keep anyone who might want to hurt me at bay. That allowed me to live a relatively comfortable life despite my *unique qualities*. But with his passing, that all disappeared. June didn't possess the same sort of clout as he and, despite wanting to, she couldn't protect me. Without Marcus' protection, my differences made me a target for some of the other students. That culminated in me being hung from a tree at night, in the freezing autumn rain."

Elsa turned toward him with a shocked look. "You were hung from a tree?"

He nodded. "Yeah, they strung me up by my feet the same as you do when dressing a deer carcass." He emphasized the point by using his hands to indicate a rope being lifted up onto something. "I nearly froze to death that night."

"That's awful."

"After that, June pushed me to fight back. I eventually got good enough at it that no one wanted to mess with me. Or at least anyone who had a brain."

"That explains your fighting experience," Elsa noted.

"That's just with my fists. Harold helped me learn a lot about fighting with a blade."

They exchanged a saddened look at the mention of Harold's name. They somberly turned their eyes to their surroundings. Hyroc crouched to get a better look at some deer tracks on the ground.

"Did things get better once you knew how to fight?" Elsa said after a long pause.

Hyroc stood before speaking. "For the most part. But that only lasted until I was thirteen." He indicated his face. "I apparently started to look more intimidating to people. They began acting as if I would attack and kill someone at any moment."

"Is that when you came to Elswood."

Hyroc sighed. "Not quite. I was fifteen when I had an *accident*."

"What kind of an accident?"

He stopped and scratched the back of his head nervously. "Well, I sort of broke another student's leg."

She gave him a sympathetically pained look. "Wow, that's pretty serious. What happened?"

"I saw him bullying another student and stepped in to stop him. He got angry, and, well, the idiot made the mistake of taking a swing at me. He missed, and I answered his attack in kind. Except, he fell, and somehow his leg got wedged in a tree, and that broke it."

"Am I right in assuming *that's* what made you come here?"

Hyroc nodded. "And you pretty much know the rest from there."

"What about June? What did she do?"

Chapter 18: Memories

Hyroc blew out a breath. "She sent me off."

Elsa gave him a confused look. "Wait, she sent you off *alone*? I thought she cared – "

"Hold on," Hyroc interrupted. "Let me explain. She was afraid of slowing me down and causing The Ministry to catch me. I know it seems that she abandoned me, but you didn't see the sadness in her eyes when she told me that. She truly thought something terrible would happen to me if she came. She believed it was the right decision, and she made me promise I would never come back because if I did, The Ministry would kill me. It was not a decision she made lightly. She cared about me, and I could tell it was the hardest decision she had ever made." He took a breath to calm some stirred-up emotions. "I promised her I wouldn't. I've hated that promise ever since. Not a day goes by that I think about breaking it, but it was what she wanted. After everything she had done for me in Marcus' place, I owed her that much in return."

Elsa's expression turned to admiration. She put a hand on his shoulder. "When someone makes you promise, you have to do it."

Hyroc nodded his appreciation but stopped when he saw movement out of the corner of his eye. He grabbed her arm and pressed down to indicate for her to lower herself. She complied without question while raising her free hand to signal for Donovan and Curtis to stop. The moving thing resolved into the shape of a deer buck with antlers. The two of them silently split up and crept into position for a shot. Elsa got there first and shot it in the chest. It was a kill shot, but Hyroc loosed another arrow into the animal for good measure as it turned to flee. Their quarry dropped before it made it a full stride. When they arrived to secure the carcass, their target was already dead.

Elsa and Hyroc exchanged a jubilant look and breathed a sigh of relief. The animal they had just slain was large enough to make up the difference with the food they lacked to reach the other side of the forest. They now had enough to get there. Neither one of them had fully believed they could do it until now. They retrieved their arrows and cleaned the blood off the heads when Curtis and Donovan arrived with the donkey. Everyone quickly got to work skinning and butchering the animal. It was nearing dusk when they had finished their work. They resumed heading west with the remaining light to put some distance between them and the kill site to avoid any entanglements with hungry scavengers during the night. When they finally stopped, they built a large fire and cooked a haunch of venison.

"It'd be nice to have something besides some crusty bread to go with this," Donovan said as he finished roasting the meat. "Some potatoes and carrots would do nicely."

"And some garlic for seasoning," Elsa added.

Donovan paused and studied Hyroc thoughtfully.

"What?" Hyroc said, taking notice. "Why are you looking at me that way? Don't go thinking I can just up and conjure a clove of garlic out of thin air. My Flame Claw doesn't work that way."

"You said there were a few tricks you could use to help us get food, or was that whole spiel a bunch of bluster," Donovan prodded.

"No, I'm pretty sure I can help. I just can't make food for us."

"Well, show us what you can do. Remember, this helps you as well as us."

"Alright. Give me a second."

Hyroc rose to his feet and swept his eyes through their surroundings. Pretty much every tree he could see was pine and spruce. It seemed reasonable to think he could use that. He closed his eyes and lifted his arms. Both his hands glowed blue. He focused his thoughts on the trees around him, then on the pinecones. His concentration descended not just to all the pinecones in the vicinity but only to the ones that were still closed and untouched. Next, he focused on the seeds within the scaly casings. He made a cradling motion with one hand and a pulling motion with the other. A rising crackling sound echoed through the trees like that of the innumerable wingbeats of an insect swarm. Seeds poured through the air toward him from every direction. Donovan ducked down as several whizzed over his head. Kit started leaping through the air playfully, trying to catch

Chapter 18: Memories

one. The seeds congregated in the air in front of Hyroc. He used his hand that had been making the cradling motion to reach down to his side and pull up his knapsack and open it. As soon as he opened it, the seeds streamed into it. The sack swelled and gained a considerable heft.

Hyroc ended the spell moments later. He felt a considerable strain on his Quintessence. The sudden loss of that amount of strength caused him to stumble and become momentarily dizzy. He remained standing, and the two sensations rapidly vanished. When they had passed, he moved closer to the fire. He unslung his knapsack and dropped it beside Donovan. It landed with an audible thud. Hyroc sat with his chin resting on one knuckle with an expected look. Flabbergasted, Donovan reached into the sack and retrieved a handful of seeds.

"Now, that's a pretty neat trick," Donovan said, awestruck. He shook a few seeds back into the bag and dropped a handful into his mouth. The seeds made a satisfying crunch as he chewed. He nodded happily at Hyroc. "They'd be a lot better roasted," he said with a full mouth.

"Don't you dare," Hyroc said half-jokingly.

He gave Hyroc a wolfish grin.

"Food is food," Elsa said, reaching into the bag. "We appreciate anything you give us." She looked at Hyroc thoughtfully with her handful of seeds. "How hard on you was that?"

"That took a lot out of me," Hyroc said. He waved dismissively when Elsa's expression turned concerned. "But it's fine. I'm going to be eating soon and sleeping. That will replace any Quintessence I just used. I'll be good as new by morning." She nodded her understanding. "Just don't ask me to do that very often. It's taxing, but I also want to leave enough seeds for the trees to spread and the animals to eat." He paused. "Is the deer done?"

Donovan divided the scolding hot meat into even portions for everyone, including some for Kit. The big cat sauntered over and tore a huge chunk out of it. Shimmer descended beside the meat and pecked morsels out of it. An irritated growl emanated from Kit at the bird's intrusion.

Hyroc nudged his companion's shoulder with the palm of his hand. "Hey, be nice," he said. "There's plenty to go around. He can have some if he wants." Kit's growl faded, but he replaced it with an angry look fixed on Hyroc. Shimmer bobbed his head at Hyroc in what seemed an appreciative gesture before he resumed eating.

"Hyroc, look," Curtis said excitedly. He walked over to Hyroc, cradling something in his hand. He held a bright crackling amorphous blob of lightning. Spikes of lightning erratically jumped out of the blob before snapping back into it. The unstable mass seemed to be trying to form into something but couldn't quite make it.

"I finally got it to stop exploding," Curtis said.

Hyroc gave him a congratulatory nod. "That's very good," he said. "See, you're starting to get it. What are you trying to make?"

"A Robin." Curtis loosened his fingers, and the shape shrank out of existence. He gave Hyroc a thoughtful look. "Hyroc, what kind of magic am I using?"

"What do you mean?"

"You're an Anamadguy – an Anamackerel –"

"Anamagi?" Hyroc offered with a mild laugh.

Curtis nodded. "Yeah, that. You can make blue fire, but I make this." He held his hands up, and a flash of lightning jumped between them. "Do you know what I'm called?"

Hyroc tapped his finger on his knee as he thought about it. "I think you're a lightning wizard or a lightning mage. Yeah, you're a lightning mage. If I remember correctly from Ursa's lessons, everyone who uses magic has a propensity toward a single element. Mine is fire, and yours is lightning. You can still use all the other elements and do everything anyone else can do with magic, but, in your case, your best with using lightning. I think it's sort of like being left or right-handed. You can use both hands well, but you tend to use one more than the other unless you're one of those oddities that can use both hands equally well. But they probably made a deal with a shadow demon for that ability."

"Lightning mage," Curtis said, testing the sound of the word. He nodded his satisfaction. "Thanks."

Chapter 18: Memories

Hyroc nodded his response, then returned his attention to his food. He chewed a handful of seeds before taking another bite of venison. An unpleasant feeling slowly materialized in his mind. He glanced over his shoulder. It was dark, and the orange flickering of the fire danced across the trees. He couldn't see anything out there, so he listened more carefully. Beyond the popping of the fire and the murmur of a conversation between Donovan and Elsa, all was silent. He looked at Kit, and the big cat's more sensitive ears didn't seem to be hearing anything. Hyroc shook his head and resumed eating.

Chapter 19
Shadows

Hyroc walked beside the Shackleton's donkey in the sunlight of a warm, cloudless day. Black spruce trees surrounded them. Their leafless branches offered little shade, making the travelers feel uncomfortably hot. Kit moved close by, sticking to the shade of the low-hanging branches of the trees as much as possible.

The ground steadily rose at a moderate angle. The donkey jolted to a stop, seemingly surprised. It pulled irritably with one of its back legs, but the limb was ensnared beneath an exposed tree root. Hyroc carefully crouched beside the animal to avoid it accidentally kicking him, reached down, and freed its trapped leg. Unencumbered, the donkey continued forward. As Hyroc rose to his feet, out of the corner of his eye, he caught a shift in the shadows of the trees farther down the incline. When he focused on the area, he didn't see anything.

"Did you see something?" Donovan said, walking up beside him.

Hyroc used his hand to indicate the place where he thought he saw movement. "I thought I saw something move down there," he answered.

Donovan put a hand over his eyes to block out the sunlight and scrutinized the indicated area. He lowered his hand and shook his head. "I don't see anything. Keep an eye out, and let us know if you see it again. We don't need a scavenger trailing us to get at our food. We'll

Chapter 19: Shadows

have to take care of it if that's what it was." He turned to catch back up to the donkey. Hyroc studied the area a little longer before doing the same.

The incline merged into a shallow ridge before flattening out on the other side of it. Here, the ground was sandy and gravelly, forming a space where no trees grew, then returned to spruce trees. To everyone's relief, leafy trees soon dominated their path, giving them somewhat of a respite from the uninterrupted sun. They stopped to take a short rest at the base of a steep hill where an oak tree grew with gnarled branches that vaguely resembled reaching arms.

A stream flowed nearby, and Hyroc used the opportunity to see if he could catch some fish. He baited the hook with a dark green caterpillar he saw creeping up a plant. He cast his line into the water and used a gloved hand to slowly reel it back in. While he readied his third cast, a snapping sound startled him. Instinctively, he wheeled around, his hand reaching for his sword. He stopped, seeing Kit plodding through the underbrush over to him. The big cat halted to regard him curiously before coming over to sit beside him. Kit watched the stream expectantly. Hyroc shook his head, feeling silly about his reaction.

When he returned to fishing, he noticed the caterpillar was missing from his hook. He scratched Kit's ears as he moved past in search of bait. "I'll be right back," Hyroc said. "I need more bait." As he combed through the plants beside the stream, he spotted a beetle. The insect's smooth, shiny shell possessed an iridescent greenish sheen that would be irresistible to a hungry fish. He grabbed it, slipped it onto his hook, and cast a line.

Two casts in, he felt something pull on his line. He landed a colorful trout that was disappointingly small. It was only big enough for him to make a single unsatisfactory meal out of. He dispatched it with his knife and began cleaning it. As he finished, Kit begged with an insistent yowl. Hyroc sighed and tossed it to his companion. The mountain lion instantly snatched it out of the air.

Hyroc used the leftover innards as bait when he made another cast. Nothing touched his line as he reeled it in. The sound of footfall in the bushes caught his and Kit's attention. When they looked, they saw the white and rusty orange colored coat of a fox. That had been what he had seen earlier, a fox hoping for scraps. Kit tipped his head in intrigue as he observed the animal. Hyroc collected a rock from the edge of the stream and chucked it into the bushes. The fox yipped in alarm as it disappeared into the foliage. Hyroc then heard Elsa call out to him that they were ready to leave. He disposed of the fish remnants in the river to lessen the incentive of the scavenger to follow before joining Elsa, Donovan, and Curtis.

"Found out what that thing was I saw," Hyroc said. He indicated the spot by the stream where the fox had been. "There's been a fox shadowing us."

"That figures," Donovan said, unsurprised. "They'll take whatever crumbs they can get."

"I scared it off, but that won't deter it."

"We'll have to take care of it if it keeps that up," Elsa added. "I don't want to have to worry about our food."

"I'll set a snared tonight that'll probably catch it," Donovan said.

"It'll be a shame too," Hyroc said. "Its pelt would sell for a nice amount if we had the time to stop and prepare it. I hate wasting that, especially when we could use the money."

Elsa and Donovan nodded their agreement.

The rest of the day came and went with a dusting of thin clouds that did nothing to block out the sun. At dusk, under the glow of an unobscured sunset, they made camp beneath some cottonwood trees. Donovan set his snare and used the bloodied remains of a magpie Hyroc forced Kit to donate as bait. They hoisted their food above the ground using one of the cottonwoods as an anchor. Then they all settled down to sleep. It had been nearly two weeks since last they saw any indication of The Ministry, so they no longer kept a watch at night. The only thing of concern were animals, but everyone figured their fire should keep any away. On the off chance that this deterrent failed and a particularly brave animal started poking around their camp, Kit or Shimmer would alert them to the danger.

Chapter 19: Shadows

Hyroc was drawn awake by a persistent feeling. He grudgingly rolled onto his other side, trying to go back to sleep. Was it that stupid fox again? After a few minutes of trying, he was still unable to sleep. He stared at the glowing embers of their diminished fire. Their fire was too small to reliably keep any curious four-legged things away. He rose to his feet and moved over to add firewood to it. The fire gained life with a subdued woosh as it burned the fresh wood. He stoked the fire with a stick to further strengthen the blaze.

He turned to return to his sleeping mat, but he noticed that the persistent feeling felt strange. It wasn't the unnerving paranoid sensation of being watched by some unseen creature; it was demanding. Was it coming from the trees? Beyond a shadow demon, a forest fire was the only thing he could think of that was capable of getting their lethargic attention. He sniffed, but all he smelled was the smoke from the campfire. He needed to check the trees to see what he was dealing with. He moved away from the fire to one of the cottonwoods at the edge of its light and placed his hand on it. His mind merged with the forest.

An icy bolt of pain shot through his head. It felt as if the trees were screaming at him. Darkness covered everything around him. A shadowy figure entered his awareness right behind him. He yanked his mind free of the tree and lurched backward as a dagger sliced into the bark at the same level where his head had been. He backpedaled away from another strike while he drew his sword. His attacker sliced downward, and he parried it with his blade. His adversary stepped back, allowing Hyroc to finally get a look at it.

The figure was hooded, covered from head to toe in ratty dark blue clothing. They wore gloves on each hand and brandished a dagger with a leather handle. Their face was concealed behind the same plague mask with a downward beak he had seen on the Ministry soldier in Elswood.

"EVERYONE UP!" Hyroc yelled as loud as he could to alert his friends. Kit roared, and a flurry of muffled curses from Donovan and Elsa filled the air.

The figure lunged at Hyroc. He deflected a flurry of strikes, but when he parried, his attacker swept his legs out from under him. His adversary was on top of him the instant he hit the ground. The person stabbed the dagger down at his chest. Hyroc seized the person's wrist to immobilize their hand and slammed it into the trunk of the tree beside him, knocking the blade from their grip. His attacker hissed in frustration, but the noise they made almost didn't sound human. The person reached for him with their other hand. Their glove blazed with fire as it burned away. When his attacker's hand emerged, Hyroc realized the skin was a deep dark gray, it was larger than the other, and the fingers had claws. Veins of purple light danced across the skin, and it crackled with deadly energy.

Hyroc raised his other hand and formed a buckler-sized barrier to block his opponent. The hand slammed into a blue shimmer, but the impact put much more of a strain on his Quintessence than he expected. If his attacker had touched him, he was certain he would have died. Hyroc turned his head and yelled out, "don't let it touch you." He saw Elsa and Donovan embroiled in a fight with a second figure armed with a sword, wearing the same plague mask. Elsa wielded a seax knife, and Donovan held his spear. An arrow protruded from one of the figure's shoulders, but it was close enough to render a bow useless. The figure deflected a stab from Donovan's spear as Elsa slashed at it.

Hyroc returned his attention to his problem. He used his hand that held the figure's wrist and started bending it backward, trying to break it. The figure growled in anger and relaxed its wrist to free its hand from Hyroc's grip. As the figure pulled back, Hyroc grabbed it by the shoulder, yanked it back toward him, performed a kicking motion, and flipped it over his body. Hyroc scrambled to his feet while his opponent was still disoriented by the move. He used the reprieve to spare a glance at his friends. Donovan held the second attacker at bay by swinging his spear wildly, and Elsa moved backward with her bow in hand to take a shot.

Chapter 19: Shadows

"I'll kill you for that, worm!" the figure snarled as it rose to its feet. The person's voice was cold and angry, but there was a tone to it that didn't seem to belong. It was a noise humans didn't make. It drew another dagger from its belt and rushed toward him.

A shrieking roar split the air as Kit leaped onto the back of his opponent. The figure yelled out in pain as the big cat tore into the person's flesh. In a flurry of movement, his opponent desperately twisted its upper body and rocked its shoulders, trying to throw off Kit.

In its determination to escape, the figure's mask was knocked off. Hyroc was aghast by what he saw. The person's head was covered in black scaly skin with no hair, and dark pointed teeth filled its mouth. Their cheeks and eye sockets were sunken, and deep violet flames blazed out of their eyes. It was a shadow demon!

The demon reached for Kit with its enlarged hand. "Kit, get back!" Hyroc commanded. Kit jumped free, digging his hind leg claws into the back of the creature as he did so. The demon arched its back in pain as it wailed out. It was a piercing cry filled with hatred that sent an icy chill down Hyroc's back. The creature snapped its gaze on him, and its eyes glowed brighter.

"I'll cut your heart out," it said as it charged toward him.

Hyroc formed a blue fireball in his hand and threw it at the demon. His opponent shrieked in agony when the ball struck and ignited the cloth on its upper body. As Hyroc moved in for a killing blow with his sword, the creature mastered itself and returned its attention to him. With its body still ablaze, it swung its dagger at him. Hyroc knocked its aside with his sword and stabbed it through the chest. The demon sucked in a ragged gasp. It stared at him in what seemed surprise.

"How, you –" the demon trailed off before the flames in its eyes went out.

When Hyroc pulled his sword free of the body, it came away covered in charcoal colored blood that seemed to be smoking. He turned his attention to the second attacker. An arrow protruded from the demon's shoulder, but its aggressive movements seemed unhindered by the wound. Donovan thrust his spear at the creature. It ducked sideways to avoid the strike, then grabbed the shaft of Donovan's spear to immobilize it and reached for him with its enlarged hand. Hyroc cursed as he ran toward his friend. He wasn't going to get there in time.

Elsa rushed forward and rammed her seax through the demon's hand. The creature screeched in pain as it pulled its hand back. It darted away to tend to the blade sticking out of its hand. When it removed the knife, the blade glowed orange with intense heat. Donovan darted toward the creature to resume his assault. The demon threw the seax at him. Donovan dodged the projectile, leaving it to sail past his head and fly into the trunk of a tree. Elsa took the opportunity to shoot another arrow. The creature avoided the arrow and then came at Donovan. Donovan swept his spear at his opponent, but his adversary avoided the tip and batted it out of the way. Then it unexpectedly continued past him.

Hyroc entered the fray and intercepted the demon. The creature was slow to notice him as if distracted. When they finally realized he was there, it was too late. Hyroc lopped off its enlarged hand with his sword and, in a spinning motion, slashed across its throat. The creature gurgled a shriek as it reached for its neck, where smoking charcoal blood spilled out of the wound. Donovan rammed his spear through its back. The demon arched its back and died. Donovan yanked the tip of his spear free of the demon's body and gave it a few pokes to make sure it was dead.

Hyroc scanned their surroundings for movement, but he saw none.

"Anyone see anything?" Elsa called out while holding her bow with an arrow at the ready.

"I don't," Hyroc answered.

"Same here," Donovan said.

"I think it was just the two of them."

"I think so, too," Donovan said. "But I've got a question. What in the name of The Hallowed did we just kill?" he exclaimed.

Chapter 19: Shadows

"That had to be a shadow demon, right?" Elsa said. "Its hand didn't look normal."

Hyroc nodded. "Yes, they both were. The eyes gave that away." He reached down and removed the fractured mask on the creature's face.

Donovan and Elsa were taken aback. Elsa leaned in closer to get a better look at the face.

"Wait," Donovan said. "Hyroc, if these are demons, I thought you could hear their thoughts or something. You heard that Shade Hunter long before we ran into it."

"Yes, I'm supposed to be able. Though I'm not quite reading their mind, it's more that they have a different way of talking, and that's what I'm hearing."

"Then why didn't you hear these two?"

Hyroc lifted his hand and shrugged. "I have no idea. But I'm an idiot for not realizing this sooner. A day or two ago, when I was searching the trees to see what was happening around us, I found an area of darkness. I thought it was just a treeless area because it seemed to be in the same place as that marsh we passed through. I didn't think it was anything dangerous."

"Hyroc, don't beat yourself up," Donovan said. "There's a lot to be distracted about lately. We were all caught off guard by this."

"Is this thing human?" Elsa said as she hovered over the dead demon's face. Hyroc and Donovan gave her a curious look.

"No, there's no way these could be human," Donovan stated. "They can't be."

"I only say that because its head seems human-shaped."

"No, and yes," Hyroc said darkly. Donovan and Elsa shot him an astonished look.

"How can it be no and yes?" Donovan questioned. "It's either one or the other."

"Marcus taught me about them. From what I understand, Faygrotha used creatures such as these during his rule. They were called The Hand of Death."

"That's a comforting name," Donovan said sarcastically, "but I can see why they're called that."

Hyroc nodded in disturbed agreement. "They're humans that are infused with shadow demon essence," he continued. "Faygrotha liked to turn prisoners into these."

"That's awful," Elsa said with disgust.

"That's about all I remember from Marcus; the rest comes from Ursa. She warned me about the dangers of their touch, which I think we all fully understand. But beyond how deadly they are in a fight, they have a darker use. People also use them to get at what someone knows. So, let's say a person knows where a certain treasure is located. They don't want to tell anyone about it, even if someone tortures them and whatnot. So, someone turns them into a Hand of Death. Whoever turned them now controls the person – if you can even call them that anymore – with the knowledge. But remember, these are shadow demons, and in order to control them, you have to bind them with a sacrifice of flesh.

"And with that sacrifice, that person can simply ask the demon where the treasure is, and it has to tell them. But there is kind of a catch. The demon will hate that person and want to kill them, not only to free themselves but because they really want them dead. The infusion process or whatever you want to call it twists everything good about that person into malice and absolute hatred."

"Wait, are you saying that person is still in there?"

Hyroc nodded. "Unfortunately, yes, but the demon is a mere shadow of the person it came from. You might as well not even think about that part. These things will kill you without remorse. They are also under someone's control, so they really can't stop trying to murder you even if they want to run away.

"That also might explain why I didn't hear them coming. Since these things are still partially human, that's negating my ability to hear them. Humans can't communicate in the same way shadow demons do. So, we can't rely on me knowing they're coming."

Elsa nodded. "But here's the question," she said. "Where did they come from? I've heard stories that witches and other nasty things are supposed to live in these woods."

Chapter 19: Shadows

"Yeah, we're far enough from Elswood for that to make sense," Donovan said. "Maybe these two were just marauding demons looking for a victim."

"No, I don't think so," Hyroc said. "If we ran into two witches, maybe, but not demons, it's too much of a coincidence.

"Okay, then *he* must've sent them. That other guy that's after you."

Hyroc shook his head. "It wasn't *him*." He reached over to the demon's body and unfolded a large wrinkle on its right shoulder. The cloth held the raven and scythe symbol that represented The Ministry of the Silver Scythe. "These were sent by The Ministry." Donovan and Elsa's expressions turned alarmed."

"How – how could they possibly be from The Ministry," Elsa said.

"Yeah, I really don't know that much about The Ministry, but from what little I do know, they kill these kinds of things," Donovan said. "That doesn't make any sense."

"Then what are we looking at?" Hyroc said indignantly. He indicated the mark with his hand. "That's the symbol of The Ministry right there."

"I don't know. Maybe they stole those clothes," Donovan suggested.

Hyroc gave him a flat look. "They stole these clothes, and we just happened to run into them? This would have to be the most amazing coincidence in history for that to make sense. No, these definitely came from The Ministry. You and I saw one of these things in Elswood. Their plague masks are meant to hide their faces and make everyone think they're a leper. People tend to stay away from lepers. It makes a lot of sense."

"Okay, I understand what you're saying," Elsa said. "But The Ministry's whole purpose is to kill witches and these kinds of things. Which is why they were originally chasing you, so why would they suddenly throw that all away and start using shadow demons willingly?"

"Desperation."

"Desperation?" Elsa said skeptically. "After all these years they left you alone, you think someone is now that determined to find you?"

Hyroc nodded. "I know of someone."

"Who?"

"A man named Keller. I met him once when I was younger, right after Marcus passed away. He saw me as an evil creature that nothing good would ever come from, and I needed to be destroyed to protect everyone. Luckily, June knew some people within The Ministry, and she was able to get them to help with protecting me from Keller. It worked, that is, up until that *accident* I had in Forna. But before that, I learned bits and pieces about his ceaseless efforts to convince his superiors to kill me. He's almost fanatical in his belief that I'm evil."

"Alright, that sounds like a horrible person and an unpleasant experience to go through," Donovan said. "But what does that have to do with these two shadow demons?"

"Everything. He is so determined to get me that he no longer cares how he does it. The ends justify the means."

"And what about the other people in The Ministry?" Elsa said. "If we're dealing with just one person, then the whole Ministry isn't responsible for these monsters. Wouldn't they destroy these things as soon as Keller started using them and come after him because he's acting like a witch?"

"Only if they knew about them. He's probably been hiding them from The Ministry. These creatures are dressed to appear as lepers. And if you've never seen what's underneath, beyond avoiding contracting their disease, you wouldn't think anything of them. Even I didn't know what they were until I knocked their mask off. So, if they were properly controlled, soldiers working with them wouldn't even know what they were. There's likely only a small number of Keller's lackeys directly involved with these creatures and controlling them. If they think I'm pure evil and know the consequences of their actions, they have an excellent reason to keep this quiet."

Donovan studied the two corpses thoughtfully. "So, what you're saying is if we can show these bodies to someone in The Ministry who's not involved, we wouldn't have to deal with Keller anymore."

"That would work if they didn't think all of us were murderous outcasts," Hyroc noted.

Chapter 19: Shadows

Donovan sighed, deflated.

"Okay, so we've figured out the hypocrisy of this Keller guy," Elsa said. "But how in the Sunless Planes did these two find us? We haven't seen so much as a smoke trail from The Ministry in nearly two weeks, and you're doing that thing that removes any signs of our presence."

"Hyroc, you're certain that's been working properly?" Donovan asked.

Hyroc nodded. "Yes. I felt the energy drain from doing it, and I saw it start working with my own eyes. I'm just as baffled as the two of you."

"Could it have simply been an accident?"

Hyroc shrugged. "Maybe. They might have already been in the area and simply got lucky when they ran into us."

"Already been here?" Elsa prodded."

Hyroc nodded. "They could've been pursuing us without lighting a fire. I assume demons don't care about the heat from a fire. They could've also been traveling night and day without stopping to rest. I learned from Ursa that they would have to stop eventually, but these creatures have far more stamina than regular people. They could cover the distance we traveled in a fraction of the time."

"If this Keller guy wants you so badly," Donovan said. "It's probably safe to say there is more than just two of these things searching for us."

"It seems best for us to err on the side of caution for now," Elsa said. "Let's only do a small fire at night if we need to cook something, and, Hyroc, you should resume getting rid of our trail."

"I agree," Hyroc said.

"Well, we should get moving." Donovan urged."

Chapter 20
Persistent Trail

Hyroc put his hand above his eyes to block out the bright midday sun. He crouched at the edge of a hill, looking toward the trees he had already passed through. Scraggly spruce trees ringed the hill, but none grew at the top. Fireweed, punctuated by some flowering plants, covered the ground here, which gave an unobstructed view of his surroundings. He watched for any signs of pursuers. Elsa crouched beside him, doing the same. He was perfectly capable of relaying what he saw without her, but she thought with the two of them watching, there was a chance one of them might see something the other had missed.

"I don't see anything," Hyroc said.

"Same here," Elsa said. "Which means either no one's there, or we just can't see them." Hyroc nodded his agreement. She turned to look at him. "How about the trees? Did they tell you anything?"

Hyroc shook his head. "No. They don't seem to be screaming at me anymore, but the only thing I can see from them is still darkness. I'm practically blind when it comes to sensing anything else that's going on. Which means we either haven't moved far enough away from where we killed those Hands of Death –"

"Or there's more of them out there," Elsa finished. Hyroc nodded. "Okay, we should catch back up to Donovan and Curtis. Are you okay

Chapter 20: Persistent Trail

to erase our trail?" Hyroc nodded again. "Join us as soon as you're finished with that." She sidled backward down the hill to keep herself less visible in case someone below them hadn't already seen them. She stood when she was far enough down the incline for it to obscure her as she headed off.

Hyroc lifted his arms and, with his eyes closed, focused on removing their trail as he cast the spell. He felt the required Quintessence leave his body, and he opened his eyes. He'd been doing this about every hour since the attack last night. This made each cast of the spell less demanding, but overall, it was far more taxing. His strength was beginning to wane, and he didn't know how much longer he could keep it up without rest. In likewise fashion to Elsa, he moved down the hill. As he headed off, he ate a piece of dried venison from his knapsack. The food would help his body regenerate his Quintessence a little faster, but without rest, the process was far less effective.

He moved swiftly through the forest and quickly rejoined Elsa, Curtis, and Donovan. Not long afterward, they arrived at the shore of a river. The water came up to their waists as they waded out into it. It had a mild current and didn't give them much trouble. Curtis had more difficulty walking through it, and Hyroc hung back to help him. Hyroc stopped and turned toward the shore when he heard an angry growl. Kit stood at the water's edge, bobbing his head from side to side irritably.

Hyroc waved his arm in a beckoning motion. "Come on, you need to get over here," he said to the big cat. His four-legged companion yowled, showing his fangs. "I know you don't want to, but if you don't want us to leave you behind, you had better get over here." He protested again before tentatively stepping into the river. The mountain lion paddled toward him. Despite Kit's hatred of water, he was a strong swimmer.

Instead of heading for the opposite shore, the group turned into the current. They moved downstream through the river to ensure they left no trail behind. They did this until their legs began to tire from fighting the current, then went to the other side. Once on dry land,

OUTCASTS

they dumped the water from their boots and rang out their clothes as much as they could before continuing. Hyroc took a moment to erase their trail when they reentered the trees.

Shimmer guided them to a patch of rocky ground. The hard surfaces prevented any footprints from remaining. When they reached softer terrain, it was nearing dusk. The group continued for as long as they had light before stopping for the night.

Hyroc and Donovan dug two shallow holes next to each other, then connected them with a draft trench. They sparsely filled one hole with firewood, and Hyroc used his Flame Claw to ignite it. It was safer for them to avoid a fire, but they wanted it more for the light than the heat. If more Hands of Death found them, they would need the light to fight. The hole where they lit the fire would help keep it concealed while it still provided the illumination they needed. A hole was a poor place to build a fire due to it restricting the flow of air to the fire. The flame would essentially suffocate itself and go out, but the draft trench provided the required ventilation to keep it going. Then, they piled branches, rocks, and whatever debris they could scrounge up in a half-circle around the fire. This further reduced the fire's light from reflecting off the trunks of the surrounding trees.

The group arrayed their sleeping hides on the ground opposite the half-circle, so they had the fire to their backs. Donovan took the first watch, followed by Hyroc. Elsa relieved Hyroc when his watch ended without incident.

When morning arrived, cool and mostly clear, they disassembled their camp. As usual, Hyroc used his Flame Claw to remove evidence of them staying here. To ease the strain on his Quintessence, they manually scattered the materials used to make the half-circle amongst the trees, and Hyroc omitted them from the spell. The ashes swirled out of the hole in a tornado before dissipating in the air. Dirt flowed across the ground like water to fill in the depressions. Soon, it looked as if the area had never been disturbed. Hyroc felt a significant amount of Quintessence leave him and sap his strength. He breathed out uncomfortably.

"More than you expected?" Elsa said.

Chapter 20: Persistent Trail

Hyroc nodded. "Yeah," he agreed.

"If it took too much out of you, we could go without the hole-fires, so you don't have to do extra work getting rid of them."

"That might be best. I didn't think removing those would be that bad."

Elsa nodded. "I agree. Try to be more careful about doing those kinds of things. You're no good if you can't fight if another one of those *things* finds us." She grabbed the reins on the donkey and led it onward.

The coolness of the morning lazily parted into the afternoon warmth. The group stopped to rest in a shaded clearing between two cottonwoods. Hyroc removed their trail before relaxing. He sat down with his back against the trunk of one cottonwood, but he did so more haggardly than he could hide. He hadn't used enough of his Quintessence for him to feel overly weak, but his fatigue was steadily growing worse with each cast of the removal spell.

"Hyroc, remember what we discussed this morning," Elsa said indignantly, taking notice of his condition.

Hyroc waved his hand dismissively. "It's not as bad as —"

"Not as bad as what?" Elsa said, cutting him off. "Your mistake with the holes? Or what you did an hour ago? You're going to keep saying that until you have nothing left"

"I —" he managed to get out before Elsa interrupted him again.

She jabbed a finger at him. "Don't you try to give me any more of *that*. You already seem to want to take a nap. It's taking too much out of you. You can't do this any longer."

Hyroc angrily indicated in the direction they had already come. "And what if something picks up our trail because I stopped getting rid of it? Getting in a fight with a Hand of Death would take a lot more out of me. Out of all of us. This is the safest option. It's tiring me out a little, but I can handle it."

She stared at him with hands on her hips. "No, you can't. Hyroc, I know staying hidden from those things is the safest option. But if we run into another one, or Hallowed forbid, something more powerful, and you're exhausted from using your Flame Claw to cover up our trail, you'll be useless. It would be up to Donovan, Curtis, and me to fight. Not only will we have one less person, but we won't have your magic. I feel a whole lot safer knowing we have that on our side than I do with you exhausting yourself and assuming we won't run into anything dangerous. There's still plenty of ways for us to hide our trail without resorting to magic. It's easier to do it that way, but it's not the only way."

"So, you'd rather risk them knowing where we are than for me to use magic," Hyroc scoffed.

"No, that's not what she's suggesting," Donovan interjected. "We absolutely want you to keep removing our trail. It's a whole lot more reliable than us trying to keep our trail hidden, but not at the expense of having you in a fight. You're pushing yourself way too hard to keep this up. We can all see it. Use your strength more sparingly. Do it when you have some energy to spare."

"You want me to keep doing it, but not as often?" Hyroc questioned.

"Yes." Elsa agreed. "You can't wear yourself out. We need you in a fight. I don't know if we can kill those things without you."

Hyroc considered Elsa and Donovan's words. "Alright," he agreed after a long moment. "I can give it a break."

"Thank you," she said, relieved.

"But I'm doing it one more time after we leave here, then I won't do it again until we stop to make camp tonight. Deal?"

Elsa sighed and shook her head in annoyance. "If you promise me to only do so when you feel up to it, and you won't use your Flame Claw to fill in any fire holes we dig."

"Deal."

"You're stubborn as a bear," Donovan noted.

"Thank you," Hyroc beamed mischievously.

"That wasn't a compliment."

"If you're not a bear, it wasn't."

At dusk, they made camp beneath a rock overhang. They dug a fire pit, but there was no need for them to build a barricade to reduce the light from the fire as the overhang already did so.

Chapter 20: Persistent Trail

When it was Hyroc's turn to watch, he scaled a cottonwood to get a better view of the top of the overhang. Kit joined him later, laying on a branch above him with his head resting on his paws as he tried to sleep.

"Wish I could sleep," Hyroc scoffed.

The big cat merely twitched an ear in his direction. Hyroc returned his attention to their surroundings. All was silent. He yawned, then sharply shook himself to chase away the urge to doze. He looked for something to keep himself occupied and settled on the stars. Lazily, he searched for the constellations. He found Ferma, the serpent, and Anol, the wolf. Was Kaska the hawk up at this time of year, he wondered? He lowered his gaze back to the forest below. An owl hooted in the distance, but that's all he heard. He returned to the stars and drummed his fingers absentmindedly on the branch. His thoughts slowly turned toward the tree he rested in. It could probably tell him if there was something closing in on them.

He placed his hand on the branch and let his consciousness flow through it. Darkness surrounded him as he expected, but it seemed heavier, and he couldn't see anything outside of it. Before, he could catch glimpses here and there of something beyond its reach, but there was nothing. It was so concentrated he could barely tell the tree was screaming at him. Wait, screaming?

His eyes flew open as he scanned the forest. He saw a shadow moving through the trees to the right of the overhang. Then, he saw a second. The trees were too thick for him to identify the shapes, and he couldn't get a clear shot from where he sat. He nocked an arrow and sent it whistling into the ground beside his friends. With a yell, everyone scrambled to their feet.

"We've got to get down," Hyroc urgently said to Kit. The big cat immediately became alert. He gracefully descended down the tree, and Hyroc followed.

Hyroc got a start when an arrow thunked into the cottonwood where he had just been. He jumped behind the tree and frantically searched for where it had come from. These things used bows? The two Hands of

Death they had killed used blades, and he guessed he should have been prepared for this possibility. The only question was, how good of a shot were they? That big hand of theirs would undoubtedly hinder their aim, so probably not a good one. He then wondered why they would want to use a bow if their power came from their hand. Why waste their ability with less dangerous arrows when they could kill simply by touching someone. A well-placed arrow would still kill him, and he supposed it didn't matter; that was just another way of making him dead.

Hyroc severed the branch of a leafy bush and stuck it out from behind the cottonwood to bate his enemy into taking a shot so he could figure out where the arrow came from. An arrow skirted the edge of the trunk, sending flecks of bark into his face. That Death-Hand was a much better shot than he expected. Fortunately, he now had a bearing. He nocked an arrow and prepared to step out. Kit came into view, walking through the foliage toward him.

Hyroc used his hand to indicate for Kit to stop. "I need you to stay right there," he whispered. "Don't come any closer." The big cat stopped and gave him a confused look.

Hyroc returned his attention to the enemy archer. He stepped out from behind cover in one sharp motion and let his arrow fly before stepping back. The Death-Hand yelled out in pain, but it didn't sound right. It sounded normal, like a man. Hyroc stole a glance around the tree to see a shape disappear into the darkness. What had he just shot?

Kit roared. Hyroc turned to see a hooded Death-Hand swinging a sword at him. He deflected it with a barrier from his Flame Claw and moved in a half-circle away from his opponent as he unsheathed his sword. He blocked a series of strikes with his blade before countering with a flaming fist to his enemy's face. His adversary yelled out in a mixture of pain and alarm before casting off its flaming mask, revealing its purple eyes and black scaly skin. Hyroc feigned a step to the side, catching his enemy off guard and creating an opening. Kit exploded out of the bushes and leaped onto the creature, sending it to the ground. While it thrashed as the big cat mauled it, Hyroc flipped his sword

Chapter 20: Persistent Trail

downward and shoved it through the creature's shoulder blade. His enemy's body tensed, and it made an angry hissing noise as it died.

Hyroc caught movement out of the corner of his eye and lurched backward to dodge a spear thrust. He grabbed the shaft of the spear and rammed it back toward his attacker. His opponent stumbled, and in a twirling motion to utilize his momentum, Hyroc slashed his sword across them.

When he focused on his opponent, he was surprised to see a young man not much older than he, clutching a wound to his abdomen. He was human. The man looked at him, stunned as he fell to the ground. The two of them locked eyes, unblinking. The rustling of bushes beside him snapped him out of the trance. He turned just as a growling hunting hound plowed into him. He grabbed its head to hold its snapping jaws away from him. Kit roared and tackled the dog, knocking it off of Hyroc. Hyroc scrambled to his feet as the big cat fought with the beast. Kit went for the back of its neck but abruptly jerked his head back. Around the hound's neck, Hyroc saw nails driven through its collar with the points facing outward, preventing his companion from delivering a killing bite. Hyroc drew his bow horizontally and shot the dog. With a yelp, it collapsed sideways.

Hyroc swept his eyes through his surroundings to find his friends. The man he had struck was still alive, but disabled was good enough to remove him from the fight. He forced thoughts of the young man from his mind as he approached the sounds of fighting.

He ventured into the area where they had made camp to find Elsa and Donovan fending off two soldiers armed with clubs and shields. Two bodies already lay on the ground with arrows through their chests. He saw three Hands of Death emerge from the shadows around the rightmost flank of the overhang. They were armed with short swords, and one wielded a two-handed broadsword.

Elsa fired an arrow that stuck harmlessly into a shield as the men moved closer. Hyroc darted toward the two men. He threw himself into their exposed side, ramming his shoulder into one man. His target stumbled and fell into the other, tripping them. Both lost their footing, falling to the ground. Donovan wasted no time rushing forward and plunging his spear into one soldier's chest. Hyroc made a stomping motion on the remaining man to keep him from regaining his balance as Elsa moved over to stick her seax into him. By the time they finished these off, the Death Hands had arrived.

Elsa picked up a shield from the dead soldiers as the three of them fanned out to engage the new arrivals. Hyroc moved toward the one with the broadsword as he was the most capable of dealing with the long sword. His target rushed toward him and thrust its sword at him. He sidestepped the attack and then deflected a sideways slice with his sword. Hyroc darted inside the reach of the creature's sword and swung his blade. He caught his opponent in the shoulder with a glancing blow. The creature growled in pain as it pulled away from him. It swiped its enlarged hand at him, but he backpedaled out of its reach.

"You'll suffer for that, wretch!" the Death-Hand snarled.

It swung its sword at him wildly. Hyroc leaned out of the way of the strike, then used his sword to defend against a series of quick blows that drove him backward toward the campfire. He deflected the next strike but did so at an awkward angle, creating an opening in his stance. The creature nailed him in the chest with a full-footed kick, knocking him onto his back almost into the fire. Hyroc rolled out of the way of a killing blow from his enemy's sword. He scrambled to his feet and lurched out of the way of a one-handed swing from the creature. There hadn't been enough time for him to grab his sword when he stood. When he drew his hunting knife, the Hand of Death laughed mockingly.

"How do you expect such a pathetic weapon to keep me from killing you?" it said coldly. Hyroc flung his knife at the creature, but it effortlessly ducked its head out of the way. "I'll enjoy seeing your head mounted on a wall." The creature moved toward him, waving its sword in a menacing flourish.

Hyroc's sword was behind his adversary. He tried to dart around the creature, but his enemy fended him off with two sweeping sword strokes. Hyroc put one hand behind his back to conceal him forming a fireball in it while backpedaling. Seemingly irritated by him prolonging

Chapter 20: Persistent Trail

his death, the Death-Hand walked quicker to close in on him. Hyroc moved his hand out from behind his back and threw the fireball. It struck the creature, immolating its leg and half its body with blue flames. Hyroc ran for his sword as the creature wailed out in agony. When he retrieved it, he was shocked to see the creature bearing down on him as it burned. He parried a strike, stepped to the side of the flaming monster, and slashed its leg before moving out of its reach. The Death Hand stumbled when the injury prevented its leg from properly supporting its weight. Hyroc swung his blade, shattering the creature's mask as it turned its head to look at him. He then finished his enemy off with a strike down the center of its back. The creature limply fell to the ground face first, laying in a burning heap.

When he turned his attention to his friends, he saw Elsa and Donovan fighting with one creature while the second hung back a few paces. Suddenly, the second dashed past Elsa and Donovan toward Curtis, who stood close to the overhang.

Hyroc formed a barrier around his hand before reaching into the fire and scooping up a piece of flaming wood. Doing so required less Quintessence than it would have if he had created the fire himself. The fire fed off the wood instead of his Quintessence and required no effort toward its creation on his part because it already existed.

Hyroc flung the fire at the creature. It sailed through the air and exploded when it hit. Fire blossomed across the creature's head and shoulders. It shrieked in pain and frantically patted its body as it tried in vain to extinguish the flame. Hyroc rushed over and dispatched the creature with several quick strokes of his sword. When its flaming body lay on the ground unmoving, he turned his attention to the last remaining enemy. He saw the creature lying on the ground an instant before Donovan stabbed it with his spear. It clutched the shaft of his spear with both of its hands, appearing almost angry that it had just been stabbed. Elsa rushed over and stabbed it multiple times in the chest with her knife. The creature crumpled into a heap and went still. They turned their attention to Hyroc when they were sure it was dead.

"You okay?" Donovan called out as he and his sister approached Hyroc.

"Yeah," Hyroc answered.

"You saw it too," Elsa said. She glanced toward the two dead soldiers. "That there were —"

"Yes, I saw," Hyroc said, interrupting her to save time.

She nodded and rushed over to retrieve Curtis while Donovan moved for the donkey. Hyroc used his Flame Claw to harvest a glob of dirt and drop it on their campfire to extinguish it, while Elsa and Curtis stamped out the smoldering remains of the two Death-Hands. Then he and his friends disappeared into the trees.

They stopped when they seemed a safe distance from their campsite to catch their breath. They staked a torch into the ground they had lit to light their way after leaving their campsite.

"I think this is far enough for now," Elsa said. "But we shouldn't stay here for very long." Hyroc and Donovan nodded their agreement. She took a few deep breaths before continuing to speak. "Okay, there were people with those things this time."

"They'd have to be around people for someone to tell them what to do," Donovan said. He lightly slapped Hyroc with the back of his hand. "Hyroc, I guess you called it about Ministry soldiers not knowing these things aren't human."

"I really wish I could stop being right," Hyroc said irritably.

Donovan nodded in agreement.

"I want to know how they found us again," Elsa said. "Hyroc, you're sure that spell of yours was working properly?"

"I'm sure. I felt the drain on my strength every time I cast it. It was definitely working."

"There's got to be some sort of trail we're leaving behind," Donovan said thoughtfully. "That's the only way they could find us through all those trees."

"Unless they know where we're going," Elsa suggested.

Chapter 20: Persistent Trail

Donovan shook his head. "I don't see how that's possible," he said skeptically. "We're not following any kind of road or trail out here. We're following the lead of a magical blackbird, and with all the twists and turns we've been taking to avoid rough terrain, they can't have any clue where we're going."

"Well, it's got to be something. They found us twice."

Donovan gave her a flat look. "Obviously."

"We've got to figure it out and figure it out fast."

Hyroc's thoughts turned to the Death-Hand that had ignored the rest of them and went for Curtis. On their first encounter with the creatures, one had done the exact same thing. He had seen them do it twice. That wasn't a coincidence. There was something to that behavior, but what? Why were they doing that? They almost acted as if they were drawn to him. What made them focus on him? He was just an ordinary boy. Wait, no, he wasn't. The thought sent a shiver down Hyroc's back. Curtis could use magic. He'd been so focused on avoiding a second Death-Hand ambush he had almost forgotten Curtis was a lightning mage. The Death-hands weren't tracking them. They were tracking him!

"Oh no," Hyroc said, tipping his head back in dismay and squeezing his eyes shut. "I know how they're finding us."

Elsa and Donovan abandoned their arguing and gave him a baffled look.

"You do?" Elsa said.

Hyroc opened his eyes to look at them. "They're not tracking us," he said. He pointed at Curtis. "They're tracking him."

"They're tracking Curtis?" Donovan said skeptically. "How do you know that?"

"Because he can use magic. That's what they're tracking."

Donovan and Elsa looked at him uncertainly. "They're tracking his magic?" Donovan questioned. "Last time I checked, that's not how The Ministry finds people. They do it pretty much the same way we do it when we're out hunting animals."

"No, that's *usually* how they find people when they aren't using shadow demons. But most shadow demons are sensitive to the presence

—191—

of magic the same way honeybees are drawn to a flower. They can pretty much smell it. The reason for this is they are more vulnerable to magical energy than swords and arrows. Think about it like footprints from an animal you're hunting. When someone can use magic, they leave a magical trail behind when they move through somewhere, and it can be followed to find them. And every time we've run into them, I've seen one ignore the three of us and go straight for Curtis. That's the only explanation for their bazaar behavior."

"Okay, let's assume you're right, and they can track magic," Elsa said. "Couldn't they be tracking you? You've been using a lot of magic, more than Curtis."

Hyroc shook his head. "No, they can't sense my Flame Claw," he said. "Simply put, since it's derived from the power of the Guardians, it cannot be tracked by shadow demons or magical means. And I've been closer to the demons when they went after Curtis. Shouldn't they have gone after me instead?"

"That seems a reasonable point," Elsa said. "And you're certain about that?"

"Yes," Hyroc said.

"If you're sure, then I trust you."

"Okay, so, if they're tracking his magical trail, what do we do about it?" Donovan asked. "Do you have a spell or something you can use to get rid of it?"

Hyroc shook his head. "I don't have any way of removing it," he said gloomily. "Ursa didn't teach that to me."

"That's fantastic," Donovan said in angry sarcasm. "So, what, our plan was doomed from the start? Do we just wait here for them to come and kill us?"

"There's got to be something we can do," Elsa said. "I need you to think really hard about anything we can use."

A thought came to Hyroc. "There might be something," he said. "I have an idea. Hold on." He placed a hand on the trunk of a tree. When his consciousness entered it, he encountered the enveloping darkness caused by the presence of shadow demons, but the black

Chapter 20: Persistent Trail

cloud seemed weaker. He could discern things happening elsewhere in the forest again. The only explanation for the darkness weakening was there were fewer shadow demons following them. There weren't as many following them, and they could use that. He opened his eyes and pulled away from the tree.

"I think there aren't as many shadow demons following us," Hyroc said.

"How does that help us?" Elsa said.

"I'm not comfortable with *any* following us," Donovan added.

"It means our pursuers are running out of them. I didn't sense any places nearby with shadow demons. The same as any physical trail, trails of magical energy decay and eventually disappear."

"So, the only ones that know our location are the ones following us at this moment," Elsa said eagerly.

Hyroc nodded. "Yes, and all we have to do is kill the ones behind us, and we should be safe," he agreed. His excitement faded when he realized what he had just said. His solution was an immensely dangerous and difficult task.

"We have to kill the monsters following us that can kill you simply by touching you with their hand," Donovan said. "Are you sure that's the best option?"

"No, it's our only option. Each ambush has gotten more deadly. It's only a matter of time before we run into more than we can handle."

"Do you know how many Death-hands we have left to kill?"

Hyroc gave him an uncomfortable look. "No, only that there are fewer."

"What about how many soldiers are with them?"

"No idea. Unless those people start a forest fire or randomly start chopping down trees, the forest pretty much ignores them."

Donovan cocked an eyebrow. "Well, this is a terrible plan."

Hyroc shrugged. "If I had a better one, I would absolutely tell you."

"It's our only option," Elsa said. "So, we don't have a choice."

Donovan sighed.

"But we do have one advantage," Hyroc said. "They won't be expecting us to come after them. We'll be hunting them."

"Even better, we could ambush them," Donovan said.

"Right, right, we could hit them at a place of our choosing. How good are either of you at making spike traps?"

Chapter 21
Determined Prey

The stars shone brightly across the night sky. Hyroc gazed at them, trying to focus his mind on the difficult task that lay before him. If he and his friends could make it through this, they would be safe. Without the Death Hands, The Ministry would have no way of tracking Curtis' trail of Quintessence. It sounded simple enough, but he knew killing those monsters would be nothing of the sort. They had nearly ended his life and that of his friends during their last two encounters. And that was mostly without the aid of soldiers. This time would be far worse. He and his friends faced the full contingent of The Ministry forces that hunted them. There would be numerous soldiers accompanying an unknown number of Death Hands. He and his friends were far outnumbered.

But they had one advantage, surprise. Their enemy had no idea of the trap awaiting them. They would not be expecting their prey to turn and fight so cunningly. They would never think that he and his friends had discovered the Death Hands could track magic, nor that this ability would be turned against them. And once their shadow demon pets were dealt with, even if more came after them, it would be too late. Any that might arrive afterward was too far away to pick up the trail of magic before it dissipated.

He lowered his gaze when his friends moved over to him to discuss the plan. Elsa and Donovan wore hoods and sashes over their faces. The sashes were meant to help conceal their breath in the cool night air and to silence their breathing so the sound wouldn't give them away to their enemy. The plan depended on the two of them going unnoticed.

"Everyone knows what we're doing?" Elsa said as she finished belting on a dagger. Donovan carried a short sword on his belt. The blades had been scavenged from the dead soldiers on their second encounter with the Death Hands. She and her brother had decided that carrying an extra weapon was necessary considering what they faced. Donovan had his spear, but if it got knocked out of his hands or damaged, all he had to fall back on was his hunting knife.

"Yes," Donovan said. "We hide in the trees and let them pass underneath us."

Hyroc nodded. "Yeah. Don't attack until they're all in front of the two of you," he said. He used his hand to indicate the campfire that burned beside him and the four sleeping mats arranged in a half-circle near it. "We need to drive them toward the fire."

"That way, they run into the traps," Donovan said.

"With you and Elsa attacking them from the back and them springing our traps at the front, they'll be in disarray," Hyroc said. "We need to create as much confusion as possible. That's the only way we have any chance against those soldiers. Then while everyone's trying to figure out what's going on."

"We take out all those Death Hands," Donovan said.

Hyroc nodded. "Right. We don't need to kill all the soldiers. We just need to kill every Hand of Death. So, once they're dead, we can pull away and leave. They won't have any way of tracking us, and we're free."

"You and Curtis will be the bait, though," Elsa said seriously.

Hyroc nodded. "Yes, we're the bait. The Death Hands will be drawn to Curtis' Quintessence."

"You're sure you can protect him?"

Chapter 21: Determined Prey

"That's my brother you're talking about," Donovan said. "I'll never forgive myself if he gets hurt."

"I'll protect him with my life. I promise I'll keep him safe," Hyroc said. "He's my brother too."

Donovan was happily taken aback by his words. "If anything happens to my sister and me, you'll take care of him?" he said.

"Absolutely. He's – you're all my family."

"Just – just keep him close."

"I will."

The four of them gathered into a close embrace. This might be the last time all four of them were alive together. Some of them or all of them might die during this. The coming fight could shatter their family. They had a small chance, but it was a chance nonetheless. Even if their plan was destined to fail, they had to try. They pulled away after a moment.

"Remember," Hyroc said. "Once we've got all the Death Hands, get out of there. If you see a blue fireball or an orb of light in the sky, head to where the donkey is. Hopefully, we will have killed all the Death Hands by then, but we'll figure it out when we get there."

She and Donovan nodded. The two of them turned and headed off to separate trees. Hyroc watched them go, knowing it might be the last time he saw the two of them alive. He turned away and placed a comforting hand on Curtis' shoulder."

"Will they be all right?" Curtis asked, his voice laced with concern.

"Yeah, they'll be fine," Hyroc said, knowing he probably just lied to the boy. "We need to get into position."

He guided Curtis to a tree opposite the ones Elsa and Donovan sat in. The two of them followed a strictly established path to avoid the traps that had been set around it.

Hyroc indicated the top of the tree. "Okay, I'm going to be right up there," he said.

"I want to help," Curtis said. "But – I lost my bow at the village, and I don't know how to throw lightning bolts. I can't even make a

-197-

little animal like you showed me. Everyone's putting their lives at risk to keep me safe. I just —"

Hyroc crouched so he was at eye level with Curtis. "I know, I know," Hyroc said reassuringly. "But I thought of something you can do." He pushed his knapsack toward Curtis and opened it, revealing it was filled with small stones. The boy gave him a confused look. "You don't need a sword or bow to make someone hurt." He unslung the knapsack from his shoulder and shook the rocks out onto the ground.

"Rocks are a lot more dangerous than most people think. Beaning someone in the head with small stones like these probably won't kill them, but they'll definitely feel it. That might daze them or slow them down, which will make it easier for me, or your brother, or your sister, to take them down." Curtis gave him a proud look and nodded his understanding. "And since you can use magic, you could use that to throw the rocks even harder. I know I haven't had any time to teach you about that, but it's the same as when you imagined what animal you wanted the lightning to turn into. Imagine the rock flying out of your hand toward someone, and use your hand to control it. Or you can imagine that while you're throwing normally. It doesn't matter how you do it. You just need to keep throwing those rocks."

"But what if I run out of rocks?"

"Then started throwing sticks or clumps of dirt. Anything you hit someone with will help." Curtis nodded energetically. Hyroc indicated the tree top again. "I'll be right up there. Will you be all right?" Curtis nodded. "Let me know if any of them get too close, and I'll be right down. Alright?" Curtis nodded. "Alright." Hyroc turned away, slung his bow over his shoulder, dug his claws into the tree's trunk, and climbed it. He stopped at a suitable branch and settled in a position to watch. He took a deep breath. It was going to be a long night.

When the darkest part of night had arrived, Hyroc noticed Kit raise his head with his ears facing forward attentively from hearing something. Hyroc followed his gaze and spotted shadowy figures moving through the trees toward the campfire. Behind those, he saw

Chapter 21: Determined Prey

points of light from torches. There was an alarming number of soldiers coming toward them. Even with the added advantage of his Flame Claw, there were far too many for them to have any hope of defeating. Surprise and confusion were their only chance of getting out of this fight alive. He hoped he had made the right choice and hadn't killed Donovan and Elsa.

"Curtis," Hyroc called down quietly. "They're coming. Get ready." Curtis leaned in close to the trunk of the tree with a stone in hand. Hyroc turned his attention to Kit. "Kit, go down there with Curtis. Stay hidden and only attack if someone gets close." The big cat noiselessly clambered down the tree, disappearing into the foliage.

Hyroc stood and pressed himself against the trunk of the tree while he nocked an arrow. He set his sights on a hooded shape that seemed to be a Death Hand. His heart rapidly beat as he held his shot. Their enemies weren't all the way into the trap yet. The plan depended on fully drawing them into it. But that was also the most dangerous part of the plan. Every step closer their enemies took increased the chance they would notice something amiss. They were all doomed if this didn't work.

A mixture of fear and excitement urged him to shoot, but he stayed his hand. He felt a slight tremor run through his arm from the strain on his muscles. The shapes drew closer. Now he could see details in their features. The one he aimed at wore the distinct plague mask of a Hand of Death meant to hide their monstrous features. Did the soldiers with these creatures even know what they assisted, he wondered? Did they think these were simply lepers dressed to hide their deformities? He forced the thoughts from his mind. Now was not the time to consider such things. His enemy was here to kill him and his family regardless of the answer.

He spotted more shapes moving at the edge of the firelight coming in to flank the sleeping mats from the side. Just a little closer! The Death Hand he aimed at stopped near a sleeping mat. It cocked its head as if noticing something. Their ruse was about to be discovered. They couldn't wait any longer! The nearest soldier arched his back and

–199–

OUTCASTS

cried out as an arrow hit him in the back between the shoulders. Hyroc let his arrow fly. They were committed now.

His arrow punched through the creature's mask as it hit its head. The Death Hand dropped to its knees before going headfirst to the ground. Another soldier went down, followed by a rapid succession of arrows that killed another Death Hand. Hyroc shot an archer that seemed to have noticed his tree before stretching his hand out. He summoned several large blue flames behind The Ministry forces. Several soldiers wheeled around and began yelling out in alarm. Two more soldiers dropped. Soldiers from the middle of the group moved toward the flames at the back and formed a defensive line. Hyroc started walking the flames slowly toward the soldiers. Cries of terror erupted from them, and the line bent away from the approaching fires. Arrows continued to rain from Elsa and Donovan's trees, and soon all organization among the soldiers evaporated. The defensive line broke, and soldiers surged away from the blue fires toward Hyroc's tree. A bolt of fear shot through him at the sheer number of approaching enemies. He needed to move!

A shrill inhuman yell startled Hyroc. He looked down to see a Death Hand with wooden spikes attached to a branch impaling its midsection. Hyroc put an arrow through its chest. When it slumped back dead, he noticed more of the creature's moving his way. They were too close for him to continue picking them off while keeping Curtis safe. The nearest creature's head jolted back when something struck its mask with an audible thud. It snarled as it held the side of its head. Hyroc finished it off with an arrow through its eye.

He dismissed his summoned fires, slung his bow over his shoulder, and descended the tree. When he reached the bottom, he found Curtis furiously chucking rocks. Kit roared and pounced on a soldier Curtis had just hit. The big cat knocked the soldier to the ground and tore into him. The soldier yelled out in pain.

"Kit!" Hyroc called out. "Get off him. We've got to move." The big cat bounded away and moved over to him with fresh blood staining his mouth. More yells filled the air as soldiers began encountering

Chapter 21: Determined Prey

more traps. Hyroc and Curtis dashed away from the tree, trying to put some distance between him and the approaching Death Hands. Hyroc knew they would be drawn to Curtis, and by getting them to move farther away from the support of the soldiers, they would be easier to kill.

The three of them weaved their way through the trees. When they had moved to what seemed an appropriate distance, Hyroc ushered Curtis behind him and drew his bow. A Death Hand burst through the foliage. Hyroc caught it in the heart with his arrow. The creature spun back and hit the ground dead. Two more creatures appeared in front of them. Hyroc shot one with a shadow killer arrow. The creature screamed out in pain as smoke roiled out of its abdomen. It crumpled to the ground and pushed out a puff of smoke when it fell.

Hyroc rapidly shot a regular arrow at the second creature. With a quick flourish of its sword, it deflected the arrow as it rushed forward. It raised its hand to block an incoming rock from Curtis. Hyroc dropped his bow and drew his sword in time to block a strike from the creature. Hyroc backpedaled as he defended against an assault of sharpened metal. Hyroc slashed at the creature, but it dodged backward. It punched at him with its enlarged hand, and he turned out of the way of its gloved fist. Out of the corner of his eye, he saw three more Death Hands rushing toward him. He had mere moments before they were close enough to threaten him and Curtis. His current adversary slashed at him and threw its enlarged hand at him with veins of purple running across it. Hyroc parried with his sword. He formed a barrier around the forearm of his other hand, which he brought up to block his opponent's attack. He felt the creature's hand slam into his barrier and unleash a powerful surge of energy. His spell held firm. Hyroc used his sword to strike his enemy in the side and slash its throat. The creature dropped its sword, and he kicked its body to the ground.

Hyroc backpedaled away from the three Death Hands that were now practically on top of him while simultaneously dismissing the barrier. They moved at him in an even line, preventing him from attacking any one of them without all three coming down on him at the same time. He held his unarmed hand out to the side to usher Curtis backward, but he didn't dare spare a glance behind him. Kit rushed to his side and roared while swatting ferociously at the approaching figures. The creatures paid the warning no heed, forcing the big cat to retreat alongside Hyroc. Kit futilely continued to issue warnings. One of the creatures moved away from the line while staying focused on Hyroc, ready to counter. Hyroc couldn't risk a look over his shoulder because even a minor distraction could leave him vulnerable to attack. He raised his sword hand toward the creature and summoned a small wall of blue fire to block its path.

The creature stopped, then let out an icy laugh. "We are aware of your tricks," it said in a cold voice. "And we will not be so easily dissuaded." It reached toward the fire with its enlarged hand, and its glove burned away. Bright purple lines danced across its charcoal skin. Then to Hyroc's surprise, an opening formed in the fire. It stepped through and continued forward. "Did you not think we would learn from the deaths of our brethren? You and your friend will not escape. Accept it. It will be less painful."

Hyroc forced down a wave of panic. These things weren't supposed to be able to do that! His Flame Claw was his only advantage over these creatures. How could he hope to win against all of these things without it? There were more of them than him, and these ones seemed more experienced and more organized than the others he had defeated. Had he sent him and his friends to their deaths? They could have kept running. They might have been able to evade the creatures that were tracking Curtis. He didn't know. They had more of a chance of succeeding with that than his suicidal plan. If only he had known – known his Flame Claw wasn't enough. He would have done things differently.

He pushed his fears to the back of his mind. If he let doubt in, he and Curtis were as good as dead! They still had a chance. There was always a chance. They weren't dead yet! He could do this.

"It'll be better if the three of you decide to turn around and leave us," Hyroc retorted.

Chapter 21: Determined Prey

The creature growled angrily at him. He knew his words would strike a nerve because even though these demons had wills of their own and possessed freedom while fighting or fulfilling their task, they were still bound to someone. They were no more than servants. Servants obedient to the whims of their master. They hated that person and would kill them if they were able. Only through the death of that person and the destruction of the amulet that controlled them could they determine their own actions. And as such, they didn't appreciate being reminded. If he could make them angry, it might give him an edge and cause them to make a mistake.

"We cannot, wretch," the creature spat. "But I will find pleasure in seeing the life burned from your eyes."

"You can try," Hyroc countered. "Curtis," he yelled. "Curtis, I need you to throw a lightning bolt."

"But I don't know how!" Curtis called back; his voice threaded with fear.

"I know you can do it."

The creature let out a frigid laugh. "You know he can't do it," it said. "He's afraid, as he should be of the darkness. He's about to die. There's nothing he can do to change this."

"Ignore him," Hyroc said. "You have to throw a lightning bolt. Just concentrate."

"But I'm scared."

"I know you are, but you can –"

He was interrupted when the two creatures that had stayed in formation charged him. He deflected the strike from one with his sword, but before he could counter, it ducked out of the way so the other could attack. When he dodged a strike from it, the first came at him again. They repeated their strategy in a continuous stream. He fended off a barrage of strikes with no time to recover. They pushed him farther and farther from Curtis while the third pursued the boy.

Hyroc yelled as he continued to defend himself. "Curtis –" *strike* "– I need –" *strike* "– that –" *strike*.

"I can't," Curtis said tearfully.

–203–

"Yes —" *strike* "— you can. Just like —" *strike* "— you did with — the werewolf. Just like — you saved — your brother — and — your sister."

The creature abruptly stepped away from each other and came at him from both sides, trying to outmaneuver him. He parried one adversary and pushed away the other with a kick to the abdomen. He formed a fireball and hit the creature he had just kicked away. It yelled out as blue fire blossomed across its body. The creature threw its enlarged hand to the side, and the fire flowed into its hand, forming a ball. It threw the ball at Hyroc. He ducked the ball, causing it to ignite a tree behind him and bathe the area in pale blue light. The second creature came at him again. He deflected the strike with his sword and backpedaled toward Curtis, trying to get back to the boy.

The Death Hand that had thrown the fireball charged him. Hyroc parried a hasty strike from the creature and nailed it in the chin with an uppercut. The creature staggered backward. Hyroc continued to punch the creature. He halted his body blows and raised his sword to strike. Before he could deliver his killing blow, the second creature sliced at him. He dodged the attack, and slashed his original target in the leg, then pulled away. The creature yelled out, holding its leg. It wasn't out of the fight, but injured was better than nothing. Hyroc formed a barrier to block the uninjured creature when it came to his side with his empty hand. Its blade collided harmlessly with the shimmering barrier. Then as Hyroc turned to counter with his sword, the creature reached for his barrier with its enlarged hand. Instead of trying to burn through it with a blast of dark energy, it made the barrier disappear. Stunned by the unexpected occurrence, Hyroc stepped away from the creature. Before he could disengage, the injured creature came at him and punched him in the stomach with its enlarged hand. Hyroc gasped and let out several choking coughs as he backpedaled, holding his abdomen with his empty hand. He struggled to keep himself from doubling over from the pain while he moved away. The uninjured creature rushed him. Hyroc barely managed to sidle out of the way of its strike. Fighting through the pain, he forced himself to stand straight.

Chapter 21: Determined Prey

A roar from Kit drew his attention toward Curtis. He saw the mountain lion swatting at the Death Hand near Curtis. The creature swung its sword at Kit, but the big cat dodged the strike and sank his teeth into the Death Hand's leg. His opponent yelled out in a mixture of pain and anger. When the creature stretched out its enlarged hand at him, he jumped out of its reach. The creature put its hand up to protect its head against the stones Curtis started throwing at it.

Hyroc blocked a simultaneous strike from his two creatures with a sweeping sword stroke. He backpedaled to put some distance between himself and the slower creature so he wasn't fighting two adversaries at the same exact time. Hyroc blocked a series of strikes from the uninjured creature. After Hyroc blocked its last swing and tried to counter, it ducked under his strike, jumped at him, and seized both his arms. He formed a barrier around his arm where the creature's enlarged hand grabbed him to keep it from destroying his flesh. The creature pushed him into the trunk of a cottonwood tree. Its slower companion moved toward him with its enlarged hand held out. A vaporous field of dark violet surrounded the hand as it surged with deadly energy. Hyroc used his foot to push away the creature that restrained him. It stumbled back, but its grip remained firm. Hyroc wanted to yell for Curtis to run, but where to? The Death Hands could track his energy trail and would find him even if he managed to elude them this night.

"Curtis," Hyroc called out in a severely strained voice. "You need to do it now! I know you can." He jerked his upper body from side to side to no avail. The hand moved closer. He felt a cold bolt of dread shoot through him. His life was mere moments from being extinguished. Were his friends about to join him? Had he killed all of them along with him?

The Death Hand laughed. "There's no escape this time," it said in a harsh voice.

Hyroc looked toward Curtis. The creature kicked Kit in the side multiple times. The big cat fell to the ground. Curtis desperately threw rocks at the Death Hand as it walked toward him.

—205—

The hand was nearly on him. "Curtis!" Hyroc yelled. "YOU'VE GOT TO – DO IT – NOW." Hyroc turned his head to look at the slower creature that had just arrived. This was it!

The air crackled with energy. A blinding light and intense heat shot over Hyroc's face and slammed into the two creatures. He felt the uninjured creature's grip pull away. Even after the light had vanished, he saw only a mixture of orange and green colors flooding his sight. Colors were all he could see for an instant; then, it resolved into the familiar view of a darkened forest. The Death Hand that had been holding him in place sat slumped against a tree with charred clothes across its upper body. Spots of orange embers still glowed along the edges of a massive burn mark on its chest. The slower creature was entangled in the uppermost branches of the same tree, smoldering.

An ear-piercing cry rent the air. When Hyroc turned his attention to its source, he saw the Death Hand near Curtis, holding its face with both hands and wailing out in pain. Hyroc darted over to it. Kit leaped onto its back and wildly bit into its shoulders. The creature stumbled forward as if disoriented. When it reached back with its enlarged hand, the big cat dropped to the ground out of its reach. Hyroc severed the creature's head with one swift stroke. A stream of oily blood spilled from the headless torso as the head and body fell to the ground.

Hyroc took in several heavy breaths. His heart felt as if it were about to jump from his chest. Curtis seemed almost in a daze as the boy stared at him. His friend's body radiated with fatigue as it tried to cope with the immense strain it had experienced from summoning such a powerful attack.

"You okay?" Hyroc asked breathlessly. Curtis nodded, and Hyroc nodded back. "Curtis, you saved me again. Thank you." Curtis opened his mouth to respond, but nothing came out. "It's okay. You don't need to talk." The boy nodded slowly with what seemed appreciation. Hyroc reached over to Curtis to resume leading him away. "Alright, we –"

His words were interrupted when an arrow thunked into the ground beside them. "Curtis, we've got to move!" Hyroc said

Chapter 21: Determined Prey

energetically. The soldiers the Death Hands had moved away from had caught back up. He shoved Curtis forward to start him moving, and the two of them rushed off as an increasing number of arrows rained down. Kit bounded through the foliage in front of them in long powerful leaps. Hyroc formed a blue ball in his hand and tossed it over his shoulder to signal for Donovan and Elsa to move toward their donkey. They dashed through the trees, barely noticing the spiny spruce bowels brushing across their faces. The three of them moved forward until they arrived at their donkey.

Curtis swept his eyes through the area worriedly. "Where's my brother and sister?" he said, concerned.

"They'll be here," Hyroc said in forced assurance, trying to keep his own fear from his voice. There was a chance neither one of them was coming. But until he was certain, he would continue with the plan assuming they would be here. He didn't know what he would do if he had lost his two closest friends.

"Go get the donkey ready," Hyroc said calmly. "I can't because he'll probably bolt if I even try." Curtis nodded and got to work getting the donkey ready for travel.

Kit moved over to Hyroc and pushed his head into his hand, wanting to be pet. Hyroc obligingly scratched between his ears. The big cat stared up at him in what seemed concern. "Don't worry. They're coming," Hyroc said hopefully, more to reassure himself than his companion. The big cat pulled away from his hand, his ears alert.

"Hyroc," a voice whispered from the darkness.

Hyroc looked around but couldn't see anyone. He glanced toward Kit to make sure he wasn't hearing things. This wouldn't be the first time that had happened to him. The mountain lion was also searching for the voice's origin.

"Hyroc," the voice repeated. It sounded like a woman's voice.

"Elsa?" Hyroc asked, still searching. "Elsa, is that you?"

"Do you see them?" Curtis said eagerly.

Hyroc held his hand up to signal for his friend to be quiet.

"Hyroc."

It was definitely a woman's voice, but she didn't quite sound the same as Elsa. "Who are you?" he said. "Show yourself." A hooded figure emerged from behind the trunk of a tree. He drew his sword and put himself between Curtis and the stranger. "Don't come any closer."

"Hyroc."

He thought he recognized the voice, but, no, it couldn't be. "June?" Hyroc said, dumbfounded. "June, is that you?"

"Yes." The figure moved toward him.

As they drew closer, Hyroc confirmed the person was more sleight of figure than a man. It really was June! He felt a thrill of excitement. He had missed her so much, thinking he would never see her again, and yet, here she was in the last place he had expected.

He lowered his sword and moved to meet her. "What are you doing here?" he said happily, not really caring what her answer was.

"Finding you," she said.

"How'd you know this was where I was going to be?"

"Your trail brought me here."

Hyroc paused. His trail? He and his friends hadn't left any sort of physical trail behind. He had made sure of that. And even if they had left one, she shouldn't have known how to follow it. She had no tracking experience, and it seemed unusual that she would have acquired any through her teaching position. The only reason The Ministry had been able to track them thus far was through the use of their Death Hands tracking Curtis' trail of magic energy. Her voice also didn't sound correct. He was positive it was June's voice, but it seemed darker and colder. Even when she had been angry about how people treated him, she never sounded remotely close to this. Then he noticed the plague mask beneath her hood.

A bolt of ice shot through him. No, they couldn't have. Why would they do this to her? She knew nothing. She was no threat to anyone. There was nothing to be gained. It couldn't be true. She couldn't be one of those monsters!

He raised his sword. "Wait, stop. Don't come any closer," he said. June stopped. "Are you still you?"

Chapter 21: Determined Prey

She was quiet a moment. "No." Hyroc grimaced. "Keller turned me," she growled, sounding hateful when she said his name.

Hyroc pushed his despair away. He couldn't focus on that right now. His grief would overwhelm him if he did, but it was becoming increasingly difficult for him to keep his composure.

"Why – why would he do this?" Hyroc said.

"To use me to find where you had gone."

"But I never told you where I was going. I didn't even know when I left."

"I knew what you were looking for. I gave you trap-making materials because you would be drawn to the forest where trapping was preferable. People never treated you well, but, despite this, you never preferred solitude and would still desire to live with others."

"How did he know I would come to Elswood? There are other settlements in Arnaira that have a forest. How did he know I would choose Elswood?"

"I led him to all the towns and villages with woods. When he didn't find you, we moved on to the next one. Slowly he's been tightening the net. And now, he's found you."

"So, he knew what to look for, but it wasn't any specific place. That forced him to simply check every place that fits what you gave him until he found me."

"It did."

"Then, why are you in this spot where we are now?"

"To warn you."

"Warn me? Keller has control over all his Death Hands. The others he sent have had no qualms whatsoever about killing me. He sent them here to end my friends and me, and they were forced to obey his will. I know it was he who sent them because he's always wanted me dead. Are you telling me you don't have to do what he says?"

"No. Even now, I fight his will."

"So, you can do what you want for now, but it won't last?"

"No, my strength to resist him is waning. Soon, I will be just like the others."

"Thank you for the warning, June."

"There is something I must ask of you."

"What? Name it?"

"Fulfill your promise."

Hyroc stared at her, taken aback. "My promise? What promise?"

"You know which one."

Hyroc shook his head. "No, I don't know. What are you –" a wave of dread crashed on him. No, she couldn't be asking him that! "No, don't ask me to do that. I won't do it. That was never part of my promise. I promised I would never come back."

"You must do as I ask."

"No, anything but that."

"Hyroc, you must kill me."

"No! I can't."

"I can track your friend. Killing me is the only way."

"There has to be another way. You're fighting Keller's control right now. Maybe you can – how do you know you can't keep doing that?"

"I cannot do as you ask. I feel him overcoming my freedom as we speak. I do not have long. His control prevents me from taking my own life. You must kill me."

"I'm telling you, I don't think I can!"

"Then I will make you." She drew her sword and started walking toward him.

"No, June," Hyroc said fearfully. "Please don't." She continued walking. "Stop, please." She was almost to him. "June, stop!" She swung her sword at him, and he blocked it with his blade.

"Don't make me do this!" he said, struggling against her strike.

"You have no other choice."

Hyroc pulled away from her, and she took another swing. He deflected it with his sword and then backpedaled. "June, stop. I don't want to fight you."

"You must." She attacked him in a rapid succession of strikes. He defended against all of them. She took another swing, and he dodged out of the way.

Chapter 21: Determined Prey

"I won't hurt you."

She turned away from him and moved toward Curtis. Hyroc darted in front of her and purposely struck at her with an easily blocked attack to return her attention back to him. She swatted it away and dashed around him. He came at her with a more determined attack. She parried and seemed focused on him again.

"June, fight it! You don't have to do this."

She sliced at him, and he blocked it with his sword. When their blades met, she shoved it toward him, driving him backward in an unexpected surge of strength. He backpedaled, trying to maintain his balance and his grip. His back slammed into the trunk of a tree. She bore down on him, attempting to knock his sword aside.

"You and your friends will never see daylight again if you do not kill me!" she snarled.

Hyroc twisted her sword to the side and kicked her off him. She stumbled backward, but as soon as she regained her balance, she rushed toward him. He rolled from the trunk of the tree out of the way of her sword and moved in a half-circle. He blocked a flurry of strikes from her.

"Stop, you're going to hurt me," Hyroc pleaded.

"You must end this! None of you will ever be free of The Ministry so long as I live. It is the only way."

"No, I'd rather die than harm you."

"Then you will die!"

She struck at him feverishly in a relentless attack. She came at him continuously and gave him no time to catch his breath. It was a pace he couldn't keep up with. She broke his stance and swept his legs out from under him. He landed on his back, and she was on him in an instant. He had almost no time to bring his sword up to block her blade. Hyroc struggled against her strength as she drove his sword down so the back of his blade was against his chest.

"June – don't – do this," he strained to say.

"It is the only way."

"Your – killing – Hyroc."

Some of her weight lifted from his sword, and she even let it retreat toward her little. A spear flew through the air and struck her in the side. It flung her off him. Hyroc scrambled to his feet. June got up on her knees. With a sharp grunt, she pulled the spear from her body. She cast it aside before rising to her feet and hobbling toward him.

"If you ever cared about me, end this." She was pleading with him. Part of him screamed to disregard her desire and any other requests she made, but part of him knew this was never going to end. "You must keep the promise I made you make that night. You must forget about me."

Hyroc grit his teeth. How could she ask that of him? That had never been part of his promise. She had made him promise in the hopes of keeping him safe, not for him to kill her. Thinking about what she was doing had been a source of happiness for him. But if he did as she asked, that would end. She'd be dead, and there would be no more to it. There was no coming back if he did this. But the idea of ignoring what she asked felt callous. She was suffering, and she wanted it to end. More than that, she didn't want to hurt him. She was under Keller's control and he would make her kill him. He couldn't simply run away from her; she would find Curtis. There was only one option open to him. He wrestled with the two sides of his mind in a fierce struggle but eventually focused his determination.

He gripped his sword tightly and stepped closer to her. Hot tears ran down his face. His heart urged him to abandon his course, but he knew he could not. It took all his will and determination to raise his sword. He struck June. She fell to the ground, and he dropped to her side. She placed her normal hand on the side of his face.

"Thank you, Hyroc," she said, her voice sounding as it had the night he had left. "Don't blame yourself. This wasn't your fault. I always loved you." Her hand fell away. She was gone.

Hyroc stared down at her lifeless body, unable to think. He felt numb as if all the warmth had been sucked out of the air. The feeling persisted even when he saw a familiar face. It was Elsa. She shook

Chapter 21: Determined Prey

him while talking urgently. Strangely, he didn't seem able to hear her. Whatever she was saying, it seemed important. His muddled mind slowly began to hear her.

"...are you hurt?" she asked sternly. "Are you alright?"

"I'm fine," he said, sounding distant. He used his hand to indicate June's body. "It was June. He made her come after us. I didn't have a choice."

"What? You're not making any sense. Are you okay?"

Hyroc nodded. "I'm okay."

Elsa nodded, but she didn't look entirely convinced. He had answered her question. Why did she seem not to believe him? What was so important anyway? He needed to take care of June.

"I need to –" Hyroc started to say.

"I need you to get onto your feet," she interrupted. "Can you stand?" Hyroc nodded, thinking that was a strange question. Of course he could stand. Why wouldn't he be able? She pulled him up onto his feet. When he stood, she grabbed his sword that he didn't even know he had dropped and shoved its hilt into his hand. He slid it back into its scabbard as Elsa pulled him toward Curtis and the donkey. Something thunked into the ground beside him. He looked over to see an arrow shaft buried partly into the ground.

The realization of the situation flowed back into his mind. He suddenly remembered where he was and what he was doing, and the soldiers rapidly moving toward him. The memories returned, but the numbness did not dissipate. When he and Elsa reached Curtis, that's when he noticed Donovan holding a spear. He knew he should be relieved to see Donovan and Elsa still alive, but he didn't seem to feel much of anything at the realization.

"Did we get all of them?" Donovan asked breathlessly.

"Pretty sure we did," Elsa said. "What do you think, Hyroc?"

Hyroc glanced back in the direction of June's body with a feeling of sadness. "I think we did," he answered.

Donovan clapped him on the shoulder excitedly. "We did it!" he said. "They won't be able to track us now."

"Let's not get ahead of ourselves," Elsa cautioned. "We don't know that for certain. We need to keep our guards up. If we missed a single creature, we're not out of danger yet." Donovan nodded.

Hyroc pulled his attention from June and followed his friends into the night.

Chapter 22
Sting

Hyroc ducked under the low hanging branch of a deciduous tree. They thinned out ahead of him, and beyond them lay the flat brown and golden planes of Forna. He and his friends had finally reached the other side of the forest! It seemed a miracle any of them had survived the journey. They had fought off soldiers and monsters to get here, all while on the verge of starvation.

Donovan clapped Hyroc on the shoulder. "Look at that!" he exclaimed. "We made it. Can you believe it? We're finally here."

Hyroc nodded absent-mindedly. As monumental and exciting as their accomplishment was, he almost felt nothing. He was numb and indifferent. Seeing the planes of Forna was no more satisfying than the events of any previous day. He had felt this way ever since their final encounter with The Ministry, or more specifically, the soldiers Keller commanded and their Death Hand minions. That precisely executed ambush had ended the pursuing hunter's ability to track them. They were free, but with as much relief as this success had brought his friends, he felt nothing.

All he could think about was his encounter with June. He held her in such high regard and had so many fond memories of her. His fight with her still felt like a dream. No, not a dream, a nightmare. It was worse than anything he could ever imagine. She'd been twisted into such a horrid form. She was a monster. A terrible trick brought about by his pursuers trying to unnerve him seemed a far more plausible explanation than what he had faced was her. Him imagining his aunt still living at his childhood home, attending to the garden, or teaching her students the day's lesson was more enticing. The thought comforted him and, even in his unfeeling state, almost brought a smile to his face. But before his desire could take root, he always saw June's frightening face from the last night he saw her. He saw her scaly face beneath her dark hood, her sharp gnashing teeth, the glowing purple embers where her eyes should be, and the glint of her dagger.

No matter how hard he tried to convince himself that the creature he had faced was not his aunt and merely some monster devised by a sick mind to imitate her, he heard what she had said. That things words were too personal, too accurate. It knew him deeply. It was only the type of depth that could come from a loving relationship. And it was asking him to kill it. Not only asking but practically begging. Why would one of those vile creatures ever do that? Even while they were bound to a master with little to no free will of their own, it was still a better alternative than death. Those creatures wouldn't willingly seek out that option. That monster almost seemed to have no desire to harm him, at least at first. It seemed only a course of action she would take.

She didn't want to hurt him, and her bond to Keller prevented her from taking the man's life or her life. In order to eliminate the threat she posed, she was forced to obey Keller's orders while she bided her time. She had to wait until she found him. Then once she did, she only had an extremely limited opportunity to stave off Keller's will while she enacted her plan. It must have been torture for his aunt to endure tracking him for who knew how long. There was even the possibility she had been forced to commit terrible acts in the name of that hypocrite.

Everything he made her do must have been an affront to her and everything she stood for. She was a gentle, caring person that wouldn't have hurt anyone. Her position as a teacher at the boarding school

Chapter 22: Sting

was her whole life. She loved bringing knowledge to the minds of her students and letting them imagine places they had never seen. The only thing she cared more about than that was him. She gave everything she could to try and keep him safe and shield him from many of the hardships he experienced as a child. Her attempts had failed to improve his life much. It comforted him to know that she had tried. That was far more than anyone beyond Marcus had done for him before he came to Elswood. It even tore her up when she was forced to send him away all by himself. That was one of the most painful and frightening nights of his life, and he felt no ill will toward her because of her choice. It seemed a tough but necessary decision. She wanted to stay because, through teaching her students, she thought she could keep what happened to him from happening to anyone else. That might have been an insurmountable task, but it was noble of her to try.

Sacrificing her life for his would have been an easy choice for her. The strength she showed in her conviction could have only come from a loving relationship. An evil creature would not have been capable of such a feat. No matter how hard he tried to fool himself, deep down, he knew that demon was June. She was gone.

"I've never been so happy to see so much open ground," Elsa said jubilantly. "Don't think I'll be needing this anymore."

She removed the scavenged dagger from her belt and threw it off into the trees. Donovan unbelted his sword and likewise disposed of it. Beyond being needless weight to carry outside of a fight, both blades were marked with Ministry insignias and would attract unwanted attention.

When they reached the edge of the trees, they made camp for the day to take stock of their supplies and figure out where to go next.

"Alright, I think I've got it," Donovan said. He sat on the ground with his back against a tree while he looked over Hyroc's map. Elsa sat nearby with the saddlebags laid out in front of her, giving their donkey a break from carrying their things and taking stock of what supplies remained. Hyroc and Curtis milled around, waiting for something to do.

Donovan made a beckoning motion to Hyroc. "Hyroc, take a look at this." Hyroc stepped over to him and crouched down so he could see the map. "So, if my judgment of our position is correct, the nearest village is to the southwest. In that direction." He used his hand to indicate the approximate direction.

"Do you know how far?" Elsa asked without looking at him. "Because it seems we've got about two days of food left for all of us. Three if we're careful."

Donovan studied the map before answering. "A day, day and a half."

"If you're correct," Hyroc said skeptically.

"Yeah, if I'm right," he said in half agreement.

"I know how we can check," Elsa said. She faced toward the tree where Shimmer stood perched on a branch and held her arm out. "Shimmer," she called out invitingly. The raven hopped off the branch and glided over to her arm. Elsa stroked his head, and he happily pushed toward her hand. "Shimmer, I need to ask you something. There's a town nearby, and we think it's somewhere in that direction –" she turned and indicated the direction for the bird "– but we can't be certain. Can you fly out and see if we're wrong? And if we are, show us where to go?" Shimmer cawed before taking to the air and flying off in the indicated direction.

"I hope he doesn't take too long," Donovan said.

"If we're close to where we're supposed to be, he'll be back soon," Elsa said reassuringly.

"What's our plan for the town?" Hyroc asked. He used his hand to indicate his face. "Remember, we're not in Elswood anymore. Anyone out here won't react kindly to seeing me."

"We'll travel together for now, then split up when we get close to the town," Elsa said. "As long as you keep your hood pulled up, from a distance, you'll look the same as the rest of us. The three of us will get supplies from the town, and we'll meet up with you afterward."

Chapter 22: Sting

"The three of you?" Hyroc questioned. "I wouldn't bring Curtis with you." He reached into his pocket and retrieved a small glass sphere with a blue glow at its center. "The guards in that town could be carrying Perception Orbs. If they are, he will be found out."

"That's a good point," Donovan noted. "Okay, the two of us will gather the supplies, then meet up with the two of you later."

"Then we can figure out our final exit from Arnaira," Elsa said. Silence settled between them as the weight of her statement sank in. They would be leaving their home, the place where every single one of their happy memories had occurred, and probably never to return. They were giving up everything they knew.

The sound of wing beats broke the silence. Shimmer alighted onto the ground near Elsa. He raised his wings and faced off to the southwest, but it wasn't quite where Donovan had shown them.

Elsa used her hand to point toward their new bearing. "I think he's saying the town is in that direction."

"Well, I was pretty close," Donovan said.

"Close enough for us to go hungry for a day," Elsa joked.

Donovan sniffed. "I can admit when I'm wrong."

"It's too late in the day for us to make any real progress before dark, so we'll head off at first light."

Hyroc awoke and sat bolt upright. A shrinking fire crackled nearby beneath a starry sky, and it was late into the night. It was the same dream again! His reoccurring nightmare had disrupted his sleep since the last encounter with The Ministry. Every time, it was his fight with June. No matter how much he tried to alter the outcome, it always ended with him killing his aunt. It continued to jar him from his slumber, and when it did, he felt intense burning anger, anger for what he was forced to do to her.

He flung the blanket from him and stalked off to the edge of the firelight. Trying to sleep with his emotions swirling around inside him was futile. He needed time to cool off before he could go back to sleep. The night air seemed the best way to do so.

When he came to a pine tree, where the lower branches seemed to have been scraped away by the antlers of a moose in rut, he placed his hand on it and squeezed while simultaneously making a fist with his other hand. His anger consumed all his thoughts. June's death felt so unfair. Justice had not been served. After everything she had done for him, she deserved justice. He knew who had turned her into a monster. It was Keller! The man who was the bane of Hyroc's existence for as long as he could remember. Just after Marcus's funeral, this man, this lackey of The Ministry, had threatened to kill him. All because Keller believed he was an evil creature that would destroy everyone around him. Years later, he had gotten the chance when Hyroc injured another student in a simple accident. Keller must have rejoiced at the opportunity, but Hyroc slipped through his fingers. During his time in Elswood, every day, Hyroc worried his pursuer would find him. It seemed Keller had always haunted him. But he never expected his reviled enemy to resort to re-creating the Hand of Death and for his aunt to get turned into one. That was a step too far.

"Hyroc," a familiar voice said. He looked over his shoulder to see Elsa. "Are you alright?"

"I'm fine," he answered, trying to keep the anger from his voice.

She looked at him skeptically. "I know something's wrong. You haven't been sleeping well the last few nights. What's bothering you?"

"Keller," Hyroc said before he realized he was speaking.

"Keller? The man from The Ministry that's been hunting you?" Hyroc nodded. "You don't need to worry about him any longer. By the time he figures out where we went, we'll be long gone."

He shook his head. "No, there's something I didn't tell the three of you." He knew his answer would lead to more questions, painful questions, but he needed to share his plight with someone, anyone. It felt like he couldn't bear it alone any longer. "The last night we fought the Death Hands, you remember the last one we killed?"

She nodded. "Yeah, it was attacking you and Curtis. Donovan threw his spear at it."

Hyroc nodded. "Well, I knew that one."

Chapter 22: Sting

She stared at him, baffled. "How? I thought all of them were prisoners that they turned into shadow demons." She pondered the conundrum. Her expression turned shocked. "No, not your aunt!" Hyroc nodded somberly. "No. I'm so sorry." She covered her mouth with her hand and had a horrified look on her face. "We attacked her. Hyroc, I'm so, so sorry, we didn't know. We would have stopped – "

Hyroc cut her off with a sharp waving motion while he shook his head. "No, no, I don't blame you or your brothers. There was nothing the two of you could've done. She was too far gone. She was lucid just long enough to –" his blood ran cold as he said the rest. "– To tell me to kill her. She could track Curtis and couldn't tolerate the idea of hurting me." He clenched his fists. "So, she made me end it."

A long silence settled on them, and Elsa eventually broke it. She gently grabbed Hyroc's hand. He didn't pull away. "There's nothing I can say, but I'm sorry. That's a terrible thing you went through, and no one should ever have to go through what you did. But you're not alone." She let go of his hand and embraced him. "We're here for you." She let go.

Her words comforted him some, but he still felt distant from them. Even after all the hardships he and the Shackletons had overcome, it seemed they couldn't understand what he was going through. They had never been forced to kill a beloved family member.

"You don't need to bear this alone. You can talk about this anytime with us." Hyroc nodded, mostly in an attempt to placate Elsa. She nodded her satisfaction. "We've got a long day ahead of us tomorrow, so you should try to get some sleep."

Hyroc nodded. "I will, and thank you." His words felt hollow as if he hadn't meant them. They were mostly for her benefit. He supposed it didn't really matter even if he might have been deceiving her.

She gave him a gladdened look. "You're welcome. The four of us are family. What use is that if we don't hold each other up." She patted him on the shoulder. "I'm going to go back to sleep now. I hope you'll do the same. I wouldn't want you asleep on your feet. And don't forget, if you want to talk, you can talk to us." He nodded, and she returned to her sleeping mat.

He felt his anger return as she left, but to a lesser degree than earlier. Perhaps it had diminished enough for him to doze off again.

When they headed off the next morning, it was a clear day, but a cool wind blew across the plains. Hyroc's anger had returned to its full strength upon his waking. No matter how he tried to push his thoughts away from June and Keller, they always returned to the painful subject. They only seemed to make him angrier when they did. He did his best to keep his anger from showing, but he was finding it more and more difficult to maintain the façade.

Just after noon, they stopped at a short hill to rest and get their bearings. Hyroc leaned against the trunk of a solitary spruce tree that grew at the top of the hill as he surveyed the surrounding terrain with his eyes.

"Hyroc," Donovan called out. He stepped up to Hyroc, holding the map. "What do you make of this?" He held the map up and indicated a tiny black line that ran north to south with several even smaller lines running off of it toward the west. "It seems to be between us and the town. Do you think it's a river?"

Hyroc studied it before answering. "No, I think it's a ravine or a ridge of hills. I don't think it's anything to worry about." Donovan nodded before turning and stepping away. Hyroc returned to looking out over the plains.

"Hyroc," Donovan's voice came again. "I had –"

"Do you have to consult me on every detail of that map!" Hyroc snapped, cutting his friend off as he spun to face him. Donovan's face contorted into a look of confusion and anger.

"Hyroc," Elsa yelled. "That's enough!" Donovan thrust a finger at Hyroc and opened his mouth to hurl insults back when Elsa grabbed his arm and turned him away. "Let it go," she ordered. Donovan walked away while looking over his shoulder. Elsa turned her attention to Hyroc. "What was that?"

Chapter 22: Sting

"Why does he have to keep bringing every question he has to me?" Hyroc said crossly.

"Because you're the only one of us that has done anything like this before." Hyroc shook his head irritably. "Our conversation last night obviously didn't fix the problem because it still seemed to be bothering you all morning. I know because I could see it in the way you were acting."

"I can't stop thinking about June and what Keller did to her."

"Alright, but there's no need for you to take that out on the rest of us."

"I'm sorry, but I can't stand the thought of that man breathing the same air as us. After what he did to my aunt, he shouldn't be alive. She deserves justice."

She gazed at him in a mixture of shock, and something he didn't understand, fear. She hadn't shown that emotion since she had first met him. Why was she afraid of him? He wasn't going to hurt any of them, no matter how angry he got. Why was she acting as if he might? He opened his mouth to tell her as much, but she got there first.

She grabbed him by the shoulder and pulled him down a little before speaking. "Hyroc, I know you're angry and have every right to be. That man took something very dear from you, and you want him to pay, but there's something more important at stake here than vengeance. My brothers and I are depending on you to get us safely across these plains and out of Arnaira. The Ministry doesn't know where we're at, but we're still not out of danger yet. If we run into any Ministry soldiers, we're going to need you. If you leave, we either have to risk taking Curtis with us into the town where he might be identified, or he'll have to hide by himself on the plains, where someone can find him. He'll be much safer with you. So, I need you to bury your anger and focus on getting us out of here."

"How am I supposed to do that?" Hyroc questioned. "After what he did to June, after he made me kill her?"

Elsa's expression was almost pleading now. "Hyroc," she said. "You need to focus on *us* right now. I know I'm asking a lot from you, alright. But as soon as Curtis is safe from The Ministry, I'll come with you and help you kill Keller." Surprise engulfed Hyroc at her offer. He had never expected her to say something so out of character for her normally gentle demeanor. "That man took our home from my brothers and me, turned us into fugitives, and I care for him as little as you do. It will be justice for them and the two of us. So, once Curtis is safe, I give you my word to help you. Is that enough?"

Hyroc studied her thoughtfully. "Yes," he said.

Elsa smiled somberly and moved her hand to his cheek. "Thank you," she said. She turned away from him and walked toward Donovan, who angrily threw his hands up in demand of an explanation as to Hyroc's reaction.

Hyroc returned to leaning on the tree. He felt guilty for having just lied to Elsa. Her proposal had been enticing, but waiting to exact his revenge against Keller was problematic. Neither of them knew how long it could take before Curtis was truly safe from The Ministry. Years could pass before they achieved their goal. By then, Keller might return to a well-fortified castle beyond Hyroc's ability to penetrate, and The Ministry zealot would escape justice. Keller was most vulnerable while he pursued himself and his friends. It could be his only chance to exact retribution for what atrocities the man had committed against June.

Chapter 23
Justice

Hyroc silently moved through the campsite in the dark early morning. It would be a few hours before his companions woke up. By then, he would be long gone. He would use the trail-removing spell to eliminate any indication of where he had traveled. His friends wouldn't have a trail to follow, and they would be forced to continue on without him.

The thought saddened him. They were the best part of his life for the past four years and had brought him more happiness than he had felt in a long time. It troubled him knowing his absence would make their journey outside of Arnaira more difficult. Though more challenging, he was confident they would manage just fine without him. They would find their way around the snag with Curtis' ability and the potential of a Perception Orb detecting him. The Ministry didn't know where they had gone, and it would be some time before word reached this part of the plains. The danger to his friends was minimal. Their supplies would also go further without him because he was one less mouth to feed. But he was dismayed, knowing he might never see them again. They considered him part of their family as if he were their brother, and he felt he belonged with them. He would greatly miss them, but he had to give June the Justice she deserved. Keller was the one responsible for separating him from Elsa, Donovan, and Curtis.

He stealthily collected his gear. Kit soundlessly sauntered over to him to investigate. Hyroc scratched behind the big cat's ears. "You ready to go, hmm?" Hyroc said. Kit turned his head so Hyroc's hand was under his chin, wanting to be scratched there. "Alright, let's go." He scratched Kit's chin before walking away, and his companion trailed him. When they were several yards out, he noticed Kit had stopped. He saw Kit looking back toward the campsite, seemingly confused why no one was following them. Hyroc moved over to him. "They're not coming with us."

Kit gazed up at him with a look that seemed to say, "Why not? Are you sure this is a good idea?"

"Yes, I'm sure," Hyroc said. "We need to keep moving." He stepped back, and Kit moved closer. Hyroc looked toward his sleeping friends. "Goodbye, everyone," he whispered before turning and continuing on his way.

The two of them moved silently across the plains toward a long dip in the terrain where a stream flowed. He needed to find something before sunrise that would obscure his presence from Elsa, Donovan, and Curtis when they eventually discovered his absence. Hopefully, when they came after him, they wouldn't waste too much time looking for him. He would kick himself if they were too determined to find him, and he ended up putting them in an even worse spot by them searching for him.

A pale glow emanated from the horizon as sunrise neared. Hyroc quickened his pace to reach the dip. If his friends found him, he wasn't fond of the scolding he would receive. They, Elsa especially, would try their hardest to convince him to abandon his search for justice for June. Then, afterward, they wouldn't let him out of their sight, and he wouldn't have another chance to get away from them. If it came to that, they would have lost a day's travel and used up even more of their dwindling supplies to find him. His guilt over that alone could override his determination to carry out his task, and June's death would remain unavenged, potentially forever. He couldn't allow that. He needed to reach that dip!

Chapter 23: Justice

The dip didn't seem to be getting any closer, seemingly for hours, but he eventually reached it just before sunrise. As he suspected, a stream flowed through the hollow. It was deep enough for him to walk upright and remain concealed. He looked back in the direction he had come and used his Flame Claw to cast the spell that removed his trail. When he finished, he followed the stream in an easterly direction. He would move through the hollow for as long as it maintained a useful course or until he was a comfortable distance from his friends. Then he would turn south. He hadn't taken his map with him, but he had memorized a fair portion of the plains on it, and he had a general idea of where everything was. There was a town a couple of days' walk south of him. From the town, he would head toward Forna. Hyroc figured since Keller was directing the hunting parties from Elswood, he would probably come that way while returning to the capital, Roranon. Then from there, well, he wasn't sure. He hadn't thought that far ahead. He would have time to figure it out once he was beyond the reach of his friends. They would know he was gone by now.

As he moved through the depression, the northern side rose up into a steep hill. The stream bent around the flanks of the hill. Beyond the bend, the stream flowed beneath an overhang of ground that had thin roots protruding out of the bottom. Hyroc's head cleared the overhang with barely any room to spare. When he came to the other side of the overhang, he stopped abruptly and grabbed Kit by the collar when he saw the shadow of a bird passing overhead. Kit let out a surprised yowl when he was pulled back. Hyroc crouched to get a better look at the thing in the sky. The bird had the wing profile of a raven, and he assumed it was Shimmer. His friends had sent the black bird to locate him. He was certain Shimmer couldn't see him or Kit beneath the overhang, but neither of them could move out from under it without being seen. They were stuck until the bird left.

As Hyroc sat there anxiously awaiting Shimmer's departure, he noticed the shape of a fish in the stream, hiding in the shadow of the overhang. Hyroc used his Flame Claw to form a barrier around the fish and pin it in place. He dropped down beside the stream as he plunged his knife into the fish. He dismissed the barrier when it stopped wiggling, and he split the fish down the middle before gutting it. He took half for himself and gave the rest to Kit. Shimmer was still circling, so, Hyroc ignited a blue flame in his hand and used it to cook his catch. As he started to eat it after it was cooked, Shimmer moved off. He finished his meal as he continued on his way.

A short way past the overhang, the stream began to deepen and spread out. Soon it filled the entire hollow. When Hyroc thought he heard the churning of a river further downstream, it seemed a good time to abandon the dip. He took a drink of water, then filled his waterskin before moving away from the stream. A flat area of yellow grasses stretched out in front of him. He rushed through the yellow plants as they waved in the breeze. There wasn't anything to take cover beneath that he could see, and he didn't want to linger in case Shimmer returned. His anxiety abated some when close to an hour later, the ground sloped downward at a mild angle. The slope would make it more difficult for anyone pursuing him to see his silhouette against the bright horizon. There still wasn't any cover, but he saw promising shapes ahead of him that might be.

A fuzzy green and white blur ahead of him resolved into a thicket of paper bark birch trees. At that moment, a winged shadow appeared on the ground. Shimmer was back! Hyroc frantically glanced around. To his left, he saw a square opening at the base of a steep rise and rushed into it. A few steps past the entrance, the ground angled downward into a short, darkened cave that came to an abrupt end. Pieces of rotting wood littered the opening, indicating it was a collapsed mine shaft. He stepped into the gloom from which he watched the sky. The dark speck of a raven zipped across the blue sky. Shimmer's course seemed unaltered, which indicated he had not seen Hyroc or Kit. But as with the overhang, he and Kit were again stuck. As they waited, Hyroc's mind wandered.

"I told you it was pointless to fight it," he heard an icy voice whisper in the back of his mind. He remembered the red-eyed bear version of himself the red Spirit Stone had shown him during his training. He could practically see the beast walking out of the darkness to stand in front of him.

"Now you understand," the red-eyed bear said. "The viciousness you faced, that you rejected, does have a place in you after all. It cannot be discarded, no matter how much you desire to do so. You cannot deny that you need me."

"I don't need you," Hyroc said. "I don't need to turn myself into the monster that you became."

"You don't?" the bear scoffed. "You're not traveling to exchange harsh words with Keller or deliver a strongly worded letter rebuking him. You're going to kill him. To snuff his life out."

"Yes. After what he did to June, she deserves justice."

The bear laughed coldly. "Justice? You make it sound so noble. But there's nothing noble about it. You're going to end a life, someone who wronged you. There is nothing more primal than the spilling of blood for revenge."

"She gave me everything that she could, and she deserved better than to be twisted into one of those creatures."

"Nothing else? No other reason?"

"No."

"You won't take any pleasure from it?"

"There's no pleasure to be had, June's gone."

"That man made your life hell. You won't take the opportunity to exact retribution? Make him feel some of what you went through?"

"No."

"And why not? Don't have the stomach for it? Too weak to make those that harmed you pay for what they did?"

"Weakness has nothing to do with it."

"That's not what I see."

"I don't care what you see. You're nothing more than an unfulfilled possibility. A teaching tool."

"Then why do you feel the need to justify yourself?" Hyroc took a breath, unwilling to answer. "Are you unsure of yourself? Don't think you can get the job done?"

"I'm plenty sure of myself."

"Use my savagery to take care of it."

"And why would I do that?"

"Because you know I can do it. No matter how much you try to deny it, I'm the only sure way you know you'll avenge your precious aunt. All that is required is for you to let go of those misguided ideals holding you back."

"No."

The bear sighed. "Your choice, but do you want to risk our aunt's killer escaping the fate he so rightly deserves?"

"I already finished your test. You have no control over me."

"Do you really believe that?"

Hyroc picked up a rock from the floor of the mine shaft and threw it at the bear. The creature vanished.

"You're nothing without me," the bear's voice whispered. "You'll need me when the time comes."

Hyroc stuck his head outside the mine shaft and swept his eyes across the sky. Shimmer was gone. His friends should abandon their search when Shimmer reported nothing for a second time. He made his way toward the birch thicket. It was a relief to be underneath the mottled shade once again. Off the open ground of the plains, he didn't have to worry about anyone spotting him from a distance. From what he saw of the thicket on his way to it, it didn't seem very wide, and he would probably be through it by the day's end.

As he moved through the trees, some of his anger departed. But instead of vanishing, that part seemed to turn into a feeling of guilt. That feeling made him think about the friends he had just abandoned. They would be concerned something had happened to him. Their anxiety would then be further heightened when Shimmer returned with nothing to share. Would they try searching for him themselves, or would they move on to the town without him? If they came looking

Chapter 23: Justice

for him, how long would they search? Would it be a day, or would they try until they ran out of food? He shook his head and forced the thoughts from his mind. They were smart. They would make a good decision.

Hyroc stopped midstep when he noticed Kit tense up. When he followed the big cat's gaze, he saw a squirrel flattened against a tree trunk. Instinctively, he silently nocked an arrow and let it fly. It struck the squirrel in the head. After retrieving the carcass and gutting it, he gathered some branches into a small pile and used his Flame Claw to ignite it. When the fire turned from blue to the normal orange, he put the squirrel on a spit and started cooking it. Using his Flame Claw to cook the squirrel would have been faster, but he wanted to give his feet a longer break. He divided the squirrel between him and Kit. The animal didn't provide much of a meal, only enough meat to stave off the hunger pangs for a few hours. When he was ready to move on, he stamped out the fire and scattered what remained.

The feeling of guilt returned. Instead of it causing him to think about his friends, he started thinking about what he was doing. He was going to kill Keller to get justice for June. That man did something terrible to his aunt and deserved to die for it. But what would change if that man was dead? He and his friends would still be pursued by The Ministry. The four of them were temporarily free from attack, but their enemies were still on the way. That fact would remain whether Kelly was dead or alive. The man was responsible for what he turned June into, but how many people were involved with that. Keller certainly had subordinates he entrusted with the details of his secret activities, and most of them probably participated directly in what he was doing. If they did, they were just as responsible for June as Keller. Should he kill them too? If he wished justice fulfilled for June, did he need to kill them as well? How many of them needed to die?

He felt a growing sense of unease toward his thoughts. If those people's actions truly made them guilty, what was wrong with ending them? Killing them would save that many more people from being twisted into a shadow demon. But how many was that, ten, twenty, a hundred? Destroying that many people felt wrong. He couldn't remember how many soldiers he and his friends had killed, but he killed quite a few of them. The shadow demons he felt no remorse for dispatching. If anything, he did those people a favor, but he felt some remorse for all the others he had killed. Though he felt some sadness, what he had done to them didn't feel incorrect. Why did it feel so different between killing the soldiers and deciding to kill Keller's henchmen for justice? He was ending lives in either case.

"...Because they had to," a voice said that Hyroc had almost forgotten. It belonged to Marcus. It was a memory from when Hyroc was a small child. Marcus was trying to teach him about the uprising that led to the overthrow of Feygrotha.

"But you told me killing is wrong," Hyroc had said innocently when his innocence was allowed to exist.

"Killing *is* wrong," Marcus had said. "But sometimes people have to. Sometimes when people want to take someone else's stuff, they don't only take their stuff. A lot of times, they're mean to the people they're taking from, and they hurt those people real bad, and sometimes they die. And the people that do this don't care what someone says to them while they're being bad. When they choose to be bad, sometimes the only way to make them stop is for people to be mean right back to them. Sometimes when they're being mean, the bad people get hurt and die."

"And that makes it okay?" Hyroc had said.

"No. When someone kills the bad people, they feel sad."

"Why do they feel sad? Didn't they do the right thing?"

"Yes, they did the right thing. They feel sad because it doesn't feel good for them to take a life."

"Then why do they do it?"

"Because they have to. They don't have any other choice if they want to keep the people they care about alive."

Hyroc focused on his surroundings. Killing those soldiers didn't feel wrong because he was protecting his family. He felt bad for killing them, as he had for Einar, but he had to do it. Going off and killing

Chapter 23: Justice

Keller's henchmen felt wrong because he didn't have to do it. A wave of guilt washed over him. Was he going after Keller to get justice, or was he after revenge and making himself feel better? What would Marcus think of him now? Would he be disappointed? Hyroc thought everything he was doing would be an affront to Marcus. The man had spent what little time they had together teaching him how to make the right choices, and here he was doing everything wrong. But he was getting justice for June. Shouldn't that mean something? He was so confused. The angry burning determination that had sustained his reasoning, and given him clarity of thought, had vanished. Everything he was doing seemed a terrible mistake.

Hyroc lifted his eyes to the sky. "I don't know what to do," he called out. "Marcus, tell me what to do. Please tell me what to do."

"You know what to do," he thought Marcus would say. He lowered his gaze and tricked himself into imagining the man emerging from behind one of the trees.

"No, I don't," Hyroc said. "Everything that seemed so clear to me this morning feels so wrong. Please tell me what to do."

Marcus shook his head. "You know I cannot. That decision lies only with you. What you do that is right or wrong is for you to decide."

"But I don't know which of those I'm choosing. Keller turned June, your sister, into a Hand of Death, and she's dead now. He killed her, and she deserves justice."

"Are you sure it's justice you seek, or is it revenge? The two can often appear unified but are separate in purpose. Justice is correcting a wrong, whilst revenge is a perceived wrong. Revenge frequently leads to the loss of more than one life through its fulfillment. When it's accomplished, the destruction may stretch far beyond the life that was lost. Those that pursue revenge can lose much that will never be recovered."

Hyroc pondered a moment. He mouthed the words, "lose much that will never be recovered." Could that be his friends? He had wondered if he would ever see them again. He shook his head and cursed. What a fool he had been! They were his family, the last remaining shred he had of one, and he had abandoned them. What stupidity had consumed him to forget that?

Something moved on the ground in front of him. He focused but didn't see anything. What had caught his attention? The ground moved again. That's when he noticed a shadow. It seemed to be some kind of bird, but the size and shape seemed incorrect. Hyroc glanced over to see Kit staring up into the branches of the trees. He followed the big cat's gaze to locate the bird. What he saw sent a bolt of fear through him. It was some kind of white and brown owl, but he judged the bird to be wider than him and at least as tall. The enormous owl flapped its wings and flew toward him. Hyroc shied into a crouch as the bird circled him once, then it landed beside him.

He reached for his sword but stopped himself when he noticed something familiar about the owl. It had a large blue swirly marking on each of its wings and a circle of silver adorned with the same shapes around each of its ankles. From its neck hung a chain of gold which ended with a ruby. The last time he had seen an animal adored this way was on his mentor, the white bear named Ursa. He had just met a Guardian.

"Greetings," the owl said conversationally in a male voice. Kit roared in alarm, seeming unsure how to react to a bird much bigger than himself. The owl extended a wing toward the mountain lion. "Peace, friend. You are safe." Kit relaxed and sauntered over to Hyroc, never taking his eyes off the owl. The bird returned his attention back to Hyroc. "Curious to find a Wol'dger in these lands. Why —" the owl trailed off. He cocked his head as if noticing something new about Hyroc. "You're no ordinary Wol'dger, are you?" The owl pushed its wings back and bowed graciously. "Hail, Anamagi."

Hyroc bowed in return. "Hail, Guardian," he said.

The owl returned to its previous position. "My name is Hoelam."

Hyroc stood straight before answering. "Nice to meet you, Hoelam. My name is Hyroc."

"It's nice to meet you, Hyroc." Hoelam used his wing to indicate Kit. "What is the name of your feline companion?"

Chapter 23: Justice

"Kit."

Hoelam gave Kit the same greeting. "What brings an esteemed descendent to such a hostile place for one with your appearance?"

"It's a long story," Hyroc said.

"That's a story I would very much be interested in learning, no matter the length."

"I don't know if I have it in me to tell you."

"Ah. It's an unpleasant one, I suspect."

"Among other things," Hyroc whispered under his breath.

"Would you wish to talk about it? Sometimes telling another can lift the burden of the knowledge you carry."

"Please don't take offense to this, but I don't know if even you, a Guardian, can help me."

"Let me try."

Hoelam's wings glowed blue. He extended one wing and made a circling motion toward it with his other. Wispy trails of mist drifted in from all directions. The mist collected into a small sphere of rippling water in front of Hoelam. Next, the water appeared to bubble as if it were boiling in midair. A stream of leaves shot toward the bubbling water. The leaves intertwined themselves around the water and formed what appeared to be a cup. Hoelam lowered his wing making the circular motions and turned toward Hyroc. The leaf cup followed in front of his extended wing, then floated over to Hyroc.

Hyroc shook out of his awe before reaching up to grab the cup. Cautiously, Hyroc lifted the leaf cup to his lips and took a tentative sip. The hot water was mildly sweet with refreshing floral notes.

"Good?" Hoelam asked.

Hyroc nodded. "Very."

"I find having something hot to drink encourages conversation. So, what is it you don't know that I can help you with?"

Hyroc briefly explained what had happened to him and his friends since escaping from Elswood, leaving out as much detail as possible without it ceasing to make sense.

"...Then, I decided I would hunt down Keller myself."

"That's quite an ordeal you and your friends have gone through. It seems a miracle that any of you are still alive."

"Sometimes, I'm even surprised we made it."

"So, it is the four of you I have to thank for dispatching the human shadow wraiths." Kit growled. "My apologies," Hoelam said to the big cat. "The five of you. I have no doubt you fought them."

Hyroc nodded before taking a sip from his cup. "Yes. I know you're supposed to burn the bodies of those creatures, but my friends and I didn't have time to do that. I hope that didn't cause any problems."

"Containing the corruption from the shadow demon essence was relatively little trouble. You and your friends did most of the work and saved me from having to eliminate the creatures myself. I merely cleaned up the mess."

Hyroc nodded. He was quite a moment before talking. "While we're speaking of those creatures. When I was fighting them, I encountered a group that was able to fight against my Flame Claw."

Hoelam seemed to become more interested. "Fight, you say?"

"Yes. One of them made a hole in a wall of fire I created. Another even tossed a fireball back at me."

"An unexpected occurrence, I would say," Hoelam said.

"You're telling me," Hyroc agreed. "If not for my friend Curtis unleashing a lightning bolt, I would have been burnt to a crisp by one of those demons." He felt a stab of sadness at the thought of his younger friend. He pushed it away. "From what my Guardian mentor, Ursa, had taught me, I thought those things couldn't do that to Guardian magic. And since my Flame Claw is similar to your type of magic, why were they able to manipulate it the way they did?"

"As you stated, our Guardian magic, as you call it, is not the same as Flame Claw magic. This difference is what allowed them to nullify your advantage. Though, you may have noticed they were unable to re-create the abilities of your Flame Claw. They were merely able to redirect your spells."

Chapter 23: Justice

"So, they could only use what I created but couldn't use Flame Claw magic to make anything of their own?" Hyroc asked.

"Precisely. When you first encountered the creatures you referred to as The Hand of Death," Hoelam stated. "They made no attempt to manipulate the attacks you made against them using your Flame Claw." Hyroc nodded. "They are vulnerable to magical energy, much more than to blades and other such weapons, as I'm sure you discovered. Most demon breeds have a different strategy for attempting to mitigate this vulnerability. Many have their own unique way of defending themselves or attacking. Since these Hand of Death are created by infusing a human with shadow essence, the creature is limited to the knowledge of the original host, including what they knew about magic."

"And because those people were clueless about magic," Hyroc added. "The Death Hands had no idea how to use magic."

The owl nodded. "Yes. They were ignorant of magic and had to learn from the very bottom the basics of that power. This resulted in the first few you killed being caught completely off guard by your abilities. But those that remained had the untapped ability to use magic, and once they learned this fact, they were able to rapidly learn how to utilize it against you. The more they encountered the remains of the creatures you had killed using your Flame Claw, the faster they learned. But beyond the deadly power installed in their enlarged hand, these particular creatures could not use magic. They could merely defend themselves against your attacks and turn them against you when they learned how."

Hyroc nodded and took a sip. "That explains what one of them meant by they had, "…learned from the deaths of their brethren.""

"Indeed," Hoelam agreed.

"I assume not all regular shadow demons are able to defend themselves against magic? I only ask because when I fought a Shade Hunter, it didn't seem to know how to react to my Flame Claw. Until I decapitated it, that is."

"You are correct. Some shadow entities, such as Shade Hunters, are closer to the intelligence of an animal and are simply incapable of defending themselves in any notable way against your Flame Claw or any other school of magic."

"Can most other shadow demons attack with magic?"

"They can. It mainly depends on what type of shadow entity you are dealing with, but most others can use magic."

"What about Guardian magic? Can they do to you what they did against my Flame Claw?"

"No. Our form of magic is repulsed by the shadow Quintessence within their forms. Guardian magic quite literally fights back when shadow demon entities try to use it, and it will harm them. Your Flame Claw does not react to them so detrimentally, but it is, however, highly resistant to their manipulation. It is more taxing for them to use abilities derived from your Flame Claw than when they use other types of magic, limiting their use of it, and in many cases, it simply is not worth the effort for them to try. It is far easier for them to turn what you create against you instead of making it for themselves."

"That's good to know. What prevents them from tracking my Flame Claw? That way, I'm prepared when and if I encounter one of them or run into someone who is able to counteract that ability."

"That seems to be the prudent decision. Because of the vulnerability shadow entities have to magic, many have developed a heightened sense for large concentrations of Quintessence indicative of the presence of a mage. But the nature of Guardian magic and your Flame Claw behaves as a sort of masking scent and covers both types of magic in a sort of camouflage the demons cannot penetrate."

"Like stalking an animal from downwind," Hyroc added.

"A fair comparison."

"Does that mean most shadow demons can also track the trails of magic that are left behind by someone who can use non-Flame Claw magic?"

"No. Though most can detect the presence of a magic user, only a small number can track those trails of magic. Those trails contain too little residual Quintessence for nearly all shadow entities to pick up on."

Chapter 23: Justice

"I don't know if that will ever be useful, but thank you."

"I'm glad to have been of assistance."

"It's been a while since I've been able to ask those kinds of questions. It saddens me to know there are so many ways for magic to help people, and The Ministry won't allow it to be used."

"A sentiment we Guardians share. Objects those within The Ministry consider as pure of witchcraft and darkness are created using magic, that which they consider as evil."

"Is this one of them?" Hyroc reached into his pocket and retrieved the Perception Orb.

"Indeed it is."

Hyroc stuck it back in his pocket.

"But there's something I don't understand about your story with your friends," Hoelam said. "If you care for your friends so much, why did you leave them? And at such a crucial point in your journey."

Hyroc sighed and took another sip before answering. "I don't quite know that myself. It seemed so important that I go after Keller."

"How do you feel about it now?"

"I don't know. Part of me seems to be saying that I should turn back, but how can I abandon my duty to June, my duty to get justice for her."

"That seems a serious dilemma. But let me ask you this; would you sacrifice your friends for your pursuit of justice?"

Hyroc gave him a confused look. "Sacrifice? What do you mean?"

"Exactly as I said it. How important is it for you to obtain justice? Would you leave your friends to be hurt if it meant avenging your aunt? Or for them to be killed?"

That seemed an odd question to ask, but at the same time, he had never considered weighing those options. He definitely wouldn't leave them to be killed. Otherwise, he obviously wouldn't have stuck with them during their flight from The Ministry. His friends were fully capable of getting along without him. They would be fine. The Ministry had no idea where any of them had gone. No one would

OUTCASTS

be coming after them for a while. And word of them couldn't have reached the nearby towns. But what if he was wrong? He pushed the thought aside. He wasn't wrong. No one knew to be looking for them here.

"I wouldn't," Hyroc said.

"How do you know you haven't?"

"I spent a lot of time thinking about it. The four of us had to have reached the plains far ahead of any courier that would have spread word about us, even on horseback. It'll be a while before they have to worry about that, and they'll be long gone before then. They're smart and resourceful, so there's no reason for me to be worried about them. They'll be fine."

"You are confident in their abilities?"

Hyroc nodded. "Yes."

"And have you taken into consideration that these lands are foreign to them?"

Hyroc paused. He hadn't actually thought about that. He was only slightly more familiar with the plains than Elsa, Donovan, and certainly Curtis. They were used to the low visibility of the woods and the ability to disappear from view when they wished to go unnoticed. Neither of those applied to the open plains. Anyone out here could be seen coming for miles, and there was rarely anything to provide cover. But his friends were capable of quickly adapting to new environments. The changes out here compared to the forest were relatively few in number, and it wouldn't take long to get used to. They didn't need him to hold their hands through the whole process. Besides, he had left them a map. They knew where to go.

"They're more skilled at hunting than I am. They'll get used to it out here. And I left them a map."

"A map is a useful aid when deciding where to travel, but navigating over a vast distance is much different than navigating trapping trails."

Hyroc shook his head dismissively. "I know they can figure it out. They'll be fine without me."

Chapter 23: Justice

"You cannot know that for a certainty," Hoelam said sternly. "Your confidence may be misplaced. How do you know they won't encounter more Death Hands?"

Hyroc felt concerned from the question. Keller couldn't have that many Death Hands. If he wished for his dabbling with dark magic to go unnoticed by the rest of The Ministry, he could only impart a small group with that knowledge for fear of being found out.

"We killed quite a few of those creatures when we escaped from Elswood. There's no way he has very many of them left. And there's no way he would have sent any here before he knew where I was." Hoelam peered at him without speaking. Hyroc's heart sank. "He can't, can he?"

"Perhaps. Perhaps not."

"Wait, you're a Guardian. You would know that."

"You overestimate my abilities sensing such creatures. I can sense them from a great distance, but not nearly as far as you seem to think. And the issue is compounded by the fact that we are several days from the nearest dwelling."

Well, even if there are Death Hands waiting in the town my friends are headed toward, the three of them have killed Death Hands before. There shouldn't be more than one or two of those creatures in the town. My friends can handle that?"

"And what if it escapes?"

Hyroc paused, taken aback by the question. "It'll bring back reinforcements."

"The reinforcements would far outnumber your friends. And what will happen if they encounter one of those creatures in the midst of the town?"

The thought sent a spike of ice down Hyroc's back. "There would be no escape."

"Your friends would surely perish."

"But that's unlikely."

"I do not know."

—241—

"Wait, you could just fly near the town. If you sense any of those creatures, you can warn my friends."

"To what end? Your friends are nearly out of food. Even after receiving my warning, they cannot bypass the town without more provisions, and they may not make it to the next one. They would be forced to leave their youngest sibling outside the town. Any Death Hands in the vicinity would be drawn to him. Without the protection of his brother and sister, his chances of survival are slim."

"And I'm the one responsible for their dilemma," Hyroc said gloomily.

"Correct. You must decide which is more important, the lives of your friends or justice for your aunt. You cannot accomplish one task without failing the other."

"But how can I abandon avenging my aunt. She was kind, goodhearted, and loving. She looked after me when Marcus, my adopted father, had passed, and she made me feel as if I were her own son. After everything she did for me, doesn't she deserve justice?"

"There is no easy answer, but if you continue on your current path, you may very well lose something irreplaceable that you have at this moment. You'll never forget what you did. What is more important?"

Hyroc stared at the ground, deep in thought. Was the safety of his friends more important than avenging his aunt? If anything happened to Elsa, Donovan, and Curtis, he didn't know what he would do. Besides Kit, the three of them were the only ones left that he cared about. But he had a duty to June. She had been threatened, tortured, twisted into a monster, and forced to hunt him against her will. How could he abandon avenging her when something so horrible had been done to her? Then a thought occurred to him. Is that what June would want him to do. Would she want him to give up on her or his friends? The answer was obvious. She would want him with his friends. He could almost hear her say, "It's okay, they need you. I once told you, 'never turn back.' Forget about me, and keep your promise. Go with them." Hyroc felt a tear run down his face. He wiped it away.

Chapter 23: Justice

"Have you come to a decision?" Hoelam said.

Hyroc nodded. "Yes. I need to go back to my friends."

"A good decision."

Hyroc had a sinking feeling. When he looked toward the horizon, he saw the sun nearing it. The day was practically over. "Oh no. It's almost dusk. It will take me almost a full day just to get back to where I left. That'll probably put me at least two days behind them. There's no way I can get to them before they reach the town."

"I believe I can assist with that," Hoelam said.

"Really?" Hyroc said. "What are –" he cut off abruptly when enormous wings enveloped him, and everything went black.

Chapter 24
Grieving

Hyroc awoke to Kit nudging him with his head. When he opened his eyes, he was lying on his back, staring up into the sunlit blue sky of late morning. The last thing he remembered was the owl, Guardian, Hoelam surrounding him with his wings. From the lack of leaves overhead, he assumed he wasn't in the thicket anymore. Ursa had used a similar trick on him at the end of his training to master his bear form. He had gone to sleep on the eve of his final task, and when he awoke, he was several days' walk from where he had been that night. What was it about Guardians that made them do those things? Did it fit into some logic beyond his comprehension, or did they simply enjoy playing tricks on him?

He sat up to find himself back on the plains in a low spot amid a growth of thistle bushes. He was grateful Hoelam had the foresight to place him and Kit somewhere that anyone in the vicinity would have a hard time spotting them.

His thoughts turned to his friends that he had selfishly left behind. What was he thinking, wandering off at probably the worst time he could have chosen on the half-baked idea that he would get justice for June? At any given moment, Keller would have multiple Hand of Death guarding him and who knows how many soldiers. Even with the advantage of his Flame Claw, he wouldn't even come close to getting

Chapter 24: Grieving

to Keller before he was killed. Did he think that's what June would have wanted? No, she would have wanted him to live. That was the whole point of the promise she made him make to her. A sudden wave of sadness washed over him. He felt himself starting to tear up, but he pushed the feeling away. Now was not the time for grieving. Right now, he needed to focus on his friends.

His friends were in danger because of his careless actions. He needed to find them before they got to the town. A stab of anxiety struck him. Elsa and Donovan would be furious with him. He had put their lives and the life of Curtis in danger because he thought revenge was more important than them. It was such an idiotic thought it amazed him that it had even entered his brain. They were his family! His life would be incredibly lonely without them. He had to do whatever it took to keep them safe. They deserved no less.

He took a swig of water from his waterskin and gave Kit a drink before getting to his feet and moving out of the low spot. When he came to the rim, he heard the distant braying of a donkey. When he looked toward the sound, he saw three people leading a pack-laden donkey down a dirt path. He realized he was looking at his friends. Further ahead of them, he saw the structures of the town. They were almost there!

Hyroc pulled his hood over his head to hide his ears. As long as he kept them covered, from a distance, he would appear to be a normal traveler. He broke into the fastest run he could manage. It didn't take him long to reach them; in fact, it surprised him how fast he seemed to move. His friends spotted him long before he arrived and stopped walking. He got a start when he saw Donovan pull out his bow and level an arrow at him. Immediately he slowed his pace so fast that he nearly tripped, threw his hands up, and moved sideways to make himself harder to hit.

"Don't shoot, don't shoot!" Hyroc yelled.

Donovan and Elsa exchanged a confused look before Donovan lowered his bow. "Hyroc?" Elsa called out.

-245-

"Yes, it's me." He pushed his hood back just long enough for them to see the profile of his head before covering it again. "Don't shoot." As he spoke the last part, he wondered if he had actually given them more incentive to shoot him because they had to be angry with him. He wouldn't blame them if they did.

Donovan waved him over. He was nearly to them when he saw Elsa storming toward him. He steeled himself for what she was about to do to him. *Let's get this over with,* he thought unenthusiastically.

"Elsa, I'm –" Hyroc started to say when a hard slap from Elsa interrupted him. She struck him again. He felt a bead of blood on his nose, but he made no attempt to defend himself, knowing he deserved every strike. She raised her hand a third time, but she unexpectedly threw her arms around him. He felt his eyes tearing up.

"I'm so sorry I left," Hyroc said.

Elsa pulled away from him. When he saw a sorrowful, sympathetic look in her eyes, it was as if a dam broke inside of him, releasing a torrent of emotions he had refused to feel from the night June died.

"He – he turned her into a monster," Hyroc choked out amid his grief as tears flowed from his eyes. "And I – and I – killed her. I had to. She asked me to do it."

"I know," Elsa said, struggling to maintain her composure with misty eyes. "I knew you were in pain. We all did. You had been forced to do something terrible."

"I was so angry. I wanted – I wanted *him* to pay for what he did. I wanted to get justice for her. She – she was – she was like a mother to me. I wasn't her –blood, but – but it didn't matter to her. She got me through so many hard things after – after Marcus – after Marcus died. I couldn't let it go!"

"I know, I know."

"I know you couldn't," Donovan said. He used his hand to indicate he, Elsa, and Curtis. "After our parents and grandfather were killed by the spiders, I was angry. I wanted someone to pay for what happened. I didn't want their deaths to be nothing more than a tragic accident, a cruel trick played by fate. So, I understand how you felt."

Chapter 24: Grieving

"What got you past it?" Hyroc asked desperately.

"Knowing it wasn't my fault. Knowing there was nothing I could have done." He took a deep breath. "I actually blamed you for a while."

Hyroc gave him a shocked look. "You never told me that."

Donovan nodded. "Yeah. I thought it was your fault our parents hadn't made it. I thought you were too slow, you made a mistake, you were incompetent in your rescue attempt, or you didn't care about them enough."

"I did the best I could," Hyroc said.

"I know – I know," Donovan said. "I know you gave nothing but your best. I came to understand that there was no better way for you to do what you did. I understood that you were fortunate to get any of us out of that terrible place. Most wouldn't have even tried. It must've taken an enormous amount of courage for you to even attempt what you did, and you nearly lost your own life in the process. How could I blame someone so selfless? I am honored to have such a friend. Without you, the three of us would be long dead. Thank you."

"You managed to get over your anger," Hyroc said. "But how am I supposed to get rid of mine? Keller did something unspeakable to June. She was an innocent victim. How can I simply let go of my pursuit of the justice she rightly deserves?"

"Hyroc, your aunt died long before that night," Elsa said. Hyroc shot her a baffled look. "What you killed that night was a shadow of her, nothing more. She died the moment Keller turned her into that thing."

Part of Hyroc didn't want to believe Elsa, but the other part of him knew, for all intents and purposes, that what she said was true. June stopped being his aunt when Keller turned her into that creature. Killing her in that twisted form was no different than slaying a wounded animal to end its suffering. What he killed was merely an echo of someone he had once known. It was a remnant that didn't want to harm him. That was something June would have done, but it wasn't her. She was gone long before he had even left Elswood.

"I now know that," Hyroc said solemnly. "The three of you are my family. I couldn't see that before. All the anger and hate blinded me to the truth. I should have remained with the ones I cared the most about. I hope the three of you can forgive me for my selfishness when I put my desire for revenge above all of you."

"There's nothing to forgive," Elsa said. "You came back."

"You came back," Donovan repeated.

"You came back," Curtis repeated next.

"I'll never leave again," Hyroc promised. His friends nodded thankfully. "I need to do something."

He gathered stones from the edges of the road into a small pile beside the path. Next, he anchored a stick in the rocks and collected a spare strip of leather from the donkey. He used his knife to cut a slit in one end, then used his Flame Claw to burn into it the name June Burk before hanging it on the stick. This would serve as her final resting place.

Hyroc dropped down to one knee before speaking, "goodbye, June. I'll miss you. Thank you for every kind thing you did for me. Rest peacefully."

It felt as if a huge weight had been lifted from his shoulders. His anger dissipated, and all thoughts of June's unimaginable fate, and his desire for revenge, faded away. He only remembered the understanding and caring person he had reluctantly departed from in Forna. After standing, he returned to his friends, who waited respectfully by the donkey to give him space to say goodbye. He was ready to focus only on what was important.

"Ready?" Elsa asked reverently.

Hyroc nodded.

"Do you still know the plan?" Donovan said.

"Curtis and I will wait outside the town while the two of you go in and get provisions," Hyroc said.

"Yes," Donovan agreed. He pulled out the map and pointed to a forested area north of the town, above where the road split into a fork. Wait for us somewhere in this area. You'll have cover in the trees, so it

Chapter 24: Grieving

shouldn't be a problem for the two of you to stay hidden. Once we get what we need, we'll send Shimmer out to find you. Got it?"

"Got it," Hyroc said.

Donovan opened a small saddlebag on the donkey and indicated for Hyroc to come closer. When Hyroc did, Donovan transferred a small portion of food into his knapsack before continuing to speak. "That's what's left of our food. It's not much, but it should hold both of you over till we get back."

"Alright. Your brother's safe with me. Oh, one more thing. Be careful while you're in town. We don't know for certain if word of us has not reached this part of the plains yet. There might be bounty posters with our faces on them or our descriptions."

"Let's hope not," Elsa said. "It'll be a really short trip if anyone recognizes us, and we'll have to figure something else out. We can't go anywhere else without food."

"If we survive our mistake," Donovan noted darkly.

Elsa shook her head in mild annoyance. "I think that's a given."

"Send Shimmer if you two run into any trouble," Hyroc suggested.

"We will," Donovan said. "But you might be too far away to help us if things go bad."

"Then let's just try to avoid getting into any trouble."

"Well, at the first sign of danger, get out," Hyroc said. "I don't want to lose either of you, especially right after I came to my senses."

"We'll be careful."

Hyroc nodded. "Okay, see you in a couple of days." The four of them exchanged a round of hugs. "Come on, Curtis."

Chapter 25
Sheep in Wolf's Clothing

Elsa and Donovan approached the main gate of the town. It was apparently named Windfell, and the only thing that made sense to Donovan was maybe this area had strong winds sometimes. A wall of dark stone surrounded the town. He had heard of places with stone walls, but he had never imagined anything close to this. The imposing fortification gave the town somewhat of a daunting appearance. Three guards stood off to one side, talking, with the downward pointed ends of a raised portcullis protruding from the top of the gate.

Two citizens pulling a cart passed him and Elsa but paid them no heed. That seemed a good sign to Donovan because such aloof behavior indicated that no one was concerned about finding them, and word from The Ministry hadn't reached here yet. Hyroc's theory seemed correct so far, but two farmers ignoring them was hardly a sign they were safe. The real test would come from the guards. They would be the ones charged with watching for them. Their plan to get food might end right here.

Donovan glanced up to ensure Shimmer was there. He saw the raven circling above them. That bird was the only way for them to signal for Hyroc's help. The only problem with that precaution was neither he nor his sister knew how long it would take their powerful

Chapter 25: Sheep in Wolf's Clothing

friend to reach them. They may be on their own for hours before he could assist them. There was only one way to find out.

He and his sister turned so their faces weren't straight on to the guards, but not so much as to risk drawing attention to themselves. Two of the guards paused in their conversation to look at them. After a tense moment, the two guards resumed talking. Donovan breathed a silent sigh of relief.

Beyond the gate, the town opened up to a sprawl of buildings that spread out around them. Just from what he could see down the street in front of them, Windfell dwarfed Elswood. His father had taken him and his sister to the town of Flatwood from time to time to trade furs, and that town had seemed huge, but this one made even that appear small. The sight of so many bodies bustling about and the intrusive sound of so much activity was almost overwhelming. He forced himself to start walking to snap himself out of his stupor. The two of them didn't have time for dallying. Their safety in going unnoticed could disappear any day now.

"We need to focus on getting food," Elsa said. "Things that'll last for a while because we don't know how long we'll be traveling."

Donovan nodded. "I know," he said. "There's something I wanted to check first." He wouldn't feel safe in the town until he did.

He wound his way through the town until he found what he was looking for. After sweeping his eyes from side to side to make sure no one was showing an unusual amount of interest in them, he moved over to a wooden billboard covered in pieces of parchment. Most of the parchment ranged from messages describing the dangers of the surrounding area to shopkeepers requesting services. One section, however, was full of bounties that offered rewards for capturing or killing people. Several had rough drawings of the individuals in question. He was relieved when he saw no pictures of him, Elsa, or Curtis on display. There was, however, one bounty that caught his attention. It had a drawing of a savage-looking, snouted, and snarling creature. Above it read the name, "High Wrasse."

"High Wrasse?" Donovan questioned while quietly snickering. "They didn't even get his name right."

Elsa covered her mouth with her hand to keep herself from laughing aloud. "Look at this here," she said, pointing at the message written below the drawing of Hyroc.

"High Wrasse, extremely dangerous witch half-breed. It is believed to have once been a farmer's goat that a witch twisted into human form. The creature has been reported to stand seven feet tall. Its hands and feet are covered in large, tearing claws. It has razor-sharp teeth and jaws powerful enough to crush a horse's skull. It has powerful abilities derived from witchcraft. Some have reported it throwing bolts of shadow that can kill with the slightest touch, and others indicate it can suck the life from a grown man, leaving only an empty husk behind. Use extreme caution when approaching this creature, and do not attempt killing it alone. Report any sightings immediately to The Ministry."

"That's not even close!" Donovan quietly chortled as tears welled up in his eyes from him containing his laughter.

"I know," Elsa agreed, also trying not to laugh. "Seven feet tall? Were they drunk?"

"What about them saying he's a goat?"

"I like the part about him sucking people's life out." They suddenly turned and feigned showing serious interest in the billboard when two men passed close by. When the men had gone, they resumed talking.

"Oh, wait till Hyroc hears this," Donovan said. He wiped his eyes on his sleeve. "I think he'll get a kick out of it. This trip was worth it just for that."

"Okay, we've had our fun," Elsa said as she regained her composure. "Now, let's get out of here and get what we need as soon as possible. I don't want to spend a minute longer here than we have to."

The two of them led their donkey away from the billboard. They navigated the maze of streets and found their way to a butcher. They bought several strips of dried meat and arranged a later pickup of the good before heading out. Next, they found a baker which they bought some bread from. After that, they bought a variety of foodstuffs from several more shops, followed by one where they purchased a hefty

Chapter 25: Sheep in Wolf's Clothing

supply of cold flour. The tasteless flour simply required water to turn it into a barely palpable gruel. As unappealing as it was to eat, the food would keep for much longer than anything else they purchased, and it seemed a necessary precaution.

"The sight of this isn't going to make Hyroc very happy," Donovan said, peering over at the bag of cold flour.

"Well, considering the weight of this, we're actually getting quite a bit of food out of it," Elsa said. "And since we don't know exactly where we're going or how long it will take to get there, it's a reliable food supply."

"Unless the taste kills him first," Donovan joked.

Elsa rolled her eyes. "We can always throw berries into it or anything else edible we find to make it have somewhat of a taste. Besides, he's eaten it before. And after he told us that Ursa made him eat raw meat and fish, not to mention all the other things I don't know I could've stomached, I'm sure he won't mind."

The heads of a few nearby people snapped toward her. They stared at her and Donovan with disturbed faces. Donovan promptly put an arm around Elsa's shoulder and turned her away from the onlookers before leading her and the donkey away.

"Could you have said that any louder?" Donovan whispered.

Elsa wore a mortified look on her face. "Sorry, I got carried away," she admitted sheepishly.

"And here I thought I was the brash one. Did you forget people don't usually eat raw meat unless there's something wrong with them? I'd rather not get our heads chopped off today."

"Alright, I think our supplies are restocked," Elsa said. "All we have to do is pick everything up, and we can get out of here."

Donovan was about to agree with her when something caught his attention. It was a shop ahead of them, but it was more vibrant and welcoming than those around it. Above, in golden emblazed letters, read the name, "Thornythistle's, Exotic Emporium." The name struck an idea in him. If the shopkeeper had gathered their wares from outside of Arnaira, they might have a map that showed what lay beyond its borders. Hyroc's map had been an invaluable tool thus far, but beyond how to get out of Arnaira, it gave no indication of what terrain lay outside the country's borders. For all they knew, they could choose a course that seemed to make perfect sense for crossing the border into Mastgar, only for them to encounter an impassable cliff that forced them to backtrack. Wasting time on an improper course was dangerous because, at any moment, The Ministry could know they were here and come after them.

"Hold on," Donovan said. "I want to look at something first." He moved to the shop. "I'm going to have a look inside," he said, handing the reins of the donkey to Elsa. "I'll be quick. Yell if anyone starts giving you any trouble."

When he came through the shop's door, he was greeted by a man his height with black hair and a medium-length beard, and he wore a rust-colored robe with long sleeves, gray trousers, and black boots. The man had tan skin, and his unfamiliar facial features marked him as a foreigner.

"Hello, my good sir," the man said happily in a thick accent.

Donovan nodded a greeting as he glanced through the shop's wares. He saw on a display rack numerous blades in a style he didn't recognize. Then, spread throughout the shop were exotic jewelry, fabrics, rugs, spices, trinkets, and much more.

The man paused, taking notice of Donovan's hunting gear and semi-homemade clothing. "Ah, a hunter, I see," he said excitedly. "I have an array of fine traps, bows, arrows, and other hunting tools that might interest you." He used his hand to indicate a corner of the shop with a display full of unusual but dangerous-looking hunting knives. At any other time, Donovan would definitely have investigated what he saw, but the tools were of little concern.

"Thank you, but no," Donovan said. "Do you have any maps?"

The man seemed somewhat puzzled by his request. "Why yes," he answered. "I have a fine assortment of the best hunting and trapping grounds in the area."

"I'm looking for a map that shows what's to the west. In Mastgar."

Chapter 25: Sheep in Wolf's Clothing

The man gave an even more puzzled look. He seemed confused why someone here would be interested in Mastgar. It seemed to suggest that everyone's mentality within the country was everything outside of it was dangerous and evil. Donovan desperately hoped that Ministry dogma was responsible for such views and that it wasn't true. Their whole plan would be an incredible mistake if it was. But, as Hyroc had suggested, most ideas the Ministry had about what it portrayed as evil were false. Hyroc's use of the Flame Claw would fit into what they considered witchcraft, but beyond its offensive uses, he had used it to heal and frequently used it to help the four of them in more ways than Donovan could count. Then, there was Curtis. His younger brother had never shown any sign of being a danger to anyone. Even after he had hurled a lightning bolt at the werewolf, his brother acted no less caring than he had the day before.

All of that, taken together, seemed a good indication that The Ministry's portrayal of the people of Mastgar being monsters was untrue. The only exception to Ministry falsehoods might have been what they said about the North Landers. The whole raiding and pillaging thing didn't seem to be something that good people would do. He was pretty sure that's why Hyroc never suggested they go North. The west appeared the best place to go, and it would be a shock to the four of them if it wasn't.

Donovan laid Hyroc's map on the table and indicated the northwestern edge of the map. "I have business in that direction, but this is all I have of that area," he said. "I don't know what lay beyond the Western border and cannot plot any reliable course."

The shopkeeper rubbed his chin, deep in thought. "I might have what you're looking for over here," the man said, shaking a finger. Donovan followed him to a back room. The shopkeeper opened a large dusty chest and rummaged through it. He pulled out a rolled piece of parchment and blew the dust from it before setting it on a table and unrolling it. It revealed an unfamiliar landscape with foreign names, but Donovan recognized the western Arnaira border, shown on the eastern portion of the map.

"Is this map suitable?" the man said.

Donovan nodded excitedly. "Yes, that's what I was looking for," he said.

"Very good, sir. The price is thirty flecks."

Donovan kept the surprise from his face. That was expensive, but he knew it was extremely unlikely he could find a similar map anywhere else. He felt a strong reluctance to accept the price, but he knew he had to pay it. He handed the coins to the shopkeeper and was dismayed to know there were hardly any coins remaining in the coin sack.

"Thank you for your business," the man said.

"Thank you," Donovan said.

As Donovan reached for the far edge of the map to roll it up, the shopkeeper grabbed his arm. The man swept his eyes through the shop, making sure it was empty. He leaned in a little, speaking in a hushed tone.

"A word of caution, my friend." He motioned for Donovan to lay Hyroc's map on the table. He pointed to a patch of forest north of the rightmost split in the fork near where Hyroc and Curtis were hiding. "I've heard of strange happenings in those woods."

"Strange, how?" Donovan asked curiously. *The kind of strange I've seen lately would probably beat whatever you think is strange*, Donovan thought humorously.

"Some speak of trees that move, and others say the very ground itself comes to life. But what I know for certain is that non-who venture there is ever heard from again. It is a cursed place. You would do well to steer clear of it." He pointed to the leftmost split in the road. "Stay on the western road."

Donovan nodded. "I appreciate the advice."

"Safe journey," the man said.

Donovan rolled up the map, turned, and walked out the door.

"What'd you get?" Elsa curiously asked when he came out.

"I got us a map of what's to the west in Mastgar," he said quietly but proudly.

Chapter 25: Sheep in Wolf's Clothing

"Really? I hadn't even thought of that. I've been so distracted focusing on our food it never occurred to me to get a map."

Donovan beamed. "I know."

She rolled her eyes. "Don't let it go to your head too much. How much did it cost?"

Donovan's heart sank. "30 flecks."

"What!" Elsa nearly yelled.

"Keep your voice down," Donovan hissed.

"30 flecks," she whispered angrily. "That's pretty much all the money we had left from buying our food."

"I know, but we have no idea what's to the west. Heading on a blind course is extremely dangerous. Trust me. We needed this."

Elsa sighed. "Alright," she said unhappily. "We've spent too much time here already. No more stops. We've got to go." She stopped, indicating the sky with her hand. "No, wait. It's almost dusk. There probably won't be anyone leaving this late in the day, and it will look strange that we left so close to night. It might seem that we're trying to avoid something. That could look suspicious, or at the very least, it will cause the guards to remember us. And if anyone from The Ministry questions them, we'll stand out. They'll know we were here and if we're not to Mastgar by then, they'll know where we're heading and come after us. Let's spend the night here, collect our provisions at first light, then head out."

"Alright," Donovan said.

They headed off to find an inn with a stable. When they came across one, it was a quaint establishment named "The Pine Martin inn." After paying to house their donkey in a stall, they headed inside. The interior was packed with patrons, a group of which boisterously sang a drinking song. The establishment reminded Donovan of the Black Spruce Tavern in Elswood, but it didn't seem to have as much of a friendly feel. That may have been due to him and his sister being hunted fugitives and that their anonymity could vanish at any moment. This had proven somewhat of a hindrance to relaxation. He felt a stab of longing for his home of Elswood. His home he, his

OUTCASTS

sister, and younger brother could never return to. Donovan pushed the feeling aside.

He and Elsa moved over to the inn's front desk, where a large open book full of names lay. After a moment's wait, the inn's owner arrived.

"Welcome to the Pine Martin inn," the man said happily.

"Do you have any rooms?" Donovan said.

"I have one available, but I have a feeling the two of you won't mind it much." The man said the last part in a strange jovial manner that made Donovan uncomfortable.

"She's my sister," Donovan said protectively.

The man stared at him, mortified. "Oh, uh, uh, did – did you want the room?" the man stuttered.

"Yes," Donovan said irritably. The man quickly opened a box and handed Donovan a key before hurrying through the door that led into the kitchen. Elsa and Donovan exchanged a look. They moved over to a table that sat away from the loud singing group, then ordered a plate of bread and cheese and a pint for the both of them.

"Well, that was an interesting conversation with the owner," Elsa said, trying not to laugh.

"What an idiot," Donovan said, shaking his head.

"When we get up to the room, we can take a better look at that map." She took a drink from her stein, then turned sideways in her chair to watch the rest of the inn. "We should at least try to enjoy this while we can," she said. "We're completely out of coin. Who knows when we'll eat a hot meal or have warm beds to sleep in again."

Donovan nodded. He took a bite of bread and drank from his stein. "Speaking of that map," he said. Elsa looked at him. He thumbed over his shoulder. "Back at the shop where I bought it, the shopkeeper said something about the forest near where we told Hyroc and Curtis to go. Something about the ground attacking people and that anyone who goes into it never comes out."

"If anyone who goes into it never comes out, then how do they know what goes on in it?" She questioned.

Chapter 25: Sheep in Wolf's Clothing

Donovan raised his hand and shrugged while shaking his head. "You've got me there," he admitted.

"I don't think we have to worry about scary stories. Those Hand of Death were something right out of a fireside ghost tale, and we dealt with them just fine."

"I'm not worried about it. We've got a friend that can light things on fire with his hands and a younger brother that can shoot lightning. I don't think there's anything for us to be concerned about."

Elsa leaned in and talked quieter. "Well, besides The Ministry finding us," she noted. Donovan raised his stein toward her in agreement before taking a drink. "But I'd rather play it safe and avoid someplace where people supposedly think bad things happen when there's another choice. After we meet up with Curtis and Hyroc, we'll take the western road.

Donovan nodded and started humming along to the tune of the drinking song.

Chapter 26
A Step into the Unknown

Hyroc leaned against a tree as he finished fashioning a piece of an alder branch into a toothbrush. He put the part of the branch he had frayed into his mouth and began scrubbing the plaque from his teeth. It was late morning, and the sun shined brightly from a clear blue sky. He and Curtis had taken shelter for the night behind a small hill that lay right next to the forest he'd been instructed to head for. There had been an unexpected chill during the night that prompted him to start a fire. Luckily, the hill hid the fire from view and the dark color of the forest would make it hard for onlookers to spot the smoke from it.

While he brushed, he turned to look toward the southeast to see if he saw anyone coming from that direction. It was clear as far as he could tell, but his eyes were drawn over to a portion of the forest to the north. It seemed darker and the trees looked strangely thicker than the forest leading up to it. He got a cold feeling when he looked at it and it seemed uninviting. A disconcerting feeling came over him, and it almost felt like the forest was watching him.

"Hyroc," Curtis said, pulling Hyroc's attention from the forest.

"ress?" Hyroc said, looking toward his younger friend with the branch in his mouth. Hyroc took the branch out of his mouth and turned and spat. "Yes?"

Chapter 26: A Step into the Unknown

Curtis moved over to him, cradling something that glowed brightly in his hand. "Look," he said excitedly. "I think I finally got it!" In his hand, Hyroc saw a fully formed bird made out of lightning flapping its wings in place above his palm.

Hyroc nodded happily. "Good job," he said. "See, I knew you could do it." The bird darted out of Curtis' hand toward Hyroc. Hyroc twisted and turned, trying to keep his eyes on the bird as it spiraled upward around him. The bird winked out of existence with a loud pop.

"That was fantastic," Hyroc said.

"You liked it flying away?" Curtis asked hopefully.

"Absolutely. I never thought to make my stag come out of my hand. I'll have to give that a try. Your brother and sister will be excited to see that."

"I can't wait to show them."

"I hope they won't take too much longer getting to us," Hyroc said. He put a hand over his eyes to block out the sun as he scanned the sky for Shimmer.

"I wanted to ask you something," Curtis said.

Hyroc returned his attention to Curtis. "Anything," he said.

"How come when you use your Flame Claw, it doesn't affect you as it does me when I use lightning? I almost faint when I use any magic other than my bird, and you don't. Why?"

Hyroc stared at him thoughtfully. "I think it's because you're using lightning," he said. "Lightning is a much more potent type of magic than, say, me throwing fireballs. It takes so much more out of you because it's so much more powerful. When I hit something with my fist-sized fireballs, it mostly just lights my target on fire. Maybe it will also make them stumble from the force of the impact. But when you hit something with your lightning, it almost instantly kills your target, and it blows them away. I once saw you put the body of a Death Hand you hit into the branches of a tree several yards out."

"So, it makes me tired because I hit so hard?" Curtis said.

Hyroc nodded. "Yeah."

"Do you know how to fix that?"

—261—

Hyroc scratched his chin, pondering the problem. "I think you need to try learning how to control it better. You should try dividing your Quintessence into less powerful attacks. That way, you're not using most of your reservoir in a single powerful strike that nearly causes you to faint. It's the same situation as how you learned to make your bird. You've got to control it and make it do you want. That's all I can think of."

Curtis nodded thankfully. "Well, thank you."

"Anytime."

The fluttering of wings caught their attention. Shimmer alighted onto the ground in front of them.

"Hey, look, your brother and sister are back," Hyroc said. "Good thing too. I finished off the last of the bread this morning. Where do we need to go, Shimmer?" The raven turned toward the south and excitedly cawed multiple times. "That's to the south so they must be waiting at the fork in the road. Shimmer –" Hyroc pointed to the east "– there's a road and right here, we're closer to that than the fork. Can you tell Elsa and Donovan to meet us farther up the eastern fork in the road?" Shimmer hopped excitedly and took flight.

Hyroc, Curtis, and Kit headed to the road. When they reached its flattened surface, they spotted three figures moving toward them. They walked to meet them. Several yards out, the two groups began waving at each other, and soon, they were reunited.

"Glad to see you two are all right," Hyroc said. "You had us worried about you in that town . Run into any trouble?"

Elsa shook her head. "No, no problems," she said. "We're just a day late because we took too long getting our supplies and then ended up spending the night in a tavern."

"Oh yes, having warm food and sleeping in a bed was a terrible inconvenience," he said sarcastically to Hyroc. Hyroc shook his head and lightly shoved Donovan's shoulder. "But I did get something for you that I'm sure you'll appreciate." Donovan unrolled the new map.

Hyroc gave him a surprised look. "You got us a map of what lay to the west," he said happily. "I didn't even think about that." Donovan

Chapter 26: A Step into the Unknown

handed him the map, and he laid it on the ground to begin looking it over.

Donovan sniffed. "I'm a lot smarter than everyone gives me credit for," he said.

Hyroc and Elsa rolled their eyes. "That's still up for debate," Elsa said, slightly annoyed. "Okay, now that we're all together, let's have a look at both our maps so we can figure out where we're going."

Hyroc retrieved the old map from the donkey and lined it up beside the new one. "Okay, from what I can see," he said. "The two splits on this road we're on go to the west and lead out of Arnaira. The road over to the west stays in Arnaira longer while this one is shorter and gets us out of the country much faster."

"The man I bought the new map from," Donovan said. "Warned me about the forest to the north of the eastern split in the road." He pointed northward farther down the road. "Something about it being cursed, and that non-who go in every come out."

"Did he seem believable?" Hyroc questioned. "Was it just some story meant to scare children?"

"No, he seemed pretty serious about it."

"Well, I've been getting a strange feeling about the forest there."

"Strange how?" Elsa asked.

"I'm not sure. Something just doesn't feel right about it."

"Between your Flame Claw and Curtis' ability, we could probably deal with anything we run into, but it'd probably be best to avoid it since there's another option."

"I agree," Donovan said. "After running into all of those Death Hands, I now know to pay attention to strange feelings. We probably shouldn't chance it."

"I think so, too," Hyroc said. "I don't relish the idea of getting into a fight when we don't have to."

"Then I think it's settled," Elsa said. "We're taking the western road."

Hyroc had barely started walking when he noticed something in the distance. It appeared to be a large cloud of dust floating in the air. Then a line of shapes appeared over the crest of an area of lower ground. A lump formed in the pit of his stomach. Those shapes were horses!

"We've got a problem!" Donovan yelled. "Look." He pointed toward the dust.

"They've found us," Elsa said disparaged.

"Damn them," Donovan said.

Hyroc turned to face his friends. "I'm sorry," he said. "I thought I was right. I thought we had more time."

Donovan slapped his forehead. "No. The shopkeeper. It was the shopkeeper I bought the map from. He must've told The Ministry about us. That's how they found us. How could I have been so stupid."

"We can figure out who's to blame later," Elsa said. "Right now, we've got to move! Head for the trees back behind us. They won't be able to use their horses in there."

When they turned around to the east, they saw another even closer line of horses. They were trapped!

"Those horses will trample us out here in the open," Hyroc said. "We've got to get to cover."

"The trees on either side are too far away for us to reach in time," Elsa said. She looked at the forest to the north. The tree line bowed out toward them, and it seemed close enough for them to reach. "Our only chance is to get in there."

Hyroc's heart sank. Something wasn't right with that forest, but their only other choice was to die out here on the road. There was no choice at all.

"Alright, everyone, into the forest to the north." Everyone rushed toward the forest. Hyroc could feel as well as hear the thunder of hooves as he darted into the trees. He desperately hoped those stories were nothing more than tales meant to scare children into behaving.

CHAPTER 27
THE DEVOURING THICKET

Hyroc rushed through the leafy forest foliage that grew between the trees. He felt his heart hammering away in his chest, and its rhythmic thump filled his ears. The farther he and his friends penetrated into the forest, the less effective The Ministry horses would be. That would force their pursuers to follow him and his friends on foot. The process of stopping and dismounting would slow down The Ministry forces, even if only by a little, and allow the five of them to gain somewhat of a lead. Hyroc could then use his trail-removing spell. Without any indications of where they had gone, they should be able to lose anyone trailing them.

Most of the trees here were deciduous, and the canopy was steadily thickening. The trees were becoming more and more numerous, giving the whole forest an enclosed feeling. That was good because it would increasingly hinder mounted soldiers and make it easier for them to escape their enemy.

The ground rose up into a moderately steep hill. It wasn't steep enough to cause the five of them much trouble, but it would be for their donkey. The animal moved at an agonizingly slow pace as it navigated the incline. It was moving too slowly and would cost them their lead, but it carried their supplies. Unless Hyroc turned into a bear and relegated himself as a glorified pack animal for their food, they had no choice other than to accept it. But if the donkey cost them too much time, he would make the unpleasant decision. His pride wasn't worth their lives.

Hyroc stopped and waited anxiously farther up the hill. He drew his sword and started hacking away at a clump of bushes where the donkey was heading to try and hasten its journey up the hill. When he had chopped as much as he could, he looked out toward the base of the hill, trying to spot their pursuers. He didn't see anything moving. That seemed strange. Those horses were right behind him. He thought he should be able to see something. Maybe he and his friends had gotten more of a lead than he had realized. He raised his hands, figuring he might as well take advantage of their lead and cast the trail-removing spell.

The donkey was a couple of steps from the top of the hill. Curtis lost his footing beside Hyroc. Hyroc immediately reached down and helped his friend to his feet. The donkey had arrived, and the group quickened their pace. The ground remained flat before sloping downward but at a gentler angle than the other side. Hyroc stopped at the edge of the hill, noticing a bed of red flowers stretching off in both directions. Everyone hurried past him. The line of flowers was far too neat to occur naturally. It was as if someone had placed them there. Hyroc reached down and snapped off a flower to take a closer look at it. It was some kind of rose, it had the smell of a rose, but there didn't seem to be anything unusual about it.

"Hyroc," Elsa called up from farther down the hill. She waved him toward her intently. "Come on. We don't have time to stop."

Hyroc raised an acknowledging hand and stuck the flower in his pocket before joining Elsa.

"I think we're good, for now," Donovan said, looking back the way they had come. Close to an hour had passed without any sign of pursuit. In fact, they hadn't seen anything of The Ministry soldiers since entering the forest.

"Good," Elsa said. She leaned forward with her hands on her knees and heavily breathed while she caught her breath.

Chapter 27: The Devouring Thicket

Donovan took a drink from his water skin, then offered it to Elsa. Hyroc put his hand on a tree and leaned into it. Kit collapsed at his feet, panting rapidly. Curtis sat down next to Kit and scratched the big cat's head.

"Am I the only one that finds it odd how easily we got away?" Hyroc said. "Those horses were right behind us. I know those soldiers dismounting would slow them down, but nothing anywhere close to this."

"I'm glad I'm not the only one that was wondering about that," Donovan said.

"Yeah, something feels off about that," Elsa said.

"Don't get me wrong, I appreciate not seeing anyone following us, but that shouldn't have happened. Not like this. The shopkeeper's story is eating at the back of my mind."

Elsa and Donovan looked at Hyroc. "What do you think?" Elsa asked. "Have you gotten anything from the trees?"

Hyroc shook his head. "I wouldn't learn anything," he said. "A few dozen soldiers following us wouldn't make enough of an impact for the trees to notice. I don't know any more about this place than any of you do." He paused. "Wait, actually. I might have something." He fished the red flower out of his pocket and thumbed over his shoulder. "Back when we were coming off that hill. I found a whole bunch of these in a line."

He handed it to Elsa when she held her hand out, wanting to take a look at it. She shrugged with her hand out. "It seems to be just an ordinary flower," Elsa admitted. She passed it to Donovan.

"There might be something else I can try," Hyroc said. "Hand that flower back to me." He ignited a blue flame in one hand and dropped the flower into it. The flower turned to ash in a puff of acrid smoke.

"What was that supposed to show you?" Donovan said.

Hyroc shrugged. "I don't know," he said. "I thought it might do something."

Elsa laughed. "Sorry, that was kind of funny."

A disconcerting feeling struck Hyroc. It felt as if something had just looked at him. He scanned his surroundings but didn't see anything.

OUTCASTS

"Well, unless someone thinks there's something else we should do," Donovan said. "I guess we keep going."

"We can't go back, so that's the only thing we can do," Hyroc said.

Elsa nodded. "I agree," she said. "Besides, we may have simply had a bit of luck, and those soldiers are still coming after us."

They continued forward. A short time later, they came upon an open area. A stream of clear water flowed through it, and dandelions and other forest flowers grew throughout the area. There were clumps of what appeared to be vibrant and immaculate roses. They seemed out of place in the untamed forest. The flowers were different from the ones he had seen earlier. They were much larger and very beautiful. A florist would clamber to incorporate these into their crop.

Elsa, Hyroc, and Kit moved forward while Donovan and Curtis stayed back to fill the waterskins and give their donkey time to drink from the stream. They moved toward the nearest clump of flowers.

Elsa pointed at it. "How are so many of these roses able to grow here?" She asked.

"I was thinking that same thing," Hyroc said.

"They're beautiful."

"I don't really care much for flowers, but I have to agree with you."

Hyroc's foot caught on something. When he looked down, he saw the shape of something enveloped in some grass. It was straight, too straight to be a fallen branch. He pulled the grass back and prided the object out with his fingers. It was a leg bone that might have belonged to a deer. Then he noticed emanating from the direction of the roses was what seemed to be a thick vine the same color as the grass. Sharp thorny protrusions lined the vine. Following the vine with his eyes, he discovered numerous tendrils coming off the roses. He stopped at a rounded white object just shy of the roses. When he focused on it, he got a start when it resolved into the shape of a human skull.

"Hey, Elsa, you're, umm, you're going to want to see this," Hyroc said, unable to take his eyes off the skull as he rose to his feet. Elsa didn't answer. He repeated himself, thinking she hadn't heard him. When he turned to her, he saw her reaching for one of the roses. Her

Chapter 27: The Devouring Thicket

eyes were wide, and she seemed transfixed by the flowers. Hyroc seized her wrist an instant before she touched the flower.

Elsa shook her head as if waking herself. She gazed at him, confused. "I – I don't know what I was doing," she said. "It was the strangest thing. I was looking at them, and I had an overwhelming urge to pick one." She turned to look at them, but Hyroc stopped her.

"No. Don't," he said. "They're enchanted. I think they're made to make you want to touch them when you get close." She gave him a confounded look, wondering how he knew that. He pointed down at the skull. She jolted back in surprise, but Hyroc kept her from moving. "Don't do that either." He indicated a vine right where she would have stepped. "Pretty sure we don't want to touch those." Elsa nodded and the two of them gingerly stepped over the vine before moving over to Donovan and Curtis.

They found Donovan restraining Curtis with one arm while he used his knuckles to messy his younger brother's hair. Both were smiling. Donovan released Curtis when they noticed Elsa and Hyroc. Curtis playfully shoved his older brother's arm.

"Donovan," Elsa said. "There's something wrong with those roses."

"What do you mean something's wrong?" Donovan said.

"Just – just umm, watch this," Hyroc said. He picked up a rock from the stream and tossed it into the nearest rose clump. The vines immediately started writhing, searching for something living to grab onto. A flurry of activity enveloped the area with the roses. They shook violently. Then the entire clump began moving. The four of them gaped in astonishment when the clump started uprooting itself. The roses lifted, and their middle peeled back to reveal a mouth that split into four sections. Row after row of teeth-like thorns filled its floral maw. An incredibly thick dark green stem supported the head. When the roots came into view, they appeared almost to function as fingers reaching out to grasp the edges of the hole the plant extricated itself from. The roots, in combination with the vines, pulled the plant the rest of the way out of the hole. The roots went from fingers to legs the plant used to walk, and it used its vines to help pull itself across the ground. The whole process occurred remarkably fast. The plant moved slowly compared to the animals of the forest, but it was fast enough to be a threat.

Elsa drew her bow and put an arrow at the center of the plant's stem. It stopped for an instant as it absorbed the impact of the arrow, but it seemed otherwise unaffected. She shot it again, followed by an arrow from Donovan. Neither arrow was effective. A vine shot out, seized Elsa by the leg, and yanked her off her feet. She yelled out as the vine drew her toward the plant's gaping mouth. She used her knife to slice through the vine. Donovan grabbed her and pulled her back. He used his spear to sever a vine reaching for their donkey.

Hyroc formed a fireball in both hands and flung them at the plant. It erupted into blue flames, and its vines wildly spasmed as they reached skyward. Then, the vines went still, and the main body of the plant slumped down. The plan gave off a foul smell as it burned.

Before anyone could celebrate their survival, every rose clump in the clearing started shaking. A roaring sound like that of a windstorm filled the area. Dozens upon dozens of the plants ripped themselves out of the ground and moved toward them.

Hyroc raised his hands above his head and brought his arms down off to the side, palms flat. He turned his hand, so his palms faced each other and slowly drew them together. A mist flowed in from the trees, settling in midair above the plants. The mist turned to water and splashed down on the creatures in a sheet.

"Curtis, light it up!" Hyroc yelled.

Curtis stared at him, baffled. He glanced from the horde of carnivorous plants back to him. Then a wicked smile crept across his face. He took a deep breath before throwing his hands toward the plants. Lightning shot from his hand and slammed into one of the plants. With a thunderous boom, everything in that area exploded into light. Blue arcs of lightning darted from the plants and the ground. The plants twitched rhythmically, their vines almost appearing as green snakes. The light vanished, and every plant collapsed limply. A burnt floral stench invaded the clearing.

Chapter 27: The Devouring Thicket

Before Hyroc could breathe a sigh of relief, a powerful presence rammed his mind. It hit with such force he almost felt as if he had just been punched. He stumbled, but Donovan caught his arm and kept him from losing his balance. A sharp pain pierced his head. He held his hand to the side of his head and grimaced.

"Hyroc, are you okay?" Donovan asked, but Hyroc barely heard him.

A voice inside Hyroc's head drowned out everything around him. "You burn that which was never meant to burn!" a commanding voice angrily said. "The blood moon rises over the fields of man. The animals sing of your sins. Your flame darkens the world. Your flesh will fertilize the fruit trees that are fruitless, Guardian."

Hyroc pushed the voice out of his mind. The pain faded, and sound returned to the world. He suddenly became aware that Elsa was shaking his shoulder and talking to him.

"...What's wrong?" she asked urgently. "Is something happening?"

Hyroc shook himself. "I'm fine," he said." Elsa breathed a sigh of relief. "But we need to leave right now! We should have never come here."

"What gave that away?" Donovan said. "Was it the army of man-eating plants?"

"There's *something* here," Hyroc said urgently. "I heard it talking to me, and it didn't sound happy."

"All who say we should leave, raise their hand and say aye." Everyone raised their hand and said aye. "I believe that settles it."

"I'd rather take our chances out there with The Ministry than whatever is in here."

"I agree," Elsa said.

They turned around and rushed out of the clearing back the way they had come. Soon, they felt the ground start to rise beneath their feet. It wasn't far to the top of the hill. Then, they had to go down the other side, through a short stretch of forest, and they were out. But the tricky part would be dealing with The Ministry soldiers waiting for them beyond the trees. Hyroc hoped he could scare them with some flashy Flame Claw magic. He only needed to distract them long enough for everyone to get to the trees away from the part of the forest where there was something that wanted to kill all of them. That *something* was probably why the soldiers hadn't followed them in.

They still hadn't reached the top of the hill. By Hyroc's reckoning, they should have been there by now. Maybe their descent down the hill had taken longer than he realized. He waited, and waited, and waited. They still weren't at the top. They should be able to see the line of red flowers, but they couldn't. Then, strangely, it felt as if they were walking down the hill. That didn't make sense. The incline was much too shallow for it to be the other side of the hill where they had climbed up. A pungent order permeated the air as if something foul-smelling was burning. He could have sworn the area around the hill didn't smell this bad.

They entered a clearing with a stream, and a blackened mass smoldered beside the flowing water. Hyroc got a start when he realized it was one of the plant creatures. Maybe The Ministry soldiers had followed them into the forest after all, and they too had a run-in with the creatures. The sight of these things might have frightened off The Ministry soldiers. That was good for them. The area of the plains outside the forest might be clear for the time being. Then he noticed numerous dead plant creatures grouped together. There was something familiar about that grouping. How could the Ministry soldiers have killed the creatures in a way that caused them to pile up in one spot so similar to how he and Curtis had killed them? A surge of ice ran down his back. The Ministry soldiers didn't do this. T*hey* did. This was the same clearing where they had killed all the plant monsters!

"How in the Sunless Planes did we get back here?" Donovan said flabbergasted. "I swear we were heading uphill this whole time."

"We were," Hyroc said.

"Then how did we end up back here?" Elsa asked.

Hyroc shrugged. "I have no idea."

Chapter 27: The Devouring Thicket

Elsa turned around and used her knife to carve a mark on a tree in the direction they had come. "Okay, everyone see this mark?" she said. "Everyone see it's back the way we had come?" Everyone acknowledged her. "I'm certain that's the way we came. Now, let's try this again."

Everyone moved out of the clearing back the way they had come. They encountered the incline of the hill and began climbing it. Hyroc focused on the sensation of moving uphill. Then, without any indication, they were going downhill again. They arrived back at the clearing. They looked at the tree Elsa had marked, and the mark was there.

"I know for a fact we were backtracking," Elsa said. "And somehow, we ended up back here again. What's going on?"

Hyroc cursed. "I think this whole forest has an enchantment over it," he said. "There was one on those roses on the heads of those plant creatures that made you want to touch them, so they could eat you. It's basically a fishing lure, but we're the fish. So, since something keeps happening that doesn't make any sense, it's got to be an enchantment."

"What, an enchantment that keeps you from leaving?" Donovan said.

Hyroc nodded. "Yeah."

"So, how do we get rid of it?"

"I don't know. We probably can't."

"Wait, we're stuck here?"

"No. Not exactly. We just can't go back."

"Right, we can go farther into the forest where there's something that wants to kill us. What an ingenious idea."

Hyroc thumbed over his shoulder. "I think those red flowers we passed on the top of the hill were a warning to stay out. It probably marked the threshold of the area with the enchantment."

"And we were too busy running from The Ministry to notice," Elsa said. She shook her head. "It's just one thing after another."

"The only thing we can do is find what's casting the enchantment," Hyroc said.

"The thing that spoke to you is a good bet," Donovan said. "We need to find whatever it is and kill it."

"If we make it that far," Hyroc said.

"You are mine," the voice said. "You will feed the roots, Guardian."

Epilogue

"What do you mean, they're all dead!" Keller yelled at a Light Walker in front of him.

He leaned over a table with a map of Arnaira laid across it, and a fire crackled in a fireplace behind him. He had appropriated an establishment by the name of the Black Spruce Tavern as his headquarters in Elswood. The business's original owner was currently being interrogated and had no use of the structure. If he was found to have no connection to the witchcraft of the Hyroc creature, he would be allowed to resume management of his Tavern once Keller no longer required the use of it. But that seemed doubtful since the owner had already admitted to the creature frequently visiting this place. Someone in such prolonged contact with the aberration would likely pick something up of the dark arts.

"Yes, Inquisitor," the Light Walker said. "The entire contingent of lepers is dead. The fugitives laid an ambush for us. We didn't see it coming. They slaughtered the lepers before escaping."

"Of course, you let it escape," Keller said crossly. "I've been tracking it for four years. Four long years! I had it within my grasp, and your incompetency let it slip away." Keller furiously swept everything off the table, sending a wave of map markers and inkwells clattering to the floor.

"We also lost numerous Ministry regulars and several Witch Hunters along with the lep –"

"I don't give a damn about the soldiers," Keller said, interrupting the Light Walker. The man shot Keller a derisive scowl but said nothing. Keller held his hand toward the Light Walker, his index finger and thumb almost touching to show how close he was to achieving his goal. "I was this close," Keller said. "This close! I had that abomination on the edge of my sword. Then, your soldiers that were probably too drunk to see straight, let my quarry get away."

"My soldiers did nothing of the kind!" the Light Walker said, letting a portion of his anger show. "They conducted themselves with dignity and honor. Do not belittle them in front of me."

Keller threw his hand out in a dismissive wave. "You are dismissed, Light Walker," he said coldly. "Get out of my sight."

"Yes, Inquisitor," the Light Walker said venomously. He gave a curt salute and stormed out of the tavern.

Keller turned toward the fire with his hands on his hips. "Shadow! How could this happen," he whispered toward the flames, seething. "I had *that* creature. I had his aunt. She told me everything I needed to know. I even brought back The Hand of Death, the tool of Feygrotha."

He crossed his arms and held his chin with one hand as he pondered the conundrum. The Hand of Death could track the witchcraft that the Hyroc creature utilized. It had killed every single one that could track it. He had thought the sheer number of creatures was enough to overwhelm his target, but he was mistaken. He had more Hand of Death, but those he had held in reserve were too far away to pick up the Hyroc creature's trail of energy. How had it known? How had it picked up on the main danger his weapons posed to it?

A shadowy figure wearing the plague mask that marked it as a Hand of Death stepped into the tavern and moved over to Keller. Keller turned to face him. The figure glanced at the objects from the table that now littered the floor.

"In light of your current losses," it said in a cold voice. "It may be advisable to replace those that are now dead."

Epilogue

Keller nodded. "I agree," he said. He indicated for the figure to follow as he walked outside through the tavern's main door. "Travel to Roranon, and *gather* more recruits. I'll stay here to see if there's any way of salvaging this disaster."

"I would advise you do so carefully," the figure said. "Lest your underlings turn on you."

"Let me be concerned about that."

"As you wish. There is another matter to bring to your attention. You have nearly exhausted the supply of Ministry prisoners in the capital. You will have to find another source if you wish to fill your ranks."

"There are always those that can be turned into enemies of The Ministry. If it is, say, discovered that the majority of the townsfolk here participated in witchcraft, those empty cells will soon be filled."

The figure laughed coldly.

The yelling from a group of Ministry archers caught their attention. The archers frantically pointed skyward. Keller looked up to see something white above him screaming toward the ground. White feathered wings burst from the thing, rapidly slowing its descent. An enormous white owl touched down on its legs in the open center of Elswood. The archers took aim and let their arrows fly. The owl extended a wing toward the archers, and their arrows curved around it. A group of soldiers came charging toward the bird with their weapons raised. The bird extended its wings and swept them to the ground. A tsunami of air shot out from it, knocking everyone off their feet.

While Keller got to his feet, the shadowy figure darted toward the owl. The owl swept its wings toward the figure, and a fuzzy distortion of heat enveloped it. In an instant, the figure turned to ash. Its sword and anything else made from metal dropped to the ground, blazing orange with intense heat. A group of Hand of Death appeared, rushing toward the owl. It raised its wings, and a blue fireball formed at its wingtips. The bird brought its wings down. The ball slammed into the ground and a wave of blue fire consumed the creatures, leaving nothing but ash and metal behind. The owl raised its wings and a tornado of blue fire swirled around it.

"Leave now, or you will die!" the owl said in a booming voice. It held its beak open, appearing to be a screaming demon wreathed in azure flames. Ministry soldiers dispersed in terror in all directions.

Keller turned to flee, but a wave of air knocked his feet out from under him. The owl jumped over to him and pinned him beneath its talon. Keller drew a dagger, but with the sweep of a wing, the bird sent it flying out of his hand.

"Ah, it seems that abomination found someone to do its dirty work," Keller spat. "Now, it shows its true colors. I knew it would one day."

"You know nothing!" the owl said. "You only see what you wish to see. Your world is so small. And the Anamagi you speak of did not send me. But he would have been well within the dictates of justice to do so. He chose something far more valuable than snuffing out your life."

"You're twisted kind has always sought to justify your atrocities, witch," Keller said.

"Fool, you don't even know what I am. Your forefathers remembered us until their dogma, born out of fear, snatched away all reason."

"You may kill me, but know. Others will take my place."

"It is precisely your dabbling with powers you do not understand that must be made to end. You seek to revive the darkness of Feygrotha. The darkness that almost consumed your ancestors."

"What I did was necessary to stop the darkness."

"The darkness spread by an Anamagi, they who were worthy to receive a portion of our power for their loyalty? He fell beyond your limited purview of what you thought was evil, despite his kindness showing the opposite. You have eyes that can see, but you do not see the truth. You thought using evil, no matter how heinous, was the way to protect your people. But you were damning them to the Sunless Planes. How many of your people did you sacrifice to a terrible fate? And all in the name of a meaningless cause."

"I did what was necessary. I don't expect someone with your corrupted mind to understand."

"I understand far more than you ever could. But as you have done what you thought was necessary, so I must do what justice demands.

Epilogue

You have disrupted the balance with your hubris, and order must be restored. Keller, son of Halnim, and Malef, Your fate will serve as a warning to anyone who may ignorantly follow in your footsteps." The owl lifted one foot, and its talons glowed blue. It slammed its foot down. So ended, Keller, son of Halnim and Malef. Bane of Hyroc.

Appendix

Locations

Elswood – a small village located in the Elswood forest on the edge of the wilderness near Wolf Paw Mountain. Its remoteness attracts witches, necromancers, and fugitives.

Arnaira – kingdom where the Ministry of the Silver Scythe rules. It's surrounded by heavy forest and rough terrain and is relatively isolated.

Mastgar – kingdom west of Arnaira. The rulers are opposed to The Ministry. The kingdom is rumored to openly accept magical abilities, but its citizens are said to be brutal savages.

North Lands – subarctic region home to the North Landers. It has brutally cold winters and a short growing season. Because of a scarcity of resources in the region, North Landers send out raiding parties to neighboring kingdoms.

Wulfren – Wol'dger kingdom. Far to the northwest of Arnaira

Flatwood – town on the northeastern end of the Plains of Forna, south of Elswood forest.

Forna – large town on the southern edge of the Plains of Forna. The home to several notable Arnairan schools.

Appendix

Roranon – capital city of Arnaira. Located to the southeast of Forna. The seat of The Ministry of the Silver Scythe and Council of Seven ruling body.

Sunless Plains – realm where shadow demons reside. Sorcerers summon shadow demons into the world from here, but sometimes one finds a way through on its own.

Creatures

Wol'dger – furry human-like creature with a face and head similar to a Wolverine. Often have dark-colored fur ranging from black to brown and gray and often have long stripes running across their body. Beyond their physical features, they are basically human. Live in the kingdom of Wulfren. Have slightly more sensitive noses than humans and can detect certain sicknesses by smell. Their fur makes them resistant to the cold. They have clawed feet and hands, making them dangerous in a fight. They have four toes and are immune to certain types of transformation magic. Were once humans that were cursed due to disobeying the orders of the Guardian Wearla.

Guardian – powerful magical creature with the body of an animal, possesses human-level intelligence and can speak. Their bodies have blue markings. They wear engraved silver on their legs and a necklace with a gem. They utilize the ancient magic of The Flame of the Sentinels (Flame Claw). They are generally kind and helpful to strangers and will aid those in need, but they can be irritatingly cryptic. They prefer to go unnoticed and avoid interfering in the affairs of people. If a Guardian is brought to anger, they are incredibly dangerous. They seek to maintain the balance of nature. They punish those who threaten the balance and will swiftly eliminate any shadow demon intrusion.

Giant spider – very large and aggressive arachnid. They are usually about the size of a large dog. Have eight eyes and eight legs, each with a claw. They have black bodies with flecks of iridescent reds and purples, and are covered in many thick bristly hairs. They kill prey using two enormous venomous fangs.

OUTCASTS

- **Jackalope (deer rabbit)** – rabbit with antlers year-round (females have smaller antlers). Docile creature unless in rut.
- **Boenake** – dark brown moose-like creature. Bluish-green moss covers its body and hangs off its paddle-shaped horns in strands. Seeing one is rare and considered a sign of good luck.
- **Shade Hunter** – wolfish-like shadow demon. It has pale gray skin, razor-sharp black teeth, flaming purple eyes, spikes running down its back, and a spiked tail, ending in three sharp prongs. Shade Hunters can mind control animals and use these animals to defend themselves or help kill whoever they're after.

Historical figures

- **Feygrotha** – a powerful sorcerer who used shadow demons and witchcraft to overthrow the King of Arnaira and appointed himself ruler. He was cruel, and his subjects suffered greatly under his rule. The citizens revolted against him. After a bloody conflict Feygrotha was defeated.
- **Wearla** – powerful Guardian who aided the kingdom of Wulfren against a devastating North Lander invasion by gifting them the ability to transform into an animal. Later she cursed the kingdom because the people misused her gift. The people then became the Wol'dger.

Factions

- **Ministry of the Silver Scythe** – commonly referred to simply as The Ministry. It was created after the overthrow of the sorcerer Faygrotha. They are based in Roranon. They are charged with eliminating dark influences and judging those accused of using witchcraft or other such dark magic. In the kingdom, all forms of magic, even beneficial ones, are seen as witchcraft.
- **Anamagi** – Wol'dgers that remained loyal to the guidance of Wearla. When Wulfren was cursed because of their loyalty, they were offered the choice to remain uncursed. They refused her offer because they didn't want to be separated from their people. Because of their choice, Wearla bestowed upon their bloodlines The Flame Claw, so they could lead their people in her stead.

Appendix

Miscellaneous

Quintessence – the name of the energy source within someone that enables them to use magic. Found in all living things and is vital for life. It exists in everyone, but it is rare for someone to have a large enough reservoir within them to use magic. Using Quintessence will drain someone's strength and weaken them the more they tap into their reserve, similar to someone exerting themselves.

Magic – the mechanism that allows someone to use their Quintessence to make something. A person creates something by imagining it, but a high amount of concentration is involved in making the thing come into existence. The hands are natural focusing points for Quintessence, and the person must move them in certain ways to mold their creation into what they want or make it do what they want. This is similar to a potter turning a lump of clay into a pot.

Mage – magic-user proficient in the five schools of elemental magic, fire, water, earth, lightning, and wind. They are still able to perform other types of elemental spells but have a preference for one element.

Witch – magic user who uses dark magic. The term witch includes males and females. No form of magic is inherently evil, but witches have a preference for causing pain, suffering, and death through curses, enchantments, and other harmful spells.

Necromancer – magic user that raises the dead. Necromancers bind the dead to their will, and the dead obey them completely. The most hated of all magic users.

Summoner – magic-user who summons shadow demons to do their bidding.

(Anamagi) Flame Claw – a potent ancient magic. A less powerful version of the Guardian's Flame Claw. Anyone with the Flame Claw has a preference for fire magic and it manifests in a blue flame. Whoever possesses the Flame Claw has several advantages over other magic users. (1) It renders the person immune to all but the most powerful of tracking magic. (2) They can perceive the language of shadow demons. (3) They can discern information through the trees when they're in forested areas. (4) The Flame Claw allows them to easily communicate information to animals that are familiar with them. (5) If they have the animal transformation gift, they can use the Flame Claw while in their animal form.

(Guardian) Flame Claw – a potent ancient magic used by the Guardians. It has the same capabilities as the Anamagi Flame Claw but has many more mysterious uses that Guardians rarely share.

Power Runes/Words – a rune/runes or word/words that have been infused with Quintessence to perform a certain task independent of the caster. A rune can be made to explode when someone steps on it or afflict someone with a curse when they touch it. Multiple runes or words can be linked together to create incantations to perform complex tasks, tasks simply too precise and complicated for the caster to imagine. Some may even require the caster to speak the words aloud.

Bindings Magic – magic used to control the undead and shadow demons. In order to bind a shadow demon, the caster must sacrifice a part of their flesh (usually a finger). After obtaining the sacrifice, a binding charm can be used on the caster, or the sacrifice can be placed inside of an amulet so the control of the demon can be transferred to others.

Characters

Marcus – the man who adopted Hyroc (Book 1). He found Hyroc as a baby in the arms of his dead mother. Retired Ministry Light Bringer. He was respected among their ranks and was able to keep The Ministry from killing Hyroc. Hyroc was raised by him till nine years old when Marcus passed from sickness. Hyroc was fond of him and greatly missed him.

June – Marcus' sister (Book 1). She looked after Hyroc after the passing of Marcus. She had less influence with the Ministry than Marcus but had enough to keep Hyroc from being killed. Though his life was safe, she couldn't protect him from severe bullying. Despite this, the bond between Hyroc and June only strengthened as time went on. She looked after Hyroc until he was 15. Hyroc had to run away after an unfortunate accident which sent The Ministry after him.

Ursa – white Guardian she-bear that trained Hyroc to use his bear form and his Flame Claw (Book 2). She saved Hyroc from two Witch Hunters that were trying to execute him after he ran away (Book 1). She revealed herself to Hyroc when he arrived in Elswood. They developed a friendly relationship. She departed after Hyroc's training was complete shortly before the events of Book 3.

Shackleton Family – Svald, Helen, and Walter, father, mother, and grandfather of Elsa, Donovan, and Curtis (Book 1). The family unofficially adopted Hyroc after his arrival in Elswood. They helped him develop his survival skills, and they developed a friendly relationship. They were killed by spiders that were corrupted by shadow demon essence (Book 2).

Harold – an ex-witch Hunter that was friends with the Shackletons. He was extremely cautious about Hyroc's presence in Elswood. Later, he became much more trustful of Hyroc and taught him how to fight with a sword.

Pronunciations

Wol'dger – (wol + ger)

Anamagi – (anna + maj + eye)

Wearla – (where + la)

Feygrotha – (fay + grr + aww + tha)

Wulfren – (wool + fren)

Ministry Rankings (lowest to highest rank)

Initiate – lowest Ministry rank.

Soldier – initiate that received basic training.

Witch Hunter – soldier specially trained to hunt witches and fugitives.

Captain – mid-level Ministry official that commands soldiers.

Light Walker – mid-ranking Ministry soldier that participates in challenging assignments.

Light Bringer – they research witchcraft and the techniques witches use in order to help better fight them.

Knight – heavily armed Ministry soldier.

Inquisitor – high-ranking Ministry official responsible for major decisions.

High Inquisitor – highest Ministry rank. Only High Inquisitors are allowed membership in the Council of seven.

Other

Shadow – in certain contexts shadow is considered a curse word in the story.

Hallowed – refers to the religious figures The Hollow Knights that are worshiped in Arnaira. Hallowed can be used as a curse word which is equivalent to saying God's name in vain.

Sunless Plains – refers to the place where shadow demons reside, and when used as a curse word is equivalent to the word hell. I.e. "What the Hell."

Hyroc, Book 1, Tree of Memories, Book 2 are available at
https://www.adamfreestone.com/
https://authormasterminds.com/
https://www.amazon.com/
https://www.bookdepository.com/

Made in the USA
Middletown, DE
11 November 2024